MVFOL
D0034261

TWO PASSIONATE LOVERS . . . ONE MAN OF GOD . . .

PRINCIPESSA GIULIA FARNESE—Proud and beautiful, the master of not one, but two powerful dynasties, she once devoured the love of Bryan Cavanagh. Now she beseeches his help.

BRYAN DE COURCY CAVANAGH—A near-penniless adventurer turned internationally successful attorney, he's about to walk into the void of forty lost years—and the rich harmonies of his love for Giulia.

SANDRO MOLLOY—A bishop elevated inside the Vatican hierarchy, he shares a secret with Giulia Farnese—one that will transform the life of Bryan Cavanagh forever.

Also by Morris West

Gallows on the Sand
Kundu
Children of the Sun
The Big Story
The Concubine
The Second Victory
The Devil's Advocate
The Naked Country
Daughter of Silence
The Shoes of the Fisherman
The Ambassador
The Tower of Babel
Scandal in the Assembly (with R. Francis)
The Heretic, a play in three acts
Summer of the Red Wolf
The Salamander
Harlequin
The Navigator
Proteus
The Clowns of God
The World Is Made of Glass
Cassidy
Master Class
Lazarus
The Ringmaster

MORRIS WEST

Published by arrangement with Donald I. Fine, Inc.

THE LOVERS

Library of Congress Catalog Card Number: 93-70904

ISBN: 0-312-95346-1

Printed in the United States of America

Donald I. Fine hardcover edition published 1993
St. Martin's Paperbacks edition/November 1994

St. Martin's Paperbacks are published by St. Martin's Press, 175 Fifth Avenue, New York, N.Y. 10010.

10 9 8 7 6 5 4 3 2 1

For

Joy,

Companion of so many voyages,
Earth-mother to a scattered family,
and for

Finn,

Latest addition to the tribe,
with much, much love

Author's Note

This is a fiction, but a fiction transmuted from many realities: fragments of personal experience, portraits of men and women met along the pilgrim way, landscapes of islands and continents, where I have sojourned in a traveling life.

I have come now to an age, when the curtains between fact, fiction and the final mystery are wearing thin; so the reader must beware of too hasty identifications. He is not he: she is not she. It's a trick done with mirrors!

The Farnese family became extinct in 1731. I have given myself the pleasure of resurrecting it by the addition of an ennobling predicate "di Mongrifone."

The heraldry of this resurrected family has been designed by Archbishop Bernard Bruno Heim, who for nearly forty years has been the accepted authority on all matters of heraldry in the Roman Catholic Church. He has designed the coats of arms of four popes, and the seals for their administrations.

He bears no responsibility at all for the follies of my Giulia or the machinations of her family and their modern peers. He lived through the epoch as I did. Unlike me, he has been bound by a clerical discretion not to record it.

—Morris L. West

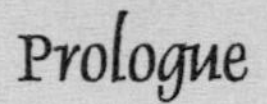

Prologue

A Letter from Rome

Manhattan 1992

BRYAN DE COURCY CAVANAGH HAD A CHAMELEON reputation. The austere brass plaque outside his chambers in the Rue St. Honoré in Paris described him, inadequately, as Counselor in International Law. His wife, Louise, who was a very witty lady, described him as "a floorwalker in the Tower of Babel," because his life was spent in a series of displacements: Beijing, Buenos Aires, London, Sydney, New York, Moscow.

He defined himself with a certain irony: "My clients think I'm a magician. They pay me large sums of money to negotiate impossible bargains between incompatible characters under mutually contradictory systems of law. Of course there's no magic! It's a parlor trick I learned at my children's birthday parties. Everyone has to get a slice of the cake. I make a big ceremony so they all feel uplifted by the sublimity of the occasion. I've got a good eye and a steady hand and I cut clean. For the rest, I'm an agreeable fellow who listens more than he talks and kisses ladies' hands, never tells Irish jokes and sleeps with his own wife and not his client's."

He was born under the sign of Taurus and this was his sixty-fifth birthday. He had spent seven weary hours of it in a Wall Street boardroom trying to mediate an agreement between his own clients, a group of European bankers, and their counterparts in a U.S. consortium. Both parties had lent heavily to an international corporation cobbled together out of a grab bag of small but profitable enterprises which, the prospectus had promised, would merge into a single giant organism, spawning money as a termite queen spawned offspring by the millions in her anthill.

In fact, the investors and the bankers were landed with a genetic freak, doomed to disaster from day one. Within three years, the shareholders' funds were all gone, loan covenants were in massive breach and the monster was dying on its feet, bleeding money by the minute. Unfortunately, the demise was a slow and expensive event because the bankers could not agree whether to dispatch the animal at one stroke or dismember the living body limb by limb for an extra margin of salvage. The Europeans wanted a swift execution. The Americans favored a slow butchery. At five in the afternoon, Bryan de Courcy Cavanagh decided he had had enough. He invoked the Chair:

"By your leave, sir! I have a statement to make, a final statement on behalf of my clients. They consider this debate has gone on long enough. They want the matter put to the vote forthwith. Before the motion is tabled, I beg to remind our colleagues of two lessons they all learned at business school: lesson one, never send good money after bad; lesson two, never try to butcher your own beef. It's a bloody business. Leave it to the professionals. My advice, which my clients accept, is that at opening of business tomorrow, you file all necessary documents in all jurisdictions for the appointment of liquidators to wind up the company. Now, my clients have given me permission to withdraw. Today is my birthday. I'm going to spend what's left of it in a private memorial service for my vanished youth. No flowers by request. Cash donations or contributions of liquor may be sent to my hotel. God keep you from harm in this wicked city! I bid you good evening!"

The exit raised a laugh and a small round of applause. It also took the last heat out of the debate, so that before he reached his hotel the bankers had voted by a comfortable majority for the immediate dissolution of the corporation.

The concierge handed him his key with a bunch of faxes and mail, most of it from his office in Paris. All of it could wait until he had washed the dust of the city out of his pores and the sour taste of business jargon out of his mouth.

Finally, bathed, shaved and fortified with a drink, he began to work through the messages: birthday greetings from Louise and the family, vacationing together in Ireland, sundry letters and a fax from an Italian company—Impresa Romagnola:

> We wish to retain your services as special counsel in certain matters affecting Italian shareholders of this company and their relations with American interests.
>
> Our need is urgent. It would be necessary that you arrive in Rome not later than Saturday the fourth of May and remain at least until the evening of Monday the sixth. You are kindly requested to confirm your acceptance and your arrival time by fax to this office. You will be met at the airport and lodged in comfortable accommodation just outside Rome. During your stay all our communication facilities will be at your disposal.
>
> In respectful anticipation of your consent, we enclose a bank draft for fifteen thousand U.S. dollars to cover an initial retainer and your trav-

eling expenses. We hope most earnestly that you will accept our brief.

I have the honor to be, sir,

Pietro Lombardi
President.

The tone was impersonal and a touch peremptory, but fifteen thousand dollars was somewhat more than a courtesy deposit.

He checked his diary and the airline schedule which he carried always in his briefcase. Today was Thursday, the second of May. He could fly out of New York on Friday evening and arrive in Rome early on Saturday the fourth. He could be back in Paris on the Monday evening, a full week before Louise returned from her holiday. He was about to call her when he remembered that in Ireland it would now be after midnight. No matter. Tomorrow would be soon enough. She was used to his sudden moves and quite incurious about his business affairs. Their lives were conducted in a good-humored shorthand perfected by thirty years of intimacy. Louise had defined it once and for all: "Bryan reserves his eloquence for paying customers. I'm happy with his table talk and his pillow talk and his silences, which are sometimes more interesting anyway."

Immediately he began to organize. A call to Alitalia secured him a first-class seat to Rome on the Friday flight. A fax to Impresa Romagnola confirmed his acceptance of their brief and his arrival time at Fiumicino. It was the way he liked to run his life: Tac! Tac! Decide and do. And when the act was done, tip your hat over your face, drowse and dream in the sun.

He was going through the rest of the correspondence when a hotel messenger delivered a document package in the plastic container of a courier company.

The envelope inside it was made of heavy hand-milled paper, embossed with a coat of arms, sealed with red wax and addressed in a bold, cursive hand.

For a long moment he sat, staring at the envelope, weighing it in his hands, running his fingertips over the embossed emblem on the paper and on the seal itself. He had not seen it for forty years, but he recognized it instantly, as he recognized the handwriting.

The coat of arms was a shield surmounted by a coronet and draped with tasseled cords. The charge on the shield was a pattern of *fleurs-de-lis*. The coronet itself was a female one and the knotted cords also were a female embellishment. They signified that the bearer belonged to an ancient princely house—the Farnese of Mongrifone.

There was a paper knife on the desk. He slit the envelope with great care and took out the letter.

My dear Friend,

For the past forty years I have made it my business to know where you would be on your birthday. I have never written to you, though I have often wanted to do so. Instead, on each anniversary I have gone to the chapel at Mongrifone, made a prayer for you and, afterwards, sat in the villa garden listening to the small sound of the water and remembering the journeys we made together in that long-ago springtime.

This time, however, I find myself in great need of your presence and your support. So I am asking you to visit me at Mongrifone. We are both long past the age of indiscretion, so there can be no question of scandal. Nevertheless, I would not, for a moment, risk an embarrassment to your wife or your family. Therefore, I have arranged for you to be invited to act as Special Counsel to Impresa Romagnola, which is one of our family companies.

I still have the medallion you gave me. I have worn it like an amulet every day of every year. So, the gold is much rubbed; the Graces have aged somewhat; Mercury has lost some of his sparkle. However, the inscription is still legible: *vocatus extemplo adsum*!

That's how I've remembered you always: as the lover with wings on his feet, who would come instantly to my call. I hope I haven't left the call too late.

Ti voglio ben assai,

Giulia

Time was suddenly suspended; space was emptied about him. Every sense was quickened by a swift surge of memories: the drift of her perfume, the texture of her skin, the pulse and passion of her voice. Her urgent, imperious script invoked them all, like the score of a symphony, read in silence, yet heard in rich harmonies through all the caverns of the soul. Even after forty years of separation and silence, the music had power to tempt him back into the perilous uplands of the love-country.

Long practice in the law had made him a skeptic. Thirty years of stable marriage had taught him that love was a plant which needed patient nurture if it were to survive the stresses and erosions of time. In spite of his Celtic origins, he did not believe in ghosts; yet far back in his subconscious was a region haunted by unexorcised memories and dilemmas still unresolved.

This letter, for instance, was both pleasant and poignant to contemplate over a drink at the end of a long business day in New York. On the other hand, it would take a deal of explaining to Louise who, for all her good humor, would tolerate no trespass on her family turf. She had enough Italian to know that *"Ti voglio ben assai"* did not mean "Have a nice day," and the spectacle of Bryan de Courcy Cavanagh as a winged messenger hurrying to the call of an old lover would please her not at all!

Immediately he reminded himself that there was no way in the world Louise could possibly know about Giulia. That affair had ended years before Louise had come into his life—which made it only the harder to explain, even to himself, why he felt obliged to honor a promise made in the heat of passion forty years ago.

Why indeed? One of the rewards of age was that the truce between the present and the past was easier to maintain. Time dulled the pain of all grieving, took the edge off most guilts. Nonetheless, his encounter with Giulia had left him so wounded in his self-esteem that he had locked the memory away in the deepest recesses of his subconscious, determined never to contemplate it, never never to discuss it. He had held to his resolve. He was a natural and entertaining storyteller, but on this subject he had never indulged himself in anecdote or allusion, even of the most trivial kind.

Now, totally unprepared, he was beset with memories, besieged by phantoms: himself, a big, freckled red-head, with a Navy discharge and a brand new law degree, leaving his home place in Sydney, Australia, for the Grand Tour of postwar Europe. The ship that carried him was a Greek rust-bucket called the *Kyrenia,* which came out loaded with migrants and went back half-filled with cut-price tourists, while she tramped the intervening ports for bodies to fill her vacant cabins.

In those days and in that shuddering hull the journey from Sydney to Athens and Genoa took six long weeks; but for Bryan de Courcy Cavanagh, with two hundred pounds sterling in his pocket and five hundred more in a circular letter of credit on Coutts Bank, every hour of every day was a new adventure.

His pulse-beat had always been in rhythm with the swing of the sea. Even in his callow days as junior watch officer on a corvette, he had the reputation of a man who could smell the weather and find a sea for the helmsman in the most turbulent stormwater. This voyage was like a chaplet of recollections—the jeweled islands and cays of the Great Barrier Reef, the misty shorelines of the East India archipelagoes, the slow enveloping smell of Asia as they came at midnight to drop anchor in the Singapore Roads, the bare cliffs of Aden giving off heat like an oven.

His early masters—the Brothers and the Jesuits—had packed him full of learning, Latin and Greek and Romance languages and ancient history and the geographies of the great voyagers. All of it had lain fallow during the war years and the postwar ones when he was running to catch up with learning and with life. Now, suddenly, it was blooming like a flower patch in spring.

He could sit on the bridge at midnight and make disjointed but comradely talk with the second mate, who came from Samos in the Dodecanese. He could curl up in one of the leaky lifeboats—God help all if they should ever be needed!—and make love with the young Portuguese widow wending her way homeward from Timor. He could huddle over an ouzo with the old bearded missionary from the uplands of New Guinea, who told him strange tales of the women who offered their first born to the pig-god and then took a piglet to the breast, of the man who could change himself into a cassowary and run faster than the wind along the mountain trails, of the sorcerers who were seen to be in two places at the same moment . . .

But all this was overture to what he knew in his flesh and bones would be the grandest opera of all—*The Passionate Pilgrim.* It would tell the tale of de Courcy Cavanagh, the Boy Wonder from the Antipodes, going back to his roots in Europe, then scrambling happily among the spreading branches of his family tree which, so his elders had told him, spread far and wide: to Halifax in Nova Scotia, and Boston, and Manhattan, and even to the vineyards of Bordeaux, where the de Courcys and the Cavanaghs had come with the first flight of the wild geese.

Well, maybe it hadn't all been grand, but sure as hell there had been some high operatic moments, big passionate arias, moments of dark tragedy, muted in the end to safe, perennial operetta, in which the freckled-faced boy from down under won himself a bride from the old quality and they bred themselves beautiful children and lived happily ever after, with himself a Docteur d'Etat in the European Community on which he had placed a bet while it was still a dream in the mind of Jean Monnet.

It had been a gamble—Mother of God, what a gamble! He could have accepted to dine in the temple and thence been called to the bar in London. He could have accepted Lou Molloy's invitation and done postgraduate law at Harvard, made himself an American citizen and been hoisted to a lucrative partnership in Manhattan. Instead, pigheaded bog-trotter that he was, he had opted for the long slog for his master's degree at the Sorbonne, the year in Moscow wrestling with the Marxist legal system, the time in Rome and Madrid preparing his doctoral thesis on the mutations of the Codex Justinianus into modern times.

It was Giulia who had urged him to walk this long way round to get the eggs. "You're a hybrid," she told him. "You're a native twig grafted on Celtic stock. In Britain, you'll always be the outlander. No matter how high you rise, you'll always be the upstart, the Wild Colonial Boy, patronized and damned with the same compliment. In America, you'll be caught in the old trap, the immigrants at war with each other and the Brahmins against them all. Of course you'll be among the winners, like the Kennedys and the Fitzgeralds, with money running out of your ears; but you won't like yourself any more. So it's two choices only: go home and be king in your own cabbage patch, or come to Europe, with all the other displaced tribes, and build it anew from the rubble upwards . . . Don't you see, you were bred for this, because this is the country in which your mind lives. This is why you and I struck fire the moment we met . . ."

He had believed her. His whole career attested to the wisdom of her advice. The irony was that a scant two weeks after she had offered it, she had thrust him out of her life and closed the door in his face.

She had done it calmly and lucidly. It was an act already understood and agreed between them. Their golden days were over; now she was summoned back to the world of business and statecraft to which the Farnese had been dedicated for centuries. Bryan de Courcy Cavanagh could have no place in their convoluted lives. He had feared that and fought it from the beginning; but he was still unprepared for the bitterness of the end.

Now, forty years later, Giulia was telling him that for her the loving had never ended and that she still counted upon his promise to come instantly at her call.

In his hotel room in Manhattan, Cavanagh found a grace of laughter. God damn the woman! She hadn't changed. She was still as arrogant and imperious as the long-dead princess for whom she was named—

Giulia Farnese, called The Beautiful. He could still see the proud lift of her chin, the fire in her dark eyes, the toss of her lustrous hair as she demanded "Do this! Do that! Take me there!" He could still hear the ripple of her laughter when he poured eloquent derision on her for a spoiled brat and a Roman snob and a chattel put up for auction in the marriage market by a down-at-heels prince. But she wouldn't give him an inch of ground. She taunted him: "Giulia the Beautiful was sold by her brother to the Borgia Pope when she was fifteen, but the Romans fell in love with her and called her the Bride of Christ—or the Pope's whore, according to their mood! And her gift to him on his deathbed was a third child, while her profligate brother finally became Pope himself! So, can you match that, my young vagabond? Can you?"

Of course he couldn't and he had to confess it. So, after the fight was the lovemaking, wild and wonderful, and after that the peacemaking and the whispered hopes that dawn would never come and the moonlit enchantment would last forever.

It didn't. Bryan de Courcy Cavanagh was a fledgling attorney with the wanderlust still on him and all his hopes in his head and nothing but small wages in his pocket. How the hell could he compete with Lou Molloy and all his millions and his high connections in the Democratic machine, with Spellman and the Vatican and, through those, to Adenauer in Germany and Franco in Spain and the Farnese and their like in Italy and even to de Gaulle, walking on the water at Colombey des Deux Eglises?

Lou Molloy! Now there was a character for you, a Black Irish buccaneer if God ever made one, supple as silk, with a smile like a summer's day, full of dignities when he chose to be and dangerous as a cocked pistol if you crossed him. He was what the old folk used to call "a fine figure of a man," flat bellied, straight backed, not an ounce of fat on him anywhere. He had big, innocent brown eyes and behind them a brain like a fine Swiss watch.

His family was in the machine-tool business, essential reserved occupation, but he had served time as a volunteer in the coast guard, using his own boat as an off-shore patrol vessel.

After the war, everything was easy. The family fortune devolved to him. In the period of postwar shortages he doubled then trebled it. The Democrats wanted to run him for the Senate. He waved them off. That was the Kennedy playground and he'd rather pay to watch than get his nose bloodied in their family game. Besides, politics under the spotlight was not his style. He preferred the chess matches played in boardrooms and clubs and chateaux in France and villas in the Tuscan Hills. Half his interests were in Europe now and he was convinced that Western Europe could develop into a viable political and economic entity, a land-bridge one day, between the Soviet states and the American continent.

He had had a variety of lovers in his life and had treated them all—except one—with a tyrant's disdain. Now it was time for him to take a wife and he would do it in the old dynastic style, with a union blessed by the Church and ornamented by tradition.

Wise in the ways of Irishry in America, he sought—and paid handsomely for—counsel from the man they called "the American Pope," Francis Cardinal Spellman, Archbishop of New York. By way of insurance he also talked with old Joe Kennedy and the McDonnells and the Cuddihys, who headed the Irish social set in Manhattan.

In due time, a smiling Spellman conveyed the news that the Pope himself was nodding towards a possible bride, a twenty-four-year-old Italian princess with an ancient name and a father eager to establish his own transatlantic connections. Molloy, in his careful fashion, took the suggestion under advisement and agreed, that subject to pre-nuptial agreement and the provision of a papal decoration for himself—the Order of St. Gregory would serve quite nicely, thank you—he would commit to the sacrament. It was typical of the man that he doubted neither his power to charm the lady nor his potency to match her in bed and endow her with beautiful children.

Bryan de Courcy Cavanagh had been witness to the wooing and was safely gone before the wedding. Of the marriage itself he knew nothing, save that a son had been born to the happy couple and that Lou Molloy had died in New York a week before his sixty-seventh birthday. Cavanagh read the obituary in the Paris edition of the *Herald Tribune* while he was holidaying with Louise in Amalfi. For a brief moment he was tempted to send a telegram of condolence to Giulia; then he thought better of it. The past was safely buried, why open the vault and set the ghosts walking?

Alone in his hotel room, looking over the long traverse of his past, Cavanagh was invaded by a winter chill. Not all this was pleasant reminiscence of young love and passionate encounters and lyric duets. There were guilts in it, too, betrayals and treacheries in which both he and Giulia had played their special roles. There were lies and shabby little stratagems, the games of spoiled children who cared not at all for the hurts they inflicted. He wondered how much Molloy had seen at the time or guessed over the years, how much he had chosen to ignore to maintain his honor and the stability of this most convenient marriage.

Suddenly his own company was intolerable to him. He tossed off the lees of his drink at a gulp, put on his street clothes and headed up Madison to a small bistro where the patron served drinks at an old-fashioned zinc bar and madame dispensed onion soup and coq au vin and a wraithlike girl played piano and sang Piaf songs. He was known. He was welcomed. He could sit quietly over his food and not feel too solitary while he remembered his first encounter with Lou Molloy, on a June day forty years ago.

Book One

The Cruise of the Salamandra d'Oro

Summer 1952

BY THE CALENDAR IT WAS LATE SPRING, but it rained that morning: hard, driving squalls which brought flurries of hail from the foothills above the town. The Old Port was deserted. The freighter-men from Italy had unloaded their wicker baskets and were waiting for the delayed deliveries of rose blooms and carnations from the hothouse growers. The fishermen had sorted and sold their catch, washed their nets and gone home. Their painted boats rocked gently in the tideless basin. In the dockyard, the shipwrights were working under cover. The trawler, hauled up on the slips for scraping and painting, looked like a hulk abandoned after a tempest.

As abruptly as it had begun, the rain stopped, the clouds lifted and the Old Port was bathed in pale spring sunshine. Bryan de Courcy Cavanagh finished his coffee, paid the score and walked out of the Bar Felix, through the Porte Marine and along the Esplanade to the lighthouse at the entrance to the harbor. He was a big fellow in those days, red-haired, tall, deep in the chest and broad across the shoulders, with ham fists and bright blue eyes and an easy grin. He was only twenty-five but he had the weathered, young-old look of a man with a certain amount of living behind him. Even Felix, the patron, who had small faith in mankind, less in women and none at all in God, treated this one with reluctant respect.

He had fetched up in Antibes a week ago, looking for a place to rest his feet. He let it be known that he had made his way on foot across the frontier. He had landed in Genoa from Australia and was fully resolved to spend the summer tramping around Europe—unless of course he could find a berth as a crewman on a pleasure yacht.

"I wish you luck," Felix had said, dismissing the notion with a flick of his dishcloth. "How many pleasure yachts do you think we get in here nowadays? The war's been over since 1945 but we're still up to our necks in shit! Indochina, the Russians blockading Berlin, the Chinese pouring their troops into Korea. We've still got that great cesspool on the edge of the port where the Boche blew their mines! And they call this a peace?"

Nobody had bothered to answer. Felix was entitled to gripe in his own bar. His problems were well known. His first wife had divorced him. His second had run off with a cigarette salesman from Paris. His only son had stepped on a Vietminh land mine.

But Bryan de Courcy Cavanagh had his own reasons to be hopeful. In Madame Audiberti's pension he had met Marie-Claire, who came from Corsica and who worked with the Société Glémot: yacht brokers, ship chandlers and provedores. Marie-Claire had an angel face and a happy devil in her dark eyes, and a ready lust for Bryan de Courcy Cavanagh. She had told him of the imminent arrival of the motor yacht, *Salamandra d'Oro,* Boston registry, heading from Alicante to prepare for a Mediterranean cruise. Her master had wired ahead for fuel, fresh water and a list of provisions as long as your arm—all luxury stuff, liquor, pre-cut meats, deep-frozen foods, fresh fruits and vegetables. They also wanted local labor for two days of scrubbing, painting and bright-work. The port captain had her listed for berth number three.

So, experienced by now in the ways of dock rats and five-dollar-a-day hitchhikers, Cavanagh perched himself on a bollard at berth number three, ready to take *Salamandra*'s stern lines, run the hose from the water hydrant, and then, either pick up a tip or offer himself for hire. To which end he carried always on his person his passport, his Navy discharge papers and the final captain's report on his competence as a navigator and watch officer.

The only value of the latter document was that it was authentic and, given half a chance, he could demonstrate the skills it described. However he had learned early that the whole Mediterranean littoral was crawling with ex-Navy types driving all sorts of craft from motor torpedo boats to clapped-out freighters, all running contraband, guns, cigarettes, whiskey, and warm bodies from North Africa to Europe. That sort of job was easy enough to find and it paid good money; but Bryan de Courcy Cavanagh had survived one war and he had no desire to get his head shot off by a trigger-happy customs man or to spend his precious sabbatical in a Mediterranean jail. So, perched on his bollard, he fished out a battered copy of Mistral's lyrics and waited for the *Salamandra d'Oro* to poke her nose past the gray bulk of the lighthouse.

At ten o'clock precisely she slid into the basin: a hundred feet of sleek white hull with a clipper bow and a square transom with a golden salamander displayed in relief under her nameplate. She had a low profile and a broad beam, acres of afterdeck and a sheltered area for sunbathing abaft the wheelhouse. This was a real sea boat built for cruising comfort and nothing stinted in the way of craftsman work. The crew moved and worked like trained sailors: a winchman in the bows, ready to let go the anchors, one man aft with a heaving line, a deckhand laying out the fenders, although there was not another vessel within hailing distance. Whoever was running this craft did things by the book—starboard anchor dropped well up into the wind, a good spread for the port hook, then a slow steady reverse into the berth. Cavanagh held up a hand to signal that he was ready to take the stern lines. Two minutes later, the vessel was made fast, the gangplank was lowered and the deckhands were coiling ropes on the afterdeck.

A few moments afterwards, a tall dark fellow in immaculate whites came to inspect the stern moorings. Cavanagh hailed him.

"Excuse me, sir. Are you the master of this beauty?"

"Owner *and* master." He had a flat Boston intonation with a touch of the Irish in it. "What can I do for you?"

"The word's about that you'll be hiring day labor through Glémot. I'm your first applicant and the best you'll get by a country mile."

"Are you now?" A faint vinegary grin twitched at the dark one's lips. "And who may you be?"

"Bryan de Courcy Cavanagh, sir, Australian passport, ex-Navy, clean discharge and a captain's report which says I'm a good bridge officer with two years of combat duty."

"But now you're on the beach?"

"Not quite. I've just finished a law degree and I'm giving myself a working holiday in Europe."

"And you're looking to bum a free ride round the Mediterranean for the summer?"

"On the contrary," said Cavanagh agreeably. "I was offering for day labor, scrubbing, painting and varnishing. I doubt I'd want to serve under you at sea.

I'm a good humored fellow and I'd have trouble with that sharp tongue of yours. I bid you good day, sir."

He was already five paces down the esplanade when a shout stopped him in his tracks.

"Cavanagh."

"Sir!"

"I'll expect you aboard at seventeen hundred hours. You'll get an apology and a drink."

Cavanagh gave him a wide grin and a snappy salute.

"It's a gentleman's offer. May I know the name of the man who made it?"

"Molloy. Declan Aloysius Molloy."

"I'll accept the drink, Mr. Molloy, but I'll make the apology. I've been on the road too long. I'm forgetting my manners."

"I look forward to our drink, Mr. Cavanagh."

"And a very good day to you, Mr. Molloy."

It had been an edgy little exchange: two Irishmen playing "waltz-me-round-Willie," each waiting for the other to tread on the tails of his coat. Even so, it had ended well—oh yes, by God! Better than well—though he still wasn't sure whether Molloy was inviting him to discuss a job or setting him up for a fall to pay for his impudence. Either way, he'd best come to the meeting well groomed and with all his wits about him.

His first call was on Marie-Claire at the Glémot establishment. For a modest fee she signed him on to their crew register for service on foreign vessels. Then she helped him choose a pair of white trousers, a white shirt, white deck shoes. She gave him a discount of ten percent and a passionate embrace for good measure—which left him no choice but to invite her to lunch at the Relais de la Galette. After lunch he suggested an hour in bed, but she declined. Too long an absence would get her fired. Good jobs were scarce;

eager lovers were much easier to find. So Bryan de Courcy Cavanagh took his siesta alone and dreamed of white sails on a wine-dark sea and brown girls leaping over the horns of bulls in the sunshine of ancient Crete.

At seventeen hundred hours he presented himself at the gangway of the *Salamandra d'Oro*. Molloy was seated on the afterdeck, reading a book, with a tray of drinks beside him. He snapped the book shut and stood to greet his guest.

"Welcome aboard, Mr. Cavanagh."

Cavanagh walked up the gangway and paused to slip off his shoes before stepping on to the teak deck. Molloy noted the courtesy, but said nothing. He waved Cavanagh to a chair.

"What would you like to drink?"

"I'll join you with the Scotch."

"Water? Ice?"

"Please."

Molloy made him a generous drink, then raised his glass in a toast.

"*Slainte!*"

"And your health too!"

Molloy looked him up and down with a critical eye, then gave him that sour grin and a grudging approval.

"I must say you scrub up well, Cavanagh. I'm impressed."

"You shouldn't be." Cavanagh was relaxed and amiable. "I don't know how far the Molloys go back in Boston, but in Australia the Cavanaghs have had lace-curtains for three generations."

To his surprise Molloy burst out laughing.

"You're an impertinent young bugger, Cavanagh, but I begin to like you! Lace-curtain Irish! I haven't heard that in a long time, but yes, that's what we were too, I guess. What did your people do?"

"My grandfather struck it rich on the Ballarat goldfields; but he had ten children so the inheritance was somewhat dispersed. My father put his share into the liquor business—country pubs in the big towns. My mother taught me manners. I had three sisters to coach me in the ways of women. The Christian Brothers ground religion into me and the Jesuits introduced me to the liberal arts—and they all left it to the Navy to knock the rough edges off me. One way and another I've been a lucky fellow."

"Which makes me wonder why you're doing this trip the hard way."

"Hard! This isn't hard! What am I doing at this moment, but drinking good liquor in good company on a beautiful boat—with half an expectation that I might be offered a job at the end of it."

"That's my point. With a background like the one you describe, how come you need a job?"

"Or more precisely, how do you know I'm not some Mediterranean cowboy fresh from drug running or smuggling cigarettes from Casablanca?"

"That's about the size of it."

"According to the strict rules of evidence, I could be selling you a can full of smoke. But if you knew the Cavanaghs—and I'm told there are a few cousins and near cousins in Boston—then you'd understand that they're godly folk who give handouts to the poor and needy, and are hard as iron to their own. My old man—God love him!—had it figured out for all of us. He'd paid for our education, the rest was up to us. I did my law course on a Service Grant and paid my room and board and the rest of my living, working as a barman, a fruit packer and penciling bets for a bookie at the tracks. That filled up a lot of gaps in my liberal education. I didn't mention, by the way, that I have French, Italian, German, Greek and Spanish—which may be a help to you."

"I'm sure it could be," said Molloy, "but right now I want to know how good a seaman you are."

Cavanagh fished in his pocket, brought out a battered wallet and laid out the documents on the table:

"Passport, discharge, service record. They'll tell you as much as I can."

"More, maybe!" Molloy gave a short, barking laugh. "I was Navy myself. I used to write these things."

Cavanagh sipped his liquor and waited in silence until Molloy handed the documents back to him and announced:

"I'll walk you round the ship."

"I'd like that. She's a beauty. Who designed her?"

"A friend of mine. The best naval architect in Quincy." There was a ring of pride in the answer. "I had her built in Glasgow at half the price she would have cost me at home. She did her sea trials in the Baltic and her shakedown cruise from Plymouth to Gibraltar. After that we took her round the Balearics and into Alicante. Let's take a look at the bridge first."

The change in Cavanagh's demeanor was abrupt. He studied every item in the console layout with a cool professional eye, counting off the items, touching each one as he did so.

". . . throttles, automatic pilot, electric log, depth sounder, forty mile radar, D.F. loop, medium wave and V.H.F. transceivers, chart index, a full Mediterranean list of pilot books, everything well positioned for a one-man helm-watch. A man would feel very comfortable up here, Mr. Molloy."

"And you could handle it all."

"Sure. But to do it properly I'd make myself familiar with your construction and wiring plans."

"Let's go look at the engine room."

When he stepped into the head-high chamber and saw the twin diesels and the big generators and the banks of knife batteries and switch-gear, Cavanagh gave a whistle of admiration.

"You've done yourself proud. Who's your engineer?"

"An old shipmate of mine, Boston Greek, Giorgios Hadjidakis. Do you have any engine room experience?"

"Very little and very basic. I can read a manual, use a wrench and an oil can and do exactly what the engineer orders in a damage control situation. That's as far as I go. How many crew do you carry?"

"On the voyage over we had five. Myself, Giorgios, Marcantonio the chef and two deckhands. When our guests come on board they'll double as stewards, and I'll be bringing in a cabin attendant for the ladies of the party."

"By my count," said Cavanagh "you're short one bridge officer. You'll have very little time to spend with your guests, especially if you're making long runs and overnight passages."

"You're right of course. We do need a third officer. Interested?"

"Eager would say it better."

"Eager enough to wear a sharp-tongued skipper?"

"Well, now!" Cavanagh gave him a big smile and a small shrug of deprecation. "Let's say I could offer you enough skill to hone the edge off your tongue, and you're enough like my old man to teach me the manners I lack."

"Prettily said." Molloy was a little amused. "But that doesn't get you the job. It gets you the next drink and another set of questions. Let's go topside."

"After you, Mr. Molloy."

This time all the questions had barbs in them.

"Tell me about your sex life."

"With respect, Mr. Molloy, it's none of your goddamn business."

"You'd better be goddamn sure it is my business!" Molloy's anger was swift and cold. "This is my ship, mister! There's nowhere off limits to me! So, answer me, man! What's your preference?"

"Women."

"Have you ever had any sexually transmitted diseases?"

"No. And I'm bloody careful to avoid 'em."

"If you were offered the job, would you be willing to undergo a full medical—at the ship's expense of course."

"Why not? But why should you care?"

There was a sudden dark anger in Molloy's eyes and a savage rasp in his voice.

"Because my principal guest is the young woman I'm going to marry. So every man jack about this vessel is going to have a clean body, clean hands and a civil mouth to welcome the lady and offer her the respect and service she deserves. Are you answered, Mr. Cavanagh?"

"I'm answered." His tone was mild and respectful. Inside, an imp of laughter was plaguing him. This was too much altogether. It was archaic, incongruous, overblown, like a bad sermon from a ranting preacher. He waited in silence until Molloy demanded curtly:

"So, do you want the job?"

"I'd like to know what you're offering."

"Four months' contract. Discharge in Antibes. I'm booking a permanent berth here—buying a share in the new harbor. You get seventy-five dollars a week, paid in U.S. currency, which means you do very nicely in drachmas and lire. Ship's rations, all found. You get two free uniforms and a set of working coveralls. You buy liquor and cigarettes from ship's stores at duty-free prices. You're insured against accident and sickness while on duty. You will not accept gratuities from guests. An end-of-voyage bonus may be paid for meritorious service. That's it."

"When do I sign on?"

"As soon as you present a clean bill of health. Glémot will make a doctor's appointment for you tomorrow." He poured another generous shot of whisky and handed it to Cavanagh.

"Let's drink to a pleasant voyage."

"And a happy homecoming! Maybe I could polish up my Greek enough to write you an epithalamium."

"Which would be what? Instruct me, Cavanagh. I have no Greek and only Mass Latin."

"A marriage song, a nuptial hymn."

For the first time Molloy laughed: an open, happy sound.

"Cavanagh, you're a clown!"

"I am that!" Cavanagh grinned, ruefully. "My old man stuck the label on me a long time ago. My mother—God rest her—made a virtue out of it. 'A clown,' she said, 'makes people laugh; so he has his proper place in God's universe. It's your drunken buffoons I can't tolerate.'"

"Wise woman."

"She was. I miss her."

"Do you have any steady woman in your life?"

"I've a lot of women friends; but none I'd call a friend of the heart."

"I should warn you," Lou Molloy surveyed him with genial malice, "you'll be seeing a lot of ports on this trip, but we won't be lingering too long in any of them. In harbor, half the staff is always on duty to serve the guests, and those off duty stay within easy call in case we want to make a quick getaway. So your playtime will be strictly limited."

"I expected nothing different." Cavanagh was a model of good humor. "It's a small price to pay for a berth on a beautiful ship—and on a lovers' cruise no less!"

"And just so you'll never say I didn't give you a true bill of goods, there's some dirty work to be done before we put to sea: scouring bilges, checking all the toilet systems, bleeding water from the fuel tanks. Giorgios Hadjidakis is a hard man to please."

"And I'm the new boy; so he'll have me swimming in grease and bilge water."

"That's about the size of it, Mr. Cavanagh. But you'll have the midnight watch, so you'll breathe the clean night air and get the stink of diesel out of your nostrils."

"The Lord giveth," Cavanagh intoned with mock solemnity, "the Lord taketh away. For seventy-five bucks a week all found, the skipper doth what pleaseth him. Amen."

Declan Aloysius Molloy let out a huge bellow of laughter.

"We're well met, Cavanagh! If you're free of the pox and your lungs are clear, you're hired! When you meet your shipmates ask them about me, they'll tell you I'm a bad man to cross, but I look after my own!"

"I'm happy to hear it," said Bryan de Courcy Cavanagh. "My thanks for the job and your hospitality. I'll report for duty the moment I have the doctor's certificate in my fist. I bid you goodnight, sir."

He saluted smartly, picked up his shoes and walked down the gangplank without a backward glance. He sat on a bollard while he slipped on his shoes, then set off down the marina, whistling the jaunty little tune which is called "The Low-backed Car." From the afterdeck Lou Molloy called after him:

"My father used to sing that tune to me. Five dollars if you know the words, Cavanagh."

"You've lost already, Mr. Molloy! 'Twas my mother

that taught them to me!" and to prove it, he began to sing in a clear, true baritone.

When first I saw sweet Peggy,
'Twas on a market day,
A low-backed car she drove and sat
Upon a load of hay.

The song rang out, sweet but alien across the sleepy little port. The sea birds rose clattering from their roost along the ramparts.

Declan Aloysius Molloy smiled happily to himself as he watched his new bridge officer stride jauntily down the dockside. He believed in the luck of the Irish, who were the favored children of the Church, beloved by the Pope and by God. This young sprout of the Cavanagh clan was the latest proof that God looked after his own.

Bryan de Courcy Cavanagh also believed in the luck of the Irish, but he was a mite more skeptical about divine intervention in his personal affairs. Even in his own short life he had met a dozen Lou Molloys in as many settings and aliases: wearing the black cassock of the Brothers or the clergy, or a bookie's check suit at the track, making secret corner-of-the-mouth talk at the Hibernian Club or bluffing their way out of a brawl with the shore patrol in Trincomalee.

All of them had the same leery eye, the same ready smile, the same dash of the bully and the opportunist. Sober, they could charm the birds out of the trees; drunk or with the black angers upon them, they were bad and dangerous company. In love? Come to think of it, he had never seen one of them in love—which accounted for his shock at Molloy's sudden ranting outburst about his bride-to-be, which also raised the question of who she was and where she came from and why Lou Molloy was making such a song and dance about his late spring wooing.

Properly speaking, Cavanagh admonished himself, none of it was his business. For seventy-five bucks a week, all found, in a soft berth, he should be deaf, dumb and blind—and if Lou Molloy wanted to marry Medusa herself, so be it, Amen! Alleluia!

For himself, he was planning a celebration. He would take Marie-Claire into Cannes. They would dine in a small but chic Indochinese restaurant, and then try their fortune at the casino. Afterwards, win or lose, they would climb to his attic room in Madame Audiberti's pension and make what Marie-Claire called in her Corsican dialect, little love games, which in English translated into long and very passionate encounters. Marie-Claire had already told him she would regret to see him leave Antibes. On the other hand she was betrothed to a Corsican cousin, and was working to supplement the modest dowry her father had promised. So, much better to make a happy ending than a messy one, no? With which simple proposition Bryan de Courcy Cavanagh had no quarrel at all. His own Irish luck was holding better than he deserved.

Within forty-eight hours, he was signed on to the ship's manifest and took up residence in the crew's quarters of the *Salamandra d'Oro*. Giorgios Hadjidakis, lean, dark and laconic, introduced him to his shipmates:

". . . Leo and Jackie, deckhands, bunkmates, members of the corps de ballet in the Boston dance ensemble . . . "

They were a good looking pair, lithe as cats, muscular as feral animals. Leo was the spokesman and his speech was brief but loaded.

"Welcome aboard, Bryan. Good to have some

young blood in the forepeak . . . Anything we can do to make you comfortable . . . anything at all."

"Thank you, Leo. Thank you both." Cavanagh offered a firm handshake and a guileless grin. "Which of you is the helmsman?"

"I am," Leo blushed and bridled at the admission. "Jackie's the front-of-house person. He knows how to pour wine and which side to serve the vegetables and how to keep the chef happy in the kitchen."

"Our chef." Giorgios made the announcement with a spartan dignity. "Our chef is Signor Marcantonio Caviglia, late of the Grand Hotel du Lac, Lugano, Switzerland."

"I offer you my most profound respects, maestro." Bryan de Courcy Cavanagh was already in vein with the occasion. "I was bred in Australia, which rides on the sheep's back, and where the most important and highly paid functionary is the shearer's cook. He lives and works at great risk, since hungry shearers have been known to turn violent. So, maestro, you have my respect, my very great respect."

"And if you, my friend, have any special dietary needs . . ."

"Thanks for the thought, maestro. I'll try to spare you any problems."

The introductions over, Hadjidakis spelled out the laws of his narrow kingdom.

"Topside and aft, Lou Molloy is God. Down here in the forepeak, I, Giorgios Hadjidakis, am God's anointed. There's not much space, so we eat, sleep, shave, shower and use the head according to the roster pinned on the door. We don't like noise. We don't make arguments. We stow our gear neatly and dump our dirty laundry in the container provided. Each man's locker, his drawer space and his bookshelf are sacred. Any problems or questions?"

"None. I'm housebroken and Navy-trained."

"That's what you told Lou. That's what Lou told me. So here's the program. First light tomorrow, we take ourselves out for a little cruise. On the way we pump the bilges and flush out the sewage holding tanks. After that you get down under the floorboards and sluice down with disinfectant. While you're down there, you'll inspect the drive shaft bearings and glands, and make yourself familiar with the plumbing and electrical layouts. By the end of the day we'll have the whole plant greased and polished so that you could eat your dinner off the engine blocks. How does that grab you, Navy man?"

"Right where I live," Cavanagh assured him cheerfully. "I like a tidy ship. Lighten up, Mr. Hadjidakis. Stop trying to scare me. I've been hazed by experts. Besides, some of my best friends are Greeks."

He offered his hand. Hadjidakis hesitated a moment, then a reluctant smile dawned on his dark, saturnine features. He accepted the handshake and offered an invitation.

"Chef and I are eating ashore tonight. Would you like to join us?"

"Sure! I'd like that; but seeing I've just signed on, Mr. Molloy might want . . ."

"Lou's spending the next two nights in Monte Carlo. You're not rostered for duty until tomorrow. Besides, it's the custom of the ship: on the *Salamandra d'Oro* we embalm you first and let you die afterwards!"

The embalming was a long but painless operation. It began with drinks on the afterdeck, served by Leo, with canapés prepared by Jackie, which earned high praise from Chef. Then followed a taxi ride to Biot, followed by more drinks in a roadhouse where the patron was an old friend of Chef and the meal was a Provençal epic, three hours long.

Chef, in his cups, proved a garrulous tale-teller.

Hadjidakis, on the other hand, displayed a waspish temper and an oddly proprietorial attitude towards the ship and all who sailed in her. Cavanagh, schooled from his youth in wardroom etiquette, listened respectfully, and asked only an occasional discreet question. Somewhere between the fish and the fowl, the talk turned to Lou Molloy and the significance of this cruise in his life history.

Chef announced emphatically, "I know you don't agree, Giorgios, but I think this marriage a good match, wealth on one side, on the other a noble and ancient lineage. Lou Molloy always does things in style."

"That's his problem," Hadjidakis gave a gloomy assent. "He's obsessed with bloody style. So much of him is genuine, I can't think why he stoops to the fakery. He doesn't have any illusions about himself. He'll tell you straight that he's a peasant who's going to be a prince—I understand that. My grandfather was a dirt farmer from Crete. In his cups he'd swear he was descended from the Kings of Mycenae."

"Whatever his origins," Chef persisted in his argument, "Molloy has the presence of a great actor. From the moment he makes an entrance he dominates the company. You talk of him as a peasant. I see him as one of the great *condottieri*, a mercenary if you like, but one who has earned his own title and his own fiefdom. This marriage he's about to make is in the same grand manner."

"You're cooking up fairy tales," Hadjidakis mocked him testily. "Lou's a very rich man. He has money spawning money. But that isn't enough for him. He wants gilt icing on the cake. The Brahmins of Boston won't accept him. So he's marrying back into the old aristocracy—spent bloodlines in a Europe that's already dead. He doesn't seem to understand that he's making himself ridiculous in all sorts of ways."

"Forgive my ignorance," Cavanagh posed the mild question, "but whom exactly is he marrying?"

Hadjidakis shrugged.

"You tell him, Chef. I'm bored with the whole business."

"You're jealous," said Chef, amiably. "You and Lou Molloy have been roistering bachelors ever since the war. Now, you can't bear the thought of breaking up the party."

"That's not true. I happen to believe he's making a big mistake."

"So it's his life. He'll live it the way he wants!"

"Why don't you tell Cavanagh the whole story? You know the bride's family. You worked for them at one stage, didn't you?"

"Look! There's no hurry!" Cavanagh felt the need to damp down the argument. "I'm the new boy. It's none of my business anyway."

"Oh, but it is!" Hadjidakis was emphatic. "Tomorrow we clean ship. The day after we take on water, fuel and stores—and my lady's personal stewardess arrives from London. She used to be a first-class cabin attendant with Cunard no less! Then we leave for Monte Carlo to pick up Lou Molloy and his guests. Our cruise begins from there. So, my young friend, you'd better know exactly what you'll be dealing with for the rest of the voyage. Go on, Chef! Tell him!"

"Pour me more wine, Giorgios. This is a complicated story and you always read it upside down!"

"How so?"

"You make Lou Molloy the hunter, instead of the hunted. He didn't come to Europe looking for a bride. He was looking for business: reconstruction projects using Marshall Plan dollars and local partners. The Farnese were eager to make an alliance with American capital. So they offered him a bonus, the daughter of the house, the little princess Giulia Farnese."

"And Lou leaped at it, like trout at a mayfly."

"Of course he did! It was a match made in heaven—or at least by the Vicar of Christ and a bunch of his most powerful henchmen, Cardinal Spellman of New York, Count Galeazzi of the Vatican Bank, Prince Pacelli, the Pope's nephew, the Cardinal Secretary of State, not to mention the father of the bride, Prince Alessandro Farnese di Mongrifone."

"That's a heavy group of matchmakers." Bryan de Courcy Cavanagh was impressed. "But why did they need so much muscle? Is the bride a bearded lady or what?"

Giorgios Hadjidakis groaned in theatrical despair. It was Chef who supplied the answser.

"O God! The ignorance of the man! Even I know that Giulia Farnese di Mongrifone is one of the most beautiful women in Italy. The Italian gossip magazines are full of her. Every so often Visconti or Rossellini makes a big song and dance about offering her a film role—which of course she always refuses. Noblesse oblige! She's named for her ancestor, Giulia the Beautiful . . ."

"So explain please!" Cavanagh made a dramatic appeal. "I come from way down under—next door to the Antarctic penguins. What do I know about Boston carpetbaggers and bartered brides in the Holy City?"

"What indeed!" Chef was gentle with his ignorance. "On the other hand you're a Roman Catholic, so you'll understand when I tell you that in this doubtful and dangerous time, the most stable organization in Europe is the Vatican. It controls or influences a huge body of international sentiment. All its wartime sins, all its shabby bargains with the Nazis and the Fascists, are conveniently forgotten because the new bogeymen are the Communists. It has a new crop of martyrs in

Eastern Europe and China. It has brought out the Confessional vote for Christian Democracy in Italy. It's funded from all round the world; so it encourages wealthy and loyal adherents like Lou Molloy and if they're hard-nosed carpetbaggers as well—which Lou most certainly is!—then so much the better. Money has no smell anyway; but good Christian money like Lou's earns a special blessing in Rome. Now, does it make sense to you, young man?"

"It begins to, yes." Cavanagh ruminated on the idea for a few moments. "But everything you've told me is general. What's the precise ground of business interest between Prince Farnese and Lou Molloy? And what's the relationship between Giulia herself and Lou? A woman with a history like hers would hardly let herself be bartered like a chattel—or would she?"

There was a long moment of silence, then Chef burst into laughter.

"Now it's your turn, Giorgios. Answer the man!"

"There's nothing to answer! It's Lou's business. If he wants to discuss it with Cavanagh, he will."

"Giorgios is right." Cavanagh was swift to placate the irascible Greek. "I'm the new boy. I do my job and keep my trap shut! It seems to me, we need another bottle of wine for the cheese. If you'll be good enough to choose it, Chef, I'll be very happy to pay for it . . ."

Hadjidakis gave him a swift, grateful glance while Chef buried his nose in the wine list. Bryan de Courcy Cavanagh was suddenly aware that he had just missed making an enemy and might, just possibly, have made a friend.

It was two in the morning before they stumbled back on board the *Salamandra*. Now that he was thoroughly embalmed, Cavanagh thought it would be a sweet and decorous end to die quietly in his sleep. That mercy, however, was denied him. He thrashed about for hours in a series of nightmares in which he pursued a naked Marie-Claire through the alleys of Antibes, while Lou Molloy thundered at his heels with a cleaver from the galley and Giorgios Hadjidakis laid bookmaker's odds on whether he would bed the lady or be butchered by Molloy.

At six in the morning, bleary-eyed, dry-mouthed with a head full of rattling stones, he was rousted out of his bunk and ordered to report to the bridge, showered and shaved, in fifteen minutes flat. Hadjidakis, spruce already in clean coveralls, was implacable. He wanted to be out of the harbor and heading south by six-thirty —and now was as good a time as any for the new boy to demonstrate his skills at pilotage and ship handling.

Cavanagh made it to the bridge with a minute to spare. Hadjidakis had the charts laid out for him. Chef was ready with coffee and croissants. Jackie was standing by the anchor winch, Leo was ready to slip the stern lines.

"Ready when you are, Mr. Cavanagh," said Hadjidakis.

"Aye, aye, sir!" said Bryan de Courcy Cavanagh. He switched on the intercom and announced, "Stand by forward. Stand by aft. Acknowledge loud and clear, please, gentlemen!"

He knew exactly what Hadjidakis was doing: handing him a million dollars worth of vessel to maneuver at close quarters, in the middle of the worst hangover of his life. If he failed the test, no harm would come to the ship; Hadjidakis was standing only a pace away from the control console, and the seamen fore and aft could go through the motions in their sleep; but Bryan de Courcy Cavanagh would be finished as a bridge officer, paid off probably in Monte Carlo.

If he made no mistakes—fine!—he would have passed the first test. He had been embalmed and still woke up with all his wits about him. But every day would bring new, and subtler tests, because Hadjidakis was a Greek and jealous of anyone, man or woman, who intruded into the private domain of his friendship with Lou Molloy.

When they had cleared the harbor, Hadjidakis told him to head for Cap Camarat, a forty-mile run southwestward along the coast. Just before the Cap they would anchor in the quiet bay of San Tropez. Cavanagh laid off the course on the chart, wrote up the log and took over the wheel. Hadjidakis went below with the two deckhands to lift the carpets in the cabins and expose the entrance hatches into the underbelly of the ship. Grinning like a satyr, he warned Cavanagh that there was no way he could escape his crawl through the bilges. Cavanagh shrugged and laughed.

His hangover was on the wane. The ship handled like a contented woman. There was a small breeze off the land, bearing with it the faint, elusive scent of spring flowers and mountain herbs. The saddles of the Maritime Alps were dark against a bright sky, the ruffled sea sparkled like champagne in the morning sun. The radar screen was empty of traffic. Cavanagh perched himself in the helmsman's chair, switched to autopilot and settled down to enjoy the dead straight run fom Cap d'Antibes to Cap Camarat.

In his Navy life these were the hours he had loved; the quiet sunlit times with a fair wind and an easy sea, and the battle, no more than an uneasy murmur left far astern. There was a block of blank paper on the chart table, to be used for course calculations and for watch-keepers' notes, which might later need to be copied into the log. Cavanagh set it in front of him and began to make a series of fluent but precise sketches of the landmarks on his route. It was one of the oldest maritime arts, and the products of it still adorned the British Admiralty charts: carefully hatched drawings of capes and bluffs and inlets and rocky outcrops that warned of hidden reefs. It was also a tranquil exercise in coastwise navigation, dead reckoning by time and speed and available landmarks, all of which could be checked against the radar screen and the shifting graph of the depth sounder, which traced the contours of the underwater shelf.

Suddenly, Chef was standing beside him with a steaming mug of beef broth, laced with cognac. Cavanagh blessed him eloquently.

"God love you, Chef! May he give you health, wealth, cheerful women and a long life to enjoy them."

Chef, however, was not listening. His attention had been caught by the sketches scattered on the chart table. He asked:

"Are these yours?"

"Yes."

"They're good."

"They're passable. The Navy put me through a crash course in mapping and topography."

"Mr. Molloy would be very interested. He is himself a skilled draftsman. He has sketchbooks full of drawings of every port we have ever visited."

"It's an agreeable hobby."

Cavanagh altered course to pass under the stern of a tanker heading southward from Saint Raphael. Chef pursued his own thought.

"With him it is not a hobby. It's all connected with his master plan in Europe."

"And what would that be?"

"Molloy believes there will be an explosion of pleasure boating all through the Mediterranean. So, he plans a series of marina developments in Italy from Portofino in the north, to Anzio in the south, then out to the Islands—Sardinia, Elba, Ponza, Ischia, Stromboli. Already the boat designers and builders are gearing up; wartime shipyards are being modernized. Once the craft start coming off the slips, there will be need of all the ancillary services: harborage, fuel points, provisioning, dockside accommodation—everything! This is what brought Molloy and Farnese together. Molloy has the money connections, the business experience, and high friends like Cardinal Spellman in New York. Farnese served in the Ministry of Marine. He is one of the old Black Aristocracy, a close friend of the present Pontiff and of Galeazzi, who runs Vatican finances. He sees this as a splendid chance to liquidate coastal real estate which has become a liability on the Church's books: old monasteries and convents, unproductive peasant farms, rundown fishing ports which can be dredged and redeveloped."

"It sounds like a gold mine." The tanker had gone now. Cavanagh eased the *Salamandra* back on course. "Why is Hadjidakis so hostile to it?"

Chef gave a small but eloquent shrug.

"He is hostile not to the business, but to the marriage. Molloy and Hadjidakis are old shipmates. They have never been equals; but in a democratic America it was easy for them to be friends. Most of the year they lived in separate worlds. In the summer they cruised together, drank, chased women, shared the company of sailing folk. You know how it is at sea. There are no half-measures. You are blood brothers or sworn enemies."

"But now it's changing?"

"How can it not change? There is a new woman, a permanent one this time, born to the old feudal traditions of Europe. Once the Farnese and their entourage come aboard, there will be no easy comradeship anymore. We will be invited to an occasional cocktail. That will be the end of it. Already Hadjidakis is resentful. Already he is working up an anger about old wrongs: the Italian invasion of Greece, the German occupation which followed it. A pity he wastes so much energy on things he cannot change. I am very fond of Giorgios but he is like a man beating his head on a stone wall just so he can feel better when he stops."

Cavanagh asked another question.

"Did I understand that you yourself once worked for the Farnese family?"

"That was the way Hadjidakis put it. The facts were slightly different. Long before the war the Farnese owned a large villa property in Lugano, on the Swiss side of the lake. When the war began to go badly for Italy, the prince moved his family across the border. I had known him a long time. I had organized business luncheons and political dinners for him at the hotel. Now he offered me, rent-free, a house in the villa domain, if I would act as unofficial majordomo and manage the domestic affairs of the Princess, hire the servants, keep the accounts and so on. I was happy to do it. I was well paid. The hotel profited from the extra business I brought in. It worked well for both sides. Unhappily, the Princess died in 1943. That was a bad time. The Allies had just invaded Sicily; the Germans were the real masters of the peninsula. So I had to arrange the funeral and act as temporary guardian of the young family."

"So you know Molloy's fiancée?"

"Since she was a young girl."

"What is she like?"

"Beautiful, intelligent, very spoiled. Her father indulges all her whims; but in traditional style he also exploits her."

"How?"

"As a family asset, negotiable in the marriage market."

"I thought you approved of this match, Chef?"

"I do. I most emphatically do! It's a marriage of convenience, yes! But, by all I know of history, it will work better than most romantic follies. Giulia la Bella will lead the dance for a while, but Molloy's had enough women in his life to know all her moves by heart. He's strong enough to tame her, wise enough to give her a loose rein when she needs it, and cold enough to shame her and keep her jealous, if she misbehaves. But what's much more important"—he gave a short, dry chuckle—"and what's the core of the whole argument, is the marriage settlement. I know the lawyers have been haggling over that for months. There's no divorce in Italy, the Farnese are too close to the Vatican to countenance an offshore arrangement. Molloy's an Irish Catholic. So he's going to make an annulment by church or state too expensive even to dream about. Therefore, according to me, Marcantonio Caviglia, if this isn't a marriage made in heaven, it's the next best thing! But why the hell should you care? You're the luckiest of us all, my young friend! No ties, no regrets—and whatever you own of history is twelve thousand miles away, south of the equator! Pass me your mug. I have to get back to my galley."

"Thanks, Chef! You're one of God's good men!"

"Present me to him one day! We haven't been introduced yet."

Then he was gone. Bryan de Courcy Cavanagh watched the landfall open up on the radar screen and altered course to make the dark axe-cut that marked the Bay of San Tropez. With half an hour cruising time on his hands he tried to work out the permutations and combinations of life aboard the *Salamandra d'Oro*: an owner-skipper who demanded clean hands and hearts in the service of his betrothed, yet maintained a jealous Greek friend of the heart, a bachelor chef from the Grand Hotel du Lac in Lugano, two comely athletes from the Boston ballet—and himself, the passionate pilgrim under scrutiny by them all.

It took him no time at all to decide that, apart from the social comfort, their opinion didn't matter a damn. He had a soft berth, on a sweet ship, all found with seventy-five dollars a week to jingle in his white duck pants. Softly at first and then, more strongly, he picked up the refrain of "The Low-backed Car."

But when the hay was blooming grass,
And decked with flowers of spring,
No flower was there that could compare,
With the charming girl I sing,
As we drove in the low-backed car,
The man at the turn-pike bar,
Never asked for the toll,
But just rubbed his old poll,
And looked after the low-backed car!

Ten minutes after they had dropped anchor off San Tropez, Bryan de Courcy Cavanagh stripped down to his jockey shorts, buckled on a tool belt and, armed with a torch and a plan of electrical circuits and plumbing conduits, started his long, claustrophobic crawl through the bilges of the *Salamandra d'Oro*.

He began right at the stern where the propeller shafts pierced the hull, and the cables of the steering system were connected to the rudder. He inspected the bearings and the watertight glands. He ran his fingers over the shafts in search of telltale irregularities. He shone his torch on the plumbing outlets in search of leaks.

He was just about to climb out of the well and move on to the next section when he caught a dull gleam of metal in the torchlight. He reached for it and his groping fingers found a gold coin, a Swiss twenty-franc piece coated with oil and dust. He studied it for a moment, then shoved it into the small leather container clipped to his tool belt, which held a miscellany of small nuts, bolts and assorted fasteners.

On the next stage of his journey he had to lie on his back with his nose against the bottom of the fuel tank, draining off water from the sump where it had settled out from the diesel oil. There was more of it than he expected, which meant that, somewhere along the line, the *Salamandra*'s fuel supplier had pumped in watered stock. There was only one remedy, to refuse to accept delivery until the consignment had been tested by pumping a sample into a clean glass demijohn and waiting until any water content settled out. Many tanker drivers raised a stink about the slow procedure. Most came swiftly to see reason, under the threat of a complaint to the company and to the police.

The most complicated area was under the engine room itself, where the big diesels were bedded and all the electrical wiring converged on the main fuse box. By the time that was all checked, Cavanagh was black as a coal miner and greasy as a fairground pig. Only two more areas remained to be inspected, the plumbing under the forepeak and the chain-locker. No sooner was he down in the darkness again when Hadjidakis called to him.

"The crew toilet's backed up. I'll pass you down a bucket and a wire probe, see if you can clear it, like a good man!"

Cavanagh said nothing. He unwrapped the sweat-rag from his forehead and tied it in a mask around his nostrils. Then he prayed quietly that he wouldn't throw up . . .

Later, when the last chore was done, he dived overboard and swam a thousand yards down the bay and back again, purging his angers with the long, flailing crawl stroke which had won him a long distance championship in his last year at college. Later still, shaved and showered and dressed in clean shorts and a tennis shirt, he sat on the afterdeck and ate asparagus and fresh lobster washed down with a local blanc de blanc that lay clean and crisp on the palate.

When the coffee was served, he took the gold piece from his pocket and slapped it on the table in front of Hadjidakis.

"I found that under the owner's cabin this morning."

Hadjidakis glanced at it, then pushed it back with the tip of his index finger.

"Finders keepers. It's yours."

"I don't want it, thank you."

"The offer offends you?"

"You offend me, Hadjidakis."

"How so?"

"You planted the damn thing! You've got wealthy guests coming aboard. You need to be sure the new boy isn't a bandit. I understand that; but you insult my intelligence with a childish trick!"

"Don't take it too hard, Cavanagh." Hadjidakis gave him a big happy grin. "I've met a lot of dock rats in my time. I've learned to be careful."

Cavanagh gave him grin for grin and added a piece of advice for good measure.

"You've had your fun, Georgy-boy; but now the game's over! Next time anyone stops up the plumbing with cotton waste from your engine room, I'll personally shove it down your gullet and stand by while you eat it. Do I make myself clear?"

"Anything else you want to get off your chest?"

"No. That's the lot—except to pass a compliment to Chef. That was a splendid lunch."

"You earned it," said Giorgios Hadjidakis, amiably. "Now can we call a truce?"

Bryan de Courcy Cavanagh thought the word was ill-chosen. A truce signified only a temporary break in hostilities. However, he raised his glass and toasted it in the dregs of the wine.

Early next morning they took on fuel and water, and the tankerman waited, cursing, until his product was tested. A van-load of provisions was checked and stored. Bedrooms and bathrooms were made up with fresh linen and expensive toiletries. Flower arrangements were delivered for the saloon, the dining room and the guest cabins. When the last messenger had stepped ashore, the decks were scrubbed and pumiced, the brass and brightwork polished, the windows and portholes wiped mirror-clean.

Just after lunch, a taxi drew up on the dock and decanted one Miss Lenore Pritchard, late of the Cunard Steamship Company Limited. She looked like a very superior nanny. She carried herself straight as a guardsman. She wore a blue serge costume, low-heeled black shoes, a white blouse and a basinlike felt hat that hid the upper part of her face. Hadjidakis handed her aboard with more than casual respect and took her immediately to her quarters—a small single-berth cabin opposite to his own and separate from the rest of the crew's quarters in the forepeak.

Half an hour later, she emerged a different woman. Dressed in summer whites, she looked five years younger, with auburn hair, a peaches-and-cream complexion, an athlete's figure and a devil-may-care look in her bright blue eyes. She was obviously at ease in shipboard company. She raised a ready laugh from Leo and Jackie. She gave Cavanagh a thorough inspection and a final grin of approval. She managed a passable French and a fluent Italian with Chef. To Hadjidakis she delivered a set of trenchant judgments.

". . . So far, no complaints! The deckhands are good-looking. The navigator can read. The chef knows how to make English tea. The engine room is as clean as a new pin. I only hope the guests are able to live up to the crew!"

"We'll soon know." Hadjidakis had summoned all hands to the afterdeck for coffee and a final briefing. "I spoke to Mr. Molloy last night. These are his orders. We leave Antibes at sixteen hundred hours and coast quietly down to Monte Carlo, arriving at seventeen-thirty. All crew will wear summer whites, and in addition to the courtesy flags we'll fly the pennon of the Farnese family. Cavanagh, you'll take us into harbor. Our berth is number seven; that's on the starboard hand as you enter. I know you'll give us a classy docking, because Mr. Molloy will be waiting with his guests to see us in. The moment we're secure, all personnel will assemble on the afterdeck to welcome Mr. Molloy and his guests. There will be two ladies, the Princess Giulia Farnese and her aunt, the Countess Lucietta Sciarra-Tebaldi. Miss Pritchard, you will take them below and get them settled. Leo, you'll look after the Prince and his friend, who is Count Galeazzi from the Vatican.

"The moment they're all below, we clear harbor and set course for Calvi at the northern end of Corsica. It's a hundred-mile run, and the forecast is for light and variable winds with low seas; so it should be a comfortable shakedown cruise for the guests. Cocktails will be served on the afterdeck at seven, dinner in the saloon at eight. That's all for now. All hands will be ready to winch out at sixteen hundred hours . . ."

The small gathering dispersed. Cavanagh went up to the bridge to mark up his charts and read the pilot books for the ports they were to visit. Hadjidakis had made it clear that, unless Molloy decreed otherwise, Cavanagh should act as navigator on the voyage. It was a left-handed compliment which at once affirmed Cavanagh's competence and relieved Hadjidakis of responsibility for piloting the vessel in unfamiliar ports and seaways.

A few moments later, Miss Pritchard came up to the bridge and perched herself in the pilot's chair. She announced calmly:

"I thought we should get acquainted before the circus begins."

"Good idea." Cavanagh gave her a cheerful grin. "How do you like to be called?"

"In front of the guests, Miss Pritchard. In private, Lenore. And you?"

"For the guests, Mr. Cavanagh. The rest of the time I answer to Cavanagh, Bryan, hey-boyo, whatever the mood dictates."

"Are you moody then?"

"No. Most of the time I'm a happy chappie."

"Good! I'm a happy soul myself, and I like clear signals. Are you married?"

"No. Are you?"

"Not any more. Tried it once and didn't like it. Don't get me wrong. I like men and I like sex. And I like the job I do, which is coddling the wealthy and the famous for the Cunard Line. With the wages and the tips, it pays well. What I don't like is me making the money for some layabout husband to spend. How do you feel about women, Cavanagh?"

"I love 'em all. I have sex with some of them, by mutual consent for mutual pleasure. Does that answer the question?"

"It will do for now. But listen, Cavanagh! I've been working the Cunarders for a lot of years now. I'm good at my job because I know it's a chameleon act. You change colors to suit the customer—and the crew too, for that matter, because you serve the customer but you have to live with the crew. Leo and Jackie, for instance, they're as camp as a canvas tent, but we'll get along fine. Live and let live is my motto. The Greek fellow—Mr. Hadj-whatever—he's much harder to read. He's all dark and screwed up inside. Mr. Molloy on the other hand . . ."

"You've met Molloy?" Cavanagh stared at her in surprise.

"Sure I've met him! How the hell did you think I got this job? Won it in a parish raffle? Molloy made several trips with Cunard. Each time he had the same cabin suite, but a different woman. Each time I was the stewardess. He liked me. He had friends in top management. He arranged with my boss that I could take a summer leave to do this job . . . So here I am!"

"Obviously Mr. Molloy gives very clear signals too."

"Clear as a bell!" Miss Pritchard gave a high, happy laugh. "With him it was always simple: 'Do you, don't you? Will you, won't you? If the answer's yes, lock the door and let's have your skirt up and your knickers down. I'll pay a hundred quid for your time and my pleasure.' I like that sort of man. He must like my sort of woman, otherwise he wouldn't have offered me this job, would he?"

"I guess not. Our Mr. Molloy is a man who knows his own mind."

"But he needs someone who knows how his mind works."

"Which is you?"

"Which is me, of course. He told me so in plain words. 'Listen, Lenore,' he said, 'I'm marrying a young and beautiful woman, the flower of the old nobility in Europe. This is tradition with a capital T. We're going to be cruising for three months, and Giulia's going to be chaperoned every hour she's on my ship. That's fine. I wouldn't expect less. I wouldn't want it otherwise; but if I'm going to last the distance

I'm going to need some regular relief from an understanding woman. I'm going to need discretion too—and that's what I'll be paying for, and paying generously . . . .' "

"So why," asked Bryan de Courcy Cavanagh, "why would you be telling me all this, when the whole essence of the deal with Molloy is discretion and secrecy?"

"Not secrecy, Cavanagh! You've got that part wrong. How do you keep a secret on any ship, let alone one this size? The answer is that you don't try. The crew are one world; the guests are another. The crew see everything and say nothing because their jobs are on the line. The guests see nothing because they're too busy with the scenery and their own gossip. And why am I telling you? Because Mr. Molloy pays well, but he plays rough. He knows I'll need a change, and I won't get it from the dancing boys, or the Greek—and Chef just isn't interested."

"But you're sure I will be?"

"I'm sure." Her eyes were bright with cheerful malice. "It's going to be a long cruise. Mr. Molloy promised me a playmate for when he couldn't be around. You're the chosen one, Cavanagh!"

"And if I have other ideas?"

"Feel free. Enjoy, enjoy! But remember, I'm the only woman available on board and you're too lusty to waste your nights baying at the moon! Never fear! We'll get together sooner or later! *Ciao* for now, Cavanagh!"

She touched the tips of her fingers to his mouth, then left him staring into the empty space where she had stood. Suddenly, the madness of it all hit him, and he found himself choking with uncontrollable laughter.

So this was the great Molloy, banker to princes, friend of cardinals, betrothed to a princess, soon to be dubbed a knight by the Pope himself. This was the stern moralist, demanding clean hands and hearts of all who would serve his virgin bride, while he himself brought in a whore to be her chambermaid, and picked a vagabond from down under off the beach to be a gentleman of the whore's bedchamber.

And yet, and yet, Chef was right. Molloy did have style; but it wasn't the wild baroque excess of the Borgias or the Farnese themselves, but rather the finicking conspiratorial ruthlessness of the Black Irish, who would rather win than enjoy the game, who would rather surround themselves with complaisant minions than risk their potency in the jousts of love.

Bryan de Courcy Cavanagh knew them well; he had, after all, been born into the clan; but he himself was still untested. Now, like a character in an old-time melodrama, he was faced with almost comic questions. What would he do when Lou Molloy clapped him on the shoulder, man to man, and told him to keep Pritchard happy because the last thing in the world Molloy needed was woman trouble on the *Salamandra d'Oro*? Came then a more sinister query: what would Molloy do if he felt himself betrayed or his great project jeopardized?

For the moment, however, it was all theory and conjecture, based on the dubious word of Miss Lenore Pritchard, who might well turn out to be the most monumental liar since Baron Münchhausen. So, Bryan de Courcy Cavanagh turned back to his charts, laid down the short courses to Monaco and Corsica and then began to study the Admiralty directions for pilots entering the harbor of Monte Carlo and mariners homing from the northeast on the Calvi light.

The boarding ceremony for Molloy's princely guests turned into a minor disaster. In the late afternoon there was a buildup of local weather behind Monaco.

The clouds piled up over Mount Mounier and a small treacherous wind began searching down the valley of the Var. Hadjidakis ordered extra speed, and Cavanagh was safely tied up in Monte Carlo harbor fifteen minutes before the appointed time.

Exactly on the half-hour a big limousine arrived; the chauffeur handed Molloy and his guests on to the quay and then began unloading a small mountain of suitcases. Hadjidakis went down the gangplank to welcome them. Jackie and Leo followed him to deal with the baggage.

The party was still bunched on the quay, admiring the vessel, when the *rafale* hit: a flurry of wind and rain and hail that swept across the exposed quay and sent them scurrying like drenched cats up the narrow gangplank and into the shelter of the lounge. As soon as the last piece of baggage was on board, Hadjidakis snapped out an order.

"Start engines, Cavanagh, and let's get the hell out of here. This is local weather only. There'll be clear skies to the south."

Which was how it came to pass that Bryan de Courcy Cavanagh was presented in private audience to the Principessa Giulia Farnese di Mongrifone. He was at the wheel, heading southward into sunlight and quiet water when Molloy brought Giulia up to the bridge. Beside Molloy, she looked small, young and very vulnerable. Then, as if by some inner transformation, she was suddenly imperious and full of fire. Her glance was a mockery; her smile a condescension. Was she beautiful? Cavanagh made silent answer to the unspoken question. Yes, by God, she was beautiful; but arrogant as one of Lucifer's angels, demanding deference, quizzing anyone presented to her like a royal visitor. Cavanagh bowed over her hand and greeted her in Italian. She gave him a small smile of approval and a patronizing compliment.

"Your accent is very good. Where did you learn?"

"There are many Italian immigrants in my country. Some families have been there for several generations. I was taught by a distinguished scholar, a friend of Pirandello."

"That's a surprise!" She was teasing now. "I thought all Australians walked upside down and talked out of the side of their mouths."

"Regrettably, my dear Principessa, you have been cruelly deceived. But that is the fate of many beautiful women."

"Perhaps you may find time to instruct me more accurately, Mr. Cavanagh."

"I, too, am in need of instruction. I have always been interested in the history of your illustrious namesake, Giulia the Beautiful."

It was a risky line; but she took it without a blush. Molloy, excluded from the talk, cut in abruptly.

"What's he telling you, my dear?"

"He's showing me—very politely, I must say—that he knows more about my country than I do about his."

"He's a surprising fellow, our Mr. Cavanagh. We haven't seen half his talents yet."

To change the subject, Cavanagh suggested that the Princess might like to take the wheel. She agreed readily. Cavanagh snapped off the autopilot and stood back, while Molloy demonstrated the feel of the steering mechanism and showed her how to manage the swing of the sea, to read the radar screen and the depth sounder.

Watching the small sexual rituals between them, his lips brushing her cheek, his hands smoothing a trailing wisp of her hair, Cavanagh felt a sharp pang of jealousy, a sudden irrational urge to wrench them apart and take Molloy's place beside the woman. The swift onset of the madness startled him. He had to mock himself back into sanity.

What was Giulia Farnese to him? What could he ever be to her? Her betrothal to Molloy was already half a sacrament, contrived and blessed by God's anointed, ratified by the ministers of mammon in a pre-nuptial agreement. The three circles of religion, family and money were already linked together and closed. There was no standing room within them for a vagabond lawyer from the Antipodes.

Then, mercifully, the little interlude was over. With a nod and a murmur of thanks, the couple left the bridge. Ten minutes later Molloy returned, alone. He asked:

"What time are you due to be relieved?"

"In about ten minutes."

"Good! I'd like you to join us for cocktails. I need some help."

"What sort of hclp?"

"Giulia says your Italian's very good. I want you to help me entertain her aunt. She says she doesn't like speaking English, although she can rattle along in most European languages. The fact is, she doesn't like me. She thinks I'm too old for Giulia, too American, too vulgar—but still rich enough to be tolerable. The dislike is mutual. I happen to think she's a royal pain in the arse. Like a lot of Italian women with too little to do, she's always complaining about her liver, her migraines, the weather, the decline of manners and morals. However, I've got to put up with her for Giulia's sake. Also, I've got serious business to discuss with Farnese and Galeazzi. I can't have the old girl moping about like Lady Macbeth. So, you're elected to keep her happy. If it gets too tough, maybe you can enlist Leo and Jackie to amuse her for a while."

"You hired me as a bridge officer, Mr. Molloy, not as a lady's companion."

"Correction, Mr. Cavanagh!" Molloy gave him a wide shark-toothed smile. "I hired you as a bridge officer on a pleasure cruise. That entails certain social responsibilities. This isn't an ocean liner. It's a small, private world—my world, Cavanagh—and it runs to my rules. Remember our first talk in Antibes?"

"I do."

"You offered me your skill in languages."

"I did."

"Now I'm calling on it. So why the fuss?"

"You took me by surprise: I was out of line. I apologize. I'll do the best I can."

It was his first admission of defeat and it lay bitter on his tongue. Molloy laughed and clapped a comradely hand on his shoulder.

"You never know what you can do until you try. It's my risk, not yours. Besides, you're not the only one doubling in brass. Miss Pritchard has to help entertain the males of the party, at least until Galeazzi leaves us. He's the laconic type, hard going at the best of times, but Pritchard will handle him. She's good value."

"I'm sure she is. We haven't had too much time to get acquainted."

"It would be a kindness if you'd spend a little time on her. She's the only woman in the crew. She's got all the guest cabins and two ladies to look after. I'm sure she'd appreciate a little tactful attention. A word now and then, that's all that's needed."

"Of course."

"Good man!"

Abruptly as he had come, he left. Cavanagh cursed him in a silent tirade:

Who the hell do you think you are? What the hell do you think I am? The cruise has hardly begun and already you've set me up with a whole dance-card. I'm navigator, interpreter, surrogate lover to your surrogate lover and fan-car-

rier to an elderly Italian lady with a melancholy disposition! Goddamn your Irish eyes, Molloy! Goddamn you!

It was Lenore Pritchard who described the first cocktail hour as "a sticky mess, like overcooked rice." The Countess Sciarra-Tebaldi anchored herself in a deck chair and forced the rest of the party to coagulate around her. The talk limped along until Molloy ordered background music and Miss Pritchard mounted a frontal assault on the uneasy little group. It was she who instructed Cavanagh on the tactics.

"You take the Countess. Get her out of that damned chair. Walk her round the deck and show her the moonrise. The lovers can take care of themselves. I'll draw off the males. I'm interested in Farnese anyway. He's a handsome brute with a roving eye and a nice, crooked smile. Galeazzi's closed up like an oyster at low tide; but I'll try to prize him open. Christ! Three months of this and I'll be overboard and swimming with the dolphins. Let's move!"

Together they converged on the group with smiles, champagne, canapés and coaxing. Within three minutes, Lenore Pritchard had Farnese and Galeazzi leaning on the taffrail on either side of her, while Cavanagh and the Countess perched themselves on the rope locker on the foredeck and watched Leo and Jackie play out a chess game on the hatch cover under the rising moon.

After two glasses of champagne the Countess was a changed woman. Her liver trouble seemed to have subsided; her migraine was in remission; her down-drawn mouth twitched upward into a smile and her talk became more voluble and less discreet.

". . . Your Mr. Molloy thinks I'm just a crotchety old woman who talks fashion and fiddle-faddle . . . I do that just to annoy him because he annoys me so much I could scream! . . . He is so certain of everything—including himself. America is the saviour of the world. The dollar is a passport to heaven . . . I think this is the thing that angers me most of all. He has no curiosity about anything that does not touch his own affairs . . . That's why my brother and Papa Pacelli and that terrible little American, Cardinal Spellman, have been able to put a ring through his nose and lead him round like a stud bull. He trots wherever they tell him—which is always to the bank for more investment to create employment, to keep the Communists from taking over the country . . . Stalin is the big black bogeyman. Communism is the reign of the Antichrist! What everyone's conveniently forgotten is that it was Churchill and Roosevelt who handed him half of Europe on a platter . . . My brother would kill me if he heard me talking like this; but I find you very sympathetic. You don't tell tales out of school, do you?"

"No, Contessa, I don't tell tales. But you must do something for me."

"What's that?"

"Smile a little! Enjoy the cruise. This is a beautiful vessel and you are a beautiful woman—especially when you smile."

"It's hard to smile when I think of my lovely Giulia marrying that . . . that crude upstart."

In spite of his anger against the man, Cavanagh was moved to defend him.

"I don't know Mr. Molloy very well. I've only been working for him for a few days, but I think you do him less than justice. It's one thing to inherit a great name and a long history and a clear place in an old society; but to carve out a career in the new world of industry and commerce, that requires a special kind of talent—courage too, and toughness. Your own family had it in the old days. They were upstarts too. They were soldiers, adventurers, traders, rough fellows with strong women as well . . . Besides, with great respect, the Principessa, your Giulia, is a free agent. Surely she can marry whomever she chooses?"

"Naturally, you would think that. You're a very young man. You live far away at the end of the world and your history is very short. My country is old. It's been overrun many times by many invaders. Now, once again it has been reduced to ruin; but it still survives, and the secret of that survival is the family. The family isn't just a bloodline. It's a whole complicated network of relationships, of debts, favors, duties, insurances against future disaster . . . Giulia is as closely bound as anyone, more so perhaps because of the attachment to her father . . . I have said enough. This is a painful subject for me . . . I like you, Mr. Cavanagh." She held out her hands so he could steady her as she stepped on to the deck. "I like young people. They're so full of hope and bright illusions. Will you walk me back, please? I'm feeling much happier now!"

As the guests filed in to dinner, Cavanagh helped Miss Pritchard to reset the afterdeck and clear away the glasses and ashtrays. It was a function of the small closed economy of shipboard that no task should be deferred, no mess should be allowed to accumulate. Pritchard asked:

"How did you make out with the old girl?"

"I liked her. She relaxed and seemed to enjoy talking. She's much shrewder than she looks."

"Like all of us," said Pritchard with dry malice, "she needs a little attention."

"You seemed to be commanding quite a bit of it yourself—and I mean that as a compliment."

"Thanks. Farnese was easy. He's a very accomplished womanizer. All the words, all the moves! With Galeazzi it was like talking to an abacus. I know he works at the Vatican. It was on the tip of my tongue to ask whether he had to be celibate, too. Luckily, Molloy came along and rescued me . . . Can I ask you to take the glasses to the galley?"

"Sure."

"I've got to go below, straighten the cabins and bathrooms and turn down the beds. After that we could have supper on the foredeck."

"Not tonight, I'm afraid. I have the midnight watch. I need some sleep."

"You still have to eat."

"There'll be sandwiches and a thermos of coffee for me on the bridge. You can join me there if you feel like it."

"After midnight? You must be joking. By then I'll either be sleeping or screwing Molloy. He won't know and I won't know until he's put the gentry to bed. That's the only problem when you go on the game this way—you're a disposable item!"

To which Bryan de Courcy Cavanagh had no adequate response; but it gave him something to muse about as he climbed into his bunk, set the muted alarm on his wristwatch and slid gratefully into sleep.

At five minutes before midnight he woke, sluiced his face, ran a comb through his hair and climbed into the thermal jumpsuit which he had bought in Singapore, and which was both light and warm enough to be comfortable in the chill of the small morning hours.

To reach the companionway which led to the deck level and thence to the bridge, he had to pass Lenore Pritchard's cabin. Above the steady throb of the engines, he heard voices and then a burst of woman's laughter, quickly stifled. He paused for a fraction of a second, then climbed up to the deck to breathe in the sharp night air and take a quick turn around the deck before going up to the bridge.

It was an old habit. On a small ship the new officer of the watch made sure that all was secure topside before he took over the bridge. On the deck there was another combination of sounds; footsteps in brisk rhythm, a low voluble exchange of talk in Italian. Galeazzi and Farnese were making a circuit of the deck together. As Cavanagh approached, Farnese greeted him.

"Good evening, Mr. Cavanagh. I hope we have not disturbed you."

"Not at all. I'm just taking over the watch from Mr. Hadjidakis."

"What time do we arrive in Calvi?"

"If you'll give me five minutes, sir, I'll be able to tell you exactly and show you on the chart where we are. Why don't you come up to the bridge when you've finished your stroll?"

"Thank you. We'll do that. *A presto*: see you shortly, Mr. Cavanagh."

Cavanagh turned about and hurried up to the bridge. Hadjidakis was just making the last entries in the log. Cavanagh interrupted him.

"I think we've got a problem, Georgy-boy."

"What is it?"

"Farnese and Galeazzi are taking a stroll on deck. Molloy, I think, is screwing Miss Pritchard in her cabin. A meeting might be embarrassing."

"You're damn right it would! What makes you so sure it's Molloy?"

"Chef and the boys are asleep. You and I are here. Who else is there? I've invited Farnese and Galeazzi up to the bridge when they've finished their stroll. As soon as I've got rid of them, I'll buzz down to Lenore's cabin; but you'd better warn Molloy when you go below."

"I will." Hadjidakis was weary and irritable. "Christ! This was a crazy idea from the start; but it's the way Molloy has always played the woman game."

"A pretty risky game!"

"To him? Not at all. His motto is that if he's rich enough to pay, he's rich enough to play."

"He's engaged to a beautiful young woman, for Christ's sake!"

"His answer is that she's not available to him yet; so why should he sleep alone?"

"And if she or her family finds out?"

"They'll be like the three wise monkeys: no hear, no see, no say. There's too much money at stake. Molloy knows that. Therefore, he resents the way they try to patronize him, especially the Countess and Galeazzi. So he cocks a snoot at them, gives them his own whore as a chambermaid!"

"A pity she's a whore." Cavanagh quoted the old tag. "I like her."

"So do I." Hadjidakis was equally frank. "She makes no secret about what she does; she's amusing and gives value for money. Molloy likes her and trusts her, which is good for us all. When he's out of humor, he's dangerous. Farnese doesn't know it yet, but he's riding a tiger."

"And you'd better get below and tweak the tiger's tail!"

"This is nothing," Hadjidakis shrugged. "We've both played wilder games than this one, in much more dangerous places." He switched on the small spotlight to illuminate the chart table: "Our heading is a hundred and twenty-five. We're forty-five miles off the Calvi light, which has a ten-mile visibility and occults to green every six seconds. You should pick up the loom about sixteen miles out. I've slowed us down to eight knots so we can drop anchor by six. We'll stand off in mid harbor, because the dock is reserved for mainland ferries and freighters . . . The best spot looks to be about two cables offshore, right in front of the Hotel de Ville . . . All systems are functioning . . . I'm out of here."

"I'm impressed." Cavanagh offered a sober compliment. "It's a pleasure to take over from a tidy watch keeper, and that's not bullshit, Mr. Hadjidakis!"

Hadjidakis gave him a swift, suspicious glance: then his drawn, sallow features relaxed into a rare smile.

"You show a certain promise yourself, Mr. Cavanagh . . . She's your ship . . . Goodnight!"

When he had gone, Molloy switched off the chart light so that the view outside became clearer and the only illumination on the bridge was the faint glow from the binnacle and the instrument panel. The radar was masked, but when he thrust his face into the mask he could see only the sweep of the vector across a blank screen; but somewhere in the next half hour the first outlines of the Corsican coast would show up on the outer rim. Outside, the sky was black velvet and the stars were like a runnel of diamonds.

He toyed with the idea of taking a star-sight, just to refresh his mathematics; then he decided against it and addressed himself instead to the coffee and sandwiches. Chef had scribbled a note on the napkin: *Hai fatto una conquista. La contessa canta i tuoi lodi. Sei bello, cortese, colto* . . . You've made a conquest. The Countess is singing your praises: you're handsome, courteous, well educated . . . Molloy, of course, takes the credit. He recognized all your good qualities at first glance."

Cavanagh chuckled over the message, then crumpled the napkin and wiped his lips with it when he heard Farnese and Galeazzi mounting the steps to the bridge.

He offered them a light-hearted greeting and what he was pleased to call "the five-dollar tour of the nerve center of the vessel." Farnese entered immediately into the spirit of the moment. He moved around the chart table and the console, examining each item with a practiced eye. Galeazzi pursued a line of private inquiry.

"You interest me, Mr. Cavanagh. I understand you have seen war service and that you now have a degree in law."

"For what it's worth, yes sir."

"And what sort of career do you plan for yourself?"

"I don't know yet. That's why I'm here, doing something I know, while I cope with all the things I don't know. The whole world's in a mess, but sooner or later the mess has to be sorted out. Diplomatic relations have to be normalized, trade patterns established and enforced. I'd like to be part of that process. How, I don't know yet . . ."

"Good!" Galeazzi was suddenly alive and interested. "I like that! Did you hear, Alessandro? Here is a young fellow who doesn't know! Splendid! May I offer you some advice, my young friend?"

"Of course."

"So long as you can work and eat you should keep traveling and learning. Come to Rome and I will find you a scholarship of some sort to study Canon Law for a year. Go to France, master the Code Napoleon. Go to Russia too, see how closely the Soviets have copied the Codex Justinianus . . ."

"It's late, Enrico," Farnese interrupted. "You lay too much all at once on our young friend."

"Please! I'm grateful, believe me. I'm very much the innocent abroad."

"I believe you are," said Galeazzi. "Therefore, I seek to instruct you before you lose your innocence—as inevitably you will."

"I suggest," said Farnese with smiling malice, "he may have lost it some time ago. What say you, Mr. Cavanagh?"

"I'll say anything you want, sir," said Cavanagh,

amiably. "So long as you don't require it to be the truth."

"In other words," said Galeazzi, calmly, "Mr. Cavanagh is offended. I can't say I blame him. He invited us to the bridge. He did not offer us his private confession."

"Then we should apologize. We do, most humbly, Mr. Cavanagh."

"No apology is necessary, sir. I am employed to navigate you safely and, in between times, serve you in any way I can. For the rest, my private life is exactly that—a reserved matter. I'm sure that's a familiar phrase to you both."

"Very familiar, Mr. Cavanagh." Galeazzi gave him a sour smile of approval. "We thank you for your five-dollar tour. It was cheap at the price. Goodnight."

"Before we go." Farnese was suddenly a commanding presence in the narrow space. "This man you are taking us to meet tomorrow, what do you know about him?"

The question caught Cavanagh off guard. "What man? What meeting?"

"Mr. Molloy told us . . ."

Instantly Galeazzi cut him off.

"Whatever he told us, Alessandro, he has not yet communicated it to Mr. Cavanagh."

Cavanagh was in command of himself again. He gave them a smile and a shrugging gesture of deprecation.

"Nothing unusual in that, gentlemen. Mr. Molloy doesn't waste words. When he wants something done, he'll tell me. If he wants me to know the why of it, he'll tell me that too. I've always been comfortable with that kind of skipper."

"And from what he tells us," said Farnese blandly, "he is equally comfortable with you. Thank you again, Mr. Cavanagh."

"Think about my advice, young man," Galeazzi insisted quietly. "You have a good mind. It would be a pity to waste it . . . Goodnight."

Cavanagh waited, while their footfalls receded along the deck and were finally cut off by the closing of the heavy bulkhead door into the saloon. Then he lifted the intercom and buzzed the signal to Lenore Pritchard's cabin—one short, one long—repeated three times. Miss Pritchard might not grasp the irony, but Molloy most certainly would: in Morse code the signal meant "Full stop. Period. End of conversation." It was perhaps a subtle piece of wit to waste upon a man sated with sex; but Cavanagh himself had wit enough to know that Molloy's own games in this love match were only beginning, and that, like it or lump it, Bryan de Courcy Cavanagh was one of the pawns on the board.

At four in the morning Lou Molloy came to the bridge, freshly shaved, clear-eyed and smiling, smelling of bath soap and after-shave. He carried two mugs of black coffee and a basket of hot croissants. His greeting was cordial, if a shade theatrical:

"The top of the morning to you, Mr. Cavanagh. I trust you had an easy night. If you'll show me where we're at, I'll take over the watch, while you drink your coffee in peace."

Cavanagh recited the helmsman's litany: course, speed, position.

". . . Fifteen miles from the light, sir. The loom is visible now. The radar gives us a clear picture of the approach to Calvi. There are no hazards. We should have anchors down at 0600 hours, as near as bedamned. I've spoken to the harbor-master's office by radio. No pratique is necessary for vessels coming directly from mainland France or Monte Carlo . . . I've signed off the log, as you see."

"Tired?"

"No. I'll wait up until we enter harbor. Everything is new to me. I don't want to miss any part of it."

"In that case, I'd like a chat with you."

"Now?"

"Any problem about that?"

"None. What's the subject of discussion?"

"Last night's little party. You handled yourself very well. I owe you one."

"It was on the house." Cavanagh was studiously casual.

"Whatever." Molloy gave him a conspirator's grin. "I liked your little touch on the buzzer: *dit-dah, dit-dah, dit-dah*. It made—what do they call it in music?—a nice coda to the evening. Very dramatic."

Cavanagh sipped his coffee and reached for a croissant. Molloy gave him a long, searching look, then challenged him.

"I take it you don't approve of my shenanigans?"

"No comment." Cavanagh bristled with sudden anger. "I thought we finished this discussion yesterday. This is your ship, your world. They run to your rules. I don't question that. Now may we drop the subject?"

"Sure. You seem to have grasped the elements of it very well. We pass to the second item."

"Which is?"

"Immediately after breakfast, I want you to take a message ashore for me and bring me back the answer. It's a private matter, so you'll go alone. You may have company on the way back."

"It sounds simple enough."

"It is. It's also very important."

"In that case, I have a request."

"Which is?"

"Don't tell me anything more than I need to know. That way, if anyone questions me, I don't have to lie and there's no chance of my dropping an unguarded word about your private business."

"That would make good sense for both of us. Now let me ask you a question. How well are you read in recent church history?"

"How recent?"

"The last twenty years."

Cavanagh laughed in genuine amusement.

"What could I know, for Christ's sake? I stepped straight from college into naval training and war service. For four years after my discharge I was chasing a buck, an education in law, and women—in that order . . . I haven't even begun to fill all the gaps in my experience and education."

"I like that. I like it a lot!" There was genuine pleasure in Molloy's tone. "No better pupil than a man who knows the depth of his own ignorance. It'll be my great pleasure to give you some personal instruction, beginning now. We've got the best part of two hours of plain sailing, and since you're waiting up, let's talk about the two gentlemen you had on the bridge. Count Galeazzi is officially known as the 'Architect of the Sacred Apostolic Palaces.' That, of itself, makes him an important man, a high Vatican official. However, and much more significantly, he is an old friend and adviser to the Holy Father. Because he's a layman, he is not bound by clerical constraints and he deals, at the highest levels, with banks and other financial institutions all round the world. He is also Giulia's godfather—although that's not the reason he's on board now. Prince Farnese, Giulia's father, is head of one of the old papal families. He is a consultant to the Pontifical Commission for Vatican City State. He is connected to most of the old Catholic aristocracies of Europe. That's the circle I'm marrying into: old families, old alliances, Vatican politics. Let me tell you, Cavanagh, I've had to do some very fast study to bring myself half-way up to pace with these people. They need me; but they think they can bend me to all their purposes. They're wrong! I don't have any illusions about them. I'm important to them only because I'm one of their lifelines to the power and the money and the political networks of the United States. Also, they trust the Irish. We're like the Poles—undiluted Catholics, with all our prejudices intact. We're totally impervious to reason or the virus of the Reformation. Spelly taught me that—Francis Cardinal Spellman—God bless his cotton socks and his devious Irish soul. He also taught me that the only loyalties you can count on in Rome are those you buy on the installment plan—because you know they'll stay bought until the last installment is paid. And the most important lesson of all, perhaps, was the one he repeated over and over: 'Lou, this Church of ours, Holy, Roman, Catholic and Apostolic, is an empire, bigger and more complicated than the Roman or the British or any other in the last two thousand years. You can live in it for a lifetime, as I have, and never figure out the complexities of it and the conflicts and contraditions that go on within it everyday. How do you cope? I'll tell you. You make your profession of faith, loud and clear, and you make sure everybody hears it. That makes you part-way safe. Nobody can accuse you of heresy or schism—no matter what else they can cite against you. Next you come out hot and strong against the Communists. They're the real Antichrist, and the Holy Father is committed to a worldwide crusade against 'em. The United States is in the forefront of that crusade, with the President and Joe McCarthy and John Foster Dulles and me too, by God! With those two points on the board, you're halfway to winning. But,' says Spelly, 'when you get to Rome, you have two other rules to learn: never assume that what you see is what is; never believe that what you're told is the whole truth. It's only when you've grasped that—and the Romans know you've grasped it—that you begin to win respect and make progress . . .' Do you understand what I'm telling you, now?"

"I think I do." Cavanagh gave him an embarrassed grin. "But I'm asking whether it's worth walking such a long way round to get the eggs. I'm a simple soul. I learned my first religion from the penny catechism—and asked my first real questions when a torpedo hit us and I lost four shipmates. I have no intention of marrying into the Almanach de Gotha or staying celibate and getting my name in the *Annuario Pontificio* as a household prelate!"

"The latter I can understand." Molloy laughed. "The Almanach de Gotha? Don't knock it, Cavanagh! You're young yet and you've still to learn how many secret rooms the law can open to you. A simple soul, is it? I hope I'm not around when you discover how devious you really can become. Anyway, let's finish your briefing for this morning's excursion." He pulled the note pad towards him and began to jot down the names for Cavanagh. "First item: you go ashore and walk to the Café Aleria in the square. You'll find a man sitting alone at one of the sidewalk tables. He'll be drinking a Pernod and reading a copy of yesterday's *Nice-Matin*. He's American. He answers to the name of Jordan. You tell him Lou Molloy sent you and that you'll pick him up on the way back. Grab a taxi and head out to the Mas de la Balagne, which is a farm about half-way to Ile Rousse. At the Mas you ask for a man called Sampiero Paoli."

"Let's hold it there a moment. What language are we speaking? The name is obviously Italian."

"The family is old Corsican. The language is Corsican dialect, or French."

"Who am I? How do I identify myself?"

"You're nobody, a messenger, a mailman. You hand over a letter. You wait for the answer."

"Which should be?"

"A man, a Frenchman. You deliver him to Jordan and bring them both back to the *Salamandra*."

"And that's it?"

"That's it. Any problems?"

"No problems, just a question."

"Ask it."

"Why the double shuffle? You need me to drive the boat, sure; but why do you need a go-between to deliver an envelope and pick up a live body?"

"I quote," said Lou Molloy, softly. "I quote verbatim, from young Bryan de Courcy Cavanagh himself. 'Don't tell me anything more than I need to know. Don't explain who, why or wherefore . . .' Did I get it right?"

"You did, Mr. Molloy. I must be wearier than I thought. If you'll excuse me, I'll take the coffee mugs down to the galley, then freshen myself up with a shower and a shave."

"If you need to get laid as well," said Molloy cheerfully, "call on Lenore. She'll oblige you anytime. I like to keep a happy ship. Remember that, Cavanagh! A happy ship!"

From the deck of the *Salamandra d'Oro* the harbor of Calvi looked like a large, landlocked lake, surrounded by broad sandy beaches, with the old town tucked into the northeast corner out of reach of the winds. The flat hinterlands of the Balagne were closely farmed, with olive groves, orchards of citrus, almonds and peaches, plots of vegetables, and flocks of goats grazing on the coarse pastures near the seashore. It looked peaceful and prosperous, but Galeazzi, in his trenchant fashion pronounced it ". . . unhappy, unhealthy and economically unsound. Italy occupied it during the war with eighty thousand troops. The Germans sent in about fifteen thousand. Their casualties from malaria were much higher than their combat losses. The population has been halved since 1936 by emigration and, although they've got rid of the anopheles mosquito, the place is still rent by family feuds and vendettas. Most of the criminal activities on the French Riviera are run by Corsican families . . . If the place has a future at all, it must be in tourist development . . ."

Which raised again for Cavanagh the elementary question of why they had come here. No one else was going ashore. The boys had put out the swimming ladders and stretched the sun awnings on the afterdeck. Molloy had given him what he had been pleased to call "the envelope," which was in fact a flat sack of unbleached cotton, containing unspecified materials, taped like an old-fashioned poultice around his chest and covered by his shirt. Cavanagh protested mildly.

"It's bloody uncomfortable and it makes me feel foolish, as though I've strayed into a B-movie."

"You'd feel a lot more foolish if you dropped it in the water or left it in the taxi."

"Aye, aye, sir!" said Cavanagh glumly, and made his way to the waiting dinghy. He was ashore within a couple of minutes and tied up at the little stone jetty near the fishing basin.

The town itself was already as hot as an oven. The striped awning of the Café Aleria provided a small relief from the glare, but none from the eddies of hot, dusty air that rose from the cobbled sidewalk.

The café was clearly a resort for local fishermen, who had wisely occupied the shady interior. The solitary fellow drinking Pernod at a sidewalk table looked like Marcello Mastroianni with a crew cut. He was dressed in cotton slacks and shirt and a pair of local espadrilles, and he had an engaging schoolboy smile. Cavanagh approached him and put the question:

"Are you Mr. Jordan?"

"I am." The accent was eastern seaboard U.S.A.

"I'm from the *Salamandra d'Oro*. Mr. Molloy sends his compliments."

"That's nice; but I hope you'll be bringing me more than compliments."

"I'll bring what I'm given. Those are the only instructions I have. You'll be waiting here?"

"I'll be waiting."

"Where can I pick up a taxi?"

"You have to telephone." He flipped Cavanagh a *jeton*. "Inside the bar. The number's just above the telephone."

"Thanks."

"My pleasure."

The taxi took ten minutes to arrive and was driven by a laconic fellow with dark, greased hair, a drooping moustache and a leery eye. The vehicle and the driver stank of stale Gauloises: Cavanagh wound down the window, stuck his head out into the slipstream and prayed he wouldn't be sick.

The Mas de la Balagne was about five miles out of Calvi. It was approached by a driveway which wound through an impressive avenue of old chestnut trees to a stone farmhouse built four-square around a cobbled courtyard with a double door of ancient hewn timber. Outside the door was a rusted bell, mounted on a wooden pillar. Cavanagh rang the bell, which had a cracked discordant sound. A few moments later, an elderly woman appeared in the doorway at the far side of the courtyard and beckoned him to come to her. By the time he reached the door she had disappeared and in her place stood a dark, stocky fellow with graying hair and no trace of a welcoming smile. He asked in French:

"Who are you? What do you want?"

"I have a message for Sampiero Paoli."

"I am Paoli. What's the message?"

"I don't know. I'm wearing it under my shirt." He opened the buttons of his shirt to display the cotton envelope. "May I come in?"

The stocky one stood aside to let him enter a big stone-flagged kitchen with a long, scarred table, a carving block made from a tree trunk, onions and leeks hanging from the beams and a big iron stew pot steaming on an old, black wood oven. Cavanagh stripped off his shirt, peeled the strapping from his body and handed the fabric envelope to Paoli. He said:

"I was told there would be an answer."

"Wait here. There's wine on the table. Help yourself."

He walked out carrying the package and a long, pointed knife which he picked up from the carving block. Cavanagh crossed to the table and poured himself a cup of wine from an earthenware pitcher. It was white and cool but rough and unwelcoming as the country itself. The first mouthful gave him heartburn, so he sipped the rest of it slowly and carefully. He was almost at the dregs of the cup when Paoli came back, empty handed. He asked:

"What did you think of our wine?"

"It's rough," said Cavanagh with a grin, "very rough."

"It's rough country." A faint flicker of humor lit up his dour features and he beckoned Cavanagh to follow him through the rear door of the kitchen, down a long passageway that gave onto a stretch of cultivated land. Beyond the plots were a series of hillocks rising to a low escarpment. Paoli pointed upwards:

"It is necessary to walk a little."

They walked perhaps half a mile, winding through

the first low mounds, then climbing to the plateau of the escarpment. There, dark against the sky, stood three dolmens, each a flat slab of stone resting upon huge, rough-hewn uprights. Cavanagh stared at them in amazement, groping through the rag-bag of memory for fragments of archaeology. He asked Paoli:

"What are these?"

"We call them the table-stones. They are the burying places of the ancient people. There are many such, all over the island. Since the war, more and more scholars are coming to study them."

He cupped his hands around his mouth and shouted in French:

"*Holà*, Tolvier! Your man has arrived!"

There was a brief period of silence, then a man emerged from the shadow of the furthest dolmen. He was tall, but stooped. He was dressed in rough peasant clothes and he carried a shotgun. He approached with slow, cautious steps. His voice was harsh and hostile.

"Hands up. Palms towards me."

Cavanagh raised his hands slowly. He turned to Paoli.

"Who's this?"

"This is the answer to your message. You're taking him back to Calvi."

Cavanagh turned back to the armed man. Suddenly and irrationally, he was angry. He shouted in French:

"I'm putting my hands down. If you want to shoot, go ahead. I'm unarmed. I was sent to fetch you. Only a damned fool kills the messenger before he's heard the message."

Tolvier lowered the gun and took a few more steps towards them. He demanded curtly:

"What's the message?"

"You are to come back to Calvi with me. There's a man called Jordan waiting for you at the Café Aleria.

If you're the man he's expecting, I'm taking you both out to the *Salamandra d'Oro*, which is a motor vessel registered in the United States. That's all the orders I have."

"And this Jordan?"

"He could be a man from Mars. I think he's American. I had thirty seconds conversation with him."

Tolvier turned to Paoli.

"Is this true?"

Paoli shrugged.

"The money has been paid. This fellow delivered it. What more can I tell you? I kept my part of the bargain. Now you have to make your own decisions."

Tolvier stood for a moment, looking from one to the other. Then he snapped the safety catch on the shotgun and tossed it to Paoli. To Cavanagh he said abruptly:

"I'm ready. Let's go."

Walking in Indian file they made their way back to the farmhouse. Paoli, carrying the shotgun, made a sinister rear guard to the small procession.

The moment the taxi drew up outside the Café Aleria, Jordan leaped inside the vehicle and ordered the driver to make all speed to the fishing dock. During the short drive he conducted a swift but clinical check on Tolvier.

"Turn your face to the right."

As he did so, Jordan traced with his fingertip, two parallel scars on the left cheek.

"How did you get those?"

"Saber practice."

"Where?"

"A *salle d'Armes* in Lyon."

"Who ran it?"

"Louis Claude Barrault."

"Give me your right hand."

Jordan examined it carefully. The small finger had been broken at the first joint. It had been badly set and was permanently swollen with arthritic growth. Jordan released his hold and turned to Cavanagh with a grin.

"Mission accomplished. Thanks."

"What now?" asked Cavanagh.

"You take us back to the ship."

"You pay the taxi." Cavanagh returned his grin. "I'll get our friend into the dinghy. That way you can cover us both."

"A sound thought," said Jordan. "But our real threat is out there."

He pointed out across the wide bay where, far from the docks, a rusted Fairmile, flying the British flag and a tricolor courtesy pennant, was just dropping anchor. Cavanagh strained to decipher the name on her transom, but she was too far away. Jordan enlightened him:

"She's the *Jackie Sprat*. British registry, Corsican skipper. Bad news. The good news is she's later than we expected. Let's get the hell out of here!"

As he drove them back at speed to the *Salamandra*, Cavanagh could see Molloy and Giulia playing a game of water polo with Jackie and Lenore Pritchard. Farnese and Galeazzi were leaning on the rail looking at the rusted hull of the Fairmile. Hadjidakis stood watch on the foredeck with a pair of binoculars, while the Countess lay on a chaise longue under the awning, with an unread book on her bosom and a pitcher of iced lemonade beside her.

When the dinghy came alongside, Hadjidakis was there to hand the two newcomers aboard and hurry them below decks. Cavanagh hung the dinghy astern, then hurried down to the forepeak to change into a pair of swim trunks. When he came on deck he saw Giulia and Molloy swimming back to the ship. They waved to him. He ignored the signal. He was off duty. He was hot, tired and irritable. The last thing he needed was another interrogation. He hoisted himself onto the guardrail, balanced himself for one precarious moment, then dived overside and swam far out into the center of the bay.

Hadjidakis, back on deck, focused the glasses on him and frowned unhappily. He liked to keep all his brood—visitors and crew alike—well within hailing distance. Although no one wanted to admit it, there were sharks in the Mediterranean; people did get cramps and had to be hauled out of the water. Add to which, Lou Molloy was an unpredictable fellow who had been known to order engines started and anchors up at the first whiff of a weather change or a woman's wave from a neighboring cruiser.

This morning—so far at least—he seemed calm and content, enjoying an innocent playtime. Hadjidakis prayed that the mood might last, that the visitors were good news and that Cavanagh, a chancy fellow himself, would do nothing to upset the master of the *Salamandra d'Oro*. He need not have worried. After a night on watch, a troubling excursion ashore and a long swim, Cavanagh was dog-tired. He collected a plate of cold cuts and a bottle of beer from the galley, ate and drank without relish, then tumbled into his bunk and slept until seven in the evening.

That night the crew were not bidden to join the guests; so while Leo and Jackie served the cocktails, Hadjidakis, Lenore and Cavanagh ate an early supper and then sat chatting together on the foredeck. Hadjidakis had news for them:

"A change of plan. We're not cruising Corsica. We're heading for Italian waters. We leave after midnight. Your watch again, Cavanagh."

"Suits me. What's the route?"

"Northeast to Cap Corse then southeast to the island of Elba. I've laid out the charts and put markers in the pilot books."

"Thank you."

"Read the pilot carefully. There's a notable magnetic deviation around Elba because of the large mass of iron ore on the island."

"Interesting. How long is the run?"

"About forty-five miles on each leg. We'll time it to eat breakfast in port."

"Why the sudden change?" It was Lenore who put the question.

"I didn't ask. Molloy was like a bear with a toothache all afternoon. You were lucky to be asleep, Cavanagh. All the rest of us were rousted for something or other."

Lenore Pritchard pursed her lips in disapproval.

"I don't envy the bride-to-be. Once she marries him, she'll be on a real roller coaster ride."

"You might be surprised." Hadjidakis gave a humorless grin. "Just before cocktail time they were on deck together. She was giving him the rough edge of her tongue, and Lou was taking it without a murmur."

"That's bad news!" Lenore Pritchard was not at all happy. "The more he took from her, the more he'll dish out to me."

"What does he dish out exactly?" Cavanagh's concern was obvious. Lenore Pritchard tried to skate around the issue.

"I told you he plays rough games; but then so do I. I guess it balances itself out."

"You've shocked the boy!" Hadjidakis goaded her softly. "He's very young. He has a lot to learn."

"I've offered him free lessons. So far he's been too shy to accept the offer."

"It's not that I'm shy, colleen oge"—Cavanagh gave

her his widest, sunniest smile—"but I don't like pain myself and I hate to inflict it on anyone else, certainly not as a form of amusement. Which is not to say I am not grateful for your kind invitation, but who am I to be claiming privileges in my own captain's bedchamber?"

"He told me he offered them to you himself."

"Indeed he did, but he made it sound as though he owned you, which is not the way I like to receive a woman—as the gift of another man."

"But I made the offer too."

"Indeed you did."

"So why haven't you accepted?"

"Well now, that's not an easy question to answer without sounding rude, but let me try. When I was growing up and just beginning to spend money and chase girls, my father took us away for a holiday in a fashionable seaside pub. One of the first things he showed me was the notice screwed to the bedroom door. It listed the innkeeper's liabilities and also the charge for the room. He made me read it carefully and added his own footnote: 'Bryan,' he said, 'there's no such thing as a free bed or free board. Both of 'em have to be paid for, in cash or kind. So before you have lunch or get laid, just be sure you're prepared to pay the score or scrub the dishes.' So, you might say that's what's holding me back: I can't read the price tag on these fabulous offers. However"—he reached out to stroke her cheek—"if you're ever in real bother with Molloy, give a yell. I'll come running."

"If you do," said Hadjidakis, "Molloy will break your back! You'd better believe that!"

"I'd expect him to try it. Whether he'd succeed or not is another question altogether. But thanks for the warning."

"You get that for free," said Hadjidakis. He heaved himself to his feet and left them a hand's breadth apart, watching the last light fade over the black hills behind the town.

That night, the guests sat late over dinner and later still over coffee and liqueurs on the afterdeck. For the first time, they seemed to be at ease with each other. Their laughter and their talk rose high and voluble, like fountains spurting suddenly in a silent garden.

Chef had finished his work and retired. Lenore Pritchard was in bed, "alone tonight—and God! am I glad of it." Jackie and Leo were cleaning up in the galley. Hadjidakis and Cavanagh were on the bridge, waiting for Molloy to call a halt to the evening, so that they could square away for the overnight run to Elba.

Hadjidakis switched on the talk-back microphone, normally used to acknowledge bridge commands when docking or casting off. The conversation on the afterdeck was immediately audible. Molloy was at the tail end of a statement . . .

". . . If you're on the run from people with worldwide connections, like the Mafia or the intelligence services, or a freelance assassin, it isn't easy to disappear. Tolvier is wanted for at least seven murders in 1944, as well as crimes against humanity while he was acting as interrogator for the Germans and the Vichy French in Lyons. We've just lifted him out of hiding, and tonight we're handing him over to the C.I.A. while we're at sea."

"It sounds like a plot for a thriller"—Giulia's tone was dismissive—"a particularly cheap one."

"Not cheap, my love!" Molloy's laugh had an edge of irritation to it. "This was a very expensive operation."

"But an important one!" Galeazzi added a hasty postscript. "Important to His Eminence in Lyons, to the whole French Church and to our other Eminence in Rome."

To which, Farnese added his own rider.

"Most important of all perhaps to American Intelligence, who are buying up these characters like horse flesh at an auction."

"Which I find entirely scandalous!" The Countess was emphatic, if a trifle tipsy. "These people are criminals, traitors, torturers. Tolvier was a professional interrogator for the Germans and the Vichy militia. By helping him, you have dirtied yourselves!"

"My dear Lucietta!" Galeazzi was, as always, the voice of pure reason. "In war one uses whatever allies one can muster, whatever weapons lie to hand. Make no mistake, we are still at war with the Marxists all over the world. No matter that the war is undeclared or that it is fought by subversion instead of by armies, it is still a mortal combat. So, those who are useful to us in the struggle must be able to count on our protection. Whatever their past villainies, they must be able to count on the compassion and forgiveness promised by Christ, through the Church, to the repentant sinner."

"Poppycock!" said the Contessa. "I hope God can forgive the Holy Father for all he didn't do in the war and what is going on under his very nose in his own city! The French Church and Rome itself are still providing escape routes for war criminals. Now you are aiding and abetting them!"

"Enough, Lucietta!" Farnese was furious.

"It's late," said Galeazzi. "Let's leave this discussion for another time."

"We should let the crew clear up," said Lou Molloy. "We weigh anchor at midnight . . ."

Hadjidakis reached up and switched off the intercom. He turned a quizzical eye on Cavanagh.

"Well now! What do you make of that?"

Cavanagh grinned and shook his head.

"I didn't hear anything. You didn't either, because

we're too polite to eavesdrop on Mr. Molloy and his distinguished guests."

A reluctant smile dawned in Hadjidakis's dark eyes. "For a dumb Mick, you learn fast, Cavanagh! I like you, Molloy likes you too, though sometimes we both think you're a cocky young bastard—but you have to know there are no secrets between Lou Molloy and Giorgios Hadjidakis. We've shared too much to let anyone drive a wedge between us. So long as you remember that, we'll get along fine. Understand?"

"I've always understood it," said Cavanagh mildly. "You're old friends. I'm just the hired help. No argument."

"Good! Now let's give our dancing boys a hand to straighten up the deck. They've been working their pretty little tails off and I want 'em up bright and early to scrub decks and clean windows before we dock in Elba . . ."

At fifteen minutes to midnight they had the decks cleared and the ship secured for the overnight passage. At five minutes to the hour the anchors were up and Cavanagh, with Molloy and Hadjidakis beside him, was nosing out of the harbor and heading northeast to Cap Corse. The wind was light, the sea calm. The forecast promised an easy passage. Molloy, however, had new orders for him:

"We're getting rid of Jordan and Tolvier tonight."

"How and where?"

"At sea, half an hour out. I'm told there's a U.S. submarine running submerged on a parallel course. When she surfaces and signals, you heave to and wait for them to send a rubber dinghy to collect our friends. I'll be glad to get 'em off my hands. I don't like either of them very much, but at least Jordan is our spook. Any questions, Cavanagh?"

"No, sir. You've told me all I need to know. If you want to go to bed, I can handle things."

"I'm sure you can." Molloy gave him a sardonic grin. "But Giorgios will hand over the bodies. After that you'll have an easy watch. There'll be no shenanigans with Lenore tonight. I'm bushed. If the Queen of Sheba presented herself mother-naked and fresh from the bath, I'd have to send her away. God rest ye merry gentlemen!"

Abruptly he left the bridge. Hadjidakis made a pinpoint mark on the chart and told Cavanagh:

"I'll walk up to the bows and take some fresh air while I'm watching. By the way, no mention of this in the log."

"Thanks for telling me," Cavanagh was testy. "I hope we're not going permanently into the body-lifting business."

"I think you can count on that," said Hadjidakis. "Lou had some markers to pay off to the intelligence community. This took care of a whole batch of them."

"It might also make him some enemies."

"It will; but that's his problem, not yours."

"Of course. Foolish of me to think otherwise! Downright stupid of me to ask!"

"Sometimes," said Giorgios Hadjidakis, "sometimes you really are a dumb Mick!"

The transfer of Jordan and Tolvier went off without a hitch. The submarine broke surface, and lay like a great sea animal dead in the water fifty yards from the *Salamandra*. Two seamen in a rubber dinghy came to pick the men from the stern of the *Salamandra* and ferry them back to the submarine. Hadjidakis watched until they were aboard and the hatch was sealed again; then he went up to the bridge to deliver a laconic order to Cavanagh.

"They're gone and good riddance! Your ship, mister. I'll see you in the morning."

Cavanagh bade him goodnight and wished him quickly gone so that he could enjoy the purest pleasure of his life: a soft sea, a sky full of stars, the lights of a strange shoreline and himself alone and wakeful at the helm, a new Ulysses, dreaming of an ancient world which he had crossed oceans to discover.

At one-forty in the morning he was trying to identify a vessel following steadily in his wake about two miles away. He guessed it to be a trawler or, more probably, a long-line fisherman trolling for swordfish on the edges of the shallow feeding grounds and the deep trenches. Then, remembering Jordan's words on the dock, he wondered if it could be the *Jackie Sprat*. He was tempted to put on speed to see if the other vessel would try to match him, but he rejected the idea in case it might disturb the passengers.

It was not an important matter; rather, it was part of a nightly game played by a lone helmsman to keep himself awake and attentive. While he noted the event in his log, he was anchored in the small luminous pool made by the spotlight on the chart table. The rest of the bridge was in twilight, while, outside, there was only star-shine and the distant, sparse illuminations along the Corsican shoreline.

Then, sudden and silent as a phantom, Giulia Farnese was standing beside him. He had not heard her approach. Her animal heat and the heady swirl of her perfume were the first indications of her presence.

She was barefoot, dressed in silk pajamas with a woolen sweater pulled over the top, so that she looked like a schoolgirl ready for a dormitory party. She wore no makeup and there were dark shadows under her eyes. Cavanagh stammered a greeting in Italian. She answered with an apology and an oddly desperate plea.

"I'm sorry to disturb you. May I stay up here for a while?"

"Of course. Take the helmsman's chair."

He helped her hoist herself onto the high stool. She launched immediately into a babble of explanations.

"I couldn't go to sleep for a long time. I never can after a talky evening. When I did fall asleep, I dropped straight into a terrible nightmare. Even when I woke up, the cabin seemed full of it. I couldn't stay there. I had to get out."

To which Cavanagh had an instant but unspoken reaction: *If I were that scared and two doors away from the one I loved, I know where I'd be at this moment—and it wouldn't be on a ship's bridge with a stranger!* What he said, however, was quite different:

"There are no nightmares here. Just the sea and the stars—clean, beautiful things. Look out there . . ."

"You don't understand!"

"So make me understand. Tell me. Talk it out of your brain-box."

The story she told had an odd, disjointed quality, as though she were still brushing away the cobwebs of the dream.

". . . During the war I lost my only brother. He was a pilot, killed in Libya. He was a beautiful, beautiful young man and I adored him. I still dream about him sometimes, and always the dreams have been happy ones, so that I'm sorry to wake up and lose them . . . Tonight was different. After dinner we were talking about that horrible man, Tolvier. He was a collaborator who worked with Klaus Barbie, interrogating his own countrymen under torture. For some reason the Archbishop of Lyons is protecting him and hiding him. There are other high people in France who want to have him out of the way without a trial. Cardinal Tisserant at the Vatican also wants him free. That's how Galeazzi and my father are involved. Lou has supplied money and contacts with U.S. Intelligence who want Tolvier to work with them . . . But that's all by the way. Somewhere in the talk Lou said the best way to disappear was to die and get resurrected. That's what I saw in the nightmare; my beautiful brother rising out of an open grave . . . But he wasn't beautiful anymore. He was horrible, horrible . . ."

Suddenly she was out of control, her hands shaking, teeth chattering, her body torn with deep, racking sobs. Cavanagh put his arm around her and held her close, crooning to her:

". . . Easy now! Easy! It was only a dream. It's over and gone. Your brother's at rest . . . "

Her panic subsided slowly. When finally she was calm again, Cavanagh poured coffee from the thermos and steadied her hand as she held it to her lips. He wondered—not at all irrelevantly—what Lou Molloy would do, say or think if he came upon them now. Giulia Farnese gave voice to the same thought.

"Look at me! I'm a mess. What would Lou think if he saw me now?"

Cavanagh gave a small, humorless laugh.

"He'd probably try to punch me in the nose."

"And would you let him do that?"

"Let's say I'd try very hard to stop him; but what would the Princess Giulia Farnese be doing during the fight?"

A mischievous smile twitched at the corners of her mouth.

"I'm not sure. It would depend on who was winning. But I would stay until the end so I could patch you up. I'd owe you that at least, after what you've done for me tonight."

"You owe me nothing. I'm glad I was here to help."

"Aunt Lucietta told me you were good value. I have to confess I didn't believe her at first. She gets crushes on half the young men she meets. I don't blame her. She's been widowed a long time, and in the last days of the war she lost a lover who was very dear to her.

My father and the rest of the family didn't approve of him, because, although he came from an old and noble family, he joined the Communist Party and took to the hills with one of their partisan groups. The Germans captured him and he died under Gestapo interrogation. That's why Aunt Lucietta is so critical about Vatican policies and some of the things my father is involved in . . ." She broke off abruptly. "But this is old history, our history; it has nothing to do with you. Tell me about yourself. What brought you to Europe? What will you do when this summer is over?"

"I'll put on my pack and go wandering again, picking up jobs as I go. I've given myself a year before I settle down."

"To what?"

"To the law, which is what I've been trained for."

"I can't imagine you stuck in some stuffy office surrounded by briefs and books!"

"Frankly, neither can I; but there is another side to the question. We're just coming out of one of the most lawless periods in world history. Sooner or later, if we're to become half-way human again, the rule of law has to prevail. We have to be able to settle disputes without killing each other, make bargains that will hold, defend the rights of people who have neither the strength nor the knowledge to do it themselves. I'd like to find a role for myself in that process; but before I do, I have to understand history, which I'm rediscovering every day, and the present, which is why I'm working on languages and people, the idioms of their lives."

"Is that what you're doing now? Working on me?"

"This isn't work. It's pleasure. My only regret is . . ."

He broke off in mid-sentence.

"Go on. Say it!"

"My only regret," he told her gravely, "is that the

pleasure has to be brief and is constantly curtailed by social circumstances . . . and if that sounds impertinent, I trust the Principessa will forgive me."

"Please don't call me Principessa."

"Courtesy demands it."

"Not here. Not now."

"What should I call you then?"

"Giulia. That's my name, after all!"

"Giulia." The word tasted sweet on his tongue. "Giulia la Bella. Strange isn't it? I know more about your ancestor than I do about you."

"Would you believe I hate her?"

"For God's sake, why?"

"Because, even after all these centuries I live in her shadow. She dominates my whole life. After my brother was killed, all my father's hopes and ambitions for the family were centered on me. When that first Giulia became the mistress of the Borgia Pope, she became the patroness and protector of the whole family. My father dreams the same role for me!"

"That's a hell of a load to carry!"

"Sometimes I'd like to cast it off and disappear—just like Tolvier!"

"Why don't you?"

"Where would I run? To a garret in Paris?"

"Your father, what does he say about all this?"

"Nothing. He takes my duty for granted, as he takes everything else in his history and his life. This marriage, for instance; it is not by his standards an ideal one, but in today's world it is much better than any European union that could be arranged. Lou is rich. He is well-connected politically in the United States, he is a friend of the man they call the American Pope, Cardinal Spellman, who is himself a close friend of Papa Pio . . . Papa Pio will confer a papal decoration on Lou before we are married. So, for today it's a very good arrangement."

"And for tomorrow?"

"For tomorrow there are other possible arrangements. There will be no divorce, but if I am unhappy I may take a lover. Lou himself most certainly would—as he does now."

Cavanagh stared at her in amazement. For the boy from "down under," the respectable lace-curtain Irish Catholic, whose modest fortunes were founded on the gold fields of Ballarat and a string of country pubs, all this was history re-enacted in technicolor. But far beyond the surprise was a sense of pathos and of waste. He expressed it in a single, blunt statement.

"So far I've heard duty and money and arrangements; but nothing about love."

"Because love's a private matter and it's different with every man and woman. Sometimes it comes soon, sometimes late. Sometimes it wears out quickly. In the lucky ones it lasts a lifetime."

"And for Giulia Farnese?"

"She doesn't know enough yet to discuss it."

"That's a great pity."

"But you, Mr. Cavanagh, will not presume to offer her pity."

"I beg your pardon, Principessa. I should know better. Lou Molloy read me a long lecture about how I was expected to behave in noble company."

"I'll assure him you have behaved impeccably."

"Better you didn't." Cavanagh gave her a crooked Irish grin. "He might get the wrong idea."

"In what sense?"

"He might think his lady and I have something to hide."

She was smiling now, feline and conspiratorial, Giulia the Beautiful, straight out of the history books.

"But we do! Lou has never seen me as you saw me tonight. I wouldn't want him to either. So, I have to trust you not to tell him or anyone else."

"There would be no reason to tell—unless you told him first and he asked me a direct question. I won't lie for you; but I certainly won't gossip either."

"If you did, we would become enemies. I want us to be friends, Cavanagh."

"Then that's another secret that has to be kept, Giulia mia."

"Why?"

"Because I'm paid to be a servant. I made that contract with Molloy. My role, like yours, is fixed. Of course we can be friends, but it's better for everyone's peace of mind if we let the service signify the friendship."

"You talk like a Jesuit."

"I was trained by them."

"Are you afraid of Molloy?"

"No. He employs me. He doesn't own me. The worst he can do is fire me."

"Are you afraid of me?"

"No; but I am afraid of myself. A man could break his heart and his neck reaching too high for forbidden fruit."

"How will you know whether it's too high unless you stretch or jump for it?"

"Because I can measure what you're marrying: money, power, position, experience. I can't match Molloy in any of those things."

"Would you want to match him, Cavanagh?"

"One day I might just be mad enough."

"I wonder how love will happen to you?"

He laid his large hand over hers, ready to withdraw in an instant. She made no movement, uttered no word of protest as he answered her.

"For me I think it will be a swift thing, a risky one too perhaps; but it will be all or nothing, a wild ride to the edge of the world and back." He gave a small, rueful laugh. "So be warned, my little princess, don't tease the sleeping tiger . . . Now it's time you were in bed. I have a watch to keep and you're very disturbing company."

He raised her imprisoned hand to his lips and then released it. She sat silent a long moment, studying his face, tracing the structure of it with the tip of her finger. Then she said very softly:

"Some woman trained you well, Cavanagh."

"There was a house full of 'em! My mother and three sisters. Even my father, who was no pussycat, kept his shoes wiped and his temper under control and his language polished in their living room. So, yes, you might say I've been woman-trained. Maybe you'll feel moved to write me a letter of reference when the summer is over."

"You're a clown, Cavanagh."

"That's what Molloy called me. I hope, before summer's end, you'll find a better name."

"I'll keep thinking, I promise . . . "

She leaned forward, kissed him lightly on the lips, then slid sideways out of the chair to avoid any answering embrace. Instantly, she was the old Giulia, closed, imperious, cold as moonlight. Only the smile in her eyes betrayed her.

"The coffee was most welcome, Mr. Cavanagh, the talk most instructive and your manners are beyond reproach."

"My simple duty, Principessa—and my great pleasure also."

He gave her an ironic salute and watched her walk barefoot down the companionway to the deck. When he turned back to the chart table he saw that she had left her handkerchief, a small wisp of cambric and lace. He touched it to his lips, then folded it carefully and buttoned it into the pocket of his shirt. A man could be hanged on evidence like that—or he could be moved to dance a jig and shout canticles of joy. Bryan de Courcy Cavanagh checked the compass heading and the radar screen, then tuned into the radio program from Nice on which Charles Trenet was singing "La Mer" . . . it seemed a nice, romantic postscript to a very enigmatic encounter.

It was bright morning when they made the approach to Elba. Hadjidakis was at the helm. Molloy and Farnese stood beside him, studying the configuration of the northern coastline, the traffic of fishermen and ferries across the seven-mile channel between the island and the mainland port of Piombino.

Their talk was technical: of water supplies and power sources, the planned extension of the single island airstrip, the range of local agriculture, the sources of tourist traffic from the Ligurian coast and the cities of Tuscany.

Cavanagh, off watch and off duty, was standing in the prow of the vessel, sketching the foothills and the peak of Monte Capanne, the marching cypresses which wound about the slopes, and the patterns of vineyards and olive groves and vegetable plots and the dark shadows of the pinewoods near the shore. Over on the mainland had lived the Etruscans, a serene and hedonistic people, whose frescoed tombs still stood among the wheat fields. Their city was called Populonia, and there they smelted the iron ore which their galleys brought from Elba. There was smelting on the island too, and the Greek traders called it Aethalia, the smoking place, because of the vapors from the kilns . . . On the mountain he was sketching there were deposits of gemstones; beryl and tourmaline and garnet, which the ancients fashioned into ornaments.

Galeazzi stood a pace away, watching him work, making his own reminiscent commentary . . .

"There has always been a boat-building industry,

here and on the mainland, and the fishing is good: sardines and anchovies and tuna . . . But these resources are all limited and rapidly diminishing, so the economic future will depend more and more on tourism. I have recommended to Molloy and Farnese that they make their first venture here, because there is a good sub-structure already in existence: ferry services from Livorno, Piombino and Genoa, a good coastal highway on the mainland and a parallel railway system. On the island there is property available, freehold and leasehold. There are shipyards in Spezia and Livorno which already are setting up for pleasure craft. Also there are places which can be developed as tourist attractions: Napoleon's villa, the local musuem, the old Spanish fort, sites for undersea exploration. We know that there are several ancient wrecks around the coastline. My own son has dived here and brought up a few bronze pieces and fragments of pottery . . . I have advised both Molloy and Farnese that they should establish themselves on the south of the island where the development is still sparse, and where the harborage for small craft would be much safer . . . I hope they will listen to me . . ."

A comment seemed to be called for; Cavanagh tried to keep it strictly neutral.

"I can't speak for Prince Farnese; but I'm sure Mr. Molloy will be very responsive to your advice. He can be brusque and blunt, but he listens carefully and doesn't miss too many details."

"He certainly knows his own mind—and speaks it!" Galeazzi's comment was as neutral as Cavanagh's. "That is, of course, the strength and the weakness of Americans. In business they are both thorough and ruthless. In other matters like diplomacy and social relationships they often lack a certain acuteness of perception, an awareness of nuances . . ."

The words he used were "*sottigliezze*" and "*sfuma-*

ture." Cavanagh pondered them for a moment and then realized that, as a man from the new world, he was as much under fire as Molloy. So, coolly at first, then with increasing eloquence he made his speech for the defense.

"With great respect, sir, I suggest you misread all of us who come from migrant societies. My country is even younger than Mr. Molloy's. It is just as large as the United States, but there are only twelve million people in it. It is potentially very rich, but it holds both threats and promises for the future . . . You have to understand something about migrant societies. Across their history there lies a fault line, a steep escarpment which separates them from the physical and spiritual homeland of their ancestors, and effectively prevents their return to it. The continuity of their history is broken. It can never be wholly restored. Take me, for instance. Like Mr. Molloy, I have Irish forebears, but I am Australian, born and bred. I am a Catholic, but of a special kind, not French, not Roman, part Irish, yes, but not wholly that either. I've come here, on my own volition, to re-establish for myself some of the continuities. I come with a reasonably prepared mind. At this moment, I am speaking your language, I am not asking you to speak mine. But when you talk of 'subtleties' and 'nuances,' of course, you are right. I miss many of them. I am like the Dorian Greek making his first visit to Athens or Alexandria. More appropriately perhaps, I am a Roman, come from the confines of the Empire to Rome itself . . . I'm not explaining myself very well, but . . ."

"On the contrary, my dear Cavanagh," Galeazzi encouraged him cheerfully, "I find you a most eloquent advocate, and your points are well taken. Far from belittling your background, I confess myself more and more impressed by it. I hope you are giving some thought to the suggestions I made about your future career?"

"Yes sir, I am. But there's the whole of summer to run yet. I'm enjoying myself too much to think beyond that."

"Bravo! That's exactly as it should be." The Countess moved in to join them, grasping Cavanagh's arm to steady herself as the *Salamandra* rolled in the wash of a passing ferry. Galeazzi asked:

"Where's Giulia? She's missing all this."

"She's resting. She had a disturbed night. Miss Pritchard has served her breakfast in the cabin."

"She's not ill, I trust?" It was Cavanagh's question.

"No, Mr. Cavanagh." The Countess gave him a bright and tolerant smile. "She is a princess. She can be upset even by a rose petal in her bed." Then she addressed herself to Galeazzi . . . "Dear God, Enrico! This place brings back memories for me! I came here with my husband when we were first married, thirty-five years ago. He had rented a big house with a park, near the Villa Napoleone and we used to drive all over the island in an open carriage with two dapple-gray horses. . . . Later, during the war I used to meet my Corrado here. He would come across from the mainland with one of the sardine fishermen, working the nets with them. At night he would change his clothes and come up to join me for dinner and stay the night. It was a terrible risk, but none of the island folk ever betrayed us. Once I made the trip back with him. We were dropped off at night on a deserted beach and had to walk five miles before dawn to make a rendezvous with the partisans . . . I know you didn't approve of him, Enrico, but he was a brave and noble man and I loved him very much."

"I have never denied that, Lucietta." Galeazzi laid a protective arm around her shoulders. "Your loss was ours too—but ours was the greater. The Church and the Democrats and this new Italy we are trying to build, were all damaged when people like Corrado joined the Communists. I will go further and confess to you that we deserved to lose them because they felt themselves betrayed by politicians and prelates and diplomats and time-servers, fickle as weathercocks. I think—though I cannot say it publicly—that the Vatican is making a huge mistake by mounting a confessional vote against the Communists. I know all the fears they have, I know all the financial and political pressures they are under, but if democracy means anything, if religion means anything, it means making a free choice—this party or that, faith or unfaith . . . "

"I wish"—the Countess was near to tears—"I wish so much, Enrico, you had said this a long time ago!"

Cavanagh was embarrassed and made a stumbling excuse to withdraw from the group. Galeazzi clamped a surprisingly firm grip on his forearm and commanded him to stay.

". . . There is no need to be embarrassed. We are a dramatic people. We love an audience. Consider this as part of your European education. Lucietta means that I could have saved her much heartache if I had been more publicly supportive of her love affair with Corrado, or even more publicly respectful of his memory. She's right of course . . . But, my dear Lucietta, there were then and there are now, mitigating circumstances."

"During the war, yes. When the Germans were here in force, yes. All of us lived behind some kind of mask. But now that the war is over . . . ?"

"What was once my mask, Lucietta, is now my everyday face. I could not shed it, even if I wished."

"I don't believe that."

"You must. Think, Lucietta! Who am I? What do I do?" He waited a long moment for her answer. When none came, he talked on, somberly and persuasively. "I am the treasurer, the financial comptroller of a monarchy, whose subjects number more than five hundred million people, all over the globe. They all pay tribute, through the parish, the diocese, by levy and donation, and the funds come finally into my hands to be managed and invested in viable securities round the world. But consider something else—and you too should meditate on this, my young friend from the Antipodes!—What am I? I am a layman in a court full of celibate clerics, for whom the exercise of power is the only indulgence left, and intrigue is the most fashionable diversion. I have the ear of the Holy Father, I am the keeper of his public and private purse. So I am the natural object of jealousy, the readiest target of intrigue. My lightest words are memorized, reported, weighed . . . A single indiscretion on my part could start a run on the stock markets of the world. My master is a proud and princely man, an ascetic, an intellectual, an absolutist. No whiff of scandal has touched his private life—yet his household is dominated by a German nun, Sister Pasqualina, who has been with him since his diplomatic days in Munich and who, more rigidly than any Lord Chamberlain, controls the approaches to his sacred person . . . I can handle her because she is afraid of me. I am the silent one in the golden mask who comes and goes and offers no more than a nod of recognition. The prelates, on the other hand, depend on her favor: some of them fawn, some offer presents, none dare risk a hostile encounter. Do you understand me, Lucietta?"

"I understand; but I pity you, Enrico."

"Better you should pity than hate me. And you, Mr. Cavanagh, what comment do you have on my sad little tale?"

"None at all, sir. Like you, though in a much lower

grade, I am a servant of the servants of God. I too go about my tasks masked and silent!"

He laughed as he said it, turning the joke against himself. The Countess laughed too and said:

"Now there's a courtier for you, Enrico!"

"More than a courtier," said Galeazzi with cool humor. "A man with a risky talent for irony. Are you a gambler too, Cavanagh?"

"A modest one, so far, because I've played with my own life and my own money. Could I be tempted further? I guess so, if the stakes were high enough . . . I'm going to get myself some coffee. May I bring either of you a cup?"

They both declined and turned immediately to their private talk. Cavanagh took himself off to the galley where Chef and Lenore Pritchard were having their own *Kaffeeklatsch*.

"We're pulling in to Porto Azzuro," Chef told him. "With luck we may get a night ashore."

"Sounds good to me," said Cavanagh.

"Sounds even better to me," said Lenore Pritchard. "You can take me dining and dancing in Porto Azzuro!"

"If there's dining and if there's dancing, you're on, Miss Pritchard!"

"A miracle!" said Lenore Pritchard in mock wonderment. "A true, bloody Roman Catholic miracle! And you're a witness to it, Chef!"

"No miracle! It just looks like one because it always happens on the third day out. Intimacy sets in. Two more days and you'll find it hard even to get people off the ship. They'll take a turn around the docks of whatever port we're in, then they'll be back on board, content to look at the world from over the rail. You must have seen this, Lenore, even on the big Cunarders?"

"I know it, Chef . . . I know it by heart. It's the

back-to-the-womb syndrome. We're all locked in this floating world, and we really don't want to be born again—until of course we enter the stage of prenatal conflict, where we're ready to scratch each other's eyes out . . ."

"And when you're bored even with my cooking!"

"Hard to believe that could happen, Chef!" Cavanagh sat relaxed over his coffee.

"Nevertheless, it does, my young friend. Then even I, the most calm of men, am tempted to run mad with a meat cleaver."

"I'm told our Giulia is indisposed?" Cavanagh tried to make the question as casual as possible. Lenore's answer had more than a touch of malice in it.

"Our little Princess is suffering from a variety of complaints. She is bored to tears with a fiancé who is spending all his time discussing business with her father, and all his sexual energies with me. I have to tell you this is the weirdest wooing I've seen. Whether the bride-to-be is virgin or not—and I'll stake my salary she isn't—she's still a lusty young woman and she's getting precious little relief from Lou Molloy. I don't know what surprises either of them expects to get or deliver on the wedding night, but they'll need to be big ones . . . I see her every day. In spite of myself I like her, but sometimes, I feel I'm watching a package being gift-wrapped for delivery . . . Hell! why should we care? It's not our wedding!"

"I feel sorry for the girl," said Cavanagh.

"I don't." Pritchard was suddenly snappish. "She's as much a party to the bargain as Molloy. She's marrying rich and she's got youth and family on her side. Molloy's marrying a title and a whole cartload of new liabilities, not least of which will be a discontented Italian wife in a society he only half understands. No matter how hard he plays—and he does and he will—he's going to end up a lonely and bitter old man. I'd hate to see that . . ."

"So would I." Suddenly, Chef was back in the talk. "I've known Molloy a long time. He's hard and he's wild; but he enjoys life. He savors every mouthful, as if it were one of my meals. I don't agree with Lenore. I think he'll manage this Princess of his. I think in the end it could turn into a love-match—or at least into a very comfortable matrimonial contract! More coffee, Cavanagh?"

"Why not? I'm wide awake now. I'll have my sleep when everyone's off the ship."

"I'll see you're not disturbed," said Lenore Pritchard. "And I'll polish your dancing shoes. I need you bright-eyed and bullish for a night out in Porto Azzuro!"

Which seemed to answer the question he had asked himself on the day of their first meeting: what would he do when she beckoned him into her cabin? Accept, of course, enjoy; be grateful and gracious and leave no smoldering embers of anger or disappointment to mar the new intimacies of their little floating world. That decision, once made, put a new complexion on the conduct of Declan Aloysius Molloy. His was more calculated, because he could afford the extra care; but it was based on the same logic: keep the conventions and keep the peace, don't compromise a complex business arrangement by a sexual solecism. And let no one talk too loudly about the morals of it, because morals, like politics, were the arts of the possible—as the Farnese had learned very well down the centuries.

It was a real web of casuistries, conspiracies and consents; but all the threads unraveled when *Salamandra d'Oro* was moored, stern-to in Porto Azzuro and Lou Molloy addressed his crew on the foredeck:

". . . My guests and I will be out of your hair for forty-eight hours. Enjoy yourselves; but make damn sure there's a deck watch night and day and the ship is clean as a new pin when we come on board again. Chef, you get your shopping done and take a rest from the galley. The crew will eat ashore. Mr. Hadjidakis will pay each of you twenty dollars per diem, which in this place at the present rate of exchange, will keep you a long way from starvation . . . Miss Pritchard, you will collect and list the ship's laundry. Have the boys deliver it ashore and collect it before you leave port. Mr. Cavanagh . . ."

"Sir?"

"You're coming with me. Pack an overnight bag. Bring the charts and pilot book for Elba, a sketchbook and pencils, a notebook. Giorgios, get him a wetsuit and a tank. Your papers say you've had scuba training."

"They do, yes. But . . ."

"Give me no buts, Mr. Cavanagh. You live by the book, you die by the book."

"Yes sir, Mr. Molloy."

"That's all. The rest of you have a nice day and a pleasant night."

"I'll work on it," said Lenore Pritchard, glumly. "But my guess is that Leo and Jackie will score long before I do."

The conference at the Marina di Campo provided new surprises for Cavanagh. The Farnese party had taken over one whole floor of the Club Hotel (seventy rooms, golf, tennis, heated swimming pool!) and there were already in residence two architects, a Roman advocate, an American attorney, two representatives of the *Comune*, a provincial official from Livorno and two senior members of the Ministry of Marine.

They all boarded a hotel bus and rode down the winding road to the bay where the architects laid out their plaster models on a flat rock and talked eloquently of the fashionable haven which would soon spring up under the sheltering bulk of Capo Poro. Molloy listened in silence, while Farnese translated the architects' explanations. Then, abruptly, he summoned Cavanagh and instructed him in an undertone.

"I want you to get into your wetsuit and do a square search of the area marked for moorings. Tell me what the bottom's like, and whether there are any outcrops that could constitute hazards. How much air have you got in your bottle?"

"Forty-five minutes."

"You'll be back in twenty. You don't have to bust a gut. This is just a softening-up exercise. One more thing—before you enter the water, make a big scene about studying the models . . . Got it?"

"I've got it."

"On your way!"

While Cavanagh was making his undersea circuit, Molloy conducted a critical examination of the models and the accompanying plans. His interrogation was curt and impersonal and he would not leave any point until it had been clarified to his satisfaction.

"The link road from the town of Marina di Campo to the new port area is presently gravel."

"An all-weather surface, yes."

"No sir! Already it's rutted and harmful to traffic. It will need to be tarmac. The cost must be built into the estimates."

"At a later stage, of course, but . . ."

"At stage one, my friend. This is to be a yachting port. Supplies will have to be trucked in—fuel, foodstuffs, liquor, everything. That road, short as it is, will be a vital artery . . . Next point, where is your water coming from?"

"The reservoir behind Monte Capanne."

"That's clean drinking water?"

"Yes indeed."

"Does it ever have to be rationed?"

"Very occasionally in the height of summer."

"Are there any other sources of fresh water?"

"There are bores and wells, but the water is not potable."

"Could we sink a bore anywhere within our area?"

"Quite probably. The water table is not overly deep."

"Then we should do so. The bore water can be used for flushing toilets, washing decks and sluicing down the docks. Make a note to get a hydrographer on the job . . ."

"All these prescriptions are very costly, Mr. Molloy."

"Not half so costly as an empty port if everybody's parking on the mainland because our facilities are substandard. This is an island, for Christ's sake! People will have to be seduced to leave their vessels here! Now let's take a look at the dockside layout . . ."

And so it went on for the best part of thirty minutes while Cavanagh finished his circuit of the mooring area, slipped off his gear and returned to make his report. This time Molloy conducted the questioning for the benefit of the whole audience.

"What's the bottom like, Mr. Cavanagh? The answers in English if you please, Prince Farnese will translate for our colleagues."

"The bottom is weed and sand, good holding ground, except close inshore where there is a continuous rock shelf, less than a meter below the surface."

Instantly the senior architect was on the defensive.

"The rock shelf is known and calculated into my plans. It is in fact the foundation of the retaining wall of the promenade area."

"According to the plans and models," said Cavanagh, "the retaining wall is on the inner edge of the shelf. There is a further projection into the harbor area, three meters wide in some places, I swam right along it. That means that any vessel with a draft of a meter cannot moor stern-to on the buttress wall."

"That means, gentlemen," said Lou Molloy, "you have to put your buttress wall four meters further out and back-fill to enlarge the promenade."

"More cost!"

"More space also for shore installations—which we still have to discuss. Any other comment, Mr. Cavanagh?"

"None that falls within my competence, sir."

"But you obviously have a question?"

"Yes. The bottom is as I have said, weed and sand. I have no means of knowing how deep that deposit is, or what kind of rock foundation lies beneath it."

"Gentlemen?" Molloy faced his experts with the problem. Their answer was a shade less than precise.

"We estimate an average sand depth of two meters. The underlying rock will, of course, be the continuum of the central rock structure of the island: eocenic serpentine, porphyry and granite."

"Upon which you propose to lay out a series of stone finger wharves, to provide an enclosed harbor basin."

"That's right."

"Have you considered the possibility of a pontoon construction, which could be erected quickly, would be easily extendable and would almost double our carrying capacity? It would also enable us to begin the major structural work on the dockside development."

"Frankly, no. The idea was not presented to us in those terms."

"Then we'll table it for discussion this afternoon. Now let's walk over the shore site itself . . ."

As they moved away Cavanagh heard the Countess berating Farnese.

"I don't know how you can put up with that man. He's a peasant, a boor and a bully."

"Who will save us, and make us a great deal of money." Farnese silenced her angrily. "I am tired of academic fools who still think they are designing immortal monuments to their own talent!"

"I agree with Papa," said Giulia Farnese. "These are the moments when I most admire Lou. He is so much the man in command . . ."

The next moment they were out of earshot and Molloy took Cavanagh's arm to steer him away from the group heading to the proposed construction area.

"Next job, Cavanagh. Get your sketchbook. Go back to where we were standing and try to visualize a series of pontoon mooring pens—walkways to give access to all craft, to carry water and power lines, with enough turning room for entrances and exits. Use the new retaining wall as the dock space for vessels over twenty meters. Can you do it?"

"I can try . . . but don't expect Leonardo da Vinci!"

"I'll settle for a lesser name, Van Vitello, maybe? All I need is something I can slap on the conference table and say, 'There, gentlemen! That's what you should be thinking about . . .' You wouldn't think you'd have to tell 'em that the moment you put down rock and concrete, you're going to change the whole configuration of the waterway. Mediterranean tides aren't big, and the currents are minimal, so these dumb bastards have decided to discount 'em . . . Then when they see the results, the Marine Ministry will start suing us for reparation of irreparable damage. Anyway that's the shape of the problem—get working on the sketch . . . See if you can have something halfway presentable by three o'clock . . . You do know what a goddamn pontoon walkway looks like, don't you?"

"I do, sir. The Navy even taught us to make 'em. I just hope I can remember."

Molloy gave him his widest grin and clapped him hard on the shoulder.

"I told you I used to write Navy reports, didn't I?"

"Yes, sir."

"Sometimes they're bullshit; but if you present 'em in evidence, as you did, boyo, you have to live with 'em. But courage, Camille! You're not doing too badly!"

"Damn nice of you to say so, Mr. Molloy, sir!"

"I'm the nicest fellow in the world, so long as I get what I order."

He threw back his head and laughed so loudly that the group ahead turned to look at him and the sea birds rose screaming from the crannies of Capo Poro. Cavanagh didn't blame them. His own rage against the man was rising fast. Nonetheless, he delivered the drawings at the hotel five minutes before the meeting.

"They're the best I could do in the time. I used the Admiralty chart for the harbor plan and a school ruler for working out the scale. There are three drawings: an aerial plan, a perspective elevation of the walkways and a sketch of the typical pontoon float and coupling, Navy-style."

Molloy, preoccupied and irritable, studied the sheets in silence, then offered only a grunt of approval.

"Not bad. They'll serve the purpose."

"Do you want me at the meeting? I could . . ."

"Hell, no! I've got my Rome attorney and Farnese; he has to fight his section of the battle, or he loses the deal. I won't invest and Galeazzi won't put in a nickel of Vatican money unless the contracts are all our way and tighter than a fish's arse. You can do me a favor, though. Meet Lucietta and Giulia for drinks in the bar at seven-thirty and take 'em to dinner at eight-fifteen.

We may or may not join you at table. I'm going to work this bunch until their eyes are popping, and we're not leaving the conference room until our version of the agreements is accepted."

"I wish you luck."

"Luck has nothing to do with it." Declan Aloysius Molloy recited his act of faith. "You know what you want. You know how much you're prepared to pay for it. If you can't cut the deal, you walk and never look back."

To which Cavanagh added a small comment.

"I guess the trick is to judge the moment to get up from the table and head for the door."

"You might say that, yes."

"I wish I could be there to see it."

"Not tonight." Molloy's voice was suddenly flat, his eyes cold and dead as agates. "Don't reach too high, too fast, young man! There are vultures in the tree who will nip your fingers off. Just do what you're asked, when you're asked—and keep the ladies happy until we're finished our business. Understand?"

"Aye, aye, sir," said Bryan de Courcy Cavanagh—and hated the man's guts.

As the afternoon wore into evening, Cavanagh's anger against Molloy cooled, and his hatred congealed into a small pellet of ice at the root of his brain. Reason, frozen into calculation, now told him that he had no one to blame but himself. He had been well and truly warned—by Lenore Pritchard, by Molloy himself, for God's sake! Nevertheless, he had persisted in his wide-open, smilin'-Irish-laddie approach, which almost invited a clip on the jaw. Molloy had delivered it, with curt brutality. Amen! So be it! But never again, by God! Henceforth he would comport himself with politeness and reserve, working out his bond-service with total detachment. Which he admitted, with a wry grin at the fellow in the shaving mirror, would be no easy matter for Bryan de Courcy Cavanagh.

When he came to the bar, a few minutes before seven-thirty, he found the Countess already settled, with a bottle of champagne and a dish of canapés and a waiter hovering by her table. Cavanagh offered an apology for his lateness. She laughed it away.

"Nonsense! I am early. Giulia is having one of her tantrum days and I'm too old for amateur theatricals. Champagne?"

"Please."

The waiter was instantly at his elbow pouring the liquor. The Countess raised her glass.

"Will you make a toast, Mr. Cavanagh?"

"I wish you, my dear Contessa, the best that you wish for yourself."

"*Altrettanto* . . . I wish the same for you."

They drank. There was a moment's silence before she laid down the challenge:

"I would guess, my young friend, that you've had a bad day."

"Let's say I've known better."

"Mr. Molloy is an impossible man. He's boorish, brutal and . . ."

Cavanagh, rich in new, cool wisdom, held up his hand to stay the conversation.

"That's your privileged opinion, Contessa. Unfortunately, I'm not free to discuss it. I am paid to serve Mr. Molloy, not to pass judgment on him."

"I am reproved, Mr. Cavanagh!" She laughed and made a great ceremony of submission. "You must have had a very bad day!"

"So why don't we give it a happy ending and change the subject?"

"Certainly, what would you like to talk about?"

"Something romantic." Cavanagh grinned at her over the lip of his glass. "Yourself, for instance, and the man who risked his life to spend nights with you on this island."

"Now you've stepped over the line, young man!"

Cavanagh was instantly penitent.

"When I'm out of sorts—which I admit I am, because it *was* a lousy day—this tongue of mine runs away with me. I apologize. Now please, may we start again?"

"Certainly. Try one of these canapés. They're very good . . . And remember, I'm a very old hand at the conversation game—much better than you'll ever be, Cavanagh. I can make love in six languages and be a bitch in two or three more."

"You should have warned me." Cavanagh dabbed a crumb of pâté from his lips. "You win, Contessa."

"You're warned now! So, let's reset the board and begin the game again. I move first. You had a bad day, we all did, because your Mr. Molloy was being rude and boorish. He is also a bully and I hate bullies."

"No comment."

"You're not asked to make a comment. I haven't finished yet. Your Mr. Molloy, whom I hate, is about to marry my niece, whom I love dearly, in spite of the fact that she is spoiled, willful and obstinate. She's a high, proud spirit and I'd hate to see her broken by marriage to a beast."

"Do you want a comment on that, Countess?"

"If you have one to make, yes!"

"Marriage is a free contract."

"In these circumstances? The hell it is!"

"Please! I haven't finished yet. Your niece, whom I know only slightly . . ."

"But who likes you very much."

"That's pleasant to hear, but it doesn't change the facts. Your niece is, in law, a free agent and she's chosen to marry Lou Molloy. I can believe she's been pressured by her father, who, if I read the situation even half correctly, has much to gain from this alliance. But Giulia's not blind and she's not stupid, and nobody in this day and age can force her into marriage."

"In short," said the Countess mildly, "you're almost as upset about it as I am."

Instantly Cavanagh was on guard again. This was a more formidable adversary than he had expected. He set down his answer very carefully.

"I have no standing in the matter, my dear Contessa. Therefore, I can have no cause to be upset. However, there are no secrets on shipboard and everyone has an opinion about everyone else . . . This is, to say the least, an exotic union. It could hardly fail to excite the interest of the crew. It must have raised comment already in the Italian press."

"It hasn't been announced yet . . ."

Cavanagh gave a long whistle of surprise.

"Now I began to understand . . ."

"You don't understand a fraction of it! How could you? This is a piece of theater, stage-managed by Alessandro Farnese. Why are we traveling? Because the gossips can't reach us, because Molloy and Alessandro and Galeazzi can complete their investment plans and present themselves as strong financial contributors to the new Christian Democratic Italy. Thereupon, the Pope confers a knightly order on our vulgar American, the marriage is celebrated with a certain pomp but a great degree of privacy at Mongrifone. It's a business deal made in heaven, which will turn, very soon, into a hell!"

"But Giulia is a signatory to the contract."

"I know. And I will tell you a secret, young man! If I could persuade Giulia to elope with a decent young fellow of her own age, I would willingly spend what's left of my inheritance to finance their flight."

"I'd keep that offer to myself, if I were you."

"Why?"

"Because then you'd be setting another snare, and what you'd catch would be every fortune hunter from Rome to Hollywood! Any man who would accept an offer like that would be a pretty poor specimen . . . Besides, the more plans you make for your niece, the more she'll delight in frustrating them."

"You're a very astute young man," said the Countess.

"I'm an idiot," said Cavanagh with feeling. "I shouldn't have let you seduce me into this game."

"You're not a bad player, Cavanagh; but you do, most definitely, need practice. Are there any women in your life at this moment?"

"None that I'm breaking my heart over. I'm in what you might call the transit of Venus."

"The transit of Venus! What a beautiful phrase!"

It was Giulia who spoke. He slewed round in his chair to find her standing behind him. He fought back a sudden surge of anger and managed a reasonable facsimile of a laugh.

"For my part, Principessa, I seem to be caught in a Venus fly-trap!"

"I've often wondered about that," said the Countess. "How does it feel to die at the heart of a flower?"

"I imagine, it might be quite pleasant, dissolving into sweetness and then turning into a flower oneself."

"There! I told you he was a poet, didn't I, Lucietta!"

"I seem to remember that you did, child. Please join us."

Giulia sat down beside Cavanagh. The waiter hurried to fill her glass, while she bit into an elaborate canapé. Then, still eating, she demanded to know:

"What was this deep discussion about anyway?"

"I was trying to seduce him," said the Countess.

"And if you hadn't come along, I might have succeeded!"

"Now he must choose between us!" Giulia raised her glass in a mocking salute. "If we were on offer, Cavanagh, which of us would you take?"

"It's a dilemma," said Cavanagh amiably, "but it's familiar to any man with a drop of Irish blood in his veins. Tommy Moore even wrote a song about it. It doesn't scan too well in Italian but in English it says: 'How happy could I be with either, were t'other dear charmer away!' It sounds even better when you sing it . . ."

"There's a piano in the alcove," said the Countess, "why don't we take our drinks over there? You can give us a session of Irish songs—a contribution to Giulia's education for marriage."

"A most necessary part." Cavanagh was beginning to enjoy himself again. "We Celts are very much like the Italians: vulnerable to music and to tender sentiment, but hard as nails in pursuit of money. Shall we go, ladies? The waiter will bring our drinks over to the alcove."

It was there that Molloy came upon them, high on melody and champagne, with Cavanagh at the piano, leading them, *con molto sentimento*, through the final chorus of "I'll Take You Home Again, Kathleen." Cavanagh spotted him first, glowering over the piano lid. He was not encouraged by what he saw; but he finished the song with a flourish and an announcement:

"Ladies, my duty is done. Mr. Molloy is here."

As the women turned to greet him, Molloy's expression changed. Instantly he was the smiling lover, sweeping Giulia into his arms, bestowing a cousinly kiss on the Countess, and offering a double-edged compliment to Cavanagh.

"You're full of surprises, Cavanagh! An Irish bard in a bar on Elba. That's one for the books!"

"You shouldn't be surprised, sir, you auditioned me before you hired me."

"Did I indeed?"

"You did, sir. You heard me singing 'The Low-backed Car' and you bet me five dollars I didn't know all the words."

"I remember now. And—God bless my soul!—I never paid you, did I?"

"No, sir, you didn't; but I always knew you would, one day."

"And what better day than today, when we've just got our first project signed, sealed and delivered. You had your own part in that, Cavanagh: a bigger one than you know. I'd like you to join us in a celebration dinner with our colleagues."

"What a splendid idea," said the Countess.

"Please," said Giulia the Beautiful, "and maybe afterwards we can have a session of Italian songs."

"If you'll forgive me, sir, ladies," Cavanagh was studiously formal, "I'll beg to be excused. There's work to be done on the *Salamandra* before you come on board again tomorrow. Also, I promised to take Miss Pritchard dining and dancing in Porto Azzuro. If she hasn't already found another partner, I'd still like to do that. I'm sure you understand. She's the only woman in the crew and you did ask me to pay her some attention."

"Very thoughtful of you, Cavanagh. Just sign out at the desk. The concierge will call you a cab. Thank you for the art work and for entertaining these two dear ladies."

"My pleasure, sir."

"Oh, before I forget." He fished out his wallet and riffled through the notes until he found a five-dollar bill, which he presented to Cavanagh with a wide, white smile as a bonus. "The bet was five dollars. The ladies will witness that Lou Molloy always pays his debts."

"Thank you. I'll be leaving now."

"We'll miss you," said the Contessa. "Thank you for your company and for the music."

"Enjoy your evening, Cavanagh," said Giulia Farnese, "and be kind to the admirable Miss Pritchard!"

"Goodnight, Principessa," said Cavanagh; but what he really meant was an untranslatable Irishism: "The back of me hand to yez all!"

It was after ten when the taxi dropped him on the dock at Porto Azzuro. The gangplank of the *Salamandra d'Oro* was down; there was a light in the saloon and the sound of a Mozart symphony played at low level. He walked up the gangplank and peered into a scene of touching domesticity. Chef and Lenore Pritchard were curled up in armchairs sipping coffee and cognac and listening to the music. Chef's eyes were closed and he was beating time to the score. Lenore had a book laid face down on her lap. Under the muted light they looked like father and daughter in an old-fashioned genre picture. It seemed a shame to disturb them. Cavanagh waited until the movement was finished, then he tapped quietly on the door and walked in.

The welcome they gave him was like the mood in the picture, warm but muted. Lenore grinned and said:

"Hi, Cavanagh! We've had dinner but you're welcome to drink with us."

Chef stirred only a fraction in his chair and told him:

"We wondered whether you might be back. Lenore

cooked me scrambled eggs for supper. It made a change from haute cuisine."

"And what about you, lover-boy?" Lenore set coffee and brandy in front of him. "Tell us about your day."

He told them, in bardic style, glad at last to translate his angers at himself and Molloy into a Gaelic comedy.

". . . I was like a featherweight up against the champ. The moment I thought I was getting close to him, he'd pop me one, right on the snout, and then haul off and give me that big toothy grin . . . Then to cap everything, the Contessa gave me a bumpy ride; but she put some fun into it. I like that woman. I didn't mind it when she swatted me around like a shuttlecock. You should have seen Molloy's face when he saw us singing our heads off in the bar. I thought he was about to blow a fuse. But sure as be-damned, he won the last round. He invites me to dinner with all his entourage. I decline gracefully. I tell him I'm taking Lenore out to dinner. He pays off his bet as if he's tipping a bloody janitor . . . and tells me to sign out at the desk! I wanted to kill the bastard; but I couldn't even shake him. What's the matter with me?"

"Youth," said Chef, with a smile. "You'll be cured of it in time."

"Money's another problem," said Lenore, amiably. "Take my word. It's very hard to bite the hand that feeds you. Don't worry, Cavanagh. I'm rather proud of the fact that you came back to take me to dinner. If you like, I'll make you scrambled eggs, too. I've got a limited repertoire, but what I do, I do well."

"Not for the moment, thanks. I'll sit with the coffee and cognac. Where have the others gone?"

"Brothel-crawling," said Lenore.

"Here? In Porto Azzuro?"

"Why not?" asked Lenore. "Boys will be boys; girls will be girls!"

"Here on Elba they don't call them brothels." This, by way of explanation from Chef. "They are houses of appointment, and because summer's coming in and times are hard and the *Comune* is angling for the tourist trade, a couple of rather stylish places have opened up—big, old villas on the fringes of Porto Ferraio, with discreet driveways and sheltering gardens . . ."

"How do you know all this?"

"Hadjidakis sent the boys ashore to scout the scene. They found a place that welcomes all three sexes. 'Expensive but agreeable' was how they described it. However, with the favorable exchange on the dollar, and some cartons of cigarettes from the ship's store, they figured they could afford a night out. So Hadjidakis has gone ashore with them. In case we want to go to bed, he told us to lift the gangplank. One of the boys can shinny along a mooring line to lower it."

"Very athletic they are." Lenore sipped meditatively at her brandy. "I hope Hadjidakis can stand the pace."

"He's not a boy anymore," said Chef, "but he's tough, like an olive tree. He'll be on deck in the morning—how do the Americans say it?—bright-eyed and bushy-tailed."

"Bright-eyed and sore-tailed, more like."

"Whatever." Chef shrugged, indifferently. "Every man to his taste. Every woman to hers."

"Is Hadjidakis married?" It was Cavanagh's question.

"Sure. He has a wife and two beautiful daughters in Boston. He's very proud of them."

"He can afford to be," said Lenore acidly, "when they're three thousand miles away, and he's catting around with Molloy and the dancing boys!"

"So what's new?" Chef shrugged off the whole debate. "His ancestors were forced to be either dirt farmers or deckhands. They sailed to Africa with the north winds. They were away six months of the year. Provided they survived the infidel and the terrors of the deep, they came back with the first southerlies of winter. That was their life: to survive and provide. No one asked what they did with their spare time, if indeed they had any."

"You're scolding me, Chef." Lenore was embarrassed.

"You're a big girl," said Chef, mildly. "You should know better . . . But I forgive you, because you do make good scrambled eggs and you do enjoy Mozart. I'm off to bed. Goodnight, children. Golden dreams!"

He got up stiffly from his chair and walked out, a man with the first chill of age around his heart.

Cavanagh said, tentatively: "You've had dinner. Would you like to go dancing?"

"No, thanks. I'm too comfortable here."

"More brandy?"

"Just a touch."

He poured for her, then topped up his own drink and made the toast.

"*Slainte!*"

"*Slainte!*"

They drank. There was a small, embarrassed silence. Then Lenore said calmly:

"Do you know what I'd really like, Cavanagh?"

"Tell me."

"Some old-fashioned, strictly-for-pleasure sex. No strings, no regrets, no heartburn and no scuttling about like midnight mice afterwards. What do you say?"

"Your place or mine, madam?"

"Neither. We can use Giulia's stateroom. The bed's huge and I have to change the linen in the morning anyway."

"What are we waiting for?"

"I'm waiting for an old-fashioned kiss," said Lenore Pritchard.

"Happy to oblige, m'lady," said Bryan de Courcy Cavanagh, and this time, felt no shame in the surrender.

Their mating was all that she had desired of him: a bawdy, boisterous romp, with teasing and laughter, a leaven of unexpected tenderness, a high, prolonged climax and a slow pleasurable descent into languor. She told him, drowsily:

". . . It doesn't happen like this very often. I feel like a girl again . . . It was so . . . right and easy. One jump and we were both over the wall and into the apple orchard. I'll give you a reference any time . . . Any time at all, Cavanagh . . ."

The words trailed off into a vague murmur. She rolled away from him, curled herself into a fetal ball and lapsed instantly into sleep.

Cavanagh folded his hands behind his head, and lay naked in the dark, listening to the faint slap of the sea against the hull, the creak of the mooring lines and the drifts of night music from some tavern near the docks. He felt relaxed and released, not only from sexual tension, but from the irk of an unresolved social situation in the crew quarters. Lenore, in her pragmatic fashion, had expressed it perfectly: "One jump and we were over the wall and into the apple orchard." The trick now would be to resist the promptings of casual lust, and the temptation to lapse into an attachment of habit. Rightly or wrongly, he felt no fear of Lenore Pritchard. She would keep her bargains. She was a woman who expected little, was happy when she got more, and who had learned the most valuable lesson of all, not to close her hand on the butterfly when it rested a moment on her palm.

She had the primal simplicity and the courage of the born survivor.

For himself, Bryan de Courcy Cavanagh, it was not so simple. He carted around with him a whole baggage of inherited belief and education and family manners, which, even had he wished, he could not quickly shrug off. The sexual encounter troubled him little. It was an agreeable incident between needy and consenting adults. The circumstances of it lay more heavily on his conscience.

The moment he had entered Giulia Farnese's cabin he had felt like a lout invading her private domain. When he had tried to withdraw, Lenore had turned it into a joke: "I tell you, Cavanagh, I've been laid in all the best staterooms: Royal, Presidential, Owners' and de Luxe. It's my social protest. Up the Proletariat. Workers of the world, rejoice! Come on, boyo! I'm not asking you to read her diary—which she keeps every day—or wear her underthings, or anything kinky at all! It's just the bed. Look at the size of it, feel how it bounces . . ." It was easier to go along with the joke than have a resentful woman on his hands.

However, from that moment, Giulia Farnese was a presence in the cabin and in the bed and in their wildest couplings. When he came to climax it was with her and not with Lenore Pritchard. As he lay in the dark he tried vainly to remember whether he had spoken her name in the babble of the final release.

He slid out of bed, dressed hurriedly, drew the covers over Lenore and crept out of the cabin. He paused in the saloon to drink a glass of mineral water and clear away the last cups and glasses. When he looked at his watch it was three in the morning. He went out on deck. The gangplank was still up. Hadjidakis and the boys had not returned.

He was wide awake now, so he surrendered to old habit, picked up a torch from his cabin and made the rounds of the ship. Once again he found himself awarding full marks to Hadjidakis for care of his vessel. Knowing that he was going out on the town, with the working members of his crew, he had cleaned ship from stem to stern. The windows had been washed, the brightwork polished, the decks scubbed, the cordage coiled. The log was written up to date, with an engine room report and a note of fuel and water levels. There was also a record of radio traffic received during the five o'clock relay transmission from Portishead: two messages, one in clear from New York, the other in code from Washington. There was a note: "Texts delivered to owner's cabin eighteen-thirty hours."

Cavanagh picked up an orange in the galley, then went on deck again. He perched himself on the port rail and began to peel the fruit, dropping the scraps of peel into the oily water below. The port was quiet now; the music had ceased; the last lights in the tenements were going out, one by one. There was only the faint wash of the water, and the rare piping of a bat and the occasional squawk of a seabird. Then, in the distance, he heard the sound of sirens and the tinny noise of automobiles driven at high speed over the cobbles. There were lights now, flashing beacons and bobbing headlights. The next minute two cars marked *carabinieri* drew up on the dock right under the transom of the *Salamandra d'Oro*. A fellow wearing the insignia of a *brigadiere* stepped out of the car and hailed the ship. Cavanagh came forward to respond in Italian.

"Yes, *brigadiere*, what can I do for you?"

"Who are you?"

"Cavanagh, officer of the watch."

"Let down the gangway, we're coming aboard."

"An instant, please."

The moment the gangway hit the dock, the officer

signaled the other car. Leo and Jackie were bundled out, staggering onto the pavement. The officer asked:

"Do you recognize these men?"

"Yes, they're crew members, listed on our manifest. Where's the other one?"

"In the clinic in Porto Ferraio. The doctor's looking at him now. If you want to see him, you'd better come with us."

"Are there any charges against these two?"

"Not yet; but you are to keep them aboard until morning. There will be more questions."

"Let me get 'em aboard first. Would you gentlemen care for a whisky while you're waiting?"

"That's very courteous of you, sir."

Shepherding Leo and Jackie before them, the *carabinieri*—suddenly there were three—mounted the gangway and stood expectantly on the afterdeck. Cavanagh summoned up as much authority as he could muster.

"Leo, get below and spruce yourself up. I'll need you on watch while I'm away. Jackie, serve whisky for the officers, please. Excuse me, gentlemen. I'll be with you in a moment."

He hurried down to the guest cabin to waken Lenore Pritchard and alert her to what was happening. Then, while Jackie dispensed drinks, he went up to the forepeak for a hurried briefing from Leo.

"What the hell happened?"

"We were in this joint. Things got pretty wild. In the end it turned into an old-fashioned orgy. Our Giorgy was pissed out of his mind. One of the guys was making a big play for him. They went into a bedroom together. When we were ready to leave, he still hadn't showed up. We went looking for him. He was lying in a heap on the floor. He'd been terribly beaten. There must have been more than one, because Giorgios is a real street fighter . . . Anyway, I stayed with him, while Jackie got the madam to phone the *carabinieri*. They took Giorgy to the clinic and brought us back here. End of story."

"I'll go with the cops and see what's happened to Giorgy. When I'm gone, haul up the gangway and make sure no one else comes aboard. Where does Hadjidakis keep the ship's cash?"

"In his cabin. The cash box is in a drawer under the bookshelf."

"I'm on my way."

Back on deck he waited with careful patience while the *carabinieri* finished their drinks. These were no common policemen, they were military personnel, charged with keeping order inside the confines of the Republic. Courtesy was the watchword, courtesy and respect and a co-operative attitude, if you didn't want to be bounced off a wall. His Tuscan accent had already impressed them. The generous shots of Scotch had helped too. He decided to clinch the *entente cordiale*.

"Jackie, be so kind as to break out three bottles of Johnny Walker, wrap each one in a paper napkin and bring them to me, please."

He offered the bottles, one to each of the *carabinieri*, as a "compliment from the ship, a thanks for your courteous handling of this matter."

On the way back to Porto Ferraio he rode with the *brigadiere* and heard his version of the affair.

". . . You must understand, my friend, that we do not normally preoccupy ourselves with what goes on inside a closed house. If a major crime is committed, of course we must intervene; but such places are designed as the safety valves of society; so we absent ourselves. By the time we were called, the fracas was over, and because your other man was injured, we have had neither the time nor the opportunity to make further inquiries. Who is the victim, by the way?"

"He is our first mate and engineer, an American citizen named Giorgios Hadjidakis. He is a longtime friend and confidant of the owner, Mr. Molloy, and of his distinguished guests, Prince Alessandro Farnese and Count Galeazzi. I presume you are aware that they are visiting the island to conclude arrangements for a major tourist development?"

Even if he wasn't aware, the *brigadiere* wasn't going to admit it; but he was suitably impressed. He hastened to assure Cavanagh:

"The clinic is small but well-equipped. It was set up for the mining community. The director, Dr. Emilio Spinelli, resides on the premises. He is both competent and careful. You may trust what he tells you."

"That's very reassuring, *brigadiere*. One can only hope he may be able to help Mr. Hadjidakis."

"As you say, one can only hope. We should be there in ten minutes."

Giorgios Hadjidakis had taken a brutal beating. One eye was closed, a cheekbone was crushed. An arm and several ribs were broken. His head was bandaged. He was still unconscious. The doctor, a crisp, efficient fellow in his early fifties, displayed a series of X-rays.

". . . The ribs, the wrist, these we have taken care of. The face will need expert reconstruction. Most worrying of all, however, is this fracture of the skull, depressed as you see at this point. I do not have the means to estimate or repair the damage. It requires expert cranial surgery."

"Where is it available?"

"In Milan, certainly. In Livorno, only possibly, but certainly at the American Hospital in Naples. I thought that, as your officer is an American citizen, and they are fully equipped for combat casualties . . ."

"Is there a phone I can use, Doctor?"

"Through there, in my office."

It took Cavanagh five minutes to raise the night clerk at the Club Hotel and another five minutes of clattering dialogue to persuade him to connect the call to Molloy's room. Molloy was rasping and irritable.

"Don't you know what time it is? What the hell's going on?"

Cavanagh told him. Molloy was instantly wide awake.

"Naples? That's the Sixth Fleet. I know the deputy commander-in-chief. I'll try to call him now and see if he can send a chopper in to evacuate Hadjidakis to the U.S. Hospital. It would make sense for us too, we're heading south. If Giorgy is okay, we can pick him up on the way down. If he's not, then we can make arrangements to get him home to Boston. Are the police still with you?"

"Yes. The *brigadiere* is waiting outside."

"Ask him if he can nominate a landing place for a helicopter."

The *brigadiere* was helpful.

"There is a large garden at the back of the clinic. It will be light before the helicopter gets here. We can mark the place with a white cross . . ."

Cavanagh relayed the message. Molloy had other instructions.

"Stay at the clinic until I get back to you."

"Yes, sir."

"I'm going to be tied up here all morning. I daren't leave until we've got the essential documents signed. Can you handle things at your end?"

"Sure. But we should have a contingency plan in place."

"Read it to me."

"In case the Navy people don't come through, I'd suggest we put Giorgios aboard the *Salamandra* and run straight up to Livorno. I could have an ambulance waiting at the docks. It's a fifty-mile run, but the sea's flat and we could make him comfortable. After he's settled in hospital I'd come back to Elba and pick you off the beach."

"I agree, but I'm sure the Navy will come through. Can you handle the vessel?"

"Sure. I'll move Leo up to watch-keeper's duties. Then I'd like to find us an extra hand, preferably an engine-room mechanic who could double as deckhand. But you let me worry about that for the moment. I'll wait here for your call."

He read off the number and hung up. It was nearly five in the morning when Molloy finally called back.

"We're in luck, Cavanagh. There's an aircraft carrier about a hundred miles south of Elba, and heading north to Villefranche. They're sending a helicopter which will evacuate Giorgios to the ship. While the chopper refuels, the surgeons will take a look at him and then arrange to move him down to Naples."

"When can we expect the aircraft?"

"They gave me a rough estimate of 0700 hours this morning."

"Fair enough. I'd better make sure the landing pad is adequately marked . . . By the way, I've taken possession of the ship's cash—I may have to dispense some of it."

"That's fine. Call me when the lift-off has taken place."

"Will do. Next question: do you want me to bring the ship down to you, or will you come back to Porto Azzuro?"

"We'll come back. Tell Chef there'll be ten extra guests for a buffet lunch on the afterdeck. We'll give them a cruise round the island and dump 'em on the dock about five in the afternoon. Now what's the latest on Giorgios?"

"No change, sir. He's stable but comatose."

"If he wakes, give him my love—and tell him he must be losing his touch."

"Yes, sir."

"And Cavanagh?"

"Sir?"

"Thanks. You're doing a good job."

"A compliment to your own good judgment, Mr. Molloy."

"The luck of the Irish more like—let's pray we can keep it running for Giorgios Hadjidakis."

"Amen to that," said Bryan de Courcy Cavanagh.

As always with Lou Molloy, a thing promised was a thing done. At ten minutes after seven in the morning a Piasecki helicopter from the U.S. Navy set down on the pocket-handkerchief park behind the clinic. Hadjidakis, still comatose, was strapped to a stretcher and hoisted aboard. The helicopter took off, leaving one *brigadiere* very impressed and one medico glad to be rid of a patient whose prognosis was, to say the least, dubious.

Cavanagh invited them to join him for breakfast as soon as he had made his telephone call to Molloy, with whom, unconsciously, he slipped into the idiom of command.

"If Hadjidakis dies, this turns into a murder case. If he survives, the whole affair can be hushed up. I'm suggesting to the *brigadiere* that he make his inquiries, but keep them off the books for the time being . . . No, sir, I'm not pre-empting your orders, but I'm here and you're miles away. I have to make decisions. Next item: without Hadjidakis, we're traveling at risk. We need at least an engine-room mechanic . . . With your permission, I'd like to make some inquiries locally, and if necessary, on the mainland. You've got Swedish diesels. Their dealers have been operating in Italy since before the war. With luck we should be able to find ourselves a passable mechanic. It's not the perfect solution, but it reduces the risk and Hadjidakis has already walked me through the manual . . . We'll be ready at lunchtime for you and your guests."

In a bar on the waterfront Cavanagh bought coffee and pastries for the doctor and the *brigadiere*. When he offered payment for his medical services, the doctor, Tuscan to his boot soles, refused. A guest on the island had been assaulted. His service was a small amends. He wished only that he could have done more, and that he could be more optimistic of the outcome. The *brigadiere*, already recompensed, approved this magnanimity.

Next, Cavanagh broached the question of an engine-room mechanic. The *brigadiere* regretted that he could not help. It was the custom of the *carabinieri* to post their officials far away from their birthplace, so that, in theory at least, they would not become involved in local conspiracies. The doctor offered at least a possible candidate:

". . . My nephew, a good boy who has completed an apprenticeship in the naval yards at Livorno. He has also had work as a temporary engine-room hand on the ferries. The problem is that, since he has completed his apprenticeship, he must be paid a full wage . . . So in these bad times, nobody wants him."

"What is he doing now?"

"He works two days a week with Ugolini, who services the fishing fleet. He also works part-time with Fischetti, who services air-conditioning plants around the Island."

"Well, let's talk to him. Tell him to be on board no later than eleven this morning. We'll be cruising from lunchtime till evening. Even if he isn't hired, he'll be paid for his time."

The doctor gulped down his coffee and hurried off to track down his nephew. The *brigadiere* raised a more delicate question: how to deal with the brawl at the "house of appointment" and the very grievous matter of the assault on Hadjidakis. So far, no depositions had been taken, no inquiries instituted, no complaints made. However, once anything was on paper, a long, wearisome and perhaps scandalous process would begin.

Cavanagh needed no spectacles to see that hole in the ground, yet he had no intention of digging a pit for himself. So, in his best Tuscan and with his most elaborate Irish blarney, he explained:

"You and I, *brigadiere*, are in the same galley. With the best will in the world, we cannot dictate to our superiors. I cannot commit my owner, who is in fact the captain of the vessel. If Mr. Hadjidakis dies, you have a murder case on your hands. If he survives, we shall all benefit by a discreet handling of the case. These are hard times for everyone, and Mr. Molloy, with his Italian colleagues, is embarking on a huge work of reconstruction on this island . . . Certainly he will feel offended and abused by what has happened; but if I could tell him that you were prepared to conduct your own discreet inquiries with a view to identifying the culprits, and dealing with them—how shall I put it—in a local frame of reference . . . You do understand what I am trying to say?"

"Perfectly, my dear sir, perfectly. As you put it, we are in the same galley. This is the kind of affair that can quickly become scandalous. But fortunately, nothing happens until pen touches paper. So, unless your man dies or your owner lodges a formal complaint, nothing will be done officially. We do, of course, have our own method of dealing with such delinquents. May I drive you back to your ship . . . ?"

"A great courtesy, *brigadiere* . . . Thank you. And your own impression of the doctor's nephew?"

"A fine young man, of reasonable education and much good will. He promises well . . . This would be a splendid chance for him."

"Leave it to me, *brigadiere*; I'll see what I can do."

Back on board, his first act was to deliver a bulletin on Hadjidakis; his second was to announce the luncheon party. This brought a small chorus of protest, which was quelled quickly by Chef:

". . . The food and the liquor we have in abundance. All we have to do is organize the service. Let's start now, my children!"

Next Cavanagh conducted a brusque briefing session with Leo and Jackie.

"I've told Mr. Molloy exactly what you told me about the punch-up at Porto Ferraio—no more, no less, no comment. You can be damn sure he'll want to question you himself. My advice is not to lie, even if it means changing the story you told me. Next, I'm bringing in a local lad to try out as engine-room mechanic. If he's halfway good, we'll keep him. Help him, and don't play games—any sort of games. You're both deep enough in the dreck already. Leo, subject to anything Mr. Molloy may have in mind, I'm going to train you as watch-keeper, Navy-style. You'll have lives in your hands, so don't foul up on me. Clear?"

"Loud and clear, Mr. Cavanagh."

"Good. Now go make yourselves useful to Chef, and, the minute Mr. Molloy and his guests arrive, step lively! Make a ceremony of it."

Finally, he drew Lenore Pritchard aside for a very private exchange.

". . . I didn't have time to say thank you before I left. I'm saying it now. *Grazie infinite*."

"My pleasure, Mr. Cavanagh." Her attitude was guarded. She gave him only half a smile. "I wish you hadn't left so soon."

"You were dead asleep. It would have been a crime to wake you."

"I'll accept the apology but I'll be interested to see what happens next. How is Molloy taking this?"

"I wish I knew. He's very restrained, very curt. He hasn't raised any objection to my moves for damage control."

"He won't. He knows he's lucky you're prepared to move into command. What's really in question here is his whole relationship with Hadjidakis."

"I know they're very close; but that's as much as I can say."

"So leave it just like that. Don't clutter your mind with guesswork or complicate my life more than it will be."

"And what does that mean?"

"For God's sake, Cavanagh! Use your brains! With Hadjidakis gone, I'm going to be working overtime to keep the great Molloy contented. I'm not looking forward to it, not one little bit."

"If there's anything I can do . . . ?"

"Not much. It would be nice if you could take over Hadjidakis's cabin. I'd feel more comfortable knowing you were just across the way."

"Molloy will have to suggest that."

"I know. It'll be interesting to see what he does."

"If we're neighbors," said Cavanagh with a grin, "for God's sake, don't clown us both into trouble."

"I thought you were the clown," said Lenore Pritchard, soberly, "or has all this sudden responsibility gone to your head?"

Punctually at eleven, there presented itself at the gangway a tall, spindly figure dressed in blue overalls and carrying a toolbox in one hand and in the other a battered valise. The figure had a mop of brown hair, an owlish stare behind thick spectacles, a child's happy smile and a schoolboy deference. It also had a high-sounding name, Rodolfo Arnolfini, and a title, "*il meccanico*."

Cavanagh's heart sank when he saw this shambling figure, but he managed a welcoming smile and immediately swept the mechanic off the deck and down into the engine room, whose mysteries he displayed with an ample gesture and a single word: "*Ecco*!"

Rodolfo's smile widened into a broad grin of approval.

"*Eh bella, bella!*"

Cavanagh asked tentatively:

"Have you ever worked on this type of engine?"

"No. Most of my diesel experience was on MAN motors. But if I can see the manual . . .

"Our manual is in English."

"No matter. It's' the diagrams I need. I understand those."

Cavanagh laid the manual in his hands and placed on top of it the engine-room plans, the diagrams of ducts and circuits and the stabilizer system. He announced with great gravity:

"Rodolfo, I am now going to leave you alone with this beautiful machinery and all this reading matter. In an hour or two I'm going to come back and you're going to have to convince me that you are a mechanic worthy of this magnificent assemblage. If you pass that test, then you'll accompany us on an afternoon cruise, so that you see the whole thing in motion. After that, I shall decide whether to employ you or put you ashore with my blessing and money in your pocket. Do you understand?"

"I understand perfectly, sir. Now if you would point me to the toilet, I should be grateful. This kind of interview always makes me nervous . . . Not because I am ignorant, you understand, but . . ."

"I understand perfectly," said Cavanagh. "It takes me the same way. Come and I'll show you. Bring your valise. You can leave it on my bunk . . ."

As he made his way up to the deck, Cavanagh felt like a squeamish spectator at the circus, closing his eyes just as the girl was toppling off the high-wire. Still, there was not too much at risk, unless Rodolfo ran crazy with spanner and fire axe, or began chewing up the manuals into papier-mâché.

He still had time to kill before Molloy came aboard with his passengers and business guests, so he made a final round of the vessel—a "white-glove" inspection, Lenore called it—to make sure there was no dust on furniture, no cloud on mirror surfaces. All his instincts told him that Molloy, so brusque and businesslike in his telephone transactions, would return to the ship boiling with suppressed emotions. In fact, he came on board at a run, leaving Galeazzi and Farnese to hand the women out of the bus, and the waiting crew to pick up the baggage and shepherd the other guests up the gangway. He took Cavanagh by the elbow and swung him into the saloon with a terse command:

"My cabin, now!"

Cavanagh followed him to his quarters, the big stateroom which stretched the whole width of the ship and was furnished in solid teak, designed and built by master marine craftsmen. Molloy said brusquely:

"Sit down. Join me in a drink. I need one."

He splashed liquor and soda into crystal tumblers, handed one to Cavanagh, drained half his own in a single gulp, then sat down heavily in a deep leather armchair.

"So now, tell me the truth of it, boyo. How's Giorgios?"

"Not good. His ribs and arm will mend. His cheekbone can be reconstructed. The doctor at Porto Ferraio took X-rays of the skull fracture. He told me he was worried by what he saw but would not commit himself to a prognosis. Giorgios was comatose when we got him on board the chopper. The pilot told me he would be setting down on the carrier to refuel, then heading south to Naples. The carrier medics will check on Giorgios to see if he's able to make the journey . . . I wish I had better news, but that's all I've got."

"If he dies," Molloy was sunk in a dark pit of rage, "it'll be murder and I'll take this goddamned island apart stone by stone to find the people who did it. How in Christ's name could it have happened? Giorgy knows his way round. I can't imagine . . . Oh, Jesus! I wonder . . ."

"What, sir?"

"Tolvier . . . No, it couldn't be. The reaction is too fast."

"I'm not following you, sir."

"In Corsica, we lifted a man who is wanted as a war criminal. I was wondering about reprisals."

"It would have to be a very quick reaction. But, yes, it's possible. Jordan seemed worried about the Fairmile that dropped anchor in Calvi Harbor."

"I know . . . We discussed it . . ."

"What are the police doing?"

"In this case, it's the *carabinieri*."

"Police, *carabinieri*, whatever! I want to know what they're doing."

"I told you, sir. For the moment they're doing nothing. That was the deal I made with the *brigadiere*: unless and until we lodge a formal complaint, he will keep the inquiries off his records."

"*You* made a deal!" Molloy exploded out of his chair and stood towering over him. "You have no right to make *any* deal that affects me or this ship with anybody at all!"

"Correction, Mr. Molloy!" Cavanagh set down his glass carefully. "In the given time, place and circumstance I had the right and the duty to make any necessary decision. I was the ranking officer taking command from an injured senior. I told you what I was doing, whether you understood me or not. I also made it clear to the *brigadiere* that you might well countermand my decision. He reminded me that he too was subject to superiors. He also pointed out that any police action could provoke a public scandal."

"That still gave you no right to pre-empt my decision!"

"It was my job this morning to buy you time to make a prudent one. I did that. I refuse to make apologies or excuses for my action!"

For an instant it seemed as though Molloy might strike him, but slowly and with much effort, he regained control of himself. He turned back to the liquor cabinet, poured himself another slug of neat whisky and tossed the drink off at a gulp. There was a long, tense silence, during which Molloy stood with his back to Cavanagh while he stumbled through an apology and a revelation.

". . . Bear with me, Cavanagh! I beg you, bear with me. I'm bleeding. I'm hurting as I've never hurt before. I can't bear the thought of what happened to Giorgios and that it might be my fault. Do you know what Giorgios used to call us? Comrades who marched in step, fought side by side, slept under the same cloak, like the warriors of Alexander. I love the man! I can't bear the thought of losing him . . ."

"You've put him in the best hands. Now all you can do is pray."

"Do you pray, Cavanagh? Can you still do it? Do you still believe in it?"

"If it helps, I'll pray with you," said Cavanagh, calmly. "We were both taught the same words!"

"Not now. I feel like getting drunk."

"But you won't," said Cavanagh firmly. "Not at midday, in the sight of your fiancé and with all these people on board. Tonight if you like, when we're safely tied up and the ladies are asleep, I'll match you shot for shot and carry you to bed afterwards. Just now, I need you sober to interview our candidate for the engine-room . . . Rodolfo Arnolfini . . ."

"Come again? What have you done this time?"

By the time Cavanagh had made his explanation, the bad moment had passed and Molloy's brief frenzy of grief had subsided into embarrassment. He said tentatively:

"I depended a great deal on Giorgios."

"I know that. He was—he is—a fine seaman. I told him so, several times."

"I know. He was flattered by your compliments. Can I trust you, Cavanagh?"

"What am I supposed to say to that, Mr. Molloy? You'll give me your trust or you'll withhold it. Either way, I'll do what I'm contracted to do. It's up to you to decide what and how much you confide in me."

"And you're damned if you're going to plead for my trust!"

"You're damned right, sir!"

A wintry smile twitched at Molloy's lips. Before he could say anything else, Cavanagh reminded him:

"Giorgios left two messages for you. He noted them in the log—one cipher, one clear."

Molloy crossed to the desk, picked up the envelopes, took out the messages and studied them in silence. He dismissed Cavanagh with a wave.

"You go look after the guests, Cavanagh. Give 'em half an hour for drinks, then we'll get under way. Tell

Chef to serve lunch once we've cleared harbor. And, Cavanagh?"

"Sir!"

"You're confirmed as acting first-officer. You collect an extra twenty-five bucks a week for the privilege. You'll be busted back as soon as Giorgios is with us again. Have the boys pack up his gear and bring it here to my cabin. You take up residence in his berth, because that's rigged as the command center."

"Yes, sir."

"One more thing . . ."

Cavanagh waited in silence.

"I don't quite see you as a comrade of the cloak. I'm not sure how well you can keep a secret, but I am trusting you with my ship and our lives. That has to mean something, doesn't it?"

"It means I should get back on deck. Chef has arranged a buffet. He thought you'd probably want to start the cruise before the meal."

"Good idea," said Molloy indifferently. "By the way, when you see Farnese, ask him to come here as quickly as possible."

He found Farnese, perched on the taffrail with Giulia beside him, while the Countess and Galeazzi stood a little distance away, sipping champagne and dispensing small talk with the men from the Ministry of Marine. Cavanagh presented Molloy's compliments and his request that the Prince meet with him in his cabin. Farnese eased himself to the deck.

"Perhaps, Mr. Cavanagh, you would look after my daughter for a little while. She is in no mood for casual company or business talk."

"My pleasure, sir." He hoisted himself on to the rail beside Giulia and told her cheerfully: "This is the best assignment I've had in the past forty-eight hours."

Giulia's answer was a bill of complaints.

"For us it's been a morning in the madhouse. Lou

has been raging about, barking orders like a warder. When I tried to calm him and have him explain what was going on, nothing he told me made any sense. All I could make out was that Hadjidakis had been injured in some kind of brawl and had to be flown to Naples for specialist treatment."

"That's the simple truth of the matter."

"The whole truth, Cavanagh?"

"Listen, Giulia!" He dropped his voice to a murmur. "Please don't ask me that kind of question. Molloy's the man you're going to marry. Ask him. I know he's very upset at the moment because his friendship with Hadjidakis goes back a long way—and Giorgios is in a serious condition."

"I know." Giulia's tone was somber. "But what troubles me is that Lou won't share his anxiety with me—and we're supposed to share a whole life with each other."

"The sharing takes some practice." The words came awkwardly and tasted like sawdust on his tongue. "If you don't learn it in a family, it takes a long time to pick it up later."

"Why must you always defend Lou?"

"God knows! I guess I'm trying to explain him to myself as much as to you. I have to live with him too, in a very special way."

"How special?" There was suspicion and anger in her tone.

"He's the captain of this vessel—skipper under God, as they used to say in the old days. Until Hadjidakis comes back—if he comes back—I'm Molloy's first officer, his right hand, so to speak. We have to trust each other, because we're comrades and allies against the sea . . . and the sea's rage can be a frightening experience . . ."

Giulia was silent for a while; then, in a small furtive

movement she shifted her grip on the rail so that her hand lay over his. She asked quietly:

"Will you do something for me, Cavanagh?"

"If I can, sure."

"I'd like to learn scuba diving. Would you teach me?"

"Of course. I'd be delighted. First thing you should do is try on the wetsuits we have on board. If there isn't one to fit you, then you should buy one on the mainland. Second thing—just for the courtesy of it—mention to Molloy that you've asked me. I know he dives. One of the sets of gear has his name on it. So he may prefer to teach you himself."

"He says not. He said no man should teach his wife to drive a car or fly an airplane either. He's promised that we'll dive together when I'm ready; but he's happier that you should teach me. Frankly, I'm happier too . . ."

"Good. It's settled. Now I have to pay some courtesies and get ready to start our cruise. Would you like to stroll around with me?"

"Yes, please."

He eased himself onto the deck and held out his hands to help Giulia down from the rail. Her perfume and the warmth of her body filled him with sudden lust. Cold reason told him that he had to disengage from her as quickly as possible, so he steered her through the small concourse of guests, pausing to exchange a few words with each group, hoping that one or other would seek to detain Giulia. She, however, was more adept at evasion than they were at snaring her. Finally, it was Galeazzi and the Countess who came to the rescue. They were still talking with the two officials from the Ministry of Marine and the group opened up immediately to include Giulia and Cavanagh. The Countess gave him her most mischievous smile and said:

"I hear you had a rather disturbed night, Mr. Cavanagh?"

"It wasn't too bad." Cavanagh tried to shrug off the incident. "Everything was under control by breakfast time."

"And how is Mr. Hadjidakis?"

"It's too early to say. We'll be getting a report from Naples this evening."

"Meantime"—Galeazzi moved hastily to change the subject—"I understand you're taking command of the vessel."

"Mr. Molloy is in command, sir. I simply become acting first officer."

"I have a small service to ask. Could we talk privately for a few minutes?"

"Certainly, let's go up to the bridge. Excuse us please, ladies, gentlemen . . ."

The moment they were private together, Galeazzi told him:

"This is a mess, Cavanagh, a dangerous mess! If the press gets hold if it—especially the left-wing press—they will turn it into a disastrous scandal. I dare not risk involving the Vatican in—let me say it bluntly—a brawl in a brothel. I want to ask you how you think we may contain the damage?"

"I've already taken the first steps. I made a deal with the *carabinieri* that no reports will be filed unless and until we lay a formal complaint. It's to their advantage to hold to that. The two members of the ship's company who were witnesses to the affair are in virtual quarantine until we leave the island. And they know they'll be fired if they speak a word out of place . . ."

"That's encouraging, Mr. Cavanagh."

"I'm not sure Mr. Molloy wholly agrees with me. He came aboard very upset and vowing vengeance on the attackers. I pointed out that he had much to lose and nothing to gain by punitive action."

"What actually happened?"

"I still don't know exactly, and I've deliberately refrained from inquiring; but clearly it was a very wild bordello evening that ended in violence."

"I guessed as much." Galeazzi was very subdued. "What troubles me more is Molloy's reaction, which I can only describe as violent and obsessive in the extreme. With Farnese and myself he gave full vent to his rage. With Giulia he was withdrawn and secretive . . . The girl is deeply upset. Now I don't know how you read all this, but I am troubled—for myself and for Giulia, my godchild. Farnese is no help. He has made his own bargains with Molloy. He will hold to them, no matter what the cost to Giulia or anyone else."

"And you, sir? Are you not party to the same bargains?" The question was out before he understood the sheer effrontery of it. To his surprise Galeazzi did not take offense, but answered with unexpected humility.

"It may seem so, Mr. Cavanagh; but in my own mind and conscience the position is very clear. The Institute for Works of Religion, which is the banking arm of the Vatican, has taken what it believes to be a sound investment position in Molloy's development enterprises in Italy. Politically also, Molloy is a powerful ally. His politics are far to the right. He is well regarded by the administration and courted by the intelligence community in the United States. He is a close friend of Spellman and this new, very vocal person, Senator Joseph McCarthy. In short, we have applied to our association with Molloy, the strictest commercial criteria. On the other hand, I will not deny that there are long-standing, traditional links between the Farnese family, the Vatican, and those noble houses in Europe whose wealth is still intact. They, too, need alliances with the richest power in the world today, which is of course the United States of America. This shabby little service we have just done in Corsica has its own political value. It makes powerful friends within the intelligence community. But what troubles me, Cavanagh, is Molloy himself and his capacity—I do not question his desire—to make Giulia happy. His association with Hadjidakis reveals itself as . . ."

"Count Galeazzi!" Cavanagh's tone was peremptory. "Let's stop this conversation right now, before we both come to regret it. I cannot serve two masters. I'm not sure I can serve even one with the dedication of Giorgios Hadjidakis. So please don't try to manipulate me into uttering judgments on the man who pays my wages. If there are issues between him and me, I'll settle them face to face. Now, you needed a service from me. Tell me, please, what I can do for you?"

"I shall be leaving the *Salamandra* at our next mainland port. Other guests will be coming aboard. Giulia has spoken to her aunt and to me of her admiration for you. I—that is to say, her aunt and myself—would like to count on you as a protector of her interests while she is aboard the *Salamandra*."

"Do you mean"—Cavanagh was suddenly in the grip of an ice-cold anger—"Do you mean, sir, that the man she is to marry may prove an inadequate guardian?"

"No, Mr. Cavanagh, I do not mean that. I mean that I take, perhaps, a more sinister view of the Hadjidakis affair than Molloy wants to accept. If I am right, then Giulia herself may be at risk—and not necessarily a physical risk. I would not for the world discourage a friendship between you. I suggest only that you be very aware of the danger to Giulia of any indiscretion." His thin lips twitched into a smile. "I presume of course that you are old enough and big enough to take care of yourself—at least with Lou Molloy. Farnese might prove more difficult. Molloy's political enemies would be the most difficult of all!"

Bryan de Courcy Cavanagh pondered that series of propositions for a long silent moment. Finally he said:

"I'd better be sure I'm understanding this. Are you warning me off the course or asking me to be available as proxy to Lou Molloy, when he's busy with other things?"

"I should say the words 'protection to Giulia' would be more accurate."

"Mother of God!" Cavanagh gave full rein to his fury. "What kind of people are you? What kind of man do you think I am? Let me tell you something which I'll probably regret later. If I thought Giulia were halfway interested in me, I'd be off this ship tonight and driving with her, hell-bent for the frontier. But don't worry! It won't happen. Giulia's sold already, delivered and paid for. It's my bad luck I came too late and couldn't afford the bride-price. I'm too much of a hard-head to spend the rest of my life chasing a folly-fire . . . But yes, I'll keep an eye on her, and if she needs a shoulder to cry on and a clean handkerchief to dry her tears, she knows where to find me . . . Does that answer your question, sir?"

"More precisely than I expected. For a young man, educated in the outer marches, I find you quite a formidable fellow, Cavanagh. Before I leave the ship, I'll give you my card. If I can be of any help in your future career, please do not hesitate to call on me."

"Thank you."

"I give you one last piece of advice."

"Sir?"

"Molloy is a rich man and more powerful than you may imagine. However, he is also vulnerable—to his own follies and the vices of his minions. Of these, you are, or have pretended to be, happily ignorant. You may not be able to remain so. A moment may come when it is you who are called to be 'skipper under God.' I trust that moment will find you prepared."

"So it's prophecy now, is it?"

"Not prophecy, premonition." Galeazzi's eyes were hooded like those of a bird of prey. His face seemed for a moment to be carved out of granite. Then, miraculously, he smiled and shook his head as if to rid himself of a nightmare. "Forget everything I've said, Cavanagh! I've lived too long with bankers and bachelor clerics. My blood has turned to vinegar! . . . I'll leave you now, you must have work to do."

"Indeed I have, sir," said Cavanagh and wondered, not for the first time, at the devious reasonings of this old and guileful people.

It was a relief therefore to go down to the engine room and talk with the spindly fellow in the blue overalls who called himself, with singular pride, "the mechanic." Cavanagh took possession of the manuals and plans, and then led the young man through a "show-and-tell" session on the principal components of the engine room. Much to Cavanagh's surprise, his answers were delivered without hesitation and were ninety-five percent correct. There was, moreover, an engaging simplicity about him, the innocent joy of a child who has discovered that he can do handstands, or juggle oranges. When the session was over, Cavanagh told him:

"As far as I'm concerned, Rodolfo, you're hired. However, Mr. Molloy will want to see you himself at the end of the day. I'll want you on deck now to help us cast off. You'll grab something to eat with the rest of the crew, then spend the rest of the cruise down here, watching these beauties in motion. Clear?"

"Clear as a blue sky," said Rodolfo Arnolfini. "I am very happy. You treat me with respect. I am grateful for that. And your engines will have the best of care."

"I believe you, Rodolfo. Now, let's get this circus under way!"

Back on deck he stationed Rodolfo at the anchor winches and then went aft to single up the mooring lines, so that they could be slipped from the deck and hauled quickly inboard. Leo and Jackie were resetting the deck for a buffet luncheon, while Lenore was clearing away glasses and emptying ashtrays. Just then, Molloy came on deck with Farnese. Both men were in high humor. Farnese went immediately to join Galeazzi, Molloy stood by until Cavanagh had winched up the gangway, checked the strappings on the dinghy and announced:

"Ready to move when you are, Mr. Molloy."

"Good! I'll take her out myself. You should grab some sack time. You look as though you need it!"

"Thanks. I will. But first I'd like you to see this mechanic, Rodolfo Arnolfini. He's bright. I quizzed him from the manuals and on the engines and he checks out well: old-fashioned apprentice learning. I'd like to keep him on board. Between us we can provide day-to-day engine-room service and at least first-stage damage control."

"Where is he now?"

"I have him standing by the anchor winches."

"Then you'd better wait with him while we raise anchors, in case he doesn't understand my orders. I won't bother talking to him now. There'll be time later when we've got this crowd off the ship."

"I need a decision, sir. Do we hire him?"

"If you want him, hire him by all means. You have to work the ship."

"Thank you. I'll train him so he can double in brass —deckhand and helmsman. One more thing: what's the program for this evening? Are we staying in port or leaving?"

"As soon as this afternoon's cruise is over, we'll get the hell out of here and head for Porto Santo Stefano. That's about a fifty-mile run down the coast. Galeazzi will be leaving us there and Farnese will be bringing a girlfriend on board—an English actress. Lucietta wants to entertain some theatrical friends and I need to look at a proposed yacht-harbor development on the south side of the peninsula of Monte Argentario. So, count on three days in harbor. Make sure you use every opportunity to top up water and fuel tanks. Chef will see to the fresh provisions. You handle the ship's funds . . ."

"About Mr. Hadjidakis . . ."

"The U.S. Navy gave me a call sign and frequency. I'll call Naples myself. You should move into Giorgios's cabin right away, the navigation systems are repeated on a panel opposite his bunk." He hesitated for a moment and then said: "I've had some news. I'd like to share it with you . . . There were two messages, one of them was from Cardinal Spellman in New York. He tells me His Holiness will invest me with the Order of St. Gregory in a private ceremony at Castelgandolfo as soon as he takes up summer residence."

"Congratulations, sir."

"I won't say I'm not flattered. I am. I won't say I haven't earned it either. What we've done here in Elba and what Farnese and I are planning elsewhere in Italy, will trigger a whole series of similar construction projects on the western coastline: yacht harbors, residential complexes, service installations . . . It can be the beginning of an economic miracle . . . and it will give a big lift to the Christian Democrats. The other thing I have to mention is the code message. I have a four-figure one-time code for communications with the C.I.A. So, don't be fazed if you get what sounds like a jumble of numbers on the radio. The important thing is to transcribe 'em accurately. Anyway, the code was a message of thanks from Allen Dulles. Our man Tolvier 'has now been safely delivered in his care.' He's expected to supply valuable information on Communist activities in France and elsewhere. There's a warning, however, that there may be reprisals for my part in the affair."

"Like the attack on Hadjidakis?"

"It's a possibility we have to take seriously."

"I understand, sir."

But when he threw himself on the bunk in Hadjidakis's cabin, there was a sour, metallic taste in his mouth as if it had been filled with Judas money. The notion of a traffic—any traffic—in human flesh was repugnant to him; but the traffic in out-of-work spies and surgical torturers had its own special horror and its own sequelae of vendettas.

He was deathly tired; there was another night of helm-watch ahead of him. He needed sleep; but sleep would not come. Beside the bunk was a small chest of drawers on top of which lay a thick, quarto-sized volume bound in black leather. Thinking to read himself to sleep, Cavanagh opened it and found that the contents were handwritten in cursive demotic Greek. The title was intriguing: *The True Chronicle of the Voyages of G and L.* The text was a double challenge: to his curiosity and to his scholarship. The handwriting was clear enough, but the contents were a strange mixture of vivid poetic passages and slangy vulgarities which Cavanagh, rusty in the language, was hard put to translate.

However, there was no doubt about the nature of the contents: A Rabelaisian narrative of the erotic adventures of Giorgios Hadjidakis, Lou Molloy and a whole gallery of male and female companions. The entries were not written up every day, as in a normal diary. They were sporadic episodes, hooked together over a number of years from weekends, extended vacation periods, fishing excursions, business trips, each one dated and clearly located.

In spite of the fact that the vocabulary of copulation in any language is very limited, Cavanagh found himself intrigued by the variety of grotesque sexual situations recorded in the diary. No combination, male, female, animal or vegetable was left untried or undescribed. Even more intriguing were the vivid descriptions of persons, places, circumstances. There could be no doubt that they were painted from life, like the pornographies of many famous artists who sought their models in bathhouses and brothels.

What seemed to Cavanagh extraordinary was that the book should be left there, in full view, for anyone to read. Then he realized that this was the cream of the joke. Who, on board the *Salamandra d'Oro*, what casual crewman or companion, would be able to read a word of the scabrous stories? Lou Molloy himself had no Greek and only Mass Latin . . . Which raised another fascinating question: did Molloy know that the book existed? Had he any notion of its contents—and the power which Giorgios Hadjidakis held over him?

Whatever the answer to that question, Cavanagh himself was now presented with a Faustian temptation. He held in his hands Molloy's reputation, his high alliances, his noble marriage. Suddenly, Galeazzi's warning resounded like the blast of a foghorn, close and menacing in a night of swirling mist: "Molloy is a rich man . . . However he is also vulnerable—to his own follies and the vices of his minions. Of these you are, or have pretended to be, happily ignorant. You may not be able to remain so . . ."

Now the time of happy ignorance was ended forever. He was armed with a lethal weapon. He could not swear that he would be proof against a sudden temptation to use it. He closed the book; but instead of setting it back on the bedside table, he put it in the top drawer of the chest. He told himself that it was a safety measure; but deep down he knew that it was his first uncertain move towards the Faustian lure. God forbid he should ever need to use it; but the weapon was ready to his hand. Thus reassured, he turned his face to the bulkhead and lapsed instantly into sleep.

He was wakened at four-thirty in the afternoon, by a call from the bridge.

"Cavanagh, I want you up here! We dock in thirty minutes."

"I'm on my way."

On the bridge, Molloy delivered his orders.

"I want you to take us in. When we dock, there'll be transport waiting to take our visitors to their hotels. They've had a good day and they're all pleasantly mellow, so I don't want to prolong the farewells. As soon as they're loaded into the bus, haul up the gangway and slip moorings."

"Same sailing orders, sir?"

"The same. I've called the harbormaster at Porto Santo Stefano and given him an E.T.A. of twenty-one hundred hours tonight. He's reserved a berth and he tells me there are no hazards and we're well away from foul ground. The dock is on the starboard hand as you pass the breakwater and our berth is right under the second light pylon. We drop the hooks in line with the harbor entrance. There'll be a man ready to take our lines—and I've booked dinner at a restaurant, Pipistrello, which the harbormaster recommends. Chef and the crew have had a big day. They can take an easy night. And I've warned the boys I'll fire them if there's the faintest smell of trouble on shore."

"Did they give you any more information on the brawl in Porto Ferraio?"

"I didn't ask for it. I've asked the C.I.A. to make their own inquiries. By the way, our visitors have left a bit of a mess—crumbs, cigarette butts."

"I'll see to that, sir. As soon as we're under way I'll have the decks hosed down and given a quick scrub. I presume your guests will be glad of a late siesta."

"That's putting it mildly, Cavanagh: I have to say I've never seen people so easily bored as the Italian nobility."

To which Cavanagh had no adequate comment. Instead he asked:

"What news on Mr. Hadjidakis?"

"They've done the cranial operation and removed the pressure on the brain. They were beginning to clear the obstructing bone fragments in the septum. So far his vital signs are good. We should call again tonight—preferably by landline from Porto Santo Stefano."

"That's good news, thank God! What about his family?"

"I haven't been in touch with them yet. I hope to have good news to tell them—and a watertight story about how he came by his injuries. Hadjidakis has a good marriage. We don't want to put any burrs in his bed, do we?"

"Of course not."

"As soon as we have some definite word from the surgeons, I want to go down to Naples to see Giorgios myself. I need to know the prognosis and to set up whatever support system is necessary for him and his family. I'll call his wife then. That would mean you'd have to handle the ship *and* the guests for a few days. Could you do that?"

"I don't see why not, sir. The ship's not a problem. As far as the guests are concerned, we can provide whatever service they require on ship or on shore. I can put in a courtesy appearance at mealtimes and after dinner. We'll cruise quietly down the coast, do some diving and fishing and meet you wherever you want between Porto Santo Stefano and Naples. We'll keep constant radio watch, so you can contact us at any time."

"Good. That's what I wanted to hear—oh, and Giulia did refer back to me on the matter of her scuba lessons. You're a tactful fellow when you want to be, Cavanagh. I appreciate that; and your new hand performed well today—quick to execute orders and very unobtrusive with the passengers. I told him he was hired at Italian rates . . . That's about all, I think. Your ship, Mr. Cavanagh!"

He glanced at his watch, signed off on the log and left the bridge without another word. Cavanagh was not unhappy with the commendations, however grudgingly they might have been offered. However, he was left with the uncomfortable feeling that the Greek symbols in Hadjidakis's black book were already beginning to complicate the once-simple equation of his life.

Once the day visitors were gone and the *Salamandra* was clear of the harbor, a vesper quiet descended on the ship. The guests were in their cabins resting after the clatter of the afternoon. Leo and Jackie were dozing to the sound of ballet music in the forepeak. Chef and Lenore had retired. Rodolfo the mechanic was hosing and scrubbing the deck, crooning happily to himself as he pursued his solitary task. Cavanagh sat alone on the bridge with one ear cocked to the transceiver traffic from Portishead, in case the *Salamandra*'s call sign, M.U.H.Y., popped up in the transmission.

There was traffic in the sea lanes too: fishermen trawling the twenty-fathom banks of the Tuscan archipelago, small tankers serving the coastal ports, a Lloyd

Triestino liner heading northward from Naples to Genoa, a destroyer, low down on the horizon against the westering sun. Eastward were the lowlands of the Tuscan coast and behind them the misty rises of the foothills where the first lights were pricking out from the hillside towns. It was pleasant cruising, but a certain extra vigilance was demanded. Trawl nets were bad things to tangle with, and sometimes a submarine from the Sixth Fleet popped up without warning for a surface run to recharge batteries and change its fetid air.

Refreshed by his siesta, Cavanagh was alert and interested in every detail of the passage. His sketchbook was open on the console and from time to time he set down swift, nervous impressions of the shoreline and the craft that came within his scan. Normally his spells on the bridge were times of renewal, of meditative quiet. This evening, however, he had another preoccupation. The phrase which Molloy had used about Hadjidakis buzzed in his ears like an angry wasp: "He has a good marriage. We mustn't put a burr in his bed." To hell with Hadjidakis! Now there was a burr in his own bed, in his breeches too, and the name of the burr was Giulia Farnese.

At first she had seemed unattainable, as far beyond his reach as a painted lady on the canvas of an old master. Then, a series of incidents, some contrived, others apparently accidental, had brought her close enough for him to be able to nourish desire without making a fool of himself. Lucietta, the racy lady with leanings to the Left had offered—albeit in sardonic jest—to finance an elopement with an eligible suitor. Galeazzi the Godfather had accepted without reproof—though not without warning—his confession of attraction to Giulia. Soon, and most conveniently, Molloy would absent himself, leaving to Cavanagh the care and nurture of his guests—Giulia among them.

Hadjidakis's book was a manual of black magic in his hands. Most important of all, Giulia herself had made the first small gestures to tempt him into the dangerous game.

So what now, Cavanagh, me wild colonial boy? Do you want to play or don't you? No shame if you don't. You keep your eyes on the sea and the charts and the radar screen. You run the ship and the crew. You smile and say "yes sir, no madam" to the guests. You have your little fun and games with Lenore Pritchard, and at the end of the tour you collect the handsome residue of your hundred bucks a week plus a good conduct bonus, and finish your Grand Tour in style. And what's wrong with that? Not a damned thing—as any right-minded man or woman would willingly admit.

And the other choice? Well, that's a mite different; but given the fact that you're part exhibitionist, part gambler, a half-arsed scholar and a would-be lawyer and something of a sentimentalist whose brains get mislaid when the Old Adam stirs inside his jock-strap, it sounds like an interesting flutter.

What have you got to lose? Not much in the way of job or money—somthing maybe in the way of dignity, when the nobility and gentry remind you, as they will, that you're a hired hand dreaming above his station. There are also other penalties, like the vengeance of Lou Molloy, with his long reach and bottomless purse, and the enmity of the Farnese and the threat of political avengers. What's to win? No fortune certainly; but possibly, just possibly the lady, Giulia the Beautiful, who might, just might, count her world well lost for love, if Cavanagh the wild colonial boy could show her what love meant, and if—the biggest if of all—if he had the passion and the talent to teach her and she the desire to learn.

How would the outcome be determined? In symbol

if not in fact, he saw it clearly. One fine day, one night of stars or storm, Bryan de Courcy Cavanagh would find himself standing alone in a great amphitheater, ringed with silent spectators. He would be facing the door to the caverns where the wild beasts were penned. When the door opened, what would emerge? Giulia the Beautiful, running to his embrace amid the plaudits of the crowd, or Declan Aloysius Molloy, a ravening tiger bent on devouring him?

He was jolted out of his reveric by the sudden appearance of a fast, fifty-foot pleasure cruiser cutting across his bows on a collision course, a bare hundred meters away. He swung the wheel hard to pass under her stern, and cursed himself for the dangerous folly of daydreaming on watch. As he resumed his course there was a call on the intercom from Molloy:

"What was that, for Christ's sake?"

Cavanagh, Navy-trained, lied cheerfully.

"A fifty-footer, playing chicken. I had him marked, but he clapped on speed at the last moment. I had to take evasive action. Sorry if you were jolted about."

"It's not me. It's the ladies I'm worried about. Keep your mind on your job and your hands out of your pockets! Do you hear me?"

"Loud and clear, sir! Loud and clear!"

He looked up at the chronometer. It showed eighteen-thirty hours, Greenwich Mean Time. He noted it in the log and wrote a one-line notation. "Altered course to avoid speeding pleasure craft." On the open page of his sketchbook he wrote the same time, with the date, and then made a lightning sketch of a bookie at a country racetrack. Under the sketch he wrote the words he had heard from a tout at his first race-meeting. "Hurdler or flat-racer, mate, it makes no difference. You've gotta be in it to win it." It was not exactly a historic inscription. It might not be worth the cheap art-paper it was written on; but he would remember it, by God, the date, the time, the mind-set in which he first set out in pursuit of the Princess Giulia Farnese, called Giulia la Bella.

It seemed that all the omens were favorable. A few minutes later Prince Farnese himself came to the bridge and asked, with due deference:

"May I join you, Mr. Cavanagh?"

"By all means, sir. We have a clear sea at the moment. We're on automatic pilot. Please, take the chair."

"You're free to chat for a while?"

"So long as we both keep an eye on the sea and the radar screen, sure! What can I do for you?"

"Mr. Molloy has told you he will be leaving the ship for a few days?"

"Yes."

"He has also told you I'll be bringing a lady friend on board?"

"Yes."

"Has he told you who she is?"

"Only that she's a British actress."

"A very well known one, Mr. Cavanagh. Miss Aurora Lambert."

"We'll do our best to make her welcome, sir."

"I'm sure you will, Mr. Cavanagh. That, however, is not my problem."

"What precisely is your problem, sir?"

"In one word, privacy. Miss Lambert and I are not married, nor, let me say it frankly, are we likely to be in the foreseeable future. We are, as the vulgar press would put it, 'just good friends.' Even that could, if wrongly presented in the gutter journals, raise certain embarrassments at the Vatican for my friend Molloy and, of course, for my daughter."

"I understand, sir."

"I'm sure you do; but there is one very special problem. Do you know the meaning of the word *paparazzi*?"

"That's a new one to me, sir."

"Well, *paparazzi* are photographers, who make a precarious but sometimes quite rich living by taking intimate or scandalous photographs of celebrities and peddling them to the world press. They are clever and persistent and they will go to any lengths to trap their victims. Places of resort like Porto Santo Stefano are their favorite stamping grounds; but they are as likely to hire a speedboat and follow one out to a deserted cove on Giglio or Giannutri. They are equally capable of bribing a crew member to provide intimate glimpses of life on board a yacht like this one. You see my problem?"

"I do. Let's try to cut it down to reasonable size. Item one. I can make sure this crew doesn't talk. Leo and Jackie are already in Mr. Molloy's black book. Miss Pritchard has been trained on the Cunarders; she will be going back to them after the summer. She will not make gossip ashore. Neither Chef nor I has any interest in creating mischief. Rodolfo Arnolfini is a new hand desperately anxious to hold his job. So—you have a reasonable bet on everyone's discretion. Item two: no photographers or members of the press are allowed on board. However, we cannot prevent photography from near or distant vantage points. So, while we're in port or under possible surveillance, you and Miss Lambert will have to be careful . . . And if you are waylaid, well, I'm sure I don't have to tell you to handle it lightly . . ."

"You have experience in these matters, Mr. Cavanagh?" Farnese was a very practiced ironist. Cavanagh took his time over the answer.

"No, sir. My only experience was in keeping myself and my crew out of trouble in waterfront bars. I learned that it was easier to mend hurt feelings than broken heads."

"A shame perhaps that you were not with your shipmates last night in Porto Ferraio."

"Who knows?" Cavanagh shrugged off the barb. "Brothels have never been my scene."

"There's enough going free for the asking, eh?"

"I'm sure your Highness would know that better than I."

Farnese flushed with sudden anger, but managed an unsteady laugh.

"A hit, Mr. Cavanagh! A palpable hit! That's Shakespeare, isn't it?"

"If your Highness says so."

"Come now, Cavanagh! I made a joke. I meant no harm. Where's your sense of humor?"

Before Cavanagh had time to answer, Rodolfo Arnolfini eased his gangling form onto the bridge.

"Excuse me, gentlemen, please. The deck is finished, sir. The furniture is in place. I have checked the pressures in the engine room. What now would you like me to do?"

"Relax, Rodolfo!" Cavanagh gave him a grin of approval. "Take a shower! Stretch out for a while. We're still two and a half hours out of Santo Stefano."

"If you are sure, sir?"

"I'm sure. Go!"

When Rodolfo had disappeared Farnese said, without obvious malice:

"You have a pleasant way with staff, Mr. Cavanagh."

"I'm staff myself," Cavanagh reminded him. "I give what I hope to get."

"And what is that, pray?"

"Respect. Arnolfini knows more about engines than I'll learn in a lifetime. If, God forbid, anything goes wrong at sea, he'll be the one to fix it. I'll just be the man holding the lamp and handing the tools. He's working his guts out to make the jump from apprentice to journeyman. Maybe, as Europe puts itself together again, he'll have a chance to get himself an education and make the next jump to engineer. I hope so."

"Is Mr. Hadjidakis a good engineer?"

"The best."

"A good seaman?"

"That too. I'm happy to serve under him."

"Then how do you explain what happened last night in Porto Ferraio?"

"I can't. Not all of it anyway. The *carabinieri* were somewhat at a loss too. Clearly they do not normally expect violence in houses of appointment—at least not enough of it to invite police intervention. I imagine they were glad to see us gone."

"But they will have the ship marked, make no mistake about it. Their intelligence service is very good. In the absence of depositions from our side, they will make and circulate their own record of the incident, impossible to overturn."

"It seems then, I made a mistake, compounding so easily with the *brigadiere*."

"A mistake? I would not say that. I have not said it to Molloy, who now approves the action you took—as indeed I do myself. All I am pointing out to you, Mr. Cavanagh, is that in this country, the norms of judgment, the Aristotelian categories, the concepts underlying the law and its administration, are vastly different from those in Germanic or Anglo-Saxon countries. If you propose to spend any time here—to further your legal studies, for example—you must learn the idiom of life, as you have obviously learned the idiom of the Italian language. I would remind you, however, that our common tongue expresses only half the thought and even less of the emotion of the peoples of this peninsula. Their private lives are carried on in dialects, Pugliese, Calabrese, Neapolitan, Sicilian, Sard . . . Are you listening to me, Mr. Cavanagh?"

"I'm listening, sir; but I'm also watching the traffic. That big white spot on the radar is a tanker or a fast freighter. He's doing twenty-five knots and from where he is now, he has the right of way . . . I understand what you mean by idioms of language and of life. Such differences are not unique to Italy. We have them even in my country, which has less than two hundred years of recorded history—which includes the genocide of the indigenous peoples, who occupied the continent for at least forty thousand years."

"Truly, I did not know that." Farnese was genuinely surprised and interested. "Where did your indigenous peoples come from?"

"It is believed they came on the now-drowned land-bridge from Asia. They are not Negroid but Aryan. Their nearest Asian relatives would appear to be the black Tamils of Ceylon and Southern India . . . They are nomads, hunter-gatherers, with clearly defined tribal areas and a highly elaborate cosmogony, preserved by oral tradition only . . . Their treatment at the hands of the white invaders was, and still is, horrendous, an ulcer that will take a long time to heal . . ."

The tanker was closing fast now. Cavanagh took a long, easy swing to pass under her stern, and bring the *Salamandra* back on course. Farnese gave him an approving smile and a left-handed compliment.

"If you handle your women as you handle your ship, you must have a very successful love-life."

"Why?" Cavanagh demanded with a certain asperity. "Why, in God's name, is everyone suddenly interested in my love-life?"

"Do you really want the answer to that?"

"Yes, I do!"

"Because the women desire you and the men wish they could be your age again. You should be flattered, my dear Cavanagh."

"On the contrary, I'm bloody embarrassed. I feel like a stud bull in an auction ring."

"I could think of a metaphor more apt."

"Which is?"

"You are the young bull being paraded to tease the old one into activity."

"What is that supposed to mean?"

"Just what it says. Molloy is totally obsessed with business. The attention he gives to Giulia is quite minimal. So, naturally her attention is focused on you, the young scholar-adventurer from the far end of the earth. Not to marry, of course, that commitment is already made, but for diversion, yes, for the flattery of your obvious admiration . . . Don't mistake me, Cavanagh! I'm not blaming you. I'm not discouraging you. I'm just trying to play fair, because I find you agreeable and interesting. Sometimes, you remind me of the son I lost . . ."

For once in his life Bryan de Courcy Cavanagh had nothing to say. It was as if he had been punched in the belly, all the air came out of him in a long exhalation. His hands were clammy on the wheel. He changed to autopilot and dried his palms with a pocket handkerchief. Farnese crossed to the chart table, and by way of changing the conversation began making his own dead-reckoning. Finally he said:

"I make us just level with Ombrone . . ."

Cavanagh looked at the radar screen.

"A small promontory just south of a river mouth?"

"That's what it looks like."

"Is there a larger city in the hills behind?"

"Yes. According to the chart, that's Grosseto."

"So your reckoning is accurate." Then, impelled by unspent anger, he demanded: "Let's finish the other discussion. You tell me I'm co-opted as a player in some kind of game between Lou Molloy and the Farnese family. You obviously takc my role seriously enough to raise the matter with me . . ."

"Not too seriously, Mr. Cavanagh." Farnese shrugged in deprecation. "So long as Giulia is in control, which at this moment she is. I do not—let me say it frankly—see you as a fortune hunter or as a *cavalier' sirviente* in the old Byronic mode. Once Giulia is married, she will do as she pleases—or at least as much as her husband will tolerate. You are a young man of good education and breeding. I do not fear you too much. I believe you will play by the rules."

"That's the problem, isn't it?" Cavanagh reminded him softly. "Whose rules are they? Yours or mine?"

"You disappoint me, young man!"

"Why so? You told me yourself one must learn the idioms of life as well as the idioms of language. In this game, however you describe it, the deck is stacked to favor the big names, the heavy players. I'm a nobody from nowhere, a Mediterranean cowboy; but of all the folk on this ship, I have the least to lose, therefore the least to fear."

"That makes you a very dangerous player, Mr. Cavanagh."

"Not really. My resources are so small, you can bid me out of any hand."

"You could borrow to raise your stake."

"I wouldn't."

"You could conspire with another player."

"With whom, for instance?"

"Are you open to an offer, Mr. Cavanagh?"

Cavanagh was silent for a long moment, scanning the empty sea and the white mass on the radar screen that marked the mainland to the east. He turned off the autopilot and corrected his course by five degrees, west, then reset the pilot. Finally, he said almost casually:

"I have to tell Your Highness I'm not open to offers and the game itself is too rich for me. Count me out, please!"

"A wise decision," said Farnese. "You can always come back when you've saved enough money for the table stake."

Half an hour after Farnese had left him, Chef appeared on the bridge with bouillon and crackers and his usual benign smile.

"It's a long time to dinner. I thought you could use some nourishment."

"You're a messenger from heaven, Chef! Sit down. Talk to me! Tell me I'm not going crazy!"

"Tell me first what ails you, young Cavanagh!"

Cavanagh told him of his talk with Galeazzi, of his passage-at-arms with Farnese, of the interlude with the women at the hotel, of Molloy's concerns for Hadjidakis. He made no mention of the black book, but asked cautious questions about Lou Molloy and his political activities.

Chef heard him out in silence; but instcad of answering, asked a question of his own.

"Where did you spend your war, Cavanagh?"

"First on a corvette, then on a destroyer in the South Pacific."

"A good life, the Navy, eh?"

"Looking back on it, sure! A hell of a good life. Much better than slogging through bloody jungles, holing up in muddy foxholes. At least the combat was clean and there was a lot of sea to hide in . . ."

"And not too many people to dispute it with you, eh?"

"That's true."

"And after the war, how was it?"

"Well, once the prisoners were home and the first grief for the lost ones was over, it was an exciting period. We realized for the first time, I think, what a big country we had, and the enormous opportunities we had to develop it. We were no longer tied to Britain's apron strings. We had fought our own war. We had new and powerful allies in the United States. Migrants were coming in by the shipload. So, yes, it was a good time—a lucky time, for men of my age at least!"

"Now tell me what you have seen in Europe?"

"Not much. The coast from Genoa to Antibes . . ."

"The best of it. The part that suffered the least in physical destruction, in the displacement of populations . . ."

"That's right."

"But you haven't seen the rest of it—the Ruhr, the Rhineland, Dresden, Vienna? You've never been in a camp for displaced persons?"

"No."

"Then you can have no conception of what it is still like to be a conquered people, living under the law of the occupying powers, subsisting upon their bounty, while all the time, even six years after the armistice, you are trying to put together the remnants of your life, trace your scattered family—collect the shreds of your own identity!"

"What are you trying to tell me, Chef?"

"That you are a lucky young man."

"I know that."

"But because you are lucky, you can also be arrogant and opinionated. You talk sometimes as though life can be run by convent-school ethics and the do's and don'ts of the Roman catechism. How can I explain it to you? I am a Swiss, a neutral, more privileged even than you. I have seen the war like Wagner's *Twilight of the Gods*, from a box seat. Even though the opera is over, the set is still standing. The skyline of middle Europe looks like a mouthful of rotten teeth. Tens of millions are dead, millions more are rootless and in despair. It is left to the women to survive, to nurture the children, to find new partners with whom to breed again. Read the magazines and the newspapers and you will see column after column of advertisements for husbands, love-partners, a dozen different designations. And in the east, in Germany, Hungary, Poland, Czechoslovakia, the U.S.S.R. itself, it is even worse. The U.S.S.R. lost twenty million dead. Now the Party has murdered liberty itself . . . ! On this little ship, Cavanagh, you are living in a time-bubble, removed and remote from all the tragedy on land. Even so, part of the drama—and no small part of it either—is being enacted under your eyes. As always, money and power are the keys to change. Both are represented here—with one notable addition, the potency of the Roman Church; the perennial survivor, organized as efficiently as the empire of Augustus, with a codified faith that promises an explanation, if not a cure, for every human ill."

"I know what you're telling me." Cavanagh was very subdued. "I'm not really as stupid as I must sound. I know I've got little to be arrogant about—and that one-liners are no answer to the world's mysteries. But what I don't understand is why I'm being drawn into all this—given that I'm the village idiot, which I've just admitted!"

"The answer to that is the simplest of all. You are young, you are virile. You have an education and a future. More than that, you are a man from a new country which is accepting migrants from all over Europe. Your signature on a marriage contract is worth whatever you want to charge for it, because it means a passport to a new life for the woman and her close family. There is a name for that kind of arrangement, a white marriage, and there are brokers who arrange them every day."

Cavanagh laughed. "At least it's a solution if I run out of funds!"

"The trick," said Chef, good humoredly, "is to pick a woman who can pay for the privilege! Let me tell you a story—a true story, which illustrates how things are in Europe. Last year, at the end of summer, I came down to spend a couple of weeks in Sorrento with an old friend of mine who runs the Hotel Tasso, right on the cliff edge. He told me that three of his young waiters had made a pool of their money and each agreed to assist the others to find, court and marry an American heiress—a visible, provable and substantial millionairess! The one who succeeded would put the others on his payroll and sponsor them to America. You laugh? One of them did find and marry an heiress. He and his two friends are now happy executives in a large cosmetic company in New York. The same scenario is being played out in comedy or tragedy all over Europe. So, you must take yourself very seriously, young Cavanagh! Put a good price on yourself. You're not only a good stud stallion. You're a hedge investment, a small stock with great potential, negotiable in all European markets!"

Suddenly, a well-spring of suppressed humor burst inside Cavanagh and he laughed until the tears ran down his cheeks. He was still drunk with self-mockery when the beacons of Porto Santo Stefano showed clear and bright against the huddled lights of the little harbor town.

The port of Santo Stefano was putting a brave face on an unpromising spring season. There were colored lights strung along the harbor front, tubs full of spring bulbs and, along the balconies above the store-fronts, a trailing of wisteria and bursts of lilac bloom. There were few vessels in the harbor and they were mostly small run-abouts and thirty-foot cruisers and old-fashioned day-sailers, against which the *Salamandra* bulked large as an ocean liner.

The welcome she received was eager and almost regal. The harbormaster himself came to shepherd her into the berth. There were two men to take her lines. The proprietor of the Pipistrello had waiters standing by with offers of spumante and savories and a guitarist to play the company into the restaurant and make music for their meal. Even the dour Galeazzi smiled and nodded approval:

"The times are hard; but we still make a ceremony of service. This is where our strength resides, Molloy! This is what you are buying with your investment dollars!"

"Sure, it's a grand piece of theater!" Molloy's humor was on the sour side. "While we're waiting for our first dividend, we'll take 'em on tour in an opera."

To which Cavanagh added the silent tag-line: "And call it, no doubt, *The Bartered Bride*!" Almost as if he had heard, Molloy rounded on him with curt commands.

"Chef tells me the crew have had their meal. Set a deck watch and give the rest a few hours ashore. Have 'em back on board at midnight so they don't disturb the guests. You're coming with me to the post office. We have some calls to make. Alessandro, Enrico, would you be good enough to escort the ladies to dinner? I'll join you later!"

"I'll come with you, my love." Giulia moved to his side and took his arm. "Good news or bad, I'd like to be with you when you call Naples."

Molloy's answer was hardly above a whisper; but it was instant, cold and hostile.

"Please, Giulia! This is my business, let me transact it in my own fashion. I'll see you at the Pipistrello."

It was like seeing a fragile leaf stripped from a tree by a bitter wind. Giulia paled, but uttered no sound. She seemed to float away from Molloy into the protecting presence of her aunt. Cavanagh, embarrassed and angry, removed himself abruptly, to pass instructions to the crew. Lenore Pritchard detained him just inside the saloon for a private word.

"Batten down, Cavanagh. It looks as though we're in for stormy weather. Our little princess is very unhappy. Her father is obviously putting pressure on Molloy, who is in a foul temper because of Hadjidakis. Tonight may be the night you'll have to rescue me . . ."

"Make sure you can shout loud and fast." Cavanagh was still rocking with anger. "God! How I hate that surly brute!"

"When he's like this he's as dangerous as a wounded bear!"

"I know. I've just heard him snarling at Giulia. Christ knows why she takes it!"

"Because she's bought and paid for, lover! Even so, I feel sorry for her."

"Cavanagh!" Molloy shouted across the deck. "Step lively!"

"Coming, sir!" He added a muttered postscript for Lenore's benefit. "And may he choke on fire and brimstone, the black Boston bastard!"

When they arrived at the post office, they discovered they had no *gettoni* for the public telephone. Cavanagh had to race back to buy a couple of handfuls in the restaurant. Then Molloy ordered him to make the call to Naples.

"I'll go crazy if I have to listen to that '*Pronto! Pronto! Aspett un momento*' routine. When you've got the American medico on the line, call me into the booth and I'll talk to him."

"Aye, aye, sir!"

It took nearly fifteen minutes to establish the connection, by which time Molloy was pacing the cobblestones of the dock and threatening to tear the instrument out of the wall. When the doctor came on the line, Molloy snatched the receiver from Cavanagh and waved him away. Cavanagh walked to the edge of the dock, perched himself on a bollard and watched Molloy mouthing and gesticulating in the booth. A long time later, he put down the receiver and began walking towards the water. His gait was slow and ataxic, like that of a sleepwalker. His eyes were fixed on some distant star in the eastern sky. Cavanagh stood up to intercept him and to ask the vital question:

"How is Giorgios?"

Molloy's answer was flat and toneless.

"He's in intensive care. He hasn't regained consciousness yet. His vital signs are very low. The doctor says he's still at risk of total collapse or of serious residual impairment. He wouldn't go into details on the telephone. He did suggest that Giorgios's family be informed. After that, it was just mumbo-jumbo. He was stroking me, trying to calm me down . . . I've got to get to Naples. I've got to get there fast, Cavanagh. How do I do it? Think, man! Think!"

Molloy was obviously in shock, struggling with a welter of emotions which he could not, or dared not, express. Cavanagh tried to talk him through the confusion.

"I've already worked out some options, sir. While we're talking, why don't we stroll down to the end of the dock. You're in no shape for company yet."

"That's for sure, boyo! Between marriage plans and covering my arse with all these high-toned hucksters, I'm besieged, beleaguered . . . And the thought of losing Giorgios—even having him maimed and out of the game—that's the last straw! Do you ever read the

Bible, Cavanagh? We micks don't as a rule. But being at sea gives you a taste for it and an understanding. Giorgios and I are like David and Jonathan, close as peas in a pod." Suddenly, like an old-fashioned preacher, he began to intone: "I am distressed for thee, my brother Jonathan: very pleasant hast thou been unto me. Thy love was wonderful, passing the love of woman . . ." He broke off, to challenge Cavanagh brutally: "Shocked, Mister Cavanagh?"

"No, sir. I understand your distress. I'm here to help if I can . . . Let's talk about your travel arrangements."

Molloy fell into step beside him and they strolled slowly down the quay towards the harbormaster's office. Cavanagh, bland as butter, went on with his exposition.

"From here to Naples by sea is about two hundred and twenty miles. If we left at midnight, we could have you there in fifteen hours—mid-afternoon tomorrow. That would be the most comfortable way to do it."

"Not for me, it wouldn't!" Molloy flared into sudden anger. "On board every move I make is scrutinized. Giulia complains because I don't give her enough attention, while I'm hard put to keep my hands off that beautiful body of hers. Goddamn it! If I did what I feel like doing, we'd be bedded every night, having some fun and to hell with the Pope and the whole bloody College of Cardinals! Instead we're playing this old-fashioned comedy of virgin bride and noble-spirited suitor, while her daddy's going to be screwing me in daylight and Miss Aurora Lambert at night. As if that isn't enough grief, Galeazzi and his Vatican investors are driving hard and complicated bargains, a different one for every location and project, because they say the underlying titles, leasehold or freehold, are all different. My lawyers are struggling to keep up with the translations and the legal costs are escalating . . . I said it before, Cavanagh, I'll say it again. I'm beleaguered! When Giorgios was here, he'd laugh and say that the pair of us could screw anything on two legs or four. Without him, I'm adrift, Cavanagh, and after what happened to him, I'm scared too. Would you believe that? Lou Molloy scared?"

"Yes, I'd believe it. It would surprise me if you weren't . . . I know I can't match Giorgios Hadjidakis; but you can trust me to run your ship and care for your guests . . . So you don't want to travel to Naples on the *Salamandra*. The next option is to drive. It's eighty miles from here to Rome, a hundred and fifty from Rome to Naples. If you like, we can summon a taxi from the harbormaster's office. You'd have a six, seven hour drive, but you'd still be in Naples for breakfast . . . The final option is to drive to Rome and have a charter flight waiting at Ciampino to take you to Naples at first light."

"Now tell me how I can arrange a charter flight from Rome in this neck of the woods at this hour?"

"Ask Count Galeazzi. He works closely with the Pope's nephew, Prince Carlo Pacelli, who runs the Italian airline!"

Molloy stopped dead in his tracks.

"Now aren't you the clever one, Mr. Cavanagh! How did you figure that out?"

"I learn from my elders and betters," Cavanagh grinned in the darkness. "Sometimes they forget I speak Italian. Galeazzi's the money man. He's got Vatican funds spread across every enterprise in Italy. Pacelli's the front man for those interests, and he's *numero uno* in Italian airlines, which is a glamor stock in spite of their early accident record."

Molloy stood for a moment staring up at the velvet sky, sprinkled with faint stars. Finally he shook his head.

"No! At this stage I *do* favors, I don't ask 'em, especially not from anybody at the Vatican. They have to see me as the white knight riding in to save 'em from the Red Menace. Spelly taught me that. Rome is like any other political capital. You have to give to get. The trick, Spelly taught me, is to be first up with the donation . . . So! It's a taxi ride to Rome, then I'll pick up a limousine at the Grand Hotel and ride to Naples in comfort. Let's finish our stroll and have the harbormaster call us a cab. Then I'll go back to the ship and pack."

"It's none of my business, sir, but have you thought that the Princess might like to go with you."

Molloy surveyed him in silence for a moment and with cool deliberation gave him his answer.

"Yes, I have thought of it, Cavanagh. I've decided that the last thing in the world I need at this moment is the company of my betrothed. If I needed a woman's company, I'd much rather take Lenore Pritchard, but you need her on board. In any case, a telephone call from the Grand Hotel will get me the best call girl in Rome. I hope you're bright enough to understand where I'm at. One way or another I stand to lose a man I've loved since we were snot-nosed kids alley-brawling in Boston. Part of him dies, part of me dies too . . . That's what love means, Cavanagh, to me, to him too if he lives and if he can still remember. Marriage? It's a social contract, and a sacrament of the Church too, if you want to be theological about it. I'll honor the sacrament. I'll cherish the bride and the children we make together. I'll kiss the chains, but I don't have to love 'em. So how do you like them apples, Mister Cavanagh?"

"I think they're green and sour, Mr. Molloy, sir. I know they'd give me colic; but I didn't grow them and I don't have to eat them."

"Talking of sour, boyo, your own tongue's got an

edge to it I don't like at all. But we'll talk about that another time. You rustle up the taxi. I'll go aboard and pack. I'll poke my head in at the Pipistrello to say goodbye. After I'm gone, you can take my place at the head of the table and settle the bill. Look after my little family, Cavanagh. They're almost as important to me as I am to them."

By the time Molloy had made his farewells and Cavanagh had taken his place as host at the Pipistrello, the first dishes had been served and the guests were waiting on the main course, a *paillard* of veal, which the *padrone* had assured them was the best quality meat to be found in the province. The musician, a good guitarist with an agreeable tenor, was working his way through a bracket of traditional Neapolitan songs which the Countess and Galeazzi were harmonizing with him. Giulia and her father were engaged in a low-voiced dialogue, which they broke off the moment Cavanagh took his seat at the table.

The waiter poured wine and mineral water for him. The *padrone* recommended the veal with operatic eloquence. The musician asked whether he had any requests. Cavanagh answered that he would rather leave the choice to the ladies. He loved the music but was quickly lost in Neapolitan dialect.

Giulia offered to make the choice and to interpret the words in Italian, provided Cavanagh would attempt a full reprise of the number with her. Agreed? Most certainly agreed! The song of her choice was "Passione," which, Galeazzi told him, had been written in 1935, the last of the golden years in Neapolitan music. Galeazzi, it seemed, was a minor expert in the folk music of the siren lands. The guitarist played Giulia into the opening stanza:

"*Cchiù luntana me staie, cchiù vicina te sento* . . . The further you are from me, the closer I feel you."

The deceptively simple words seemed almost to betray the singer into the haunting passion of the chorus:

"*Te voglio, te penzo, te chiammo* . . . I want you, I think of you, I call you, I see you, I feel you, I dream you . . ."

That much at least he knew he could memorize. The words were alien but their meaning and their passion were his own. Were they Giulia's too? They had to be—else why had she chosen this plangent little lyric, why had she waved everyone into the last chorus, her family, the other diners in the room? Why, when the song was ended, did they all applaud so spontaneously, and afterwards turn the private supper into a riot of music and Latin sentiment?

It was long after midnight when they walked back along the dock, arm-in-arm, a quintet of happy travelers. Giulia, high on liquor and mischief, challenged Cavanagh:

"Now see if you can remember the song."

Cavanagh stopped, gathered the group around him and intoned softly: "*Cchiù luntana me staie, cchiù vicina te sento* . . . His Neapolitan sounded rather more like Tuscan, but the notes were true and the rhythm authentic and their *a capella* rendition of the chorus swept softly along the seafront with the night breeze.

"There now!" Cavanagh was riding a high wave of elation. "It strums on the heartstrings, doesn't it! We should form a singing group and take ourselves on the road!"

"We could call ourselves The Lovers," said Giulia, "and we'd specialize in love songs!"

"Don't even whisper it!" Farnese was suddenly out of humor. "That's the sort of thing the gutter press loves to print. I can just see the headlines, 'Passion in Porto Santo Stefano!' "

"What's wrong with a little passion, Papa?" Giulia

was in no mood to be bullied. "You'll be glad of it when Aurora Lambert arrives tomorrow!"

"God forgive your mother for the daughter she gave me!"

Farnese turned on his heel and stalked off. Galeazzi moved to follow him.

"Time I was in bed. My thanks for a most pleasant evening, Mr. Cavanagh."

"Mine too," said the Countess.

"It was Mr. Molloy's party. I'll pass on your compliments. He'll be more than happy to know you enjoyed yourselves."

"I don't want to go to bed yet." Giulia was reckless with mischief. "Will you walk me to the end of the dock, Mr. Cavanagh?"

"With pleasure. Give me five minutes to relieve the watch and check the ship. I suggest you bring a wrap. That breeze is quite cool."

The Countess put in a cautionary word.

"Don't keep her up too long, Mr. Cavanagh. Otherwise she'll be impossible in the morning."

"I have to be up early myself, Countess."

"I know. You have great responsibilities now. Enjoy your walk."

Cavanagh and Giulia followed her on board and then separated briefly while Cavanagh relieved Rodolfo from his deck watch and made his final round of the ship. Everything was quiet in the crew quarters, but when he went into his cabin to pick up his quilted jacket, he found a note on his pillow:

"I heard the serenade. Beautiful! Like two lovebirds in a cage. I'm happy for you; but watch it, buster! Your slip is showing. Sleep well. Lenore."

When he went back on deck he tore the note in pieces, tossed them overboard and watched them flutter away on the night wind. Giulia, wrapped in a cloak, was waiting for him on the afterdeck. She hurried him off the ship, but offered not even a hand's-touch until they were safe in the deep angle of shadow where the seawall butted into the foundations of the harbormaster's watchtower.

Then, without a word spoken, they were in each other's arms, lip to lip, body to body, trying vainly to meld their two selves into one. They drew apart, long enough to look, each at the new other and mutter the first desperate words:

"I want you so much!"

"And I want you!"

Then, they were entwined again, gasping and kneading, devouring each other with kisses until the first fury subsided and Giulia found voice again.

"Not here! Not now! I don't want it like this!"

"It's too dangerous on board."

"Then we'll find another place, another time. I'm not denying you . . . I want you. I love you. You must believe that!"

"I do! I love you too. God knows, I never expected it to hit like this . . ."

"I prayed it would! I dreamed it would. Now it's a mess, a terrible mess!"

Suddenly Giulia was weeping and he was comforting her with lips and hands and small endearments.

"There now! It's a mess, sure; but it's not beyond mending. The great, grand thing is that we have love between us. We can see it, taste it, touch it. There are no secrets now."

"Oh, yes there are, my love—more and darker ones—between Molloy and me, between my father and me."

"What about your aunt?"

"She knows. She wanted this to happen. She doesn't want me to marry Molloy."

"And Galeazzi, your godfather?"

"He sees everything, but says little. He likes you. He

says that openly; but if his masters' interests are threatened, he will act against you."

"So we wait and let others do the worrying. Don't you see? We've been given a holiday. Molloy's away. Galeazzi's leaving. Your father's going to be busy with his girlfriend. I've been commissioned to teach you to dive. We have all the excuses in the world to be together . . ."

"And that's enough for you?"

"That's all we've got until we work out something better."

"Like what?"

"All you have to do is say yes and I'll take you away and marry you."

"I will not come to you like a barefoot gypsy!"

"You can come to me stark naked if you want; just so we hit the road together. Right now I'm a poor man, but one day I swear to you I'll pull the stars out of the sky and pour them like diamonds into your lap!"

"You're crazy, Cavanagh!"

"We're both crazy, my love. So let's do what they do with racehorses. Let's put the blinkers on just so we can't see how rough the competition is!"

"I'm scared—for Lou, for my father, for me."

"I'm scared too—but only for you. I tell you truly, you could do nothing worse in the world than marry Lou Molloy!"

She thrust him away, holding him at arm's length, staring into his eyes, as she challenged him:

"Never, never say that to me again!"

"It's the truth, for God's sake! You don't love him. He's . . ."

She covered his mouth with her hand before he had time to blurt out the rest of it.

"Listen to me, Cavanagh. Please, please listen! Molloy is my betrothed. He asked me to marry him. I accepted. I don't know what it means in your country, but a *fidanzamento*—a betrothal—is a serious matter. I have to deal with that in my own way. You will hurt me and shame yourself if you begin to abuse Molloy to me."

"I saw him shame you tonight. I wanted to kill him! Now he's standing between us and the sun. I won't let him have you. You're mine. I want you."

"Not here! Not now! You're right, my love. We've been given a holiday. Let's begin to enjoy it! Hold me, kiss me! I love you so very much."

A long time later they walked back to the ship, hand in hand, with the sound of the love song soft between them, and their secret written on their faces for all the rough world to read.

He was about early the next morning, rousting the crew to get the decks swabbed, the brightwork polished, the salt dew wiped off the windows, the carpets vacuumed, the interiors dusted. There was no time to talk, the job must be done before the passengers were astir and under their feet. Afterwards, he took Leo up to the bridge, and put him on radio-watch. His instructions were precise and emphatic.

"We're tuned to Portishead and we're on a fifteen-hour watch for communications from or to Molloy. You and I will have to share it. While we're in port we'll keep the public address system switched on. Watch especially for a code transmission in figures and, if you get one, for Christ's sake, make sure you copy it correctly. I'll start training Rodolfo so he can stand helm-watch while we're cruising. We'll have a new visitor on board and we've got an owner-skipper with a lot of problems. I have to be able to depend on you, Leo!"

"You can, I promise. Jackie and I feel terrible about

Hadjidakis. Looking back now, it had to be a setup and we both fell for it."

"Say that again!"

Cavanagh snapped up the phrase instantly. Leo was startled.

"It had to be a setup."

"Explain that!"

"Well, when we first got to the brothel we were having a drink in the bar. There was this big, handsome brute next to us with a couple of English seamen. He wasn't English, though he spoke it a little. He said his name was Benetti and that he was skipper of a Fairmile called the *Jackie Sprat*. We remembered seeing her in Calvi. He told us he'd cruised behind us all the way to Elba. We made him for a smuggler; but he was good company. That's how it all got started—the drinks, the guys, the girls, and Giorgios and Benetti getting hot for each other. They split first. We picked up a couple of good-looking boys and went into their room. It wasn't until we were ready to go back to the ship that we missed Giorgios and went looking for him."

"What about Benetti and his crew?"

"They were long gone—an hour and a half at least, the madam told us. But I'll swear they were the ones. When the *carabinieri* drove us back to the *Salamandra*, we had to pass along the waterfront of Porto Ferraio. There was no sign of the Fairmile. It all adds up, doesn't it?"

"Why didn't you tell me this before?"

"Because you were following your own game plan, remember? We were confined to ship so the *carabinieri* couldn't interview us. You went back with them to look after Hadjidakis. We were ready to tell the whole story to Molloy—except he didn't bother to ask us . . . We guessed he had his own reasons; why should we stick our heads in the lion's mouth?"

"You called it a setup. Why?"

"It's like bad fish: the longer you leave it, the more it smells. Looking back now, it was too pat, too staged. But it doesn't make any sense."

"It does; but it's too long to explain now. It's a political matter. It has to do with the fellow we picked off the beach in Calvi. The C.I.A. is involved. I'm waiting on further instructions from Molloy. Meantime, while we're in port, let's be extra vigilant—and for Christ's sake, be careful about casual contacts and report 'em to me. We've got important passengers on board. Any one of them could be the next target."

"For what?"

"Kidnapping, violence, murder! Anything's possible. Meantime, I want you to stay on the bridge until I relieve you. Get me out charts from here south to Ischia and also for Sardinia and the Lipari Islands. Put markers in the pilot books. And I'm looking to you to pass what I'm telling you to Jackie. Are you hearing me?"

"Loud and clear, skipper! Loud and clear!"

His next meeting was with Galeazzi and Farnese, who were taking their morning coffee on the afterdeck. He sat down with them and announced briskly:

"I need some instructions from you, gentlemen! First, what time does Miss Lambert arrive? Do we need to provide transport?"

"No, thank you. Count Galeazzi's chauffeur is driving her up from Rome. He'll bring her directly to the ship. Galeazzi and I will be spending the morning at the port site on the other side of the promontory. We'll be back before noon."

"I shan't be with you for lunch," said Galeazzi. "I'll leave as soon as my car gets here. I have two other calls to make down the coast."

"I understand the Countess also will be receiving guests on board?"

"There will be two for lunch." It was Farnese who answered. "I should not think they will be here before two in the afternoon. Does that create a problem for the chef?"

"Not at all, sir. Will the guests be staying on board?"

"No. They're on their way north to Milan."

"Which brings me to a matter I feel bound to discuss with you both."

The two men were instantly alert. Farnese asked quietly:

"What sort of matter, Mr. Cavanagh?"

Cavanagh spelled out the information he had just received from Leo and his own immediate need of help.

"If either of you gentlemen has any information or advice on this matter, I beg you to let me have it now."

Farnese shot a quick glance at Galeazzi and then fumbled with a long-winded answer:

"I'm not at all sure that we have anything to tell you, Mr. Cavanagh, or if we did, whether we would have the right to disclose such sensitive information."

"Then let me enlighten you, sir!" Cavanagh was in nowise prepared for a fencing match. "In the absence of Mr. Molloy, I am the master of this vessel. I am responsible for the safety and well-being of all who sail in her. If there is a threat to that safety and well-being, it is your plain duty to disclose it to me!"

"Mr. Cavanagh is right, Alessandro." Galeazzi was judicious as a confessor. "Even before he assumed this acting command, he was involved in the Tolvier affair in Calvi. He has now a duty to inform himself on all its possible consequences."

"You tell him then, Enrico!"

"Very well. Molloy, Farnese, and I hold differing opinions about the attack on Mr. Hadjidakis. We are not surprised by your seaman's report that it was a setup, an entrapment. We are all agreed that it was.

The question is who set the trap. Farnese here and Molloy, possibly influenced by the climate of American and Vatican opinion, believe it was an act of reprisal, initiated by the Marxists. A wanted man, a war criminal, had been bought out from under their noses. They were underlining the fact that there is still a political price to be paid."

"But you don't believe that, sir?"

"No, I don't. From the very moment we were in Calvi I believed that reprisals would follow; but I told Alessandro that day, and I have repeated it many times since, that this is a purely French affair—French and Corsican, if you want to be quite specific. Who knows how many of his victims—men and women—have sworn vengeance against Tolvier? I believe that the men who attacked Hadjidakis had come to Corsica looking for Tolvier. They could well have had an inside tip. French intelligence is as full of leaks as a colander. The Vatican itself is a snake pit of conflicting interests. It is too convenient to do what the Americans are doing and dump every crime on the doorstep of the Marxists. Togliatti and the Italian Communist Party don't work that way. He's too shrewd, too practiced. Already he controls most of the municipalities from Florence to Turin. He runs them very efficiently on a law and order ticket. Too often it is the Right who foment violence. I do not see an Italian hand in the Hadjidakis affair."

"But either way, sir, you see the act as a reprisal for the escape of Tolvier."

"Yes."

"So, my next question. Are more reprisals likely?"

"Again," said Galeazzi quietly, "we all say they're possible. The attack on Hadjidakis was a calculated brutality. It was meant to inspire terror. Farnese believes further acts are unlikely. Molloy is reserving judgment until he's consulted with the C.I.A."

"Which is exactly the point at which I am bound to enter, gentlemen. In order to minimize the threat which we all agree exists, in order to scatter whatever forces may be disposed against us, I suggest we start our cruise tonight. I'll plot us an itinerary that will keep everybody entertained and well out of harm's way, until Mr. Molloy is back in command on the *Salamandra d'Oro*. The last thing we want to do is hang around resort areas like this one . . . However, Prince Farnese must speak for his family and his own guest."

"Let me ask you a question then," said Farnese. "Who, on board, is the person most vulnerable to any further reprisals?"

"Without doubt, your daughter."

"Why?"

"Because she is the point at which all your interests coincide—yours, Count Galeazzi's, Molloy's."

"It makes sense," said Galeazzi. "Sense enough to accept Mr. Cavanagh's advice. You and I can try to speak with Molloy this morning, by telephone. If we miss him, I'll contact him as soon as I get to Rome. Essentially nothing has changed except the balance of our personal opinions. My advice would be to enjoy your holiday but perhaps expedite the other arrangements; Molloy's investiture, the wedding . . ."

"I agree. I'll talk to Giulia and Lucietta today. I expect less trouble from them than from Molloy, who has certain grandiose ideas about the ceremonies. Meantime, I'm happy to accept your suggestions, Mr. Cavanagh. We'll put to sea this evening, after Lucietta's guests have gone."

"Thank you, sir. I'll discuss the itinerary with you later."

As he stood up to take his leave, Farnese stayed him with a gesture.

"If my daughter wants to go ashore, will you be

good enough to ensure that she is always accompanied by a member of the crew?"

"She will be going ashore, sir, to buy a wetsuit and diving gear. I myself will be going with her."

"Then I'm sure I can count on your care of her."

"Yes sir, you can. Is there anything else?"

"Thank you, no."

"Until later then, gentlemen!"

He was perhaps four paces away when he caught the tag-end of a remark by Farnese:

". . . He's always so certain of himself . . ."

To which Galeazzi added a rider of his own.

"The arrogance of youth, the raw confidence of the new world! Be patient with him—and pray that Molloy returns quickly."

He did not hear Farnese's mumbled reply. He was moving in a daze, a man who had just read the warrant for his own damnation.

The purchase of Giulia's wet suit and diving gear was a long-drawn-out ceremony, performed under the critical eye of the Countess. By the time it was over, Cavanagh was dry-mouthed, short-tempered and convinced that he was being made to pay in blood for his evening's escapade. While the salesgirl was writing the bill and Giulia was counting out lire in large denominations, he made his escape and hurried back to the ship, forgetful of his promise to guard Giulia against all harm and villainy. Fortunately, Farnese and Galeazzi were already on their way to the port site, so his only critic was Lenore Pritchard, who came to join him on the afterdeck as he stood watching for Giulia and her aunt to come out of the store. Lenore had a house-keeping problem.

"A full change of bed linen and towels. At the local laundry they tell me they can't have them dried and ironed before midnight. You tell me we're sailing straight after dinner. What am I supposed to do? Save the stuff for a week? Beat it on the stones myself?"

"We'll wait for the laundry, love. It's no big deal!"

"Will you help me carry it ashore then?"

"Where the hell's Rodolfo?"

"In the engine room. Where else?"

"Get him to do it . . . Better still, you call him. I'll explain what you want done. Does that make you feel happier?"

"You're a bastard, Cavanagh! Don't go away, I'll find Rodolfo; then I want to talk to you."

"I'm not going anywhere."

"I know. You've just been! And you're bored out of your mind shopping with the two noble ladies. I read you like a book, Cavanagh! . . ."

He waited while she fetched Rodolfo and sent him staggering down the gangway with bundles of sheets and towels, then she rounded on Cavanagh again. This time, however, she was much more subdued.

"You got my note last night?"

"I did."

"I wasn't begging and I wasn't bitching."

"I know that."

"But you are the talk of the ship—fore and aft."

"I know that, too."

"You're babes in the wood, the pair of you! Do you have any idea how many enterprises are being built on this marriage, how much money is invested in it?"

"I can only guess."

"Then double your guess and double it again! . . . Molloy talked to me about it in bed, so I have half an idea at least. Ask yourself whether anyone's going to let you ride in like bloody Lancelot and snatch the reluctant bride from the altar steps? They'll kill you first, Cavanagh! They'll tie you in a sack with stones and dump you in a thousand fathoms of water . . . Look up there! What do they call that mountain?"

"Monte Argentario. Why do you ask?"

"Because Farnese was telling me about it while I was making up the cabins. In the last days of the war those woods were a guerilla hideout, from which the partisans would swoop down, ambush the coastal road, kill a bunch of Fascists and Germans and then head back into the bush. Those were bloody times; but here and now, we're not so far away from them."

"What are you trying to tell me?"

"Back off! Go into reverse! Disengage!"

"And what do I tell Giulia?"

"That your conscience is bothering you. You're betraying a trust, coveting your neighbor's wife-to-be. She's a good Roman Catholic. She'll understand all that. Use me if you want. You've done me wrong."

"The hell I have!"

"I know you haven't. It's just a 'for instance,' if you want out."

"I don't."

"Then watch your back, Cavanagh! And may God have mercy on your simple soul!"

The next moment she was gone, hurrying through the saloon and down to the guest quarters. Cavanagh stood leaning on the rail, watching the shop-front until Giulia and the Countess appeared, followed by a small boy staggering under a mountain of packages.

Before he left the ship, Galeazzi asked Cavanagh to come to his cabin. He handed him four envelopes and explained their contents.

". . . Letters of introduction to persons of significance in Paris, London, Rome and New York, who may help you to further your ambitions in the law. Present them at your own convenience."

Cavanagh was touched, but troubled. His facile eloquence deserted him. He stammered his thanks.

"I don't know what to say. I'm—I'm deeply grateful, but . . . but . . ."

"But you feel a certain guilt, yes?"

"Guilt?" He repeated the word curtly. "No sir! Hesitation, yes. You and I are, in a certain matter, adversaries."

Galeazzi smiled and bent to strap his suitcase. He asked amiably, "But is that not the whole nature of the law? Today you prosecute. Tomorrow you defend. That should not be a bar to personal friendship or professional respect. You have been open with me. I shall be clear with you. I wish with all my heart that Giulia could make a life with you or someone like you. I know it will not happen. I do not grudge either of you one moment of whatever happiness you may find in each other. I pray that my godchild may be spared too much grief. But be sure, my friend, the grief will come to both of you."

Cavanagh acknowledged his goodwill with an embarrassed smile and a timeworn tag:

"We who are about to die, salute you!"

Galeazzi was not amused.

"It's a poor joke, Cavanagh! The omens are bad enough already." He fished in his pocket and brought out a fifth envelope, which he offered to Cavanagh. "A small something for yourself and for the crew."

Cavanagh declined the gift.

"Thank you, sir, but no! We are not permitted to accept gratuities. Mr. Molloy takes good care of us. We are honored to serve his guests."

Galeazzi put the envelope back in his pocket and said with mild surprise, "You protect the man's honor as a host; but you have no hesitation about stealing his woman!"

"Correction, sir! She is promised. She is not yet Molloy's woman."

Galeazzi stared at him in astonishment. "You're a

phenomenon, Cavanagh! A Mediterranean absolutist born far south of the equator . . . No! Don't be angry! I'm paying you a compliment. Believe it or not, I wish you luck!"

"Thank you. I wish you a good journey, sir. Let me take your bags."

On deck, he handed the baggage to Jackie and consigned Galeazzi into the care of the Farnese for the final rituals of farewell. This piece of stage-management made Cavanagh responsible for five minutes of small talk with Miss Aurora Lambert, star of West End theater and the J. Arthur Rank film organization. It was a strictly unmemorable interlude. Miss Lambert was overawed by the ambient nobility and was, in consequence, overplaying her role. Her voice was pitched half a tone too high. Her gestures were too broad, her poses too studied. She was so eager to impress that she babbled, and the babble became an unstoppable torrent of words. Cavanagh listened in a kind of hypnotic gaze, admiring the physical beauty of the woman, wondering how long her peaches-and-cream complexion would survive the wind and sun of a Mediterranean summer and how long Farnese would endure the endless inanities of backstage gossip and soundstage trivia.

He was soon answered. The moment Farnese returned, Miss Aurora Lambert was transformed into a girlish lover, leaning for support upon his noble bosom, sighing out her love in short bursts of well-rehearsed Italian phrases, in which Farnese himself had obviously coached her. He threw a protective arm around her shoulders and led her below decks. The Countess gave a long sigh of exasperation.

"My God! How that woman prattles! Luchino will carve her up and eat her for lunch!"

"On the contrary," Giulia had other ideas. "He'll drown her in charm, then have her begging for a part in his next production. That's when the torture will begin. How Tennessee Williams will behave is another matter altogether . . . I'm sorry, Cavanagh. Now we're prattling! We're talking about Aunt Lucietta's luncheon guests. Luchino Visconti and Tennessee Williams. You're familiar with their work, of course."

"With Visconti's hardly at all. He is not well known in Australia. Tennessee Williams, of course. I saw *The Glass Menagerie* and *Streetcar*."

"Visconti has directed both for Italian theater. His own latest film, the one he finished last year, is *Bellissima*. It stars Anna Magnani . . . That should give you a start for lunchtime conversation."

"We expect you there, of course," said the Contessa hastily.

"You must forgive me, Contessa," Cavanagh was quite firm on the matter. "I'll be happy to join you for a pre-luncheon cocktail; but I beg you to excuse me from the meal."

"For God's sake, why?" Giulia's protest was sharp.

"Because I think it's neither proper nor opportune to intrude myself into a family gathering at this moment."

"Is that the only reason?"

"No. There is one other. Because of what happened to Hadjidakis, because of the absence of Mr. Molloy, the crew are uneasy and off balance. I need to be with them. I'm sure you understand."

"Of course, but you don't have to sound so formal about it."

"On the contrary, my dear," said the Countess tartly. "That's exactly how he must sound unless you want your father running mad with a carving knife. When are we leaving Porto Santo Stefano, Mr. Cavanagh?"

"Tonight, at midnight, Contessa. The Prince suggests we make an overnight run to Sardinia. He tells me the country is beautiful and unspoiled and is now, mercifully, free of malaria. He also wants to look at some of the areas where new developments are proposed: Porto Cervo, Romazzino and Golfo d'Aranci."

"And you've heard nothing yet from Lou?" The question came from Giulia.

"I wouldn't expect it today. In fact I doubt he has yet arrived in Naples. We're keeping radio watch from six in the morning until nine each evening. That was the arrangement he requested. I'll let you know the moment his call comes through; but just remember, lots of other people on other ships will hear your conversation . . ."

"That's embarrassing."

"It can be, yes. By the way, I've told Chef to serve lunch in the saloon. It's air-conditioned. You won't have passersby gawking at you or *paparazzi* shooting pictures from the dock."

"You're very thoughtful, Mr. Cavanagh." This from the Countess.

"I think he's a clown," Giulia teased him. "Always in costume, always with a big painted smile."

"It's the role to which he's condemned." Cavanagh put on a face of mock mourning. "Court jester in love with the beautiful princess. He can't possess her until he sheds the grease paint and is recognized as a courtier in his own right."

The Countess laid a cool hand on his wrist and gave him a quiet warning.

"Don't be in too much of a hurry, Cavanagh. The follies of a jester are easily forgiven. A courtier who makes a fool of himself may well lose his head."

"All the more reason to skip luncheon, wouldn't you say? Excuse me, ladies."

In spite of all his special pleading he found himself, two minutes later, cornered and bidden to the meal by

Farnese himself, whose rank was much higher and whose reasons were far more cogent than his own.

". . . There will be much talk in Italian. Luchino and Lucietta will dominate it. Miss Lambert will feel put upon unless she has someone to keep her in touch with the dialogue or distract her from it! Mr. Tennessee Williams is a unknown quantity to me. He is rich, successful and notably disinterested in women. Rumor has it that Luchino is so fascinated with his work—and with the man himself—that he has even begun to imitate his dress and style . . . A word of warning, however. Luchino is trying to get financing for a new film, but because he's a member of the Communist Party and writes for *L'Unità*, Papa Pacelli and the Christian Democrats don't like him and place all sorts of obstacles in his way. I don't much like him either; but I do respect him. He has great talent and during the war displayed much courage as a member of the underground. Lucietta has promised him that I'll try to tap Molloy for some investment funds. I will try, of course, but not very hard—just enough so that the Visconti and the Farnese do not become enemies. However, the point I am making is that this part of our conversation should *not* be translated to Miss Lambert. She, too, is looking for a patron to finance a new play for her and I am most definitely not interested in that method of losing money. So, when the subject is discussed, do your best to divert her attention to other subjects."

"Do you have any suggestions, sir?"

"Miss Lambert has three abiding interests: herself, sex and money. The first quickly becomes boring. In the second, she is full of agreeable surprises, and for the third, her demands are interminable. You must know, Cavanagh, that every day we are at sea I am saving money, and the scenery in Sardinia costs a lot less than the jewelry in the Via Condotti!"

"What can I say?" Cavanagh spread his hands in a gesture of resignation. "I make no promises. I'll do my best. It's all part of the service on the *Salamandra d'Oro*!"

"So far," said Farnese, "the service is holding up very well. It's understated, discreet, but very efficient."

"Thank you, sir. I'll pass that on to the crew."

"The compliment was intended for you also, Mr. Cavanagh. I am aware that your discretion has been sorely tested by recent events . . . By the way, it is possible that the date of Giulia's marriage may be brought forward. I am anxious therefore that she should enjoy what is left of her holiday. Sardinia, for example, will be a splendid place to begin her diving lessons. The waters are clean, the sea-growth and the fish abundant. There are interesting underwater sites where Phoenician and Roman pottery have been found . . . I'll mark some of them on the chart for you . . ."

"That would be a great help, thank you."

"One small matter: Miss Lambert will be coming ashore with me to look at development sites. You and Giulia will have to look after Lucietta . . . Make a picnic of your diving excursions. It would be quite unfair to leave her moping about on board."

"Be sure we'll look after her. If she wished, I could teach her to dive, too. There's no real age limit."

Farnese laughed boisterously.

"I doubt you need go that far, Cavanagh; but I'm sure she'd appreciate the offer, just as I do. I have to confess, my dear fellow, that you continue to surprise me. I told you once, you had a lot to learn; I was not prepared for your quite charming simplicity and directness."

With singular effort Cavanagh managed a shrug and a rather lopsided grin.

"It comes and it goes. As it says in the Bible: 'Be wise as serpents and simple as doves.' With the Irish what you get depends on the weather."

"Which, at the moment and in the absence of Molloy, is mercifully calm."

"And may God give us the wit to enjoy it," Cavanagh quoted from some buried folk-memory.

"Amen to that," said Farnese fervently. "My father used to say that we surrender our youth to purchase wisdom. What he never told me was how badly we get cheated on the exchange rate!"

The strategy of the luncheon table had been set by the Countess. Farnese sat at the head with Visconti on his right and Lucietta on his left. Next to Lucietta was Tennessee Williams, raffishly elegant in a seersucker suit, hollow-eyed and pale. Opposite him sat Giulia, with Cavanagh on her right, facing Aurora Lambert. The effect of the arrangement was to support Aurora Lambert with two English speakers, and to give Visconti an attentive and understanding audience of his own. Most importantly from Cavanagh's point of view, it enabled him to engage with Giulia in a surreptitious tactile dialogue under the shelter of the tablecloth.

The table talk was lively and passionate, Visconti railing against "*i puritani*" and "*i papalini*" of the Christian Democratic Party, who were reviving all the old machinery of censorship. Mario Scelba, Minister for the Interior, had refused visas for Bertolt Brecht and the Berliner Ensemble. Even his friend de Sica was sliding into fantasy and sentimentality in his choice of material . . . "The Americans, notably my friend at this table, are the only ones getting it right . . . They have the courage to renounce the bourgeois certainties for the doubts, the fears, the agonies of those who live always on the dangerous outer edges of existence."

"As we do ourselves, let's face it." Williams was swiftly touched by liquor and emotion. "They call Rome the Holy City—that's defined by Concordat, mind you!—but when you peel off the cellophane and wave away the incense, it's such a mess of worms that it frightens even me . . . If Luchino were not here, I doubt I'd want to stay."

"And tell me, Luchino," the Countess had her own lines of inquiry, "how is la Magnani behaving herself?"

"As always!" Visconti's expression was more eloquent even than his words. "A little crazy, but God, what talent! It pours out of her like lava from Etna—then when the flow stops she is morbid and unhappy until the energy builds up again. Ask again our Tenn, here, our genius of the outer edges; he spends much time with her."

". . . But such time! Every conversation is a play in itself. Then she hauls me off to the Colosseum to feed the stray cats—hundreds of them, ghostly in the moonlight, and she's like a ghost herself—a heroic figure from another age, doomed to endure this one!"

Miss Aurora Lambert was awed by the talk, but could find no entrance into it for herself, while Farnese was seated too far away to offer any help at all. Then as the meal went on and the wine flowed, both Visconti and Williams became aware of Leo and Jackie, who were serving them with theatrical grace. The stock questions followed: where had they come from, what were they doing on board, what were their prospects after the summer? Their answers were so voluble and their body language so eloquent that Cavanagh felt obliged to intervene with a good-humored caution:

". . . I can give them the highest recommendations, gentlemen; but for the present they're contracted to the owner, Mr. Lou Molloy, who I'm sure would press his prior claims to their services. However, I know they'll be happy to give you the address of their agent before you leave . . ."

For the first time during the meal, Visconti gave formal recognition to Cavanagh's presence at the table. He asked, with a mildly patronizing air:

"And where did you learn your Italian, Mr. Cavanagh?"

"Where I got the rest of my learning. At home in Australia. My teacher was an old man who had been a friend of Pirandello—had traveled with him on his world tour in the early twenties . . ."

"And how, may I ask, have you landed here in Porto Santo Stefano?"

"The luck of the Irish. There I was, standing on the dock in Antibes when Mr. Molloy came sailing into harbor. I begged him for a job and after a certain amount of palaver he gave it to me."

"Ireland is still Ultima Thule to me, I'm afraid. I've never been there; though I have bought horses from Dublin."

"Which is about the riskiest occupation you have engaged in! I hope what you bought held up to your hopes."

"Some of it, Mr. Cavanagh, only some of it. And where do your own ambitions lead you?"

"None of them, at this moment, points me past this summer. This is the year of my Grand Tour."

To which Giulia added her own provocative postscript.

"Don't take him too lightly, Luchino. He was a naval officer during the war. He has a degree in law, and a long list of other accomplishments—including a very good voice."

Whereupon the teasing began, the quiet, poisonous

bitchery of the seasoned professionals. Williams suggested:

"Luchino's doing *La Locandiera* in Venice this year. You should audition for him. Even as an understudy it would be a marvelous experience."

"I'm sure it would be, Mr. Williams—and a privilege to work with the great man himself . . . but I'm strictly a bathroom baritone."

"Not without skills in Irish balladry," said the Countess.

"And a quick study in Neapolitan," said Farnese.

"*Qualis artifex pereo*," Cavanagh declaimed the old tag. "What an artist perishes in me! Sorry I'm not available, but Miss Lambert there has a very long list of triumphs in theater and films, which I'm sure Prince Farnese could recite for you at length."

"It's the least you can do, Papa!" Giulia picked up the cue swiftly. "Miss Lambert has been singularly modest and reticent so far."

Cavanagh and Giulia exchanged caresses under the table while they watched Farnese walk himself into a series of honey-traps: a recital of Aurora Lambert's many but modest accomplishments, the ever-present problem of angel money for new productions and a final snare set and baited by the Countess herself when she announced blandly:

". . . Of course Alessandro may not agree with me, but I believe that Lou Molloy is exactly the kind of person Luchino should have as a major investor."

"I am, of course, happy to put the idea to him, Lucietta; but there are, as you know, certain political problems . . ."

"The fact that he leans further to the right than Andreotti and Scelba, or even Papa Pio?"

"Of course!"

"But don't you see, Alessandro, that's the whole virtue of my suggestion. As an American, Lou Molloy subscribes to a constitution which guarantees free speech. Freedom of the press is the cornerstone of American democracy, which they're trying their damndest to sell in Europe and Asia. Think about it, Alessandro! It's such a beautiful paradox, it just might work."

"I most certainly shall think about it, Lucietta. I promise I'll discuss it with Molloy. However, I cannot make any commitment on his behalf."

"On the other hand, my love"—Aurora Lambert was suddenly a presence in the argument—"maybe you could persuade this Mr. Molloy to invest in a London or even a New York vehicle for me. That would be strictly unpolitical, wouldn't it? Perhaps Mr. Williams would agree to write it and the great Visconti to direct it!"

In the sudden silence that followed, Cavanagh gave Giulia a furtive pat on the thigh and then made a more or less graceful exit.

"You must excuse me, ladies and gentlemen. I'm due on radio-watch. This is just about the time one might expect Mr. Molloy to call. Happy to have had you aboard, gentlemen. With your permission, ladies . . ."

Before he had stepped out the door, the conversation had begun again and with it, the slow incineration of Miss Aurora Lambert by two very practiced destructors. Farnese, in his own interest, would have to shield her from the worst of it, but Cavanagh asked himself what kind of a job these sophisticated folk could do on him if they really set their minds to it.

That question extended itself into an infinity of others, like ripples spreading across a dark pool. Was he truly in love with Giulia Farnese? Was she in love with him? Or were they both pretenders: he, in the vulgarest sense, to sexual conquest of a reigning beauty;

she to the exaction of every last tittle of interest from the bargain she had made with her father, for premarital amusement and post-marital liberty, the latter of which would provide a convenient plea for annulment if the marriage collapsed and a case were presented to the Holy Roman Rota.

Among the Catholic aristocracy of Europe such legal devices were well known and widely practiced. From early times the Roman Church had secured a monopoly on marriage. It had outlawed divorce and created its own fictions of legal annulment, administered by its own courts. However, in spite of all protestations to the contrary, marital rearrangements were much more available to the rich and knowing than to the poor and ignorant.

Halt there! Reject such cynicisms out of hand! Accept that Giulia Farnese and Bryan de Courcy Cavanagh are truly in love, that given an hour of privacy, they will become lovers in body and soul. Then Cavanagh, the brash suitor from the end of the world, the scholar-gypsy makes his proposal: "Pack a knapsack. Let's make a run for it. I'll marry you as soon as we can find a minister to make it legal. Then we'll go wandering together. I can fend for both of us. When you're tired of traveling and you feel like making a baby, I can start my career . . . That's not so hard, is it?" Well, maybe it is a mite harder if you're Giulia Farnese, with all that history weighing you down like a jeweled cope and a father who's trading you off to restore his fortunes, and a godfather in the Papal Court and noble cousins, in various degrees, scattered like dandelions all over Europe.

And then there's Lou Molloy. We haven't talked much about him, have we? Strange that, because he's your *fidanzato*: the accepted candidate for your marriage-bed and I'm a junior officer running his ship, responsible for the well-being of his crew and his guests. I'm also in possession of a whole catalogue of unpleasant facts about him—which I'm still too proud to reveal—but, by God, I could be tempted if the game got too rough. Which reminds me, my beautiful Giulia, that you have been singularly reticent about Molloy and your own feelings towards him. Of course I understand that there's an honor in your silence, just as I claim there is in mine; but I'm getting jealous now. I want to know what attraction he has for you. You've admitted that it exists. I want to know what secret roots the man has thrust down into your soul, how friendly is the soil, how deep the tendrils may go when they are nourished by money and power and—let's have it out in the open—the stimulants of long and exotic sexual experience?

Then came the final question: When would the issue be resolved? In his own mind there was no doubt at all. There would be no better time than this voyage to Sardinia, the wild island, with Molloy absent, Farnese occupied with his actress and his land deals and the Countess, for the moment at least, a declared collaborator. So be it then! Time, place and circumstance were all favorable. When they weighed anchor at midnight the final gambits of the love-game would begin.

When he came to the bridge he found another game in progress. The radio, tuned to Portishead, was chattering out an interminable list of mechanical supplies for an oil rig in the Persian Gulf. Lenore Pritchard, who was sitting watch during the luncheon service, was bent over the chart table with Rodolfo beside her. She had drawn a series of crude sketches: a cottage, a girl, a boy, and a few animals. She was teaching Rodolfo to put English names to them in print and in sound. When she saw Cavanagh, she blushed like a schoolgirl and held up a warning hand.

"Not a word out of you, mister! Not a sparrow's

chirp. He's a good boy and he wants to learn English. I'm teaching him . . . Clear?"

Cavanagh, caught flatfooted, fumbled his return.

"I haven't said a word! It's a good idea! It helps! Thank you . . . Now tell me where we're at with radio traffic?"

"Shopping lists, most of it: construction sites, ship movements, cargo manifests, personal messages to or from crew—births, deaths, marriages, divorces even! . . . Nothing for us so far . . . How was your lunch?"

"What you might expect: show-talk, in-group gossip and scandal . . . Fortunately I had an excuse to leave."

"How would you like it as a steady diet?"

"Meaning?"

"It's written all over your freckled face. You're head over heels and gone for Giulia Farnese. You're racking your brains for ways to get her: abduction, elopement, ritual rape like they have in Sicily . . . I wish you the best of British luck!"

"Thank you, and the same to you, Miss Pritchard. You're both relieved. You might introduce Rodolfo to the galley and teach him how to wash dishes . . ."

"Isn't that just a tiny bit waspish, Mr. Cavanagh? Just because you're feeling put out, you shouldn't take it out on the rest of us."

"You're right. I shouldn't. I apologize, but Rodolfo's rostered for pot-scouring anyway." To Rodolfo he said in Italian: "Keep up the lessons! Miss Pritchard is a very good teacher. You are privileged to have her interest."

"I know it, sir." A hint of a smile showed on his handsome young face. "I am very privileged indeed. I should sign off the log now?"

"Yes, please."

"Do I write anything?"

"Yes. 'No messages received during watch.' Then you sign it." His handwriting was a traditional Italian cursive, beautifully and fluently executed. Cavanagh wondered how much it had cost him in tears and rapped knuckles to learn this dying art of calligraphy. He said to Lenore Pritchard:

"You're right. He's worth teaching."

She gave him a swift, suspicious glance and then relaxed.

"So, no jokes, no nasties, promise?"

"I promise. I didn't mean to be unpleasant. That luncheon party threw me."

"Let's hope it taught you something."

"Like what?"

She picked up the sheet of drawings and held it up for his inspection. She pointed to the male figure and parodied her own role as teacher:

"This is the head. This is the heart. These here are the cock and the balls. The head is for thinking. The heart is for feeling. The others are for screwing, as you damn well know. But if you're set on having a noble affair, never, never let your heart or your balls run away with your head . . . How do I know? I've traveled a lot further and a lot longer than you, Cavanagh—and first class is where you meet the monsters . . . Come, Rodolfo. Let's you and me go scour the cookpots!"

Twenty minutes later, while he was working through the pilot-book for the Straits of Bonifacio and the ports and havens of northern Sardinia, Portishead radio gave out the call sign of the ship: M.U.H.Y.

". . . *Mike Uniform Hotel Yankee* . . . This is Portishead calling *Mike Uniform Hotel Yankee*. Do you read me?"

Instantly Cavanagh turned up the volume and began transmitting.

"This is *Mike Uniform Hotel Yankee*. I read you loud and clear. *Mike Uniform Hotel Yankee* standing by."

A moment later Lou Molloy was on the air. His voice was flat, toneless.

"This is Molloy."

"Cavanagh here, sir."

"Listen carefully. No questions or comments until I've finished. I'm not sure I can get through this without cracking up. Giorgios Hadjidakis died two hours ago. It's a mercy he was taken. If he'd lived, he would have been a vegetable . . . I'm flying his body back to the States as soon as I can arrange it and I'll be attending the funeral with his wife and children." His voice cracked and he fought to get his emotions under control again. "Galeazzi has told me about the arrangements for your cruise. I approve them. I'll meet you in Ischia harbour ten days from now. Until then I'll be out of contact. See that Giorgios's things are crated, ready for dispatch to his family . . . I'm told by the C.I.A. that the risk situation for the rest of us still exists. So all present precautions remain in force. In the right-hand locker in my cabin you'll find the ship's firearms. I want you to carry a handgun at all times, and if you're swimming in lonely places, have a man on watch with the rifle. Jackie's a good shot. That's all. Now you can talk."

"I'm grieved for you, Mr. Molloy, as everyone else will be."

"Pray for Giorgios. Pray for me. That's all anyone can do now."

"Would you like to speak to Princess Giulia or to her father?"

"No. You tell 'em what's happened. Explain that I'm in no shape for talk. Give Giulia my love. Tell her this is not her grieving. I don't want to inflict it on her, because I want us both to make a new start. Will you do that for me?"

"I'll try. Any message for the Prince?"

"Just tell him to expedite all the Roman arrangements. He'll understand. How are things on board?"

"All's well, sir. We'll look forward to seeing you again in Ischia. Would you like me to have a Mass said for Giorgios?"

"I've already arranged it." Molloy was beginning to break up. "Giorgios always said he wanted to be prayed out by the Orthodox and not by the Romans. The Mass will be celebrated in his own parish. I'll be there. But thanks for the thought . . ." He was in tears now. "Sorry! This is all I can take, Cavanagh! Over and out!"

Which left Cavanagh standing speechless, with the microphone in his hand while Portishead called in a freighter to pick up a miscellaneous cargo from Tunis: dates, camel hides and barrels of local wine for blending in Europe. The guests were on the afterdeck now, chatting over their coffee, the talk attenuating itself to small, shrill bursts and lengthening silences.

For Cavanagh, the presence of strangers on board created an immediate problem. He could not announce a death on the tail end of a luncheon party. He could not risk a tale of recent murder and present danger in the company of fashionable gossips. Least of all could he pass Malloy's private message to Giulia and explain it to her in terms that would leave him some shred of honor to wrap around his shabby self.

For the moment the bridge was his refuge, the chattering radio was his camouflage. He resumed his study of the pilot book and then set down his predeparture checklist: the fuel and water tanks had been topped up, Chef had bought supplies of fresh fruit and vegetables. If it were not for the late delivery of the ship's laundry, he could cast off and be out of Santo Stefano before sunset. For everyone, seafarer or landlubber, that single act of detachment was a rebirth from the womb of the past into a new, mysterious future full of perils and promises. The sudden discontinuity could be confusing or consoling, healing or destructive. The outcome depended in large part upon the voyagers themselves, but much also upon the skipper under God, the reader of skies and winds and tides and charts, who must also have some skill in the reading of minds and hearts.

Did he, Cavanagh, have such skills? Could he cut through his own confusions to provide a light for his shipmates and the guests—not to mention his love, Giulia Farnese. The sea had its own ghosts. Seafarers had their own superstitions. Death, for them, always wore a face different from that which they presented to land-bound folk. So the first decision had to be made: How should he announce the death of Giorgios Hadjidakis?

Luchino Visconti and Tennessee Williams left the ship at four-thirty. As the Farnese family came back on board, Cavanagh made an announcement over the P.A. system.

"This is Cavanagh speaking. Would all guests and all crew members please come immediately to the saloon? . . . All crew members, all guests to the saloon, please!"

When they were assembled, curious and uneasy, he made a formal announcement.

"I regret to tell you all that our first officer, Mr. Giorgios Hadjidakis, died today in the U.S. hospital in Naples. This news was passed to me about an hour ago by Mr. Lou Molloy, who was so deeply distressed that he was just able to sustain the short conversation. I offered him condolences from you all. He gave me the following directions. He wishes us to continue our cruise. He will accompany the body back to the United States, attend the funeral with the Hadjidakis family and meet us in Ischia ten days from now. Meantime, U.S. Intelligence has told him that our passengers and personnel are still under threat, so this cruise is very timely. Ship's crew will be further instructed on the voyage. I now have private messages for the Farnese family, but before you go I'd like you to join me in a short prayer for our shipmate, Giorgios Hadjidakis."

Dredged up from memory, the archaic words had a strange, moving quality:

". . . Lord, enter not into judgment with your servant Giorgios Hadjidakis, our brother and our friend. Keep him always in the light of your countenance and bestow your consolations on those whom he has left, his wife, his children, his friend Lou Molloy, and on us his shipmates. Eternal rest give unto him, O Lord, and let perpetual light shine upon him. May he rest in peace."

The last amen rippled around the small assembly. Giulia and Lenore Pritchard were weeping. The Countess and Miss Lambert sat stony-faced. Farnese gave a nod of approval. Cavanagh added a small postscript:

"Jackie, we'll fly the flags at half-staff until sunset. I'm sure you'd all like us to get under way early. So let's make shipshape and see if the laundry can be ready any earlier. Crew are dismissed. Thank you all."

When the crew had filed out, Cavanagh offered an explanation:

". . . I regret springing the news on you like that; but I couldn't go whispering it about while your guests were still here."

Giulia came instantly to the attack.

"But you could have called Father and me to the bridge and let us speak with Lou! How could you be so thoughtless, so, so presumptuous."

"I was neither thoughtless nor presumptuous,

Principessa." Cavanagh was very calm with her. "I asked Mr. Molloy whether he would like me to fetch you and your father. He said—and I quote his own words: 'Tell them what's happened. Explain that I'm in no shape to talk. Give Giulia my love. Tell her this is not her grieving. I don't want to inflict it on her, because I want us both to make a new start.' I asked was there any message for the Prince. He said: 'Tell him to expedite all the Roman arrangements. He'll understand.' "

"It seems you have a very good verbal memory." The Countess's voice was dry as pebbles rattling in a gourd.

"It's my training, madam. Sometimes people's lives depend on an accurate rendition of orders. I am not called upon to defend Mr. Molloy; but I do have to tell you all that he was deeply moved, that he spoke with great effort and dissolved into tears at the end of the conversation. He did, however, inform me that U.S. Intelligence considers that we are still at risk and—even on this trip—we must take adequate precautions. That's all I have to tell you—except for a personal explanation. If my handling of this news has upset or angered you, I apologize. It was not my intention to do so. A ship is a very small society and the relationships between crew members are often very complicated. The passengers are better served if the crew's feelings are respected. Now, if you'll excuse me . . ."

"Mr. Cavanagh!" Farnese's voice stopped him halfway to the exit.

"Sir?"

"Be assured we are offering you our thanks—not our reproaches."

"I'm glad to hear that, sir. The last thing we need at this moment is contention or misunderstanding . . . Oh, by the way, Chef will be serving a light supper this evening, but if there are any special requests, he'll be happy to take care of them . . ."

Then he left them, to comfort the small huddle of people around the galley, where Chef was dispensing a medicinal dose of cognac and coffee. Chef himself was the most shaken. His hands were unsteady, his speech rambling and incredulous:

". . . A man like that, so tough, so knowing, kicked to death in a whorehouse, while his shipmates are two rooms away . . . It makes no sense! There will be a big black hole in Molloy's life from now on—in mine too, for that matter! Giorgios was a real Ulysses, straight out of Homer! To have him end like this is intolerable." He whipped off his cap and apron and flung them across the galley. "I'm not working anymore today. I am in mourning. I'm going to pour libations to the old Gods and then get drunk . . . !"

The others stood silent, waiting for Cavanagh's reaction. He laid a hand on Chef's shoulder and said gently:

"Take the rest of the day off, Chef. We'll have supper sent across from the Pipistrello. Do me one favor though: if you leave the port area, let me know where you're headed. I'd like to cast off at twenty-one hundred hours, if we can get our bloody laundry back, and I don't want to leave you behind!"

"Thank you. I've always said you have a sense of the proprieties . . ."

He stumbled over the last word, but he held his head high, and marched himself out of the galley like a guardsman.

"He's drunk already," said Lenore briskly. "He won't be going anywhere except to bed. Don't bother about the restaurant. Jackie and I will make supper."

"Thank you. I appreciate it."

"May I make a suggestion, Mr. Cavanagh?" This from Leo, suddenly deferential.

"Please, do."

"Well, sir, we've had grim news; but I still don't think we should start our cruise like a coffin-ship. I'm damn sure Giorgios wouldn't want it like that. For everyone's sake, I think we need to put some life into things, beginning tonight."

"How do you suggest we do that?"

"Very simply. We set up supper on the afterdeck, but we turn it into a supper dance, with everyone joining in—except the helmsman, of course! We turn up in dress whites, we pick a good program of dance music. Let's see how they react."

"You're talking about a wake."

"If you want to call it that, sure."

"Fine! What have we got to lose? It's going to be a long ten days if we all settle into the miseries! Rodolfo, stroll across to the laundry, offer them twenty dollars bonus if we get our stuff back, dry and ironed before nine-thirty!"

"Immediately, sir."

As soon as he had left, Cavanagh gave Leo a quick briefing.

"You and I will share the night watch. I'll be on until midnight, which should have us out of harbor and away from the coastal traffic lanes. You do twelve till four. I'll bring us into anchorage between four and eight . . . I'll have Rodolfo with me, so I can start breaking him in."

"That's fine by me." Leo was faintly hesitant. "But I do think you should put in an appearance at the dance, if only to get things going . . ."

"True. So why don't I take us out and then you relieve me for, say, half an hour."

"As long as you want. I've looked at the charts. It's an open run to Sardinia. Until we get close inshore, the only hazards are coastal traffic. One more question, Mr. Cavanagh."

"Yes?"

"Now that Hadjidakis is dead, where do we stand with Mr. Molloy and with you?"

"Who's we?"

"Jackie and I."

"Right now we're adrift and we're scared." Jackie added his complaint. "You must understand that."

"I do, but I can't speak for Mr. Molloy. For my part, I was not an eyewitness, I am in no position to make a judgment. You're both doing your job. So long as you continue to do that, we'll have no problems."

"Thank you. Jackie and I both needed to hear that."

"And you both need to hear this, too. The threat continues. The danger is real. And you're at risk with the rest of us. You are also a risk to us. No matter where we are, you can't afford to go catting around with the rough trade—or the carriage trade either! At least you've got each other for company . . . but remember what happened to Giorgios, and how simply and quietly it was done. Are you reading me, Leo?"

"Very loud, very clear, sir."

"And you're not going to argue yourself out of it, are you, the first moment you get the hots for a stranger?"

"No, sir. At least not unless he's so devastatingly beautiful that . . ."

"Get the hell out of here! Start work on the saloon and then move onto the afterdeck. Dismissed, the pair of you."

They went off at a trot, leaving only Lenore Pritchard to offer an ironic salute:

"You're growing up, buster! They'll soon let you play with the big boys!"

"And the best of the day to yourself, Miss Pritchard. You're a big girl already!"

He left her then and went out on deck, just in time

to see Farnese, the Countess and Aurora Lambert walking across the dock to a waiting taxi. He hurried after them and detained Farnese.

"Do you mind telling me where you're going, sir?"

"Not at all. I'm taking the ladies for a little drive, round the peninsula, on to Orbetello—and back again. They're upset by the news of Mr. Hadjidakis's death. A break will do them good. We'll be back in a couple of hours."

"Where is your daughter?"

"She's resting. She was very disturbed by Molloy's refusal to talk to her. I can understand it; but she finds it difficult to accept. She'll calm down."

"With great respect, sir, you will remember at all times that we are deemed to be at risk of further violence."

"I am well aware of it, Mr. Cavanagh. This cane is, in effect, a swordstick and I am carrying a Beretta automatic . . . Even while we are strolling, the taxi is instructed to stay with us. But thank you for your care and your vigilance."

"My duty, sir. Have a pleasant outing. If the laundry's ready, we may be out of here early."

He handed the ladies and Farnese into the taxi, watched them drive away down the dock, then went up the gangway at a run. After a quick glance to determine the positions of the crew working around the vessel, he hurried down to Giulia's cabin and knocked softly on the door.

"Who is it?" Giulia's voice was muffled and drowsy.

"Cavanagh."

"Wait a moment."

He waited for what seemed the longest ten seconds of his life until Giulia opened the door, drew him inside and bolted the door behind him.

The next moment she was naked in his arms, crazed as a bacchante, smothering him with kisses, pulling him onto the bed, undressing him with urgent violence, turning each movement into an act of phallic worship, almost unbearable in its intensity. The few words they spoke were swiftly stifled. Naked together, they played through every moment of the love-suite to a climax that left them panting and exhausted, begging for respite even while they gathered themselves for yet another reprise.

This time, the rendering of the maenad music was different. The rhythm was more measured, the harmonies fuller, the moments of emotion more tenderly explored.

Spent at last, Giulia lay in the crook of his arm. Her hand lay slack on his belly. His face was buried in the perfumed forest of her hair. He told her with drowsy wonder:

"I promised you we'd have a wild ride."

"To the edge of the world and back, you said."

"You weren't disappointed?"

"No, no, no! I'm still out there dreaming. And you?"

"I feel like the king of creation . . . but let me tell you something, my beautiful one. I am glad this coronation day is over."

She heaved herself up on one elbow and challenged him:

"What do you mean?"

"Until today it was all hope and guesswork for both of us. Now we know: the loving works for us. We fit each other. We don't have to explain or argue. We make music together. It isn't always like that for everybody. We're the lucky ones."

"We are, my love. Now all we have to do is enjoy each other."

"Not quite all, Giulia mia! There are a few other things we have to think about, like . . ."

"Not now!" She laid her fingers over his lips.

"We're still at the end of the earth. Let's stay here for a while."

The words were hardly out of her mouth when they heard, through the half-open porthole, the sounds of arrival; car doors opening and slamming, women's voices, footsteps on the gangway. Giulia went off into helpless laughter. Cavanagh cursed, grabbed his clothes and darted naked across the corridor to Molloy's suite, where he dressed and tidied himself in record time, and then began laying out the ship's armaments on the coffee table. When he heard the Farnese party entering their cabins, he buzzed Lenore Pritchard in the galley. He told her:

"Our guests are back on board. If they ask for me, I'm in Molloy's cabin, checking the arms-cupboard."

Lenore laughed, a lusty, husky sound.

"I presume all the weapons have been thoroughly tested?"

"Yes, they have."

"Now of course they have to be kept clean and oiled for instant action."

"That's the drill. You've been well-trained, my dear Miss P."

"Like yourself, Mr. C."

"What's the word on the laundry?"

"We'll have it back inside the hour."

"Great! How's Chef?"

"Out like a light. I've taken off his shoes and covered him up. I never realized how old he looked. How is the beautiful Giulia?"

"When last I saw her, very well, very happy."

"I'd be ashamed of you if she weren't."

Cavanagh surrendered to her cheerful mockery.

"That's why they call it 'the little death.' You get a return ticket. You're born again, fresh and beautiful after every encounter. At least that's what I'm told."

"That's half the truth. The other half is what happened to Hadjidakis; the big death, the one-way ticket to no-place . . ." The mockery was over now. Her tone was suddenly somber and brooding. "I never thought I'd hear myself say this, Cavanagh, but I wish you both well. Enjoy yourselves. Make the most of your honeymoon! Don't waste an hour of it!"

It was just after eight in the evening when, briefcase in hand, he marched down to the harbormaster's office to pay the mooring fee, the water levy and the port tax for the *Salamandra d'Oro*. As he neared the office he noticed a new arrival backing into the quay: a weather-beaten Fairmile flying the Red Ensign. The name on her transom was *Jackie Sprat*.

He had seen her like in other Mediterranean ports; bought from the Navy at war surplus auctions, hastily refitted and then put out as workhorses in the Mediterranean contraband traffic. As vessels, they were always suspect and sometimes highly dangerous. They were fueled by petrol, and driven at high speed. Leaky fuel tanks, dirty bilges, short-circuits in the electrics, incautious smoking habits on the part of the crew, were constant hazards.

Their captains were generally ex-Navy types, their crews an assortment of dock rats and discharged deckhands, all dedicated to the pursuit of a fast buck and not too particular as to how they made it. Whenever they came into port, the customs and immigration people gave them a scouring. Most of the time they came up empty, because the transhipments of contraband—drugs, cigarettes, spirits, warm bodies—took place at sea, outside territorial waters. Occasionally there were intercepts, generally due to poor navigation on the part of the smugglers. More often there were armed encounters between rivals, when one group tried to muscle in on another's territory.

As Cavanagh came level with the berth, the seamen on the afterdeck hailed him in English.

"Hey, mate! Take a line, will you!"

Cavanagh set down his briefcase, caught the two stern lines and made them fast round the bollards. More from courtesy than from curiosity, he waited until the vessel was winched in and the gangplank run out. The seaman gave him a laconic acknowledgment.

"Thanks, mate."

"My pleasure."

"You English?"

"No. Australian."

"You're a long way from home."

"You can say that again. Where have you come from?"

"Today? Elba. We laid up for a couple of days in Porto Ferraio. Which is your ship?"

Cavanagh jerked a thumb over his shoulder.

"That one. The *Salamandra d'Oro*. We're leaving tonight."

"Where are you heading?"

"South." The lie was prompted by sudden caution. "Anzio, Naples, that-a-way. Wherever the owner wants. You know how it goes."

"Don't I just. Tell me, is there any good crumpet around this place?"

"I'm sure there is, but I've been too busy to chase it."

"Too bad. In Porto Ferraio they were touting it on the docks, perfumed cards and all. We went to one place, very posh, where half the girls were boys. Our skipper and his mates liked that. I didn't. I left and found another place. I'm all for home comforts—I like a lot of butter on my crumpet . . . if you know what I mean. Come to think of it though, we met some of your fellows at the first place. Two pretty boys and a real hard-nose—Greek name, American accent. When

I left, he and our skipper were getting along like a house on fire . . . Our man's a Corsican but he speaks fair English . . ."

"Simmons!" There was a shout from somewhere below decks. "Stop your gabbing and get your arse down here!"

The seaman gave a shrug and an embarrassed grin, then scuttled down the companionway. Cavanagh picked up his briefcase and walked on to the harbormaster's office. As he was paying the bills, he remarked casually:

"I see you've got a new one. *Jackie Sprat*, English."

"Oh that!" The official made a sour mouth. "She's bad news, a smuggler—cigarettes, scotch whisky, all the high tax items. She picks 'em up in Tunis or Casablanca and sells 'em in any port round the Tyrrhenian Sea where there is a market. Nobody minds that too much. People have to eat. And State tobacco in Italy is like camel dung anyway. But the captain has a bad name, one that people speak very softly. For instance, some time ago he was arrested by Customs off Gaeta in the south. There are those who say it was an arrangement, a put-up job. What happens is this. The Customs men hail and board him. He's way inside Italian waters. He doesn't run. He doesn't fight. He surrenders peacefully. His ship is impounded, with all its cargo. He himself is given a small fine and freed. Now comes the pretty part. Under Italian law the ship —that one down there—is put up for public auction. Who wants a piece of scrap like that? No one except the captain, who puts in a personal bid and gets it for next to nothing. But he's a Corsican, so he doesn't want to register it in France. The taxes are too high! No sir! So, he gets his old British syndicate to register it in their name, put up all the money for new merchandise, and buy back half the vessel at twice what he paid for it. Now he's back in business, but with a new twist this time: prohibited migrants from Muslim countries, political people who are on the run—and always the hard drugs."

"What's the captain's name?"

"Benetti. Claude Emile Benetti. The *quaestura* have a file on him as thick as your fist; so he's not good company to be seen with . . . Where are you heading now, sir?"

"South." Cavanagh was studiously vague. "We'll probably end up in Corfu, if the owner doesn't change his mind."

"I know what you mean, sir. Have a good trip."

"Thank you. Goodnight."

As he came out of the office he saw five men trooping off the Fairmile and heading across to a small dockside tavern with the grandiose name of La Grotta delle Grazie. He waited until they had all entered the tavern and then hurried back to the *Salamandra*.

Farnese and the two women were on the afterdeck drinking cocktails. Cavanagh drew Farnese into the saloon and gave him a quick rundown on his encounter and the information from the harbormaster's clerk. Farnese took it with odd calm.

"It does not surprise me, Mr. Cavanagh. A ship like ours is as easy to follow as a circus elephant. The radio gossip on the sea-lanes goes on all day and all night. You have only to call up any harbormaster's office to get news of arrivals, departures and who's staying in port. It's part of the special courtesy of the sea. More than that, the purpose of my visit to Orbetello was to talk with Galeazzi and, if possible, to make contact with Molloy. I missed Molloy, but Galeazzi had already spoken with him from Rome. The U.S. Intelligence report was specific. We should expect surveillance by sea and, at some point in the voyage, another act of violence. Tolvier, that disreputable creature, has involved us all in a very tribal vendetta.

He is still being hunted by his victims: we are being hunted because we have helped him escape. The victims have hired themselves professional executioners to do the job which the Republic of France failed to do."

"Which brings me to my next question." Cavanagh was terse now. "Why are you keeping me in the dark? Why are you short-circuiting my communications with my owner, Mr. Molloy?"

Farnese shrugged off the question.

"Because it is easier to do that than brief you on the whole complex background of the Tolvier affair and its ramifications in French, Vatican and American politics, which are, in any case, not your business. Besides that, each party has its own means of dealing with this threat."

"But I—all of us on this ship—have to deal with it, here and now. It is very likely that the men who killed Hadjidakis are just over there, drinking in that tavern!"

"And if they are, if you are sure that they are and you are sure you have enough proof to present to a court, what will you do?"

"I don't know."

"Precisely. You are a foreigner on Italian soil. Alone you have neither status nor power to pursue the matter. I beg you to trust me, Mr. Cavanagh."

"You forget, sir. I am still in command of the vessel. It is you who must trust me. I cannot, I will not sail blindfold into danger."

"Are you saying that I am leading you into it?"

"You are depriving me of the means to deal with it—knowledge of the facts, of all the contingencies involved. We leave here tonight on a pleasure cruise. Where are we going? Sardinia. Have you been there?"

"I have."

"We haven't discussed a routing yet."

"I thought we could do that just before we leave. Frankly I don't know why you're making such a big fuss about this."

"Because you've just told me, officially, that we're going to be under surveillance by sea and possible violence by land—and the people who'll be threatening us are fifty meters across the dock in The Grotto of the Graces! This isn't the Middle Ages, for Christ's sake! I've studied the charts. Once we hit that Sardinian coast—outside a few ports, there's nothing at all but rocks and scrub. There's not even water to fill our tanks. Whoever's following us will have us literally between the devil and the deep blue sea! Use your brains, man! Stop patronizing me, and remember it's your daughter who's threatened!"

For a moment it seemed as though Farnese would burst into fury, then with equal swiftness he was in control again. He said coolly:

"Your arguments make sense, Mr. Cavanagh; but your language is intemperate. Indulge me a moment. Come up to the bridge and let's take a look at the chart together. Remember that I was not always a desk man in the Ministry of the Navy . . . And I am just as concerned for my daughter as you are—though less obviously and theatrically . . . Why don't we call a truce now and have Jackie bring us both a drink to toast it?"

On the bridge it was Farnese who laid out the chart and made the commentary.

". . . Here's where we'll be cruising: the northeast corner of the island from Capo Testa in the Straits of Bonifacio, to Capo Coda Cavallo, just south of Olbia. The landscape is rugged and beautiful, there are many islets and rocky outcrops that will require careful navigation. On the other hand, there are beautiful bays and inlets which offer shelter in all weathers and where one can swim in privacy and dive in safety, always with the hope of coming up with some antiquity or other . . . But you are right, from Capo Testa to Coda Cavallo there is nothing—Santa Teresa is a small fishing port with a ferry connection to Corsica, Palau is a village, the only town of any consequence is Olbia, which is the traditional port for trade with the mainland by ferry and freighter. However, the places that interest us are these . . ." He circled them lightly with the tip of his pencil. "La Maddalena, which is an Italian naval base commanding the Straits of Bonifacio, and Tavolara, which is now an installation under joint U.S. and Italian control. I have friends in both places, which are, as you see, less than fifty kilometers apart . . . We shall be cruising between them. Our sinister friends will presumably be shadowing us. But my friends from Tavolara and from La Maddalena will also be shadowing them, as part of their local naval exercises with surface craft and submarines . . . They will be protecting us. The sad part is that they will also be protecting a nasty type like Tolvier, who has become an embarrassment to France and a desirable prize for U.S. Intelligence."

"Which, presumably, has offered to arrange this convenient protection for us."

"Presumably, yes."

"And what will happen to the people on the *Jackie Sprat*?"

"Again, presumably, the intention of the exercise is not only to protect us, but to remove them from contention."

"Mother of God!" Cavanagh swore softly. "I don't believe this! What a stinking mess!"

"Much less of a mess, my friend, than revelations of sodomy and murder and a trade in hunted criminals —revelations which could wreck a huge pilot plan for economic reconstruction in Italy with American and Vatican financing. It is not only our plan, it is a dozen or more others which will grow out of it—new money just waiting in the wings to see how we fare . . . Again, look!" He drew a large circle round the northeast tip of Sardinia . . . "This is a plan bolder than anything Molloy or I would venture. Galeazzi thinks it's a madness; but he's willing to encourage it so long as Vatican money isn't involved. There is a buyer for all this land, all of it! His offer is on the table, one lire per square meter. A nothing, you say. But if the offer is accepted, he will pump in tens of millions of dollars every year to develop a tourist resort, to found an airline, to build a huge dam, road works, an electricity network . . . This is what I have come to see. I want no part of it. I can have no part of it—the man is a religious leader in the Muslim world, the monies are the offerings of his followers . . . But you see, my dear Cavanagh, there are other dimensions than yours and even Molloy's . . ."

"I agree," said Cavanagh somberly. "I'd be a fool if I didn't. But I tell you again, on this ship, on that sea out there, I am the master. I am responsible for you, not the other way round. Do we understand each other?"

"I hope so, Mr. Cavanagh. I truly hope so."

"Hope isn't enough," said Cavanagh flatly. "I have to know. Do you accept, with all that it entails, that I am the captain of this ship? You know what that means? Yes or no?"

"Yes," said Alessandro Farnese wearily. "I would not for the world dispute your little kingdom."

"Thank you," said Bryan de Courcy Cavanagh. "I'll try to intrude as little as possible in your business affairs."

"You are already an intrusion," said Farnese, "but that's my daughter's fault, not yours." He raised his glass in the toast: "To our mutual good health."

"Health, money and love!" said Cavanagh. "May God give us time to enjoy them."

They drank. Cavanagh asked a final question: "Where in Sardinia is our first port of call?"

"Maddalena."

Cavanagh picked up the ruler to measure the distance on the chart.

"A hundred and twenty nautical miles—an eight-hour run at fifteen knots. We can loiter until midnight and still be in for breakfast."

"What does the weatherman say?"

"Clear and calm. Fresh northwesterlies developing tomorrow."

"By then we'll be under the lee of the big island. Our cruise promises well, Cavanagh. It promises well!"

At least it began in style. The *Salamandra* left harbor on a glassy sea under a waxing moon, with music playing and her passengers sipping champagne on the afterdeck. Cavanagh was on the bridge, with Rodolfo, the apprentice helmsman, beside him.

As he passed the *Jackie Sprat*, he noted that the vessel was still in darkness and her crew, apparently, still at dinner in The Grotto of the Graces. When he had rounded the spur of Monte Argentario and turned southward towards the small island of Giannutri, he handed the wheel to Rodolfo.

"Steady as she goes, until we have the island on our starboard beam. We'll round it slowly. Keep checking for traffic, both visually and on the radar screen. Forget that I'm here. It's your ship . . ."

"Yes, sir." After a few moments silence he asked: "May I say something, sir?"

"Go ahead."

"Miss Pritchard told me you had said I was worth teaching."

"I did."

"I am very proud of that. I want to say again I am grateful for the respect you show me."

"You're earning it, Rodolfo, because you're eager to learn, because you ask questions, because you're looking at what is outside you, not always at yourself."

Rodolfo laughed, an open boyish sound.

"Miss Pritchard says it the other way. She makes me face the mirror. She says: 'Look at yourself, Rodolfo. You are young, handsome, you are not afraid of work. Be proud of yourself. You can be anything you want.' She is very understanding, I think."

"Very." Cavanagh was carefully neutral. Rodolfo went on:

"In my country, at this time, it is hard to find a road for oneself, especially when one is without money or education."

"So what do you think the answer is, Rodolfo?"

"Emigrate. But that's hard to do if you don't have family in America or Australia or Argentina. The other way . . ."

He broke off in obvious embarrassment. Cavanagh prompted him.

"Yes . . . ?"

"The other way, which my friends joke about, is to find a rich foreign lady and marry her."

"What kind of lady, Rodolfo?"

"They say, a widow, because she is more likely to be willing and eager."

"And what do you say, Rodolfo?"

The young man shrugged uneasily.

"What can I say, sir? I live on a small island. It is expected that I should marry an island girl, but I certainly don't want to get engaged or married until I can afford a family. I must not get involved with local women; so my only experiences have been in the closed houses, and I can't afford those too often. So you see, it is a problem."

"Have you discussed it with Miss Pritchard?"

"Not directly, no, sir. Do you think I should?"

"Perhaps later, when you know her better; but always, as you say, with respect."

"Always, sir. Most certainly with respect."

And there, for the moment, the teasing little dialogue ended, because Giannutri was coming up on the starboard beam, and there was still no sign of an approaching vessel. He called Leo to the bridge to supervise Rodolfo, then walked down to the afterdeck to play master of ceremonies at the supper dance. His first partner was the Countess, light on her feet and lethal always in her humor. She began with a compliment:

"This was a splendid idea, Mr. Cavanagh. I have to tell you we were about to die of ennui."

"No credit to me, Contessa. It was Leo who suggested it."

"Ah, yes. The young *ballerino* whom Luchino was admiring. I tell you, you nearly lost those two after lunch."

"I noticed," said Cavanagh.

"I noticed something too," said the Countess. "You were left in a very embarrassing position when Molloy refused to speak either to Giulia or to Alessandro. I thought you handled the announcement very diplomatically."

"Thank you."

"One understands Molloy's grief at losing a friend; but there is much to be explained in that relationship, wouldn't you say?"

"There probably is, but the relationship is now ended forever."

"But the questions for Giulia remain unanswered."

"You and I shouldn't play games, Contessa. I wonder why those questions weren't asked and answered a long time ago—long before this betrothal took place."

"Perhaps because both Giulia and her father considered them irrelevant to the text of the agreement."

"To that," said Cavanagh, "I confess I have no answer."

"Have you asked Giulia herself?"

"No."

"Why not?"

"Because there are more important questions."

"To some of which you already know the answer?"

"Some, not all . . . May we change the subject?"

"Of course."

"You're a beautiful dancer, Contessa."

She laughed and drew closer to him.

"I was in my youth, a well-turned-out young lady. I had the best of teachers and a very ambitious mother. I was taught to dance, to sing, to paint, to embroider, to make intelligent but respectful conversation with gentlemen young and old and pay deference to the mothers of eligible sons . . . Most of it was baggage that I've tossed away over the years—but some of it still comes in handy . . . May I ask you a question?"

"Of course."

"I think you're in love with Giulia. She's told me she's in love with you and I believe her. But my question is different. Do you love her?"

Before he could answer she laid a cautionary finger on his lips.

"Don't answer yet. Think about it. We'll have plenty of time to talk on this voyage. But remember something. I like you, I admire you. I think that, at this moment, you are the best thing that could have happened to Giulia. In the future, who knows? I don't. I'm sure Giulia doesn't. That's why the question is so important. Now if you'd be good enough to dance me to the bar and pour me a glass of champagne?"

"My pleasure, Contessa . . . and I will think about your question."

"Not now, please! Do me a favor and ask Miss Lambert to dance. She's out of humor with Alessandro, who is taking revenge by flirting with the good Miss Pritchard . . ."

"Your servant, always, my dear Contessa!"

Miss Lambert was very much out of sorts. The prospect of a vacation on the wilder fringes of the Tyrrhenian Sea pleased her not at all. What would she wear? What sort of people would she meet? What would there be in the way of evening entertainment? Wasn't the *Salamandra* a bit like Noah's Ark, drifting around waiting for the flood to subside—and with a very small collection of exotic animals on board . . . ?

That gave Cavanagh the first good laugh of the evening, and even surprised Aurora Lambert with her own wit. Giulia, dancing with Jackie, looked across and waved. Farnese grinned and whirled Lenore Pritchard perilously close to the guardrails.

When it came time to ask Giulia to dance, he felt a sudden, strange moment of embarrassment. He could not match the detached professional grace of Jackie. He dared not, with this audience, make open display of a lover's intimacy. All his emotions challenged him, not to a courting ritual but to a defiant discretion, a gambler's poker face. It was Giulia herself who rescued him. She declined with a smile:

"Jackie has just danced my feet off, and even the great Cavanagh can't compete with him. Let's sit this one out . . ."

For which relief he blessed her and they sat side by side watching the moon climb over the dark water and the wake foaming astern while the constellations merged themselves into the silver light of the moon-glow. Giulia asked softly:

"What happens tonight?"

"I'll have to leave in a few moments. I'm on watch until midnight. I have to sleep—and I mean have to sleep—until four in the morning. Then I'm up to bring us into Maddalena. If you want to join me on the bridge then, you're welcome."

"But I won't be welcome in your bunk. Is that what you're telling me?"

"I'm afraid so, my love—unless you want me to run you on the rocks before dawn."

"Then we could swim away and disappear, couldn't we?"

"I'm afraid it's not going to be as easy as that," said Cavanagh ruefully. "Sooner or later we have to stand up and face the whole goddamn symphony orchestra—from the fiddles to the big bassoons."

"But not yet, please!"

"No. Not yet; ten days from now!"

Suddenly she was shivering. Cavanagh was instantly solicitous.

"You're cold. Shouldn't you get a wrap?"

"No, no! I'm fine. It was just . . ."

"Just what?"

"As they say in the country: a goose walked over my grave . . . How soon can we start my diving lessons?"

"Tomorrow if you like. We arrive early in La Maddalena. As soon as your father has paid his courtesies to the naval commandant, we can go find ourselves a quiet bay and begin work."

"Will it be difficult?"

"Easy as falling out of a tree. The trick is to get the drill right and think yourself through it every time, until it becomes automatic. There's a whole new world waiting for you down there."

"That's good to hear. Just now I'm not very happy with the one I'm in."

It was the first time she had ever uttered so clear a complaint. Cavanagh, taken aback, could only murmur a platitude.

"But we're going to change that too, very soon."

"You make it sound so easy."

"In the end it will be easy."

"How can you promise that?"

"I learned it during the war. Before you've been in action, you're scared, day and night. You have no idea what it will be like or how you will behave. Once the shooting starts, there's no time for questions. The curtain's up. You're on stage. You say the lines you've learned. You move where your feet take you. It's that simple." He laughed and added a deprecating postscript. "I lie, of course. Simple it is, but easy it most certainly is not."

"That's probably why you're better at it than I am. You're a nice simple man from a big new country. Something gets in your way, you charge at it like a billy goat and butt it out of the way. On my family crest there is a gryphon, which is a much more confusing animal. It has an eagle's head, wings and talons; a lion's body and tail. So how does it get about—walk, stalk or fly? . . . Life can and does get very complicated. And you, my darling Cavanagh, have complicated mine." She shivered again. "I think I do need a wrap. I'll go downstairs and get one. You go up to the bridge. I'll come and kiss you goodnight before I go to bed . . ."

Oddly enough, that night they all came up in turn to bid him goodnight. Giulia was the first. She gave him a lingering, sensual embrace and then hurried away at the first sound of footsteps. The Countess wanted to thank him for an entertaining evening and remind him that they must find an opportune time to talk at length. Farnese wished to display to his Aurora the view from the bridge, with the moon riding high over the dark sea chasms between the mainland and Sardinia. Jackie passed by briefly to tell him that all was shipshape on deck and in the galley. Lenore brought word that Chef was awake, badly hung over, but in his right mind and grumbling that no one had bothered to wake him for the party. Half an hour later, Leo came up, refreshed after a catnap, to relieve him at the wheel. Cavanagh told him:

"It was a good party, Leo. I'm grateful you suggested it."

"It did work, didn't it? Strange! On other voyages when we've just been roistering around with on again-off again guests, Molloy has always been good fun. This time, with Farnese and the women on board, he's been quite different—broody somehow, always on a short fuse."

"Maybe he's just scared of getting married." Cavanagh tried to be offhand about it.

"You wish!" Leo gave him a mocking grin. "He wants it so bad it hurts! But not for the sex, although he'd kill anyone he thought was sniffing round his Giulia—which does mean you, Cavanagh! You're really making a spectacle of yourself, though nobody's going to tell. We're all agreed on that."

"I'm going to tell," said Cavanagh flatly, "and so is Giulia, as soon as Molloy comes aboard."

"Jesus H. Christ!" Leo swore softly. "Now that's a big, big decision to make. If I were you—either or both—I'd give it some more thought. You've seen only one side of Declan Aloysius Molloy, the one with the party manners and the golden handshake for the grandees. But there is another one, a real rip-roaring buccaneer with pistols in his belt and a knife in his teeth . . ."

"And you've seen him in action?"

"I've seen him kill a man in Cuba—in an old-fashioned duel, after a crap game. Hadjidakis was his second . . . It took place in a big private garden . . ."

"When was this?"

"Last year . . . Down there anything goes. You know that."

"It seems I don't know as much as I thought I did."

"Then I'll give you one more piece of information for free. Molloy likes a stand-up man. That's why he took to you, you were willing to dare him. But the one thing you can't ever do is let him think you're laughing at him. Hadjidakis could do it because Hadjidakis always knew how to promulgate his manhood. He taught him to fight anybody and screw anything. How do you think Jackie and I got this job?"

"I've never asked and you don't have to tell me; but why the hell does Molloy want to marry Giulia and foul up her life?"

"Because he doesn't see it that way. Don't you get it? He's *endowing* her! With all that macho history, all that money and power and influence. You're a reading man, Cavanagh. You'd know about Sir Richard Burton—the guy who translated *The Arabian Nights* and *The Scented Garden*, who explored the sources of the Nile with Speke and made the trek to Salt Lake City with the first Mormons . . ."

"I know about him, yes! A fabulous adventurer."

"Who did everything in the no-no book and had a wife who was crazy about him till the day he died. That's Molloy for you! No way you can match the personal power he wields . . . And you're going to stand toe-to-toe with him and take his woman away? You're out of your cotton-pickin' mind, Cavanagh! I don't know what Farnese would do to you, but Molloy would have you followed to the ends of the earth and then blown off the edge!"

"Why are you telling me this?"

"You gave us a break in Elba. I figure we owe you one."

"Thanks. I'll think about it."

"You do that—and keep on thinking. What's the course?"

"Two-thirty. No hazards except shipping and tuna traps, and there's three hundred fathoms of water under your keel most of the way."

"It's a long way down," said Leo, "especially with a concrete block chained to your ankles! Sweet dreams, Cavanagh!"

"Your ship, mister! Make sure you stay awake!"

Alone in his cabin, he kicked off his deck shoes and stretched out fully clothed on the bunk. On the bulkhead in front of him was a series of instruments repeating information from the bridge: compass course, engine revolutions, wind velocity. There was also a two-way communication system, with a microphone and speaker just above his pillow.

Leo's blunt warning troubled him deeply. He was the more intelligent of the dancing pair. As Chef had once remarked: "That one dances with his head as well as his feet." He was well-educated, shrewd and widely read in some very unlikely areas. So his summation of Molloy's character, history and intentions—if true, if not invented to scare the new boy—had to carry some weight. Which raised the next important question: how to prove the oracle?

Cavanagh opened the drawer of the bedside table and took out the leather-bound volume of Hadjidakis's diaries. He leafed hurriedly through the book trying to isolate any entries for the year 1951. In January of that year, it seemed, while the *Salamandra d'Oro* was still being built in the British Isles, Molloy had taken his old yacht cruising in the Caribbean: Cuba,

Jamaica, Haiti, Santo Domingo, Barbados. Those were the wild, wide-open days, just after the war, when the tourist exploiters were homing in, with the off-shore bankers and money-movers and the mobsters, to run the gambling and the girls and the drug traffic, which was just in its infancy.

For a buccaneer like Lou Molloy it was open season . . . Hadjidakis had a colorful phrase that summed it up perfectly: "wild nights ashore, quiet days afloat with the sea and the wind to purge us clean." The duel in Havana was recorded, but with an odd, nightmare casualness:

> We're in the casino shooting craps. Standing next to Molloy is this beautiful mulatto girl. He's on a run. Every time, before he shoots, he runs his hand up the inside of her thighs for luck. She brings him luck, too: fifty something thousand dollars! Then comes the surprise: this very courtly, very drunk Cuban accosts Molloy and accuses him of an indecency on his woman. He demands satisfaction. Molloy says he'll be happy to talk about it outside. We go outside. On the way out I see Jackie and Leo drinking at the bar. I signal them to follow us, in case there's a brawl.
>
> Molloy tries to placate the Cuban. He turns obstinate. He wants an apology. He wants what he calls "a share of the luck from my woman's loins." Molloy refuses. The Cuban challenges him to a duel. Molloy tells him he's crazy; but he persists and his friends back him up. Finally Molloy shrugs and agrees. He names me as his second. He asks the Cuban to put up fifty-thousand on a winner-take-all bet. He figures that will scare him off. No way! The man's got money running out of his ears.
>
> We go to his house. The duel is staged on his

> tennis court. The weapons are a pair of old-fashioned dueling pistols, beautiful things. The referee and stakeholder is his family doctor. He recites the rules and counts off the paces. Molloy fires first and kills the Cuban. He picks up the money and shakes hands with the referee. We walk out, flag a taxi and drive down to the harbor. As soon as we're on board we up anchor and leave. Molloy gives me ten thousand dollars to divide among the crew. He and I split the forty. He keeps what he's won at craps. He says we ought to stay away from Cuba for a while. My only regret is that we didn't bring the girl along with us. Lou tells me that with the winnings we can buy a much better one—even two!

Even though he was reading it in Greek, Cavanagh was chilled by the laconic indifference of the narrative and the portraits which it presented of Lou Molloy and the late Giorgios Hadjidakis, his lieutenant and chronicler.

He had always suspected that there was real reason to fear Lou Molloy, but the true dimension of the man, in power and in potential malice had, until now, eluded him; or, rather, he had chosen to delude himself about it.

Like many others of his generation, he had accepted, without question, the victorious might of the United States of America, and its dominance in global politics and atomic weapons. What he had failed to understand, what he was seeing now, dimly and with little understanding, was that the system threw up both geniuses and monsters, against whom the law was a fragile defense, and for whom the Faustian dreams of wealth, power and knowledge, were always within a hand's reach. In such a society the borderline between criminality and commerce was often indistinct and sometimes invisible. In spite of all the catch-cries of democracy and liberty under the law, the difference between the legitimate exercise of power and the oppression of the subject was sometimes very hard to discern.

The questions, therefore, were matters of life and death. Could Lou Molloy pursue him to the edge of the world and blow him off? Very possibly. Would he? Very probably. Which lent a special meaning and a special poignancy to the Contessa's question: "Do you love Giulia?"

He closed the diary, put it back in the drawer, turned off the light and drifted slowly into a troubled sleep.

At five in the morning, an hour after he had taken over the helm-watch, he was surprised to see Farnese mounting the steps to the bridge balancing precariously a cup of coffee and a plate of croissants. He was in very good humor.

". . . I thought I'd come up and keep you company. I did my cadet service on La Maddalena, so I'm a walking encyclopedia on the whole of the Straits of Bonifacio." He set down his cup and plate, then asked, "Would you do me a favor?"

"If I can, sure."

"The harbor entrance to Maddalena is quite tricky."

"I've noticed," said Cavanagh vaguely. "I've been looking at the chart and reading the pilot-book. What's the favor?"

"If you'd allow me, I'd like to pilot you in."

It was the shy, ingenuous request of a youth and, for the first time on the voyage, Cavanagh warmed to him. He hesitated a fraction of a second and then gave a smiling consent.

"Why not? I'd be fumbling my way through it anyway. You must know it like the palm of your hand."

"I do . . . but the real reason is that the Commandant's wife is an old flame of mine and well . . . What the hell! I'd like to impress her with a good entrance. You know what *figura* means, Cavanagh!"

"I'm happy to oblige." Cavanagh was grinning from ear to ear. "But for God's sake, don't bend Molloy's boat!"

"Have no fear, Cavanagh." Farnese was as happy as a schoolboy. "I'll bring her in without so much as a smudge on her paintwork. Where are we now, by the way?"

Cavanagh pointed to the chart.

"At four this morning we were sixty miles out . . . Now we've about forty-five to go. Three hours cruising time."

Farnese traced the course with the tip of the pencil:

"We come in from the east, past Capo Ferro and then head past Capo d'Orso to the eastern side of the island of Santo Stefano. That puts us right on the ferry lane from Palau, which is the easiest way into Maddalena itself . . . If you like, I'll take over at Capo Ferro and you can monitor me as we go . . ."

"Sure! And you can tell me the historic bits."

"I'll tell you now." Farnese was bright as a brass button. "Maddalena was where Bonaparte suffered his first defeat in 1793. He was only a lieutenant then, second-in-command of a French artillery company which had been landed on the neighboring island of Santo Stefano to bombard and capture Maddalena. The resistance, however, was too strong. The French general had no stomach for a fight. He left. Bonaparte had to follow him, leaving stores, guns and some of his men. Some say it was that first defeat which made him, later, a glutton for victory. Ten years later, Nelson arrived. He used the Straits of Bonifacio and Maddalena itself as a base from which to blockade Toulon. He renamed the area 'Agincourt Sound' and begged the Lords of the Admiralty to take possession of Sardinia itself for England. His words were taught to us in class. Let's see if I can remember them . . . Ah yes! . . . 'This, which is the finest island in the Mediterranean, possesses harbors fit for arsenals and of a capacity to hold our navy within twenty-four hours' sail of Toulon. It is the *summum bonum* of everything which is valuable to us in the Mediterranean. Here we are the healthiest squadron I ever sailed in . . . ' " Farnese laughed. "Well, those are just bits and pieces of what he wrote. But his lords and masters would have none of it. However, Nelson did leave a kind of farewell gift—a pair of silver candlesticks and a crucifix for the church, all engraved with the Bronte arms. I can arrange for you to see them if you like . . ."

"I'd like that, thank you."

"And while we're here, Caprera's worth a visit. That's where Garibaldi ended his days. The island is kept as a national monument . . . It's no distance: you can walk across on the causeway. The flowers should be beautiful now, not only here but all over Sardinia, lavender, asphodel, red saxifrage, rock-roses . . ."

"You sound as though you love the place." Cavanagh coaxed him quietly.

"I love Sardinia, yes; because it's still wild, beautiful and untamed. I hate it too, because it's so backward and brutal to its people. Up in the Barbagia, the families of goatherds put their children to work at a tender age. They live like troglodytes under the angles of rocks and they feed on corn bread and goat cheese, while their landlords live on the mainland and are blind to their misery. I'm one of them, I have to tell you, because my father bought holdings here, but they bring me little but shame. The people are stern and closed and there is a deep anger that sometimes flashes out like a dagger drawn in the sun—a bronze dagger, Cavanagh, made by the people who built the *nuraghi* and fled inland away from the sea raiders."

He broke off and laughed, as if ashamed of his eloquence. Cavanagh begged him to continue:

"Please, don't stop. I've traveled halfway round the world to connect myself with these things. When you talk like this, you make them come alive."

"I make myself come alive, too." Farnese was suddenly moody. "I confess to you, Cavanagh, it is much easier to tell you stories than to flog myself into ecstasies with Aurora Lambert." He threw out his hands in a gesture of comic despair. "That's ungallant, I know. I should have better manners—and more sense than to be chasing second-rate actresses! What about you, Cavanagh? What's your experience with women?"

"Limited, but on the whole, pleasant. Maybe it's the family I was brought up in, but mostly I've had pleasure with women—though, God help me, I'd never claim to understand 'em."

"No thoughts of marriage?"

"Until recently, no. As a student I couldn't afford it. For a traveling man it didn't seem necessary."

"But now, you're ready to contemplate taking a wife?"

"That's an old-fashioned phrase," said Cavanagh. "I'm not sure I've ever approved it as a definition of a love-match, which is what I'm contemplating and hoping for."

"With or without benefit of clergy?"

"With, for preference. Without, if need be; always provided the lady is willing."

"The lady in question being my daughter Giulia?"

"Since she's free to deny both the answer and me—yes!"

"Thank you for telling me."

"Thank you for asking, sir. And now since there's no one here but thee and me, can we not discuss the matter in a civilized fashion?"

"What else do you think got me away from a warm bed and an eager woman at five in the morning? By all means, let's discuss it."

"All cards face up? No platitudes, no exhortations?"

"As you say."

"Then let me clear the decks for you, sir. I love Giulia. She loves me. I've asked her to marry me."

"And she?"

"Wants to defer the answer."

"Has she told you why?"

"Only in the most general terms. I haven't pressed for details. I've simply told her we have to get things sorted out before Molloy comes on board."

Farnese gave him a thin, grim smile.

"One could say that was a minimal requirement. On the other hand, you and my daughter have already bedded each other."

Cavanagh flushed and was momentarily at a loss for words. Farnese shrugged.

"Don't be surprised, Cavanagh. Don't be ashamed. It was I who contrived the opportunity for you with my little excursion to Orbetello. Just as it was I who seized the opportunity to offer you both this short vacation together, while Lou Molloy is purging his grief over the demise of his friend Hadjidakis."

Cavanagh, in total shock, gaped at him and finally managed to utter the single word:

"Why?"

"Because, strange as it may seem, Cavanagh, I love my daughter and I like you and respect you. You are in a sense my gift to her, my thanks-offering, before she is committed to the brute realities of a political marriage—which she does understand and which she has accepted freely."

"How can she understand it, for Christ's sake? She's only a girl!"

"No, Cavanagh. She's a woman and she knows exactly what this marriage signifies."

"Then perhaps you'll spare her the pain of explaining it to me, because I don't understand it at all, and I sure as hell need to. Right now I'm like a blind bull blundering around in a shop full of glassware."

"Don't be too hard on yourself, Cavanagh! How much can any man be expected to know in his twenties, when he comes from a place where history has only begun to be made. I confess that I am amazed to find you so, so prepared for your Grand Tour . . ."

"Prepared? God Almighty! Was ever a dumb mick less prepared! But you're going to explain things to me now, aren't you?"

"I'm going to try," said Farnese. "But it's a long story and you'll have to let me tell it in my own way."

"Provided you don't mind a question now and then, to make sure I'm understanding you."

"By all means."

"The radar's clean, the sea's empty, we're dead on course for Capo Ferro. You have my total attention, sir!"

"You will understand none of this," said Farnese, "unless you follow the single thread which runs through all European history from the days of Caesar Augustus until now: the concept of '*imperium*,' empire, a single unit, or a confederation of units, presenting a united front to enemies, or potential enemies—traditionally characterized as the barbarians. The single, strongest strand in that thread—at least the one that has endured the longest—is the notion of Rome as the head of that empire, the place where the '*numen*' resides. You understand '*numen*,' Cavanagh?"

"I understand it. Please go on."

"All the follies of European history have been perpetrated by people who didn't recognize that power resides in the myth itself, in the folk memory, and not in any given person or set of circumstances. The British are, because of their isolation, natural myth-makers. They have managed to create, out of an obscure German house, a royal family upon whom their imperial dreams—even those which are now toppling into nightmare ruin—have centered themselves. Hitler and our ill-fated Mussolini failed to do that, because they denied what the British have always acknowledged, even on their coinage, that there has to be in every empire a core, a lodestone of divinity. True or false, it doesn't matter; but the fire must glow, the warmth must be felt. Only then will the complicated machinery of government work; otherwise, it will freeze into impotence. So, this is my question, Cavanagh. Where are the essential myths enshrined? Where does the true source of power reside?"

"I'd say it resides in the possession of atomic weapons."

"Would you go one step further and stipulate that the real masters of the universe are not those who control the arsenals, but those who control *their* hearts and minds?"

"I would so stipulate, yes."

"So now take a look at the northern hemisphere. America, victorious, rich, aggressive, has Japan as her eastern bastion and when the French are beaten in Indochina, she will move in there too. Australia, your country, is available to her as a base of operations. In the west, England is her dependent ally and all Western Europe is her vassal state. Who stands against her? Mother Russia and all her vassal states in the U.S.S.R. . . . and all the peasant millions of China. So how does anything work? The terror of the mushroom cloud lies over the whole planet. Administration, trade, the commerce of ideas, how do they function? . . . As they did, Cavanagh, in imperial times, through the historic instruments of power, consuls, and proconsuls, bankers and traders, whose scrip holds good, and the Roman Catholic Church, your church and mine, with its polyglot population of seven hundred million people, growing every day, and its hierarchy, good, bad and indifferent, controlling them all with the oldest '*numen*' in existence: the God who speaks through his vicar, the successor of Peter. That voice is heard everywhere, Cavanagh, even in the gulags of Siberia and the way-stations of the Long March. And, believe it or not, I'm one of its more important functionaries, because I'm a fund-raiser, a seller of stocks and bonds in the still vast equities of the Roman Church in Italy. I'm an ambassador outside the diplomatic service, because I speak the universal language of money. People deal with me, as they deal with Galeazzi, because they know what stands behind me . . . Do you understand me, Cavanagh?"

"Very well," said Cavanagh. "But what I don't understand is why Giulia, your own daughter, has to be part of the trade."

"In principle," Farnese took the question in his stride, "the answer is simple. From earliest times, under Roman law—and in Roman practice across the centuries—woman was always a chattel until she passed from the care of her father and her brothers, into the possession of her husband, when she finally achieved the status and dignity of a matron. But you're a lawyer, you know this."

"I also know it's bullshit!" For the first time, Cavanagh's patience began to fray. "I don't want a potted history of the law. I want the facts about Giulia and Molloy, the whys and wherefores of this bloody travesty!"

"Is it a travesty, Mr. Cavanagh?"

"Yes—and I can prove it."

"Indeed? Then before you make a total fool of yourself, let me give you what you are pleased to call the facts." He waited a moment while Cavanagh checked his heading and switched to automatic pilot, then he resumed his story. "There is still a little history yet to absorb. You know that the surrender of German troops in Italy was arranged by Allen Dulles and the Vatican, working with the German S.S. Intelligence Chief, Walter Rauff. What you don't know is how many side deals were made during those negotiations—deals that involved the protection, by Dulles and his O.S.S. groups, of men who were guilty of war crimes, but who might be useful to combat the rising power of the European Communist parties. Dulles had a whole group of them whom he kept on ice just outside Munich: men like Gehlen, Barbie and Dragonovich. One more step. Italian elections were slated for 1948. In 1946, the Italian Communist Party, with support from Moscow and the Communist parties in Western Europe, launched a full-scale bid to secularize Italy, break the Vatican's power and destabilize the whole republic. Two things happened. Pius XII threw the support of the Church behind the Christian Democrats. The Americans, urged along by Cardinal Spellman, weighed in with money and the invisible presence of a large intelligence group, led by the one and only James Angleton. Result? The Communists were defeated. The Christian Democrats were elected in 1948 and have even been able to establish an uneasy working arrangement with the Left. But the fundamental problem still remains. A huge mass of unemployed people, our industries in disarray—the whole country a massive breeding ground of discontent! End of history lesson! I could use some more coffee. You?"

"Thanks."

His brief absence from the bridge gave Cavanagh the chance to compose himself and prepare for a critical hearing of the only matters that interested him: the relations between Molloy and Giulia. Farnese, back with the coffee, gave a temperate and relaxed rendering:

". . . In February of last year, I was looking around, with Lucietta, for a suitable match for my daughter . . . I see you react from the idea. Relax, man! How do you think these things are arranged? By lottery? By casual encounter in a night club? They are arranged—which does not mean that they are imposed."

"Please! My reactions or opinions are of no consequence at this moment. I'm listening."

"My desire to see Giulia settled is known. The matchmakers and the noble gossips are busy spreading the news. The Holy Father himself is discreetly interested and makes sure that I am discreetly informed! Now our American Eminence, Francis Cardinal Spellman, arrives in Rome on one of his frequent visits. As always, he brings gifts, substantial gifts. As always, he brings political information and economic proposals, which can benefit both Italy and the United States and drive another nail into the coffin of the Communists. This time he brings Molloy—very rich, very Irish, very Catholic, rabidly anti-Communist, a friend and collaborator of Allen Dulles and General Bedell Smith, well connected on Wall Street and in Washington. He is interested in European investment. He is attracted by the tourist splendors and rundown assets of Italy. He has already worked out how a clever impresario could put value into them. He is also a bachelor, who has reached that certain age of anxiety, in which he begins to dream of a young wife and a son to succeed him. In short, as Spellman is eager to point out, the man is a godsend. The Holy Father agrees. I am summoned to a very private audience with His Holiness and His Eminence from New York, who rolls out the whole plan before me like a design for a beautiful tapestry! I agree to study it. I meet with Molloy and am deeply impressed. He is presented to Giulia, who is both impressed and attracted to him. Now, if you are honest with yourself, Cavanagh, you will have to admit both the man's power and his charm. He is emphatically not a barbarian. Rather, I see him as one of the great *condottieri* like Sforza, Brancaccio di Montone and the Englishman, Sir John Hawkwood. Even you, Cavanagh, would have to admit the stature of the man!"

"I admit it freely."

"And you would admit the importance of such an ally, at this perilous time, to the economic and political well-being of Italy."

"I have no scale by which to judge those things; but I'll take your word for them."

"As Giulia does . . . And now that we've come to it, let's talk about Giulia. Quite obviously you see her as being somehow forced into a destructive union with Lou Molloy. You are mistaken, Cavanagh. You have no knowledge at all of the power of the Italian matriarch. Ask any Italian woman; she will tell you that her husband is unfaithful, her children are spoiled, all society is geared to the worship of the male. Don't believe a word of it! The goddess who rules Italy and the Mediterranean is still Magna Mater—the archetypal matriarch—and in the family, as among the celibates in the Vatican, the exercise of power is the final vindication, the ultimate satisfaction. A trifling illustration: Molloy does not speak Italian. He will never learn. On whom will he depend for social communication, for secret judgment—on Giulia, of course. Don't you see, he cannot afford an enemy in the house?"

"So you're telling me that, in the long haul, it doesn't matter whether Molloy's a saint or a double-dyed bastard!"

"Exactly. In any contest on Italian soil, Giulia has to win. That's the way the dice are loaded."

"And where does love come into all this?"

Farnese took a sip of coffee and dabbed at his lips with a paper napkin. He was no longer eloquent and emphatic, but gently ruminative, a skilled actor making a sudden shift in the emotional line of his scene.

"Where, how, when, why does love come into it? I tell you truly, Cavanagh, I don't know. I know only that it does come in the most surprising ways. My father was a monster to my mother, to all his women in fact. But my mother adored him. Once, before she died, I asked her how she could have put up with him. She smiled and told me: 'I understood him, Sandro—he was just a big baby. He always needed a teat in his mouth.' The other side of the coin was, of course, that she dominated him through his own weakness and his own guilts. There are two sides to every coin, Cavanagh!"

"Unless the coin's a double-header," Cavanagh smiled, in spite of himself. "If Giulia is so bound to Molloy, why is she even bothering with me? Why are you so anxious to placate her that you're presenting me to her like a gift-wrapped candy-box?"

"Does that displease you?"

"Yes, it does. It presumes that I'm yours to dispose of—another chattel. Be assured, I'm not. May I ask you a question now?"

"Of course."

"You're Giulia's father. How important to you is Molloy's character: his public and his private conduct?"

Farnese was in no hurry to answer. He sipped his coffee, ate half a croissant, wiped his lips with a paper napkin, pondered the question with theatrical deliberation. Finally he said:

"Molloy's public conduct is most important to me, to Giulia, to all our patrons and our enterprises. Any threat to his reputation is a threat to us. We will respond to it vigorously. As to his private morals, I am more relaxed about those than you appear to be. Do you find that strange? I'm her father, you're what? Her Johnny-come-lately lover! So, I ask myself, are your concerns genuine? Or are they simply the carpings of a suitor, jealous of his own interests!"

"I believe," said Cavanagh, quietly, "I truly believe we both have genuine reason for concern."

"Have you expressed these concerns to Giulia?"

"I've told her I believe she's marrying the wrong man."

"But the particulars, Cavanagh? I presume from your remark, that you are able to recite them?"

"I am."

"Then, please begin."

"No, sir! Not to you, not to Giulia!"

"To whom then?"

"To Molloy himself, if it comes to that."

"My dear Cavanagh," Farnese addressed him with sedulous moderation. "Let me offer you a very important piece of advice. Whatever evidence you have against Lou Molloy, bundle it all up in a sack, put a large rock in the sack and dump it overboard in the deepest ocean trench. When you've done that, erase every last line of it from your memory."

"And where does that leave Giulia?"

"Precisely where she is now—a woman betrothed to a man she has chosen freely. Besides, my young friend from far-away-land, Giulia is a Farnese. In our long family history we have had more than our share of assorted rakehells, satyrs and sexual fantasies. Somehow our women have managed either to bring them to repentance, control them, or, when all else failed, to conjure up a convenient assassin—a loyal friend, a devoted page, like you perhaps. Have you ever killed a man, Cavanagh?"

"Some, I guess," said Cavanagh, flatly. "But in the Navy all our killing was at a distance. So, I'm not sure how I'd measure up in a hand-to-hand encounter—or a private execution. Let's drop the subject, shall we?"

"With pleasure; but where do we stand now? I'd hate to think we've wasted all this talk."

"We haven't." Cavanagh paused a moment to correct a slight drift on the autopilot. "First, I'd like to thank you for a civilized chat and for allowing Giulia and me to work our way to our own decisions."

"But you know those decisions have to be made."

"Of course."

"Does that mean you'll bow out of Giulia's life, when the time comes?"

"If she wants me out, yes. If she wants me in her life as a husband, then that for me is final. I don't leave without her. That's the best I can promise."

"I had hoped for more," said Farnese.

"I love your daughter," said Bryan de Courcy Cavanagh. "I'll not surrender her against her will, especially to a man like Lou Molloy!"

"Whatever he's been, whatever he's done, could you not find it in your heart to forgive him?"

"What's forgiveness got to do with it, for God's sake?"

"That's an odd question from a Christian. You did say you are a Christian, Cavanagh?"

"I did say it and I am. But forgiving is one thing—trusting is another. I don't trust Lou Molloy—not with Giulia!"

"But he trusts you, Cavanagh. He has trusted you with his woman, his ship and his friends. Do you find yourself worthy of the trust? Think about that—and do call me before we raise Capo Ferro."

Punctiliously, Farnese gathered up the crockery and carried it down to the galley, leaving Cavanagh to scan the horizon and sort out all the contradictory themes, in what was becoming an elaborate *valse macabre*.

Sardinia revealed itself slowly. The islets and headlands were first to appear, black humps rising against a pale morning sky, out of a shimmering sea. Then the headlands were joined by white ribbons of sand and tufted ridges, behind which rose the rock-strewn saddles of the hinterland. The fresh breeze off the land carried the scents of wild thyme and rosemary.

Cavanagh reduced speed to seven knots to give himself time to match the configurations of the land with his chart and with the images on the radar screen. His first landmarks were clear now: the beacon on Capo Ferro and, opposite, the rocky island of Bisce. A little to the south was the narrow gullet of Porto Cervo and the wide-open approach to Golfo Pevero.

As he scanned the shoreline through his binoculars, his heart skipped a beat. There, riding peaceably at anchor in Golfo Pevero, was the long, gray hull of the Fairmile, *Jackie Sprat*. At first he could not believe what he saw; then a piece of simple mathematics convinced him. The Fairmile had a speed of thirty-five knots and a forty-mile radar scan. The *Salamandra* had loitered for a couple of hours and then run through the night at fifteen knots. The skipper of the *Jackie Sprat* could have picked her up on his radar anywhere with three hours of Porto Santo Stefano and then, her identity and direction established, outrun her into Sardinia. Farnese was right. The *Salamandra* was as easy to track as a circus elephant. He called Farnese to the bridge and handed him the binoculars.

"Tell me what you see, please."

Farnese studied the vessel for a few moments then set down the glasses.

"It's no surprise. I'll report their presence when we get in to Maddalena. No point in broadcasting the news. That's Capo Ferro ahead, isn't it? Would you like me to take the wheel?"

"Your ship, sir."

Cavanagh noted the time and wrote an entry in the log: "Prince Farnese, at his own request, piloting vessel into La Maddalena. Cavanagh remaining in effective control."

Farnese smiled and asked:

"Covering your tail, Mr. Cavanagh?"

"Always." Cavanagh was equally good-humored. "You've done navy service. Somebody has to take the kicks. It's either the cabin boy or the ship's cat. By the way, sir, what's your program in Maddalena?"

"Lunch with the Commandant, his officers and their ladies. We'll be back on board for siesta. A light meal would probably suffice for the evening. What about you, Cavanagh?"

"We'll be cleaning ship. Chef will be shopping. We'll give the crew time off to see the town. Somewhere in all that, I'm going to sleep . . . I take it we'll be leaving here tomorrow morning?"

"Probably not. We may return the Commandant's compliment by inviting him and his staff to join us on a day run tomorrow, down to Coda Cavallo, or even over to the western end of the Straits, if the weather holds good."

"There's a northwester promised. That could make for a bumpy trip."

"Then we take the lee side of the island. It's no

problem; but in any case be prepared for visitors and a picnic, and probably a second night in port here."

"Whatever you decide, sir, I just need to give Chef enough notice to prepare the food."

Their talk was crisp and formal. They were heading now for the promontory called Cape d'Orso. Farnese was watching for traffic in the enclosed space. Cavanagh was making swift, nervous sketches of the new landscapes that presented themselves. One half of his mind was concentrated on his sketchbook, the other was dealing with a new revelation.

With surgical precision, Farnese had just subtracted two days from his private time with Giulia and there was not a word he could reasonably say to protest it.

By the time he had snugged down the ship in the Italian Navy pens, issued his orders for the day and consigned the Farnese party into the care of the Commandant of Maddalena, it was eleven in the morning and he had lost all desire for sleep. So he decided to go ashore with Chef and help him with the marketing. It was a simple, homely occupation which opened the town to him and opened Chef, too, into a whole litany of confessions.

". . . I fell into pieces yesterday, Cavanagh. You must understand that I am haunted by the thought of a sudden and lonely death. I made a bad exhibition of myself. I'm sorry."

"Come now, Chef!" Cavanagh tried to soothe him. "It happens to everyone at least once on a voyage. The days are long. The sea's always murmuring in your ear and you don't know whether you're hearing a lullaby or a siren song. The only way you can escape it is to get drunk or jump overboard—which is not recommended."

"I was mad with you too, Cavanagh."

"Everybody's mad with me, Chef. Don't worry about it."

"How can I not worry? I see you, all lit up with passion for our little Princess, riding madly into battle with my old friend Molloy. I think you're crazy—that's the privilege of youth. I don't blame you for anything except stupidity. But Molloy—that's a horse of another color . . ." He broke off, to test the lettuce on a market barrow, to press the peaches, smell the melons and deliver himself of a totally irrevelant piece of wisdom. ". . . Always in Italy they do the same thing—they put the spoiled fruit at the top of the pile, so that it will sell first. By the time you get to the bottom of the pile, that's gone off too! I tell them to sell the bad stuff at discount and make up on the good stock. But will they listen? Never! They have been doing it this way since Nero . . . Here, you can make yourself useful. Hold the sack open. Two dozen oranges, four kilos of peaches, then we'll take a look further down. It pays to spread the custom!"

As they strolled among the market stalls, Cavanagh steered him back to the subject of Lou Molloy and his strange wooing. Chef expounded in his grumbling fashion:

"You're too young, Cavanagh. Your country has not even two hundred years of history. You're just out of university, just done with a war. The future is spread like a magic carpet under your feet. Sex is wonderful, love is wonderful. The world is a garden of girls! And yet you're breaking your neck to get married. Why? This is the big game, Cavanagh, the one they play in the *salle privé* with the doors closed and all the hard men sitting around watching the jackpot get bigger and bigger. You're out of your class! You're going to get hurt. Your Giulia's going to be left bleeding for you; and Molloy will have the whip-hand over her for the rest of her life . . ."

"Not if she comes away with me."

"She won't. She can't."

"Who says so?"

"I say it, my young friend, without malice, with sadness for you both."

"I don't believe you!"

"I know. You don't dare to believe me; but I know Molloy and I know the Farnese and their like."

"So explain Molloy to me."

"No! You'll have to learn him yourself, line by line as you first learned to read . . . He comes from a new world too; but it's older than yours and richer and much more ruthless. Pass me one of those figs. Try one yourself . . ."

After a while they separated. Chef walked back to the ship, accompanied by a scrawny youth carrying his purchases. Cavanagh completed his circuit of the old town with its pink-and-white houses, ornamented with iron scroll-work. In an alley behind the main street he came upon a narrow shop-front whose window carried the legend "*Antichità.*"

Most of what was displayed behind the glass was old naval material—a telescope, a quadrant, an officer's dirk, a pair of dueling pistols, gilded buttons, medals and decorations . . . He went inside. The shop was empty. He was browsing quietly among the knick-knacks when an elderly, white-haired man appeared from the rear door and asked:

"May I help you, sir?"

"Thank you. I was just browsing, but perhaps you can help. I was looking for a gift for a lady—something curious, out of the ordinary."

"A young lady, sir?"

"Yes. A young lady of good taste and education."

"I understand. This may need a little patience, but let us see what we have."

From under the counter he produced a series of

cardboard shoe boxes, from which he brought out, in turn, an antique tear-bottle of Roman glass, a tiny nuraghic bronze figure, a gold locket in the Hungarian style, an enameled scent-vial from Vienna, sundry rings, bracelets, brooches and pendants. It was a pendant which finally caught Cavanagh's eye: a medallion of yellow gold, held in a milled circlet of the same metal and attached to a woven chain of gold filaments. The medallion was finely wrought. It carried on one side the image of a winged Mercury, under which was an inscription "*Vocatus extemplo adsum.*" On the obverse was a representation of the Three Graces embracing each other in the traditional pose.

The old man watched as Cavanagh fingered the piece. He smiled, nodded and said:

"It pleases you, sir, yes?"

"It does. What can you tell me about it?"

"Not much more than it has already told you. The medallion is older than the circlet and the chain; I would say seventeenth century Florentine. The setting and chain are nineteenth century. It was sold to me by a young naval cadet, whose aunt had left it to him in her will. That's all I can tell you. The piece is genuine."

"How much?"

The old man cocked his head on one side like a quizzical parrot and asked:

"How much is it worth to you, sir?"

"How much do you want for it, *padrone*?"

"How will you pay?"

"In lire."

"Then the price is thirty-thousand."

"That's fifty dollars."

"For American currency I could make a better price."

"I'll give you twenty-five dollars."

"Make it thirty-five."

"Make it thirty."

"*D'accordo!*"

"And you'll find me a nice box for it and wrap it in fresh tissue."

"With the greatest of pleasure, sir."

While the old man was rummaging amongst his junk for a jewel box and wrapping paper, Cavanagh looked at the medallion and pondered the inscription: "I come instantly to your call." For the moment at least, Giulia was wearing another man's ring; but, if she accepted this pendant, it would lie between her breasts and assure her that, like the messenger of the gods, he was and would always be in her service. On which there followed a sour little after-thought: he had only his love to give him wings. Lou Molloy was much more potent, with messengers, minions and men-at-arms always at his disposal around the world.

He was therefore touched and surprised when the old man took his money, handed him the medallion, carefully wrapped, then presented him with the little glass tear-vial as "a small gift for the fortunate lady!" When Cavanagh tried to thank him, he waved him away with a laugh.

"I am probably the only man on Maddalena who knows what it is: a fragile trifle from long ago. In any case, you will need it. Even in the best of loving there are tears, but they too should be kept as a precious memory."

It seemed a double omen when, turning back into the main street, he found himself ten paces behind Lenore Pritchard and Rodolfo. They were holding hands and laughing at their own disjointed talk. A few paces further on, they stopped dead in their tracks and exchanged a lingering kiss. Cavanagh, too, was forced to stop and concentrate his attention on a display of hanging sausages in a *salumeria*. The last thing in the world he needed at that moment was to involve himself in another love triangle—which, whatever its outcome, had to be much less complicated than his own.

He waited long enough for the pair to be done with their kissing and get another twenty paces ahead of him. By that time the country sausages were beginning to assume phallic shapes and the fatigue of the night-watch had caught up with him.

He patted his pockets to make sure he still had his purchases, then hurried back to the ship. The Italian Navy had posted a courtesy guard at the gangway. Cavanagh returned the lad's salute and identified himself. He popped his head into the galley to let Chef know he was on board. Back in his cabin, he stripped, shaved and showered, and slept like the dead for seven hours.

He was wakened by a cabin-to-cabin call from Farnese.

"I hope I didn't spoil your siesta, Cavanagh."

"No, sir. It's time I was up anyway. What can I do for you?"

"I just wanted you to know we've brought two guests on board. I've asked Miss Pritchard to make up Galeazzi's cabin for them. That has two bunks. They'll be quite comfortable."

"Who are they?"

"Mr. Jordan, whom you met in Calvi, and a friend of his from the Italian Navy."

"I'll need their documents for the ship's manifest."

"I think you might waive that formality," said Farnese smoothly. "They'll only be with us while we're in Sardinian waters."

"Who assigned them to us?"

"Wrong question, Mr. Cavanagh. These are our friends."

"Where are they now?"

"On the afterdeck. It's cocktail time."

"I'll be up shortly, to offer them a welcome. By the way, are we expecting more guests tomorrow?"

"No. The Commandant and his people will be welcoming a destroyer from the Sixth Fleet. So our picnic cruise is off. If you like, we can leave here in the morning. Our guests have suggested some interesting places to visit."

"Have they indeed? I'll be most interested to hear them."

As he washed and dressed, Cavanagh felt the now familiar pang of resentment at being so openly manipulated by Farnese. Yet it was difficult to frame a justifiable complaint. Farnese, friend and father-in-law-to-be of his owner, was the only conduit he had into that underground world from which they were all threatened, and from which their protectors, too, had obviously emerged. So, he chided himself. *Keep a still tongue in your head, Cavanagh! Listen and nod and smile and learn to be as practiced a plotter as the rest of them!* He was just brushing his hair when Lenore Pritchard gave a perfunctory knock, stepped immediately into the cabin and announced:

"I thought you should know. Farnese's brought a couple of heavies on board."

"He called me a moment ago; he told me they were guests."

"Whatever he calls them, I've just been down to their cabin with towels, soap and bottled water. There was a big canvas bag pushed under the bunk. I looked inside it."

"What did you see?"

"Wet suits, spear guns, pistols, hand-grenades . . . other gear I didn't recognize."

"You didn't disturb anything?"

"Hell, no! I just zipped up the bag again and shoved it back under the bunk."

Cavanagh shrugged.

"At least we can be sure they're on our side."

"I hope nobody's going to start a war, just when I'm beginning to enjoy the cruise."

"Don't worry. Nothing's going to happen. Molloy and Farnese are simply taking out insurance policies. That means the ship and crew have to be covered."

"I hope so."

"Did you do any shopping today?"

"Not much. A few postcards, a couple of pieces of local embroidery. Rodolfo and I . . ."

She broke off, blushing and embarrassed. Cavanagh chided her gently:

"Come on now! Why the blushes? I saw you both in town. I thought you made a very handsome couple."

"I can do without the blarney, Cavanagh!"

"It's not blarney. I mean it."

"Rodolfo makes me feel like a girl again."

"Good."

"Damn it all! I'm old enough to be his mother."

"The boy's got good taste. What's wrong with that? Enjoy what you've got, while you've got it!"

"Is that what you're doing, Cavanagh!"

"Not exactly. I'm trying to hang on to what I think I've got. I want to marry Giulia; but everyone's trying to warn me off the course."

"Naturally enough, wouldn't you say?"

"I guess so. Molloy has to be the odds-on-favorite."

"What's Giulia's point of view?"

"She loves me. I love her."

"And?"

"I've told her I'll marry her at the drop of a hat—and to hell with Farnese and Molloy and Papa Pacelli and all the rest!"

"So now you're just waiting for someone to drop the hat?"

"If you put it like that, yes."

"Who, for instance?"

"Giulia, for Christ's sake! I've asked her to marry me. She has to answer."

Lenore Pritchard gave a long, low whistle of surprise.

"Jesus! Do you realize what you're laying on the girl? I know she's bright. I think she's brave. I'm prepared to believe she loves you, but you can't leave her out there, standing in the eye of the hurricane, waiting for the big winds to blow! It's inhuman!"

"I don't see that!"

"Then you're blind as a cave-bat and you don't deserve the woman!"

"So, help me, please! Explain to me where I'm wrong."

"Oh brother!" She perched herself on the edge of the bunk and made him sit beside her. "You really are beyond redemption, Cavanagh. You must know all the raw power that's stacked up against you."

"You're damned right, I know it!"

"Then don't you see? You're opting out: you're leaving Giulia to face it alone. You've constructed a situation where she has to accept you, and then explain herself to Molloy and her family and the Pope and all the other interested parties! If she breaks, you'll blame her and leave. She'll be a victim to Molloy and her family for the rest of her life. You'll be fired, of course. You may even be beaten up in a dark alley. So what? You'll be home free. Your life will go on. Hers will be finished . . ."

"You can't say that!"

"The hell I can't! In my own small way, I'm in the same position with Rodolfo. I'm good enough in bed to keep him happy for quite a while yet, but that's not the point. For him, I'm the rich lady because I earn ten times as much as he does and I know ten times as much about the big wide world. I'm as good as a widow because I'm used merchandise and he doesn't owe me any fidelity. Even so, he expects me to call the tune, make the decisions for both of us; but I know that the day will come when he knows, or thinks he knows, more than I do, and he's found someone twice as rich and half as old as I am. Then it's *finito*! Kaput! . . . What I'm saying, boyo, is that if you want to hold your lady—and by me she's quite a lady, even if sometimes she acts like a spoiled brat—you have to make the moves. You have to pick some pebbles out of the brook and fit them to your sling and go challenge Goliath yourself . . . My father used to give me that advice; but his way was to get drunk and leave the giants, like the rent collectors, to my mother. She beat 'em too, in her own biblical way. She took 'em to bed and then cut their balls off—or was it their heads? It's hard to remember. Have you got a drink here?"

"Scotch?"

"Whatever."

As he handed her the glass he told her:

"I hear what you're saying. I can't duck the issue. I'm just trying to work out the right way to handle it."

"There is no right way," she told him harshly. "You're a lawyer. You should know that. I had a boyfriend once who was a very distinguished attorney in New York. He used to tell me: 'Stay out of court, kid; but if you land up there, remember one thing: it's a battlefield. You walk out alive or they carry you out dead. And we attorneys will charge you the same for the triumph or the burial!' Just hold me, will you, Cavanagh. I'm cold. I always get cold when I'm scared."

When, finally, he arrived on deck, he found that Giulia had not yet appeared, that Farnese and Aurora Lambert were engaged in some very emotional dialogue, while the Countess was entertaining the two new arrivals. She presented them to Cavanagh with a certain comic-opera flourish:

"Mr. Jordan, you've already met. He works for the State Department."

"Welcome aboard, Mr. Jordan." Cavanagh was at his most cordial. "What section of the State Department do you work in?"

"The State Department is like heaven." Jordan gave him a big flashing smile. "It has many mansions and a lot of tiny cubbyholes. I work in one of those called the Document Disposal Unit."

"Document Disposal Unit? Fascinating," said Cavanagh.

The Countess permitted herself a small, skeptical smile and completed the introduction. "And this young man bears a name famous in naval history, Lieutenant Andrea Maria Doria."

"My pleasure, Lieutenant. I trust you'll both be very comfortable on board."

"Your Miss Pritchard has already made us most welcome."

Doria's English was polished and precise, but clearly, Jordan's was the voice of authority. He was disposed to courtesy but determined not to waste too much time on it. He asked immediately:

"If the Countess would excuse us, I need a few moments with you in private, Mr. Cavanagh."

"Now?" Cavanagh was taken aback by the man's abruptness, but the Countess waived a cheerful absolution:

"Business before pleasure. You are excused."

They had hardly set foot on the bridge when Carl Jordan announced:

"I hate crap. I'm sure you do too, Cavanagh; so I'll come straight to the point. Lieutenant Doria and I are here to protect your guests and your crew. To do that, we need your full co-operation."

"You'll have it, Mr. Jordan—provided you give me a full and proper briefing, in advance."

"That may not always be possible, Cavanagh."

"Then let's start with the possible. Names and documents. Are your names real or at least do you have documents to back 'em up?"

"I have a passport. Doria has an Italian Navy I.D. card."

"I'd like to see them and they should be entered on the ship's manifest."

"We'd rather they weren't."

"We can accommodate you on that. I shall, however, make a note of your presence in the log."

"If you must."

"I must. Next question. Who's in charge of the exercise, you or Lieutenant Doria?"

"I am."

"And you're responsible to . . . ?"

"I told you, the D.D.U.—the Document Disposal Unit of the State Department."

"Who cut your orders?"

"I don't have any written orders. That's not the way we do things."

"How do you do things, Mr. Jordan?"

"Oh Christ! A hardhead!" Jordan threw out his arms in theatrical despair. "We're here to help you."

"And if I'm to co-operate, as you ask, I need more information."

Jordan ruminated on that for a few moments, then, much more mildly, he remonstrated:

"Okay. We're talking about intelligence business here. And, crazy as it sounds, information is always the problem. Who has it? Is it true or false? Who's trying to buy it? Who's selling it? Is it clean or is it poison bait? Don't push me on this, Cavanagh."

"I'm not pushing. I'm asking simple questions on a need-to-know basis. So, as you say, let's cut the crap.

I'll give you a reading. You check the boxes right or wrong. Fair?"

"Try me."

"Your work in the D.D.U. is directed by Mr. Allen Dulles."

"Check."

"Dulles is engaged in rounding up former Nazis. He's collecting them as assets and information sources for future anti-Communist campaigns. He keeps some of them stashed around Munich."

"No comment."

"In the State Department itself there's a sharp division of opinion about the morality of this policy."

"How the hell can you possibly say that? How can you know it—guess it, even?"

"Easy! Six million Jews, gypsies and so-called enemies of the Reich dead in the camps, and your Mr. Dulles is putting their torturers on his payroll! You've got a presidential election coming up. The Jewish lobby is important. Ergo—there has to be division of opinion."

"Check."

"Here, however, a vendetta has begun over a French collaborator, Tolvier. Hadjidakis is a victim because he's connected with Molloy, who helped deliver Tolvier to Dulles."

"Check."

"The men who killed him are now tracking us. Their boss, the probable executioner, is a man called Benetti."

"Check."

"And we're the bait you're using to lead them into a trap and eliminate them."

"No comment."

"But, I've got one, by God!" Cavanagh was full of cold anger. "You're not protecting us. You're gunning for Benetti and his group. And you want to use this ship as a base of operations for a political assassination!"

"That's bullshit!"

"Is it, Jordan? Let's prove it out. Follow me!"

He walked off the bridge and hurried along the deck with Jordan a pace behind him. He turned into the saloon and strode down to the guest area. Without a word he opened the door to Jordan and Doria's cabin, knelt and hauled out the large canvas bag from under the bed. Jordan made a move to stop him, but Cavanagh warned him softly:

"Don't, Mr. Jordan. Don't even think of it. Just unpack the bag and lay the items side by side on the floor!"

"Do it yourself."

"I don't need to, Mr. Jordan." He unzipped the bag, fished inside it and brought up a single disc-like object. "That, unless I'm mistaken, is a limpet mine, designed to be attached to the hull of a vessel by a scuba diver, who, in this case, is Lieutenant Doria. A couple of these in the right places will detonate the *Jackie Sprat* like the floating bomb she is . . . Check, Mr. Jordan?"

"Go to hell!"

"No, Mr. Jordan. You go to hell. I want you and Doria off this ship now!"

"You can't do that. This ship is American territory."

"And I am her master until her owner fires me! I will not permit her to be used as a base for sabotage operations in peacetime against a merchantman, whom the Italians can legally arrest if they have grounds to do so."

"Look, Cavanagh. This is madness! At least give me a hearing. Let me walk you through the situation again from square one. I'll try to . . ."

"Problems, gentlemen?" Farnese, smiling and urbane, stood framed in the doorway.

"You might say that!" Jordan was pale with anger. "This—this clown has just ordered us off the ship."

"Why, Mr. Cavanagh?" Farnese was suitably shocked.

"Do you recognize this, Excellency?" Cavanagh held up the limpet mine. "You should. It's an Italian limpet mine. You did navy service. When you were in administration you must have authorized their manufacture, purchase and use. Mr. Jordan has brought three of them on board. He has also brought hand-grenades and side-arms!"

"Has he told you why, Mr. Cavanagh?"

"On the contrary, he has refused to comment, while at the same time asking my full co-operation in his undisclosed plans."

Farnese frowned. There was a peremptory tone in his next question.

"True or false, Mr. Jordan?"

"True; but I'm caught here between a rock and a hard place. Cavanagh asked to see written orders. I don't have any. Cavanagh is a foreign national with no U.S. security clearance."

"Fair comment, Mr. Cavanagh?"

"No. A security clearance gives Mr. Jordan the right to disclose material to me. It doesn't give me the right to demand it. More importantly, even with full information in hand, I cannot, I will not guarantee compliance with Mr. Jordan's requests. I'll examine and discuss them in good faith—but I will not commit beyond that. And may I remind you, Excellency, that all this bloody mess started when I, acting under orders from Mr. Molloy, visited Sampiero Paoli at the Mas de la Balagne and handed him money. I was a junior then, doing a simple errand. I think you'll agree that this situation is radically different. I have assumed command responsibility. I cannot abdicate it to anyone else . . ."

"It seems to me"—Farnese was now the wise counselor, evenhanded and placating—"It seems to me, Mr. Jordan, that there is still a ground of compromise. Mr. Cavanagh has not refused his help. He asks full disclosure of the nature and scope of your operation. He will examine what you tell him and reserve his ultimate right to say, yea or nay. Is that a correct summary of your position, Mr. Cavanagh?"

"It is, sir."

"And pending Mr. Jordan's application to his people for your security clearance, will you withdraw your order that he quit the ship?"

"How long will it take you, Mr. Jordan?" Cavanagh asked the question.

"If I can contact my control in Munich, I should have it before midnight. If not, I'll have it by nine in the morning."

"In writing, if you please. Your signature will suffice. I'll lock the document in the ship's safe until the operation is complete. Meantime, you're welcome to stay aboard until we have decided whether or not we participate in the operation." He turned to Farnese. "That is all that's at issue here, Excellency, whether, in my best judgment, we do or do not participate in Mr. Jordan's operation. If he decides, in any case, to undertake it without our help, we shall be even better content!"

It was then that Carl Jordan exploded.

"Hell, no! I'm not buying this! Cavanagh wants exactly what he's refusing to us—the final say-so on a U.S. operation. He can't have it! No way! No how! We're pulling out, just as you wanted. Right now! From here on, Cavanagh, you're on your own!"

Farnese turned on him with icy contempt.

"You are a fool, Mr. Jordan, an arrogant, obstinate fool. I agree that it is better you be gone. You are so consumed with your own righteousness that you would put us all at risk . . . This is a dirty business at best; you, I fear, will turn it into a shambles."

"How can you say that?" Carl Jordan gaped at him in shock. "You sat with us while the whole damned . . . "

"I have since thought better of it." Farnese cut him off abruptly. "This discussion is closed. Mr. Cavanagh is in command, not I!"

Without another word he stepped out of the cabin and hurried away, leaving Cavanagh and Jordan staring at each other, mute with surprise.

Jordan was the first to break the silence. He was a man in shock. It was as if he were reciting his woes to an audience instead of an adversary:

"How do you like that? Farnese spent two hours with me and my people after lunch today. It was his idea that we eliminate Benetti and his bunch and build ourselves a big cover story about Communist violence and attempts to sabotage the recovery of the Italian economy . . . Now, just like that, he dumps us and walks away . . . 'Mr. Cavanagh is in command, not I!' That's not what he said at the meeting."

"What did he say?"

"'Cavanagh's a good officer with war experience. You'll find him easy to deal with . . .' Oh, brother! Was that the overstatement of the year! Dealing with you is like trying to screw a porcupine! Anyway, it's over now. We're gone with the wind!"

"Calm down, man! Talk to me. Let's see if there's anything to salvage."

"And then have Farnese sabotage us again? No way in the world!"

"That's your problem, Jordan. You don't listen. You try to push people around. You're the ugly face of victorious America. You draw lines in the sand and you're surprised when the wind changes and blows them away. Your people in Washington are playing one game. Your Mr. Dulles is playing another. Farnese's got his own set of priorities and Molloy's got his own problems."

"And you, Cavanagh?"

"Me? I'm a nobody. Molloy hired me off the dock in Antibes; but I do know how to run a ship and I've been in the service long enough to know that what they call intelligence is often one big foul-up. That's why I refuse to carry the can for you, unless you're prepared to tell me what's in it. I've got nothing to win here and nothing to lose. I'll be fired the moment Molloy gets back, but right at this moment I'm the only man he's got to run this ship. Farnese knows that; so he opened the way to a possible compromise. You blew it. He's handed you back to the Document Disposal Unit because he has no authority to override me and he knows it! Now that's the hand I'm holding, all cards face up. Do you want to walk or talk?"

"Right now I could use a drink—in private."

"I know exactly where to find one," said Cavanagh and led him across the companionway to Lou Molloy's stateroom.

Forty minutes and two large whiskies later, Cavanagh called the afterdeck and asked to speak to Farnese. He delivered his message with careful respect:

"I believe, Excellency, Mr. Jordan and I have reached a workable compromise."

"Which is?"

"Mr. Jordan and Lieutenant Doria will dine on board tonight. After dinner they will go ashore, removing all their gear from the ship. They will not, however, abandon their protective surveillance of us. They will simply conduct it from the shore or from their own craft, with such Italian service personnel as they may need. Mr. Jordan and I have arranged a system of communications which will bring them swiftly to our aid if we are threatened."

"Which means that our forces are split."

"It means, sir, that Mr. Molloy and yourself and we, as crew of a foreign pleasure craft, are effectively divorced from any political or quasi-military action, which may be undertaken by Jordan or those who direct him."

"Are you asking for my approval of this arrangement, Mr. Cavanagh?"

"No, sir. I'm absolving you from any connection with it. I'm informing you that a procedure has been agreed which saves face for everybody and gives us what we may well require, surveillance and protection. It carries no political cost for you or Mr. Molloy."

"You should have been a Jesuit," said Alessandro Farnese. "Will you be joining us for dinner?"

"Not tonight, sir. I think your guests will be happier to have you to themselves . . ."

"Are you suggesting Mr. Jordan is still unhappy?"

"Quite the contrary, sir. Mr. Jordan is much happier to run his own operations without foreign observers looking over his shoulder. He will, I'm sure, confirm that in person. Would you like to speak with him now?"

"There is no need," said Farnese. "As you say, I am no longer involved. You have accepted full responsibility. Tell Mr. Jordan he will be very welcome to join us at dinner."

In the small, dark hours of the morning, Giulia slipped like a wraith into his cabin, threw off her dressing gown and climbed into his bunk. All their pent-up passion was poured out in a long, turbulent, almost wordless encounter which left them, spent and breathless, clinging to each other in the narrow bed. The first coherent words Giulia uttered were:

"I nearly went mad today. I can't bear to be away from you . . ."

"Soon, very soon, we'll be together all the time."

"I wish I could believe that."

"All it needs is one word from you!"

"It isn't as easy as it sounds."

"It's easier today than it was yesterday."

"How can you say that?"

"Your father and I have talked. He knows we're lovers. In fact, he told me he'd contrived it! I've told him that if you want me to leave, I'll walk out of your life without a word said. If you want me to stay, I'll face Molloy and then we'll go away together."

"And you think it will be as easy as that?"

"I know it won't. It's complicated and it's dangerous and I could get myself killed, because Molloy and your father are both dangerous and powerful men. But that's the name of the game, isn't it? My lady or my life! We're two adults engaged in the risky business of loving and making love. Are you understanding me, Giulia? Am I reading you right?"

"I don't want to talk about it. Just hold me."

"Fine! But remember, I'm committed."

"I know. I know."

She tried to draw him to her again, but he disengaged himself and slipped out of the bunk.

"I almost forgot. I bought you a present." He switched on the bunk light and smoothed the sheet so that he could lay out the gifts: the medallion and the tear-vial. He explained them with a lover's care, embellishing the old legends:

". . . Mercury was the messenger of the gods, the leader and playmate of the Graces; but I liked the inscription most of all. It says everything I'm trying to say to you: *Vocatus extemplo adsum*—I come instantly to your call." He clasped the pendant around her neck and nestled the medallion between her naked breasts.

"I'll be here, close to your heart. The gold is soft and a little of it will rub off on your breasts every day. Do you like it?"

"I love it. I love more the man who gives it to me and the words he says to me." She picked up the small glass vial. "And what is this?"

"It's a tear-vial. It's a gift from the old man who sold me the medallion. He said that even in the best of loving there had to be tears . . ."

"Oh, God! I love you so much, Cavanagh! I can't bear the thought of life without you."

"What else have I been telling you, for God's sake! You don't have to be without me."

"Papa is very angry with you."

"Why?"

"Because of me, because you forced him to change his plans with Mr. Jordan and Lieutenant Doria."

"Did he tell you what his plans were?"

"No. He was talking to Aunt Lucietta. I was standing with Doria a few paces away. He called you a dangerous young upstart. He said the sooner you were gone, the better."

"He'll have his wish. The both of us will be gone the moment Molloy gets back. The both of us, do you hear me?"

"I hear you; but I don't want to talk any more. I want to make love again. Come back to bed!"

"Then you'd better give me the glassware. It's fragile. If it breaks in bed, we'll do ourselves a damage."

Giulia giggled and re-wrapped the piece in tissue paper. She laid it on the bedside table and wedged it with Hadjidakis's diary. It was the first time she had noticed the book. She ran her hand over the leather binding and asked:

"What's this?"

"It's Hadjidakis's journal. I have to pack it in with

the rest of his gear and hand it over to Molloy in Ischia."

Giulia picked up the book and leafed through it. She frowned in disappointment.

"It's written in Greek."

"So it is."

"Molloy told me you read Greek."

"I do."

"Have you read this?"

"Just enough to know that it's a private document."

"Come now, Cavanagh." She began tickling and teasing him. "How much more private can we be—two lovers naked in bed at three in the morning. Read it to me, please!"

For Cavanagh, suddenly—after wild and happy sex, in an afterglow of tender sentiment—there was the high, Luciferian moment of which he had dreamed. He had only to translate a few passages and all the dust sheets that covered this proposed marriage of convenience would be tatters in the wind. Giulia would be brought, untimely, to the ordeal by fire; but at least he, the lover, would be there to lead her, only lightly singed, through the flames. Giulia opened the volume at the title page and handed it to him. He accepted it, pondered awhile, then closed it firmly and shoved it into the drawer of the bedside table. He said curtly:

"I can't do it, my love. The man wrote in Greek to keep his thoughts private. He's dead now and entitled to the decencies."

Giulia was instantly in a rage—like a spoiled schoolgirl denied a lollipop. She could not scream, but her whispered abuse came out a viperous hiss:

"I don't need a lesson in manners, Cavanagh—not from you, not from anyone. This is just what Papa complains about! You presume too much. You're too big for your deck shoes! You swear you love me. I come creeping to your bed like a whore, just to be near you, but you won't share a silly thing like this. What's in the book anyway? Dirty stories?"

"Very dirty stories." Cavanagh was cold and unyielding. "Stories that I hope his wife never gets to read, that I'd rather not tell you either, for fear they'd turn the things we do so happily into something spoiled, like bad fruit. So will you please give over now and drop the subject?"

He slipped into bed again and drew the covers over them both. She turned her back to him and lay a long time, stiff, silent and unyielding. Finally, she found voice to tell him like a petulant child:

"The words on the medal are a lie. I called and you didn't come."

"Not so! I was here all the time. I'm still here. I love you. I will not offer you poisoned fruit."

"Why? Because you want to keep the poison for your own use."

"That's a very Renaissance point of view."

"We're a Renaissance family. You'd be wise to remember that."

"I'm forced to remember it, every day."

"Does my father know you have this book?"

"No."

"Does Molloy?"

"I don't know. I doubt it. After tonight, it will be locked in the ship's safe until I can deliver it to Molloy."

"That means you don't trust me."

"On the contrary. It means I'm confessing a mistake. I should have put it in the safe the moment I realized what it was. It was the most natural thing in the world for you to ask me to read it to you—and the hardest thing for me to refuse. Can we kiss and make up now?"

"If you'll answer a question for me."

"I'd like notice of the question, before I promise to answer it."

"I hate you, Cavanagh! I hate you twice over when you talk like a lawyer."

"I'm not talking at all unless I have notice of the question."

"Does Lou Molloy appear in the book? Does he appear in any of the dirty stories?"

"That's two questions instead of one."

"And the answer?"

"The same to both: *niente da dire*, no comment."

"Then no more loving, Cavanagh. I'm going back to my own bed."

"It'll be cold, Giulia my love, and full of prickles instead of rose petals. You'll be much cozier here, I promise."

In the end, she stayed dangerously late, passing through the saloon just two minutes ahead of Rodolfo with his vacuum cleaner and Chef, who came to the galley to brew the first batch of morning coffee.

By ten in the morning, they were at sea again, coasting slowly southward past Porto Cervo and Golfo Pevero and the long white beach of Romazzino and the islet with the sinister name, Mortorio, the funeral place.

It was a clear, bright day, with a high-pressure system clamped solid over the northern end of the Tyrrhenian Sea. Farnese was on the bridge with Cavanagh, scanning the coastline through binoculars and giving a running commentary for the benefit of Miss Aurora Lambert, who was looking very much the star of stage and screen in a halter top and white shorts, her hair tied back with a scarlet ribbon, her lily-white skin gleaming with suntan lotion.

". . . At the moment, everything you see is wasteland: rocks and scrub and wild herbs. There is no water, no electricity. The only roads are what they call *strade bianche*, all-weather tracks bulldozed to make connection with the main highway round the island . . . But look at the sea, sapphire blue, emerald green, with virgin beaches, and a low hinterland and all those dramatic contours behind it . . . It could be —it should be a tourist paradise. But Molloy is right, the time is not ripe. It's a fabulous development project, but a lousy investment. One would need a bottomless well of money even to put in the substructures . . . That's why he wants us to concentrate on places where the substructures are already in existence . . . Still, one cannot help dreaming."

"But why, Sandro, is it still so deserted?" Aurora Lambert prompted him to continue.

"Because, *cara mia*, until after the war, this whole island was infested with malaria. When the Allies took it over, they conducted a huge campaign to wipe out the anopheles mosquito. Walk into any village and you will see daubed on the doors of the cottages 'DDT,' signifying that the place has been disinfected . . . But there are historic reasons too. The island folk always mistrusted the sea. That's where the raiders came from, the mainland tribes, the Etruscans, the Phoenicians from Africa and later the Corsairs and all the other plunderers from Italy and Spain and France and Sicily and Malta . . . The original inhabitants built the *nuraghi* as watchtowers and forts. The later ones fled inland, leaving only a small seaboard population of fisherfolk and traders . . . I wish I knew more of the history of these names. Over there, see! That's Cala di Volpe, Fox Cove . . . Was it named for the animal, I wonder, or for some old pirate? The bay bends round behind the Cape. It would have made a wonderful ambush . . ."

Cavanagh interrupted Farnese's narrative to announce quietly:

"We've got company, sir, about a mile astern."

Farnese looked first at the radar and then astern through the binoculars. He said:

"It's the *Jackie Sprat*."

"Yes. She picked us up as we passed Porto Pevero. She'll loiter behind us all the way."

"What are you going to do about it?"

"Nothing. We proceed as planned. Have a picnic, spend the day on the beach, take a siesta, have a cocktail cruise, snug down for the night in another bay—or the same one, if it pleases you."

"Nobody's told me where we're going!"

A friendly critic had once complimented Aurora Lambert on 'a querulousness, which stops just short of boring, but in the context of this play, is sometimes dramatically effective.' So, even in her daily discourse, the tiny whine of complaint was always audible. Cavanagh answered cheerfully:

"Step over here and I'll show you on the chart. Then, if you like, you can take us part of the way yourself . . ."

"I'd love that."

It surprised them both to find that she had a steady hand on the helm and a gift of silence when she was about something that interested her. Farnese kissed her, gave the thumbs up sign to her performance, then bent with Cavanagh over the table to examine the somewhat unsatisfactory chart for their next port of call, the stretch of water defined by the two islands of Tavolara and Molara, and the hooked headland which was called Coda Cavallo—the Horse's Tail. Farnese was at once enthusiastic and concerned:

". . . For a picnic, for your diving and swimming it is a fabulous place. It has good holding ground, with sand and weed, a variety of beaches and always a prospect of archeological finds. This little island here—Molara—was once a Phoenician trading port. There are traces of an ancient shrine. The shallows are littered with fragments of amphorae and assorted pottery. Occasionally you find an old stone anchor, with the hole bored through the middle . . ."

"What about the big island, Tavolara?"

"A secret military zone. Access is prohibited. There's a tiny harbor from which tunnels go into the center of the mountain. You'll be fired on without warning if you stick your nose a meter inside it."

"So far, so good," said Cavanagh. "What other problems do we have?"

Farnese pointed to the chart. "Reefs, here and here, between the islands and the shore. You'll need to go dead slow and keep a man on bow-watch, if you get anywhere near this point."

"I'll be steering well clear."

"But remember them, for God's sake, if you have to get out fast or maneuver in close quarters."

"It's good advice, sir. Be sure I'll take it."

"Meanwhile," Farnese persisted, "what will Jordan and Doria be doing?"

"I haven't been told, sir. I'm doing exactly what was requested. I'm anchoring between Molara and Coda Cavallo. I'm taking you all ashore for a picnic while I give your daughter her first diving lessons. Miss Pritchard will come with us to serve lunch. Rodolfo will drive the tender and set up beach umbrellas for you. I'll take the small rubber dinghy with an outboard. I'll bring Giulia to join you on the beach for lunch. Leo, Jackie and Chef will remain on board. They will be armed and they will maintain a deck-and-signal watch until we return."

"And that's all?"

"Everything. We're on a Mediterranean pleasure cruise, sailing under the Stars and Stripes and the courtesy flag of the Republic of Italy."

"Then why the arms?"

"The deck-watch is always armed, sir, to protect the swimmers against sharks and other sea monsters. Your Excellency may relax. I know that I am carrying very precious cargo." He glanced across at Aurora Lambert and switched to English. "Turn the wheel to the left, until the bow is clear of that far point. That's it, now look at your compass. It should be reading a hundred and sixty-five."

"A hundred and sixty-three."

"That will do very nicely, thank you, Miss Lambert."

"Why is it," mused Farnese, softly, "why is it that I like you so much and trust you so little, Cavanagh?"

"It's called conflict of interest, sir." They were back to Italian now. Cavanagh was eloquent and cheerful. "If I were the one marrying your daughter, you'd trust me to the world's end and have brass bands out to welcome me into your house as the perfect son-in-law. As it is,"—he gave a theatrical shrug and made a rueful mouth—"As it is, I'm the cuckoo in the nest, and short of bloodshed, or a blow-up with Molloy, you're wondering how the hell to get me out of it. I've told you plainly. It's Giulia who has the answer to that problem. She knows now that it's herself who must tell me to go or stay. So, why don't you and I relax and enjoy this God-given day?"

"Why not, indeed?" said Alessandro Farnese. "Who knows how many more God will grant to either of us?"

The traffic became more active as they approached Capo Figari, the northern sentinel to the port of Olbia, so Cavanagh took the wheel again, while Farnese watched the *Jackie Sprat*, trailing a mile behind them. Suddenly he snapped:

"My God, they're arresting her!"

"Who's arresting what?" Cavanagh had his eye on a big ferry charging into port from Civitavecchia.

"Two vessels, one's a motor torpedo boat from the Italian Navy, the other's a customs cutter from the Guardia di Finanza. They're closing on the *Jackie Sprat*, ordering her to stop."

"Board and search operation." Cavanagh's tone was casual.

"Did you know about it?"

"No, sir. It was simply one of the options Jordan discussed with me. A delaying tactic, he called it. If they found—or indeed if they planted, any contraband—then they could hold and interrogate Benetti and his crew. I'd love to know what's going on below decks right now. Would you mind if we hove to for a few minutes?"

"Better we don't." Farnese was curt. "You made a great fuss about ordering him off the *Salamandra*. He won't thank you for turning this operation into a spectator sport. Let's keep moving. How long now to Coda Cavallo?"

"We'll have anchors down in fifteen minutes. The ladies can start changing for the beach if they like. Rodolfo will run the gear ashore first and put up the sun umbrellas and set the picnic site . . . That's Tavolara ahead . . . According to the chart the best way in is round the south side . . . It's a massive chunk of rock, isn't it?"

Massive it was, and curiously sinister. Its lower slopes were covered in brushwood. Its precipitous limestone crags, shining in the sun, were wreathed with chattering sea birds, while a peregrine falcon climbed high into the blue, above its summit.

On the north side of it, the tiny harbor mouth was dark and unwelcoming. All that could be seen within it was a causeway and a wall and a series of black tunnel mouths leading into the depths of the mountain. On the south, the rock walls were dazzling, the sea birds raucous, and a pair of seals sunned themselves on a wet rock. The bay itself was ringed with small white beaches, beyond which the hillocks were covered with golden broom, while a few goats grazed on the coarse grasses.

Cavanagh called Rodolfo to stand watch in the bows, while Jackie handled the winch. He turned left into a perfectly sheltered anchorage, out of the lurch of the sea, in a wide, deep basin, fringed by rocky fingers and sandy beaches. He pushed far up under Coda Cavallo and laid his anchors in a wide spread with plenty of chain to prevent dragging, if the sea breeze freshened in the afternoon.

He watched with a certain youthful satisfaction as the boys locked the winches and then hurried to load the tender and the rubber dinghy and lower them overside, ready for embarkation. He had been up early to drill them on what he wanted: a speedy disembarkation and a trouble-free day. When Farnese and Aurora Lambert left the bridge, he switched the radio to the frequency Carl Jordan had given him and announced his presence with the pre-arranged signal:

"This is Letter Coda to Cavallo. Do you read?" The answer came back a few seconds later, read in English at dictation speed. Cavanagh copied it word by word. "This is Cavallo to Coda. Operation now concluding. Ship and company under arrest for possession of prohibited substances. Three crew members in custody and under question aboard customs vessel. Captain and first mate driving arrested vessel to Maddalena under Navy escort. Enjoy your holiday. Sicily is beautiful at this time of year. Thank you. Out."

Cavanagh gave a whistle of satisfaction, shoved the message in his pocket and walked out on deck. Rodolfo was just pushing off in the tender to set up umbrellas, windbreaks, deck chairs and the picnic table on a white beach. Jackie and Leo were loading diving gear into the small rubber dinghy and fitting the outboard motor. The women were below, changing into beach wear. Farnese was leaning over the rail watching the proceedings. Cavanagh showed him the message he had just received. Farnese nodded indifferently.

"It is good that these people are in custody. I imagine they will be taken to the prison at Tempio di Pausania and held without bail, while the magistrate conducts his primary inquiries. That will take them out of the argument for a while. By the time the Navy and the Guardia di Finanza make their depositions and the instructing judge has studied them and the prisoners have made their depositions and the judge has studied those too, it will be, oh, at least six months, more than enough time to . . ."

Before he had time to finish the sentence there was the sound of an explosion, muffled and distant. It was followed by two others. Then, over the low, northward ridges that hid the city of Olbia, they saw a high, billowing cloud of black smoke, spreading at the base, its apex shot through with flames, thrusting higher and higher into the blue sky.

Cavanagh was caught in a sickening moment of horror—a moment he had lived before during the combat years: a steel ship erupting into fragments, human bodies tossed like rag dolls into the air, the sea aflame, the sky blackened by smoke, the water putrid with tarry waste and oil that choked the lungs of any who survived the blast. Then he himself was choking on his own anger. He hammered his fists on the rail and finally found voice for a torrent of curses:

"That son-of-a-bitch! That rotten, treacherous bastard! He told me he was going to stage an arrest and plant enough evidence to hold 'em and get 'em into custody, while the *carabinieri* on Elba investigated the murder of Hadjidakis . . ."

"It would seem from the message that he's kept his promise."

"For Christ's sake! You know what he's done as well as I do. Look at that smoke. There must be half a mile of seaway ablaze now. He's blown up the *Jackie Sprat*, with Benetti and his mate on board! He didn't even have to stick the mines on the hull. He could have planted them in the bloody engine room during the search!"

"But you can't prove that," said Farnese firmly, "not in a million years. Read the last line of your message . . . 'Sicily is beautiful' . . . He wants us out of here."

"I'm sure he does!"

"Whatever Jordan has done," Farnese persisted, "it all works to our benefit. A real threat has been removed. Those who ordered Hadjidakis's death have been put on notice that there is no profit for anyone in a long vendetta. Thanks to your careful thinking, we are totally divorced from anything that may have happened out there."

"We were the decoys, for God's sake!"

"No! We were the quarry pursued by predators! My suggestion now is that we begin our picnic and spare the ladies any distressing speculation. Yes?"

"We don't have much choice, do we?"

"None at all. We enjoy our day. And tonight we point our nose southward."

Cavanagh turned to go. Farnese laid a hand on his arm to detain him.

"Mr. Cavanagh, let me tell you something. There is no court in this country, or indeed anywhere in the world, which would find that you had acted badly in this matter. You co-operated with the authorities. You protected your guests, your crew, your ship. You were not involved in any way in this inter-service operation."

"How the hell can you take it so calmly? This is murder—a double murder—and I helped to set it up."

"So you did. But remember, I did warn you that you were playing in a game you didn't understand. You invoked your authority as master of this vessel. I deferred to it, because your own obstinacy made you a most convenient scapegoat."

"It's a lesson I'll remember, sir, but not one I'll thank you for!"

"The lesson's more important than the thanks." Farnese's indifference was itself an insult. "It may one day save your life!"

He had set much store upon the simple matter of Giulia's diving lessons. He was jealous of them, as a child might be jealous of a private game with a beloved friend. They would be the first open leisure they could enjoy together, the first real playtime, in which they could share looks, waves, gestures, simple bodily contacts, without the urgency of furtive mating in the confined space of shipboard. It would be his first chance to display to her his physical skills, and be there to support her while she mastered them herself.

Yet, when the moment came, in the sheltered inlet on Molara, out of sight of the ship and the people on the beach, he found himself suddenly brusque and constrained, reverting to the old routines of the Navy instructor, setting out curtly the cautions that must be exercised on entering this new element.

Giulia, on the other hand, seemed to welcome this unfamiliar attitude of professional detachment. She listened carefully, asked intelligent questions, committed herself with full confidence to each step of the drill. When they surfaced after the first practice dive, she told him:

"I thought I would be much more nervous, the way one is if a parent or relative wants to teach one to drive a car or play a game. On the contrary, you were so cool and professional, I didn't feel awkward at all."

"I'm glad. This is a dangerous sport, mistakes can be costly. Yet, how do you lecture the woman you adore?"

"I didn't feel you were lecturing me—but I didn't feel you were adoring me either."

"Enough from you, Principessa! Now, we're going back into the water. Same exercise, clearing the eustachian tubes, then we'll go out a way and swim round the rocks, diving to about fifteen or twenty feet. We'll swim together. I want you to practice looking at the depth gauge and the watch on your wrist. That, again, is like driving a car—you go through the safety motions every time—and remember that we keep signaling to each other, and the signals are standard too. Ready?"

"Ready!"

"Let's go!"

This time, the pleasure began to return. In the water she was beautiful to watch. Her movements were fluid, her breathing was regular and unhurried, her normal impulsiveness was subdued to the rhythms of this world, still quite new to her—to the movement of the sea grasses, the silver flash of the minnow schools, the slow cruise of an inquisitive grouper, the flurry of a flounder burying itself in the sand, the furtive progress of a hermit crab in his borrowed house. Finally, Cavanagh pointed to his watch and signaled that it was time to make the homeward circuit round the headland.

This time Giulia led the way, with Cavanagh trailing a short way behind her. Suddenly she stopped and pointed downwards. There, half-buried in the sand was the shoulder, the lip and the handle of a terra-cotta amphora.

Cavanagh signaled her to dive and then joined her on the sandy bottom. He motioned to her to disturb the sand as little as possible and then began gently to free the amphora. The task was easy. It was a fragment only, from one of those long, inverted cones which the old-time sellers of wine and oil fitted into slots outside their shops. It had no value at all, but its discovery was an event for both of them. When they came out of the water, they sat on the beach to examine it. Cavanagh pointed out the grooves of the potter's fingers on the inside surface and the small fragment of a seal stamped into the shoulder. Giulia smiled and kissed him.

"It's important to you, isn't it?"

"Yes, it is. It's the connection, don't you see? The connection between some long-dead mariner and me, the man from the farthest continent. I doubt he was wrecked here. The amphora probably broke and was tossed overboard as a piece of ship's rubbish . . . But we found it, you and I. So we're connected to the potter, the merchant, the sailor . . . I'd like you to keep this."

Giulia declined gently.

"No, you keep it. Our places are full of such things, much more perfect, but none of them means as much as this fragment, now that I've seen the light in your eyes and the smile on your lips . . ."

"Today is only the beginning. We'll find better things."

"But none will be as precious to you as this. Tell the truth now!"

"You're right, my love. None will be as precious as this. It puts the taste back into a very bitter day."

"What do you mean?"

He told her all of it: his deal with Carl Jordan, its brutal outcome, her father's contemptuous absolution and his curt warning. Giulia heard him out in silence. She gave no verdict upon his actions. She offered no sympathy for his distress. She said simply:

"Last night you said a thing that troubled me very much. The name of the game, you said, is my lady or my life."

"That was a bad joke. I beg you to forget it."

"No, my love, it was not a joke. What happened this morning, what Papa said to you, these were not jokes either."

"Very well! I accept that, but I cannot accept that you or I should live in fear of faceless monsters."

"I can't accept it either; but I know better than you that the monsters exist. I fear them. I fear for you, too, because I love you with all my heart, Cavanagh!"

"And I love you too, Giulia mia! So, not all the monsters in the world can defeat us."

"Oh, yes, they can! And they will, just as they did today . . . It breaks my heart, my love; but I have to say it. I cannot, I will not marry you!"

"You don't mean it. You can't!"

"I mean it. From now until we arrive in Ischia to meet Molloy, I am yours, morning, noon and night. I don't care who knows it or sees it. But the hour before we dock, you walk out of my life; I walk out of yours."

"Holy Mother of God!" Cavanagh reached out to grasp her but she stepped away. "This isn't you talking. It's your father, your aunt . . ."

"No, Cavanagh! This is your Giulia—and I'm yours as long as I live, as long as you care to remember me. But if you die—what's left to me? A ghost piping in winter among the laurels! I won't risk that. I won't risk you. Please don't be angry!"

"I'm not angry. I'm crying inside me. I can taste the salt on my tongue. I love you, for Christ's sake!"

"I'm so proud you love me, Cavanagh. Let me go on being proud of you. Let me wave you like my banner, even if it's only for these last days."

"I can't let you go to that son-of-a-bitch, Molloy. I know what he is. I . . ."

"Hush, my love! I know what he is too! You don't have to hate him so much. My namesake tamed the Borgia pope and none of his monster sons dared threaten her. I'm not afraid of Molloy—and I will not see you shamed by him or by my father . . ."

"It's myself who'll do the shaming, if it comes to that. I'll ram Hadjidakis's book down Molloy's neck and make him chew it page by page! Crazy, isn't it! I'm losing the only thing I prize in my life and all I can think of is a book written by a Greek who only half knows his mother tongue!"

Cavanagh's humor turned suddenly black and bilious. "Come on! Let's make love! Let's peel off this bloody rubber suiting and disport ourselves like honest peasants on the beach!"

"You're not a peasant, Cavanagh. To me, you are a prince!"

"That's nice to hear, Giulia mia; but I have to tell you, some son-of-a-bitch has just turned me into a toad!"

Interludes

New York to Rome

Flight AZ 611
1992

THE FRIDAY EVENING FLIGHT WAS A RED-eye, which departed Kennedy at five in the evening and landed at Fiumicino at seven in the morning. In spite of his age, Bryan de Courcy Cavanagh had developed a tolerance for long-haul overnight flying. His prescription was simple: he ate little, drank only mineral water, then blotted out the world with earplugs and eyeshades, closed all the doors of his mind and willed himself into instant oblivion.

This time, however, the formula had failed. They were three hours out on the Great Circle route and he was still wide awake, his once-tidy mind a jumble of business memoranda, family news from Louise, speculations about why Giulia had summoned him to Rome, and a whole jigsaw of forty-year-old memories which he was trying to fit back into a logical sequence.

The business matters were swiftly dismissed. He opened his briefcase, reviewed the decisions of the meeting in Manhattan, re-checked the list of documents his office had been instructed to produce, did some quick arithmetic on his own earnings, decided there was nothing to be worried about and much to be grateful for, and closed the briefcase.

The family news was neutral. Everyone was well.

Cavanagh's only anxiety was whether he had been overvoluble in his explanation of this sudden call to Rome and his new client. Impresa Romagnola. Louise was interested only in his personal well-being; she was not at all concerned with the persons or corporations which made up his client list. This time, however, she had cut him off in mid-talk and asked:

"Are you sure you're all right, darling?"

"Of course I'm all right! Why do you ask?"

"Because you've told me all the news. You're going to Rome to see a new client. Now you're burbling on and on like the proverbial brook . . ."

"Am I? I didn't mean to. It must be a reaction. Yesterday was a long, rough day. I had my birthday dinner alone at a little bistro up on Madison. The wine must have been even rougher than it tasted. Anyway, I'll see you Monday. Give the kids kisses for me—and save a couple of the best ones for yourself. I love you."

"I love you too. Godspeed."

Which brought him, by a round turn, back to the jigsaw pieces of the past, still rattling round in his head. He had to set them in order before he faced Giulia in Mongrifone. He had worked long enough in the law to know that the advocate who came to a case with holes in his brief would soon find his money and his clients leaking away through them. Somewhere in all the mess of memories was the reason for Giulia's summons and her urgent call for his presence in her life after forty years of absence.

Up to the moment of destruction and of love on the beach at Molara, everything was clear. It was the events of the aftermath which had to be set in order. As the big 747 droned its way through the night, Cavanagh made his own silent flight into the black abysses of the past . . .

* * *

From the moment they rejoined the picnic party, there was a subtle change in the atmosphere. It was, as Giulia said later—"as if they were waiting to inspect the bloody sheets after the wedding night, or to measure the bridegroom's member to prove that he was potent." No one, however, knew how to frame the question or dared to put it until Cavanagh issued a curt command.

"Rodolfo, I'd like you to take the tender and give Miss Lambert and Miss Pritchard a tour of the harbor."

Miss Lambert opened her mouth to protest, but thought better of it. Lenore Pritchard said nothing and headed immediately down to the boat, leaving Rodolfo to shepherd the reluctant Aurora. Once they were afloat and out of earshot, Giulia made her announcement.

"It's no secret to you, Papa, or to Aunt Lucietta, that Cavanagh and I love each other and that we are lovers in fact. This morning Cavanagh asked me once more to marry him and go away with him to share his life. For reasons which you fully understand, and which Cavanagh still finds hard to accept, I refused. He had promised from the beginning that, if I did not want to marry him, he would walk out of my life. He is an honorable man. He will keep that promise. But now hear me, Papa! We are lovers still. We shall be until we come to Ischia and Lou Molloy is there to claim me. Until that time you will not ask where I am or what I do with this man I love, who is breaking his heart to keep his promise. You will not shame him, snub him or belittle him in any way. If you do, I shall be gone—and all you have built on my marriage to Molloy will be in ruins. You know me, Papa. I keep my promises too."

There was a long, bleak silence before Farnese asked:

"Do you want to say anything, Mr. Cavanagh?"

"Only this. I didn't compose Giulia's speech. If I had, I should have left out the threat at the end. If anyone treads on the tail of my coat, I'll deal with them personally. For the rest, neither Giulia nor I will embarrass you on board; but I hope you won't grudge us the last drops of the happiness we have."

"No, Cavanagh. I won't grudge them to you. You may find it hard to believe, but I wish you much good in your life."

"I do find it hard to believe, sir; but it's too late in the day to argue the matter. Let's part in peace."

Farnese hesitated a moment and then nodded agreement.

"In peace. Yes, of course."

To which the Countess added her own tart little postscript:

"A few days ago, Cavanagh, I asked you a question. You've just answered it for me." She raised her glass and pronounced the old-fashioned salute: "*Salve!*"

"I hail him too, Papa." Giulia,. diminutive but defiant, stood beside Cavanagh. "I'm marrying Lou Molloy; but never forget, this is the man I love!"

After that, unless his memory was playing him tricks, they behaved, for a very short while, just like a family. They linked arms and walked along the beach looking for shells, they paddled in the shallows and skipped stones across the water until Rodolfo brought his charges back from the tour of the bay, and drove them all to the ship before returning to dismantle the picnic site.

On board, another strangeness awaited him—or was that too just a trick of tired memory? It seemed that the crew were looking at him with furtive eyes, as if he were Moses, with horns of light on his brow, coming down from the mount of revelation. But the only verbal memory he could summon up was Lenore Pritchard's remark:

"What happened to you today, buster? You look as though you've taken a real beating—or was it just too much sex under the rosemary bushes!"

After that, pictures of their last ports of call unrolled themselves like film on an endless spool.

They were all small and unfamiliar places, because Farnese was restless and very bored with his Aurora and he wanted to stay on the move, far away from big ports and tourist centers.

The names echoed in the dream like ancient incantations: Alicudi, Filicudi, Salina, Lipari, Vulcano, Panarea.

The images were not of today, with ferry docks and tourist hotels, but of forty years past, when the islands were still places of exile, their natives were small inbred tribes, their dialect a barrier against casual contact.

Their recreations on the cruise were simple too. They bathed in hot pools, they dived in blue caverns, they shopped in tiny fish markets and drank dark, sulphurous wines grown on precarious terraces. One night they made the circuit of Stromboli itself, a cone of fire with fresh lava flows rolling slowly down its slopes. After that they sailed until dawn and dropped anchor under towering cliffs, with a beach between, in the Gulf of Policastro.

Amid all these dramatic landscapes, the images of Giulia seemed the least precise, the most fleeting. She was always present, as she had been on the voyage itself, in bed during his rest time, on deck as he went about his duties, on the bridge during the night crossings. Each of her presences was a delight, but they were all in mezzotint. It was like an ironic reprise of "Passione," only this time with the words reversed:

"*Cchiù vicina me staie, cchiù luntana me sento.* The closer you are to me, the further away you seem . . ."

Then, out of all the soft-focus images, one projected itself with absolute clarity.

It was very early in the morning. They had dropped anchor off a sandy beach, in the Gulf of Salerno, just opposite the ancient ruins of Paestum, which they proposed to visit during the day. The crew were busy, washing decks, brushing carpets and polishing brass-work, while Cavanagh, just off night-watch, was drinking coffee with Chef in the galley. In his forthright fashion the Chef put the question:

"Tomorrow we are in Ischia. Molloy will be back on board. How do you feel about that?"

"I feel fine. I'll be handing him a clean ship and, I hope, a happy crew . . . Which reminds me, Chef, I'll need the rest of your accounts. I have to finish writing up the books."

"To hell with the books! Tell me the rest of it. How are things with you and Giulia?"

"They're fine."

"What's that supposed to mean. 'They're fine.' That's nothing talk!"

"What do you want me to say? It's ended, or nearly ended. Tomorrow we rule a line through it and forget it ever happened. That's what we agreed."

"Rule the line, by all means! You have to do that, but you'll never erase what's written."

"I know, but why should we erase anything?"

"Why indeed, if you can read the tale without bitterness."

"I'm just beginning to believe we can."

"I've watched Giulia." Chef was musing now. "She's been very careful of you, like a mother weaning a baby off the breast."

"Jesus, Chef!" Cavanagh spluttered over his coffee.

"That's a hell of a thing to say! Look what you've made me do! This bloody shirt is ruined!"

"Why do you make such a fuss about a simple statement? It's true." There was a gleam of cheerful malice in his eyes. "And you're a good, strong baby, Cavanagh, you're weaning well! I have respect for you —much more than I had at the beginning."

"*Grazie infinite!*" In spite of himself Cavanagh laughed. "You don't give an inch, do you, you old bastard?"

"What's to give? What's to take? We're stuck with what is. I keep asking myself how Molloy will be when he comes back?"

Cavanagh dismissed the question with a gesture.

"The Molloys of this world never change, Chef. They're hardheads. They take all, give nothing and they can charm the birds out of the trees when they put their minds to it. Dangle a profit or a pretty rump in front of Molloy and he'll be head down and charging like a bull at a matador's cape."

Chef stood back, folded his arms and surveyed him like a particularly noisome specimen in a glass jar.

"So! What have we here? A Solomon sitting in judgment! Who gave you the right to stick a label like that on Lou Molloy?"

"It's true."

"Maybe, but it's not the whole truth."

"Who knows the whole truth about anyone, Chef?"

"Then let me say, I think you still have quite a few surprises coming from Lou Molloy!"

The first surprise came late that same afternoon while they were coasting slowly up to the port of Salerno to take on water and fuel and replenish their stocks of fresh food before making their last short run to Ischia, where stores would be double the price in the high season. Molloy called up on the regular Portishead channel. No, he did not want to talk to anyone else, only to Cavanagh. What time did he expect to be in Ischia? Anytime Mr. Molloy desired. Ten in the morning then. Aye, aye, sir. Was Mr. Hadjidakis's gear packed? All of it, sir, in Hadjidakis's own sea chest. Now a message for Farnese. Galeazzi was with Molloy on Ischia. Molloy had booked accommodation for all his guests at the Regina Isabella Hotel. They should be ready to leave the ship with all their baggage and expect to stay a few days before going on to Rome. The vessel and the crew would remain in port pending further instructions. Was all that clear? Yes, sir, and how was Mr. Molloy himself? Mr. Molloy refused to broadcast the state of his health to the whole wide world. They would talk at length in Ischia. End of a forty-year-old dialogue . . .

The stewardess was tapping him gently on the shoulder. When he lifted his eyeshades, she handed him a hot towel, informed him that they were just passing over the Maritime Alps en route to Rome and asked would he prefer an American breakfast or coffee and croissants.

Awake, shaved and modestly refreshed, he sipped coffee and toyed with the tasteless croissants and looked down upon the changes that forty years had wrought along the Mediterranean littoral. The shoreline was an uninterrupted ribbon of urban sprawl. The hinterland was dotted, ever more closely, with ugly townlets where once the serried vineyards had marched, with the green pike-men of the cypresses towering over them.

The sea, once sapphire and emerald and full of fish, was now a fetid lake of sewage from which the fish had retreated to the darkest ravines, while the sea-grasses were covered with saponified slime, and human hordes disported themselves at daily peril of gastroenteritis, typhoid and hepatitis. Alas and alas, the fleeting years!

It had all been different on that early summer's morning when they slipped out of Salerno Harbor, coasted past Amalfi and Capri and headed across the Gulf of Naples to Ischia. Giulia and he had spent the night together, in the big double bed in her cabin. They had made love. They had talked disjointedly about his future and hers. They had wept together. They had made love again; but this time the passion was almost spent and they surrendered to the elegiac languors of the last mating and the last farewell that had any meaning for either of them. The rest would be postscript, dispensable, a formality.

By the time he maneuvered the *Salamandra d'Oro* into her berth in the small harbor basin, the passengers' luggage was stacked on deck, the boys were ready with the gangway and Molloy was standing on the dock, a gaunt, commanding figure in his dress whites, ready to take the lines, as Cavanagh himself had done that first day in Antibes. Behind him the van from the Regina Isabella was waiting to pick up the luggage and there was a trio of horse-drawn carriages for the Farnese party.

The moment the gangway was down, Molloy came on board at a run and swept Giulia into a passionate embrace that drew a low chorus of approval from the watchers on the dock. He embraced the Countess, kissed Miss Aurora Lambert's hand, shook hands with the males of the crew, pecked Lenore lightly on the cheek, then turned his attention to Cavanagh, who had just come down from the bridge and was waiting to offer his own formal greeting.

"Welcome back, sir!"

Molloy stared at him for a long moment, measuring

him as he had done at their first meeting; then his face lit up with a smile. He clapped his hands on Cavanagh's shoulders and drew him, too, into a long, Latin embrace. Then he held him at arm's length and proclaimed:

"Well! Well! Well! The cub's a tiger now, I hear! Did you have a good trip?"

"It had its moments, sir, yes. And how was yours?"

"That had its moments too, but we'll talk about those another time. I want to get our friends installed in the hotel. We have urgent business with Count Galeazzi. I'll visit with you sometime tomorrow, probably before lunch. Meantime, see if you can plug into a telephone circuit, clean ship and get the laundry done, then give the crew some shore leave. How are you off for money?"

"We're still in funds, sir. We don't need anything yet."

"Good! Then say your goodbyes and we'll be off."

The farewells were as brief as politeness permitted: a *baciamano* for the women, a cool handshake for Farnese, a brief expression of thanks for the pleasure of their company, a hope that soon they would meet again, a courteous but cool refusal of the envelope which Farnese handed him as "a small thanks for your service and that of the crew."

When Leo and Jackie complained afterwards that he had deprived them of their rightful earnings, he burst out:

"Rightful, be damned! You know the rules! Molloy pays, not the guests! You missed the point. He was trying to put me down with a Judas payment!"

"It was perhaps a natural mistake," said Chef blandly.

"How natural?"

"Well, he saw you and Molloy embracing. That

must have looked very much like a Judas kiss to him. It certainly did to me!"

"Oh, go to hell!"

The memory of that little exchange, forty years ago, still made him feel uncomfortable. In all truth, it had been a Judas moment. All of them had been party to the betrayal of Declan Aloysius Molloy. However, there was no way one could embellish the metaphor, because Molloy was certainly not Jesus Christ, not even an innocent victim. He was a rough, tough politico, a ruthless moneymaker, a recorded killer, a man, who, as the Irish used to say, would poke a hole in a wall. Even so, the Farnese had eaten his salt and would soon be eating his money, Giulia was committing him to a loveless marriage, and Bryan de Courcy Cavanagh had made him a cuckold even before the wedding night, put horns on him before all his crew.

The memory somehow matched with the polluted seas and the defaced landscape below him, and it was a dangerous ulcer for a sixty-five-year-old lawyer to be carrying on an already well-scarred conscience. But that wasn't the last of it. There was still one more part of the jigsaw to complete and he put it together, while the aircraft was hung up for half an hour in a holding pattern over Lake Bracciano . . .

Molloy came to the ship at eleven-thirty the next morning. He came alone. Cavanagh was alone too, sitting on the afterdeck, watching the ebb and flow of life around the dock. Once upon a time he would have had to be out there, mingling, making talk with anyone who would give him the time of day, smiling at the girls, offering them coffee and cognac for companionship. Today was different. He was different: empty inside, bruised all over. The only way he could take the crowd was to let it spread itself upon him like a healing salve. So, even Molloy's visit was a welcome diversion.

They walked over the ship together, Molloy nodding a laconic approval of what he saw. They went through the ship's accounts. Molloy approved those too, and handed Cavanagh a large wad of dollar bills by way of a new impressment. Cavanagh protested:

"That's far too much, sir. It's five months' funding. It's risky to carry that much cash on board."

"There's a reason. I want you to take the ship back to Antibes, pay out the crew contracts—with a month's bonus all round—then hand her over to Glémot for *gardienage* pending further instructions."

"May I know the reason, sir?"

"Sure! There's no secret. Giulia and I will be married as soon as we get to Rome. I'm taking her to the United States for our honeymoon. Then Galeazzi and Farnese are coming over to meet with the Wall Street financiers. So there won't be any more time for cruising, not this season anyway."

"With respect, sir, wouldn't it be a good idea to work the ship, let Glémot find some charters for you?"

"And let people I know nothing about kick the guts out of my beauty? No way!"

"It needn't be like that, sir. This is a good crew. We'd look after her for you."

"I know you would, Cavanagh; but . . ." He hesitated a moment then let the words out with a rush. "Hell! What's the use of beating around the bush! Without Giorgios Hadjidakis, I've got no heart for her any more. I'm going to sell her. I'll give you a letter to Glémot with the appropriate instructions."

"She's your vessel of course, but it seems such a shame."

"It is a shame, Cavanagh, but there it is. There's a curse on her now. She'll never be a happy ship again. Not for me, anyway."

Since that was a subject he had no wish to explore, Cavanagh asked:

"What do you want me to do with Hadjidakis's gear?"

Molloy fished in his pocket and brought out a business card with an address written on the back of it.

"Use these people, Salviati, they're international shippers. They do a lot of work for foreign residents and embassies. They have an agent on the island. The address of Hadjidakis's wife is written on the back."

"How is Mrs. Hadjidakis holding up?"

"Well, as always, She's an iron lady, that one. She married a wanderer, but she knew it when she got him. I never heard her utter a word of complaint. His kids adored him. I set up a money plan for them years ago. So they'll be doing fine. The hole in their life isn't so big as if Giorgios had been around all the while . . ."

"That reminds me, sir. There's something I have to give you. It belongs to Hadjidakis. I wasn't quite sure how to deal with it. Wait here a moment, please."

He was back in two minutes with Hadjidakis's diary. He opened it at the title page and laid it in front of Molloy, who leafed through it quickly.

"What is this?"

"It's Hadjidakis's journal. I found it lying on his bedside table when I took over his cabin."

"Have you read it?"

"Enough to know what's in it."

"Which is?"

"The title describes it accurately: *The True Chronicle of the Voyages of G and L*, that's Giorgios and Lou."

Molloy's first reaction was a belly laugh.

"Well, I'll be damned! The old bastard was always promising he'd do something like this. I never believed him. Go on, read me some of it."

"You may not like what you hear."

"That's for me to judge. Go on, man, read it!"

Cavanagh picked two entries, one a particularly brutal description of an exhibitionist brothel in Martinique and an orgy in which both Hadjidakis and Molloy had taken part. The other was the account of the duel in Havana.

Molloy was silent for a long time afterwards. Cavanagh closed the book and pushed it across the table to him.

"I thought you should dispose of it yourself. It's not the sort of thing you'd want his wife or his children to read."

"Nor anyone else for that matter. Who else has seen this?"

"I have no idea. It was lying in full view on the table beside Hadjidakis's bunk. Anyone could have seen it; but, so far as I know, I'm the only one on board who reads Greek."

"Have you talked about it or read it to anyone else?"

"No." What else could he say without involving Giulia? "I kept it locked in the safe."

"But you must realize you've taken an awful risk by showing it to me."

"I understand the risk. I have for quite a while now. In the games you're playing, people do get killed. There are three dead already. Hadjidakis, Benetti and his mate . . . I'm sure there have been and will be others. I could be one of them. There were moments when I thought of holding on to the book or at least making a certified photographic copy just to protect myself."

"That would have been the smart thing to do."

"It could also have turned me into a sort of blackmailer—a species I'd rather prosecute than promote. You have your book. If you want to do me harm, you'll do it anyway. For the rest, if you're agreeable,

I'll leave tomorrow morning. We can do the trip in two days."

"That's fine. But I'd prefer you to stay at sea for the whole run."

"We have to drop Rodolfo off in Elba. That's his home port."

"Stay the hell away from Elba. Put the lad ashore in Livorno or Piombino and give him his fare home. I know Carl Jordan thinks he's cleared out the rats' nest. I'm not so sure. The more I see of this intelligence underworld, the less I like it. They run their own kind of blackmail. Do you have anything more for me?"

"No, sir, that just about wraps it up."

"Then pour us a couple of whiskies and bring 'em out on the afterdeck. We can watch the fillies parade while we talk."

The talk was a confession, an *apologia pro vita sua*, by Declan Aloysius Molloy. He took a big swallow of whisky and then launched straight into the narrative:

". . . I need to talk about this, Cavanagh; and I'm talking to you, because you're the one who understands this whole Irish-Catholic rigmarole of sin and guilt and repentance and wanting to make a new start and never being able to, because there's an enormous great millstone hung round your neck and you can never lift your head high enough to see a single star. Now that Hadjidakis is dead, the guilts are blacker and the weight of the millstone is twice as heavy.

"I wanted to talk to Spelly about it in New York, but he ducked it. He said we had so many outside things going, he'd rather not meddle in my private conscience. Which I understood, because I think Spelly's a little screwed up himself in the sex department and he's also keeping some very odd political company with Joe McCarthy and that little prick of a Roy Cohn. He said he'd be happy to recommend me to an understanding confessor, but hell, that's the worst kind of blind date . . .

"So, I've been stewing ever since, because I really do want to make a clean start with Giulia and found a family that can have some respect for its old man. Now you hit me with this—Hadjidakis's book, which I can't read and daren't get translated, so I'll never know what my heart's true friend thought of me." He emptied his glass at a gulp and thrust it at Cavanagh. "You're forgetting your party manners, boyo. I'm out of liquor! . . ."

Cavanagh refilled his glass and put only a half measure in his own, but Molloy was quick to protest:

"Oh no, you don't! If I have to be drunk to tell it, you'll need a decent drink to make the tale tolerable. By the way, Giulia showed me the little tear-vial you gave us for a wedding present. I liked the thought and I thank you for it. It showed you have some grace about you—as my old history teacher used to say. And it's history now I'm talking about: Giorgios Hadjidakis and Declan Aloysius Molloy! We made some history! The plan was that we'd go on making it. Now he's dropped off the planet. That's why the bastards who killed him had to die too. That was the deal I made with Dulles. Those were Carl Jordan's orders, which you nearly fouled up. But that was my fault, because I didn't take you into my confidence. I'm doing it now, but it's a long time too late.

"I told you, didn't I, Hadjidakis and I were kids together and our relationship never changed. He was the contriver, the one who set up the plots and dares. I was the doer, the sucker who had to carry them out. It wasn't that he lacked courage. Never! He was there, raging like a lion every time. But he needed a leader. He was the perfect number two and he never wanted to be anything else. I needed a teacher. My old man was hard as nails and my mother was born to lace-curtains. Between them they closed the doors and held them closed against anything or anyone that might threaten our safe and sacred world. So who was there to teach me how the world wagged beyond our front porch?

"It was Hadjidakis who showed me how to steal an apple on a fly-past run in the market. It was he who taught me about sex and the nine and ninety ways you could have it, and he gave me my first lessons himself. It was he who took me to my first bar and taught me how to listen to the talk: the clerks from the law offices, the enforcers from the loan sharks, the business girls and their pumps, the cops passing by to pick up the free drink and the envelope with the Friday money in it. He taught me about trade, too—how to buy low in the flea-market and sell higher, peddling door-to-door to the housewives. He'd bargain for the goods. I'd sell 'em to the ladies. I didn't need the money—we had lace-curtains, remember?—but Hadjidakis kept it for me, so I wouldn't have to explain it at home. And somehow he managed to make it grow like a conjurer's mango tree.

"One day we made a pact. Wherever and whenever I got a job, I would find a place for him, a place near me. I would haul him up the ladder with me and he would cover my arse from the bastards below. We would share everything, vacations, adventures, lovers, confidences, everything! When he got married, things changed. They had to; but we still cruised together, until I offered him a job on my first boat as first mate, engineer and, well, master of ceremonies—whoremaster, some folks would call it; but with Hadjidakis you couldn't think of it that way. At least I couldn't.

"I asked his opinion on everything, even on my association with Farnese and my marriage to Giulia. He advised me to go ahead, to put down roots in the old world as well as the new. He understood politics.

His old man had been a ward heeler for Honey Fitz among the Greek community in Boston. He didn't want me to get involved in the Tolvier affair. He thought there were too many players in the game. I thought I knew better. Besides, Dulles and his friends were calling in some markers and I knew I'd need some favors too, once Farnese and Galeazzi and I started to work together . . . Well, this is how it ends! Giorgios is dead. And I'm making my confession to a mick from down under who, rumor has it, tried very hard to seduce my beloved Giulia. Now what would you say to that, Mr. Bryan Cavanagh?"

"I would say"—and he said it very slowly because for the first time in his life he was groping for words—"I would say, Mr. Molloy, sir, that rumor is a lying jade, and I think I can name the jade in question."

"Can you, now? Would you try it on me for size?"

"Farnese's girlfriend, Aurora Lambert. He's tired of her. She's looking for a new patron and angel, you!"

"Clever boy! Go to the top of the class!"

"It was an easy question. What's hard to understand is your need to ask it."

The question sobered Molloy for a moment. He took his time over the answer.

"Well, Cavanagh, as I've just tried to explain to you at great length, I've been robbed of the greatest love in my life. I know I'm getting a new chance with Giulia—which I'm very lucky to have. The problem is, I'm not sure my experience fits me to handle a lady of her quality and lineage. Is there any advice a young fellow like you might be able to offer me?"

"None, sir. You're the man with the years and the experience. All I can remember is what my mother used to tell me: 'Before you sit down to supper with decent folk, Bryan Cavanagh, make sure your hands are clean!' "

"A wise woman!" said Declan Aloysius Molloy. "A

wise, wise woman. Now will you watch me down the gangplank, please, and help me into a horse and buggy? I'm a mite unsteady on my feet."

Forty years on, it was the fear in the man which Cavanagh remembered most poignantly. He was like a puppet, hanging from the catwalk with all his limbs askew and no puppet-master to bring him to life.

It was a fear that Cavanagh now understood very well. The plane was coming down now on a steep descent into Fiumicino. The moment he stepped off it, he would be walking into a void, the dark backward of forty lost years.

Book Two

A Weekend at Mongrifone

1992

THE DRIVE FROM FIUMICINO TO MONgrifone was irrevocably lost to him. His chauffeur was a taciturn young Florentine, who drove the big Mercedes so smoothly that Cavanagh slept all the way from the image of Leonardo da Vinci at the airport, to the portals of the Farnese villa in the Sabine Hills.

The chauffeur handed him over to a majordomo, an elderly white-haired fellow with courtly manners, who conducted him up a wide, circular staircase to a huge bedroom which opened out onto a terrace and a panorama of vineyards, farmlands, orchards, greenhouses and vegetable gardens, with misty blue ridges in the background.

The majordomo explained that the Principessa had left early in the morning for Rome, but that she would be back for lunch about one o'clock. Meantime, after so long a flight, the *dottore* would no doubt appreciate a bath and a sleep. If he had any clothes to be washed or suits to be pressed, they would be taken care of while he rested. Meantime, he would be pleased to unpack the baggage and draw a bath for the *dottore*.

As he worked, he offered small sweetmeats of information. This was formerly the bedchamber of Prince Alessandro, dead these many years, but still remembered and loved in Mongrifone. That was the town over there to the right, on the crest of the hill. In the old days, the family had maintained its residence within the walls of the fortress; but in the nineteenth century they had moved out to this estate, which was called the Prince's Villa. It was a large enterprise, as the *dottore* could see; but the Principessa managed it with great skill.

The bathroom was large enough to parade a platoon and the bath itself was a huge porphyry tub with steps leading into it and dolphin heads for faucets. There was a dressing gown hung behind the door, a rack of thick towels and an array of toiletries in crystal bottles.

On the bedside table was a note and a gift-wrapped package. The note, which carried Giulia's personal escutcheon, read simply: "I lend to you what you gave to me. The tears are real. They are the tears of joy I shed when I knew you were coming. *Te voglio te penzo, te chiammo.* Giulia." Inside the package was the tear-vial, mounted on a tiny gold stand, and stoppered with a gold coronet. There were indeed a few drops of liquid inside it. Cavanagh tested them on his tongue. They had a salt taste to them, just like those he had tasted on her cheeks the night before they parted.

The majordomo announced that the *dottore*'s bath was ready. When he was rested he should simply ring the bell and the pressed clothes would be returned to him. There was mineral water on the table. If he desired coffee, any other beverage, he had only to call. He wished the *dottore* "*Buon riposo*" and went out, closing the door behind him.

Left alone, Cavanagh studied himself in the mirror and decided that what he saw was a mess. His skin was pasty, he had botched his shave on the aircraft and his tongue looked like the bottom of a birdcage. His brain —if there were anything left of it—must have turned to butter, because there was no gleam of intelligence in the dull, bloodshot and brutish eyes. So the whole toilet would have to be done again. He cleaned his teeth, washed his mouth, shaved with patient care, boiled himself in the bath for forty glorious minutes, dried himself on a fluffy towel as big as a bed sheet, then wrapped himself in the dressing gown and slept until twenty minutes after midday.

When the majordomo delivered his freshly minted clothes, he asked what dress might be appropriate for lunch. The answer was instant:

"The Principessa asked me to tell you, sir—very casual. There are no guests. You will be lunching on the terrace in warm sunshine."

"The Princess is back, then?"

"Yes, sir. She will pass by your room and pick you up in about twenty minutes."

"You must forgive me. I have neglected to ask your name."

"Bosco. Luca Bosco . . ."

"You've been with the family a long time?"

"Too long to think about, *dottore*. But if you have questions, I am to tell you that the Principessa wants to deliver all her news herself. She warned me that if I gossiped with you, she would have my head."

Cavanagh laughed.

"I believe you, Luca! She can be a very formidable lady."

"But not with you, *dottore*. Not ever with you!"

"Why do you say that?"

The old man gave him a sidelong, mischievous grin and refused the bait.

"You mustn't tempt me, *dottore*. It's my head that's threatened, not yours."

The next instant he was gone, leaving Cavanagh to make a momentous, solitary decision on what he should wear to lunch with Giulia the Beautiful and whether his gift to her was too trivial, or too audacious in the memories it evoked.

He had found it in a small jewellery store on Madison, one of those expensive holes-in-the-wall, which traded in estate jewelry and sold pieces on consignment for aging or needy clients. It was a Victorian piece, quite small for that period, a golden salamander with emerald eyes and a pavé of tiny rose-cut diamonds down the spine. They had asked an outrageous price for it, but he had haggled them down to seven hundred and fifty dollars—which made him feel less guilty about buying a gift for an old lover, or on the other hand, about spending too much of the fee with which the said lover had endowed him. He took one last look at the piece, closed the little velvet box and laid it on the bedside table beside Giulia's gift.

Clothes were the next problem. Hell! What was he? A teenager going out on his first date? An open-necked shirt, light fawn slacks, Gucci loafers—what else could you do with a sixty-five-year-old *conseiller d'état*, who was hard put to keep his belly reasonably flat and who could do nothing at all about his receding hair line. He was just making a final inspection of himself, when he heard the knock on the door and Giulia's announcement:

"It's me, Giulia."

"Come in," said Cavanagh, and watched in sudden fear, as the door opened and Giulia stood before him.

Time had been kind to her and she had let it do its own work in peace. She was gray now, but still trim and firm-breasted. There were lines on her face; but they were not the down-drawn strokes of melancholy, rather the patterns of contentment and acceptance. Only her eyes had not changed, those big, dark, lustrous orbs, that had charmed the heart out of him forty years ago. She wore a cream silk blouse and black silk slacks and low-heeled shoes, and her hair was tied back with a ribbon of black moiré silk. That was all he had time to take in, before she kicked the door shut and came running into his arms, and time rolled back, in the wink of an eye, to their first breathless encounter on the dockside at Santo Stefano. As it had been in that long ago, it was Giulia who found voice first.

"We're always like this, aren't we? Nothing to say—and then I have to start the talking."

"You know me, my love, Cavanagh the dumb mick!"

"Whatever else you were, my love, you were never dumb. Did you find my present?"

"I did—and thank you."

"They're real tears, Cavanagh."

"I know. I tasted them."

"Did they taste happy?"

"If you tell me so."

"I'm still wearing your pendant. I've worn it since the day we parted."

She opened the buttons of her blouse, to show him the golden medallion cradled in the cleft of her breasts. She drew it out and offered it to him to handle. It was exactly as she had described it in her letter, buffed and rubbed by forty years of contact with her body, but like the body itself, all the more precious for the defacements of time. He handed it back, and before she re-buttoned her blouse, he bent and brushed her breasts with his lips. He felt her flinch in surprise, but she did not withdraw. She smiled when he told her:

"The last time, I promise!"

"I'm glad you still want to touch me. Have I changed much?"

"Like good wine, Giulia mia—only for the better. I brought you a gift too."

He handed her the little velvet box and watched as

she opened it. The light in her eyes and the smile on her face moved him near to tears. She kissed him full on the lips and thanked him in a rush of words.

"I'm going to put this on now and wear it while you're here. The salamander's an animal that can survive in the hottest fire. We're survivors, Cavanagh, both of us." She pinned the brooch to her blouse, patted it into place, looked at herself in the mirror and then, imperious as the Giulia of old, commanded him: "Take my arm, Cavanagh! My staff are dying of curiosity. Let's give them a good entrance, shall we?"

They lunched under a pergola of vines that threw dappled shadows on the white napery. They were served by the majordomo, who poured the wine and ladled the food, a maid in a starched apron and cap, who handled the plates, and a formidably large female cook, who presented each dish as if she were Brillat-Savarin himself. Giulia had to restrain her giggles until the cook left the scene and she was able to explain to Cavanagh:

"We don't always do things with this much style; but if I hadn't displayed you to them, they'd have gone on strike."

"Who do they think I am?"

"They know who you are, Cavanagh. *La vecchia fiamma della principessa!* My old flame! They love the idea. Luca adores a little intrigue. He says this is the way it used to be in the Prince's Villa. The women have even been gossiping about whether we'd sleep together while you're here. I told Luca to knock that notion on the head immediately!"

"You might at least have offered me the refusal."

"You wouldn't want to play that game again, would you, Cavanagh?"

"I'd like to, my love, but I'm afraid I'd make a great fool of myself."

"Tell me about your life, your wife, your family."

"What's to say, Giulia my love? I have a happy family and a successful practice. I've been a lucky man."

"So share the luck, Cavanagh. Tell me what you did after Ischia?"

"We sailed straight to Antibes. We were supposed to drop Rodolfo off along the way, but he refused to quit. He wouldn't leave Miss Pritchard. He was set on going to England with her. The last I heard they were dealing with the question of a passport and a visa and how he was going to get them. I paid everybody off, and handed the ship over to Glémot. We had a wild party in Cannes and went our separate ways. Then, I hitchhiked to San Tropez where I met a girl, and then on to Toulon, where I met another girl, and then to Marseilles, where I met several girls—and not a damn one of them can I remember; because you were always there, like a candle in the window, calling me home to a feast day I'd never enjoy again.

"I'd wake in the night wondering where you were, what you were doing, how Molloy was treating you. Then I decided that the ports and docks and seaside girls were doing bad things to my spirit; so I went on to Paris, found myself a little mansard apartment on the Left Bank and started to write to the people to whom Galeazzi had given me introductions. The speed and the cordiality of the replies astonished me . . . I was so dumb then, I never understood what a powerful man he was. When I finally caught on, I decided to spend whatever it took to get myself to New York and London and Rome to meet Galeazzi's friends in person.

"The outcome was magical. Career opportunities opened to me on both sides of the Atlantic. I couldn't make up my mind, so I decided to talk to Galeazzi himself. We arranged to meet on his next visit to Paris. We sat up half the night talking in his suite at the Crillon. He was very gracious and very open. He urged me to take a longterm view, to do postgraduate work in international law in America, in Great Britain, France, Rome and in Moscow itself, if I could bear it and if I could get a visa. He advised me strongly against making a career in the United States. His reason was curious, but the more I thought about it, the more sense it made. He said: 'Remember always that the United States were built—are still being built—by Europeans in flight from their origins. You are not in flight, you are a young man surprisingly sure of his identity, who has come to discover his spiritual and intellectual roots. What you have found is a wasteland—a continent which has just seen the final sequelae of the Great Schism between Rome and Byzantium, the Reformation and the Counter-Reformation, the fall of monarchies and dictatorships, the tribal enmities that began with the great migrations across the steppes into Europe. But mark my words, Europe will recover, and slowly begin to see that its salvation lies in co-operative effort and some code of common belief and law. It might challenge you to be part of that process, a catalyst for change. If it doesn't, then I think you would be wiser to return to your own country and make your career there.'

"I thought about it for a long time and finally opted for the long haul, postgraduate studies in five countries, and a career in international law. I got myself a very junior job with a member of the International Commission of Jurists. I was half a step above an office boy, but the job enabled me to survive and study."

"Did Galeazzi tell you anything about me?!"

"Nothing, except that you and Lou had a son. He made it clear that any further questions from me would be an unwelcome intrusion."

"But your career marched forward?"

"It did, thank God and Galeazzi! Would you believe I now have a very distinguished woman client who pays me fifteen thousand dollars just to fly over to Rome and visit her! It's a madness of course, but lawyers make their money out of other people's follies!"

"Cavanagh, my love, you haven't even begun to earn your fee! Tell me about your wife. What's she like? Where did you meet her? Are you happy—both of you?"

"Yes, we are happy and I thank God every day of my life for the woman he finally gave me."

"That's quite a testimonial." Giulia gave him a small, dubious smile. "Do you have any photographs?"

"Of course." He gave an embarrassed grin. "Never travel without 'em. That's Louise, with our two sons and our daughter and their respective spouses. These in front are our four grandchildren."

"That's already a tribe, Cavanagh!"

"Fortunately, none of them lives with us. They join us sometimes for holidays. And Louise is on permanent call as matriarch—which I tell her is crazy."

"Where did you and Louise meet?"

"In Paris. She was studying at the Conservatoire, cello and composition. She and three other students had formed a quartet which played each night in a little *boîte* on thc Left Bank. They were all classical players, but they had developed a comedy act, skits and musical parodies, which went down well with the audience. I dropped in there most nights and—God help me!—I conned them into letting me join their act as a vocalist. After that, I conned Louise into letting me be the man who walked her home. *Et voilà!* We married. We settled in Paris. My career started to prosper. We bred a trio of our own musicians!"

"Very romantic! Now tell me what your Louise is really like. I can see she's beautiful! I expected that. You always had good taste in women, Cavanagh. But tell me the rest of it."

"The rest of it is so simple you'll laugh at it." Cavanagh stared out acoss the sunlit land towards the misty hills. "With Louise, life is always and only 'now.' She refuses to brood on the past. She tells me I'm so good at worrying about the future, that she doesn't have to bother about it. She says to our children: 'All you have is this moment. Make the most of it!' Nothing frightens her . . ."

"I might, if she knew I was back in your life."

"I doubt it. Besides, this is a weekend visit, not a sojourn."

"Are you going to tell her about the visit?"

"She already knows I'm here in Rome."

"But you haven't told her about me?"

"No. It's an agreement we have. I don't bring my business home. We entertain only our friends. Besides, you've paid me a fee. You're a client. I have no right to discuss you or your business." He cupped his chin on his hands and studied her face. Then he challenged her: "Why are you playing this game, Giulia?"

"Because, suddenly, I'm jealous."

"You have no cause to be."

"You mean I have no right to be."

"Put it either way, it's true!"

"I know. I had first offer on you, Cavanagh. I turned you down. I shouldn't have any complaints."

"That's not what I meant."

"I'm teasing you, Cavanagh."

"I'd rather you didn't."

"I won't do it again."

"You're forgiven. Now, I want to hear about you."

"It's a long story. I don't know where to start."

"Start where it ended for us."

For a woman at once compulsive and calculating, she seemed to have great difficulty in framing a simple narrative. Cavanagh waited in silence, until finally she found the opening phrase:

"After we left Ischia for Rome, everything happened in a rush. Everyone seemed to want the wedding over and done with. I did myself; that would force me to go forward, instead of looking back all the time. As soon as we got to Rome, Molloy was summoned to a private audience with His Holiness at Castelgandolfo, where he was created a Knight of St. Gregory. It was really a trivial occasion, as Molloy was quick to realize. He got a scroll and a medal and a Papal blessing—and fifteen minutes' conversation with the Pontiff, mostly about the Communist plot and the defects of U.S. policy in Europe. The Vatican, like the British monarchy, makes much use of these old-fashioned honors, which cost nothing but a little paper and metal and colored ribbons, but keep the illusions of monarchy alive. After that, Lou demanded a very quiet wedding, which Papa and I were very happy to give him. By the time state and church documents were ready, another month had passed. Lou and I were married in Mongrifone with the local bishop celebrating the nuptial mass for a small congregation of close relatives and friends and a church full of local townsfolk. We were all glad when it was over. The wedding party was held here at the Villa and we spent our honeymoon night in the Royal Suite at the Grand Hotel in Rome. The day after that, we left for America. There, the money men laid out red carpets for him everywhere. Back in Europe, the old families and our European cousins ignored him as much as they dared; but Lou did a better job of ignoring them, and I had to acknowledge his courage."

"But the marriage itself, how did all that work out? Or would you rather not talk about it?"

"I need to talk about it, Cavanagh, if you are to understand why I asked you here. The truth is that I was totally unprepared for what happened on my wedding night. I was expecting—how shall I say it?—

at least a vigorous encounter, possibly a violent one. I wasn't afraid of that. You know what I'm like in bed—or used to be! I was even looking forward to the experience. If the sex was good, life with Lou would be at least halfway tolerable. In fact the night was a disaster—not because he wasn't potent—he was as strong as a bull!—but because he was so tender and caring and protective! The last thing I needed was protection for the innocence I didn't possess. It was a laughable situation, but I didn't dare laugh. I couldn't confess to my past, while he was trying to shield me from his. So, I pretended. I went on pretending that I was getting what I needed, that Lou Molloy, the penitent Don Juan, was conducting me gently through the rose gardens of love. All the time I was hating him and trying to dream you back into my bed; but you just drifted further and further away and all I could feel of you was the medallion between my breasts. Lou used to complain about it and say it got in his way when he fondled me, but I refused to take it off and made up some fairy-tale about a love-spell which great-grandmother Farnese had attached to it. I tell you, Cavanagh, I was not a happy bride or a good wife, but Lou didn't deserve what I inflicted on him, because for those first twelve months at least, he was really trying to be a good husband, and a better man. However, in my own defense, I do have to say I was pregnant. I had a lot of minor ailments. I developed some kidney problems and in the end the baby was delivered by Caesarean section in Professor Peroni's private clinic. Lou was traveling a lot at that time and he was in New York when Sandro was born."

"Sandro?" Cavanagh was intrigued. "I can't imagine Molloy giving up his naming rights to the first-born."

"Oh, he didn't surrender them easily, by any means. The original nuptial agreement specified that the child, if a boy, should be named by him, without prejudice to the child's rights to continue the Farnese name and any titles that might devolve to him. So, because Papa was ailing, I worked hard on Lou to have him agree to naming the baby for my father. Lou argued a lot but finally consented. The baby was baptized Alessandro Aloysius Molloy Farnese. When you meet him, he'll tell you himself, it's a large mouthful to cope with. He prefers to call himself Sandro."

"Where is he now?"

"He's in Rome. He'll be here for dinner tonight."

"What does he do?"

"He's a diplomat, well advanced in his career, too."

"How old is he now?"

"Work it out for yourself. He was conceived in the summer of 1952."

"That makes him thirty-nine or thereabouts. Whom does he take after?"

"The Farnese, I'm glad to say, though he does have a lot of his father's mannerisms and an occasional expression round the mouth and eyes. But looking at his photographs, you'd swear, boy and man, he was a Farnese."

"How did Lou take to him?"

"He adored him. Whenever he was home he would croon over him for hours, insist on being present at his bath, caress him, answer to his slightest cry. I was surprised at first, and always touched, when I saw how much he loved the child."

"Didn't that make any difference to your relations with him?"

"You'd think it would have, but it didn't. All my attention was focused on Sandro. I had a nurse, of course, but I wanted to rear him myself. I breast-fed him, I changed diapers, I played with him and laid him down to sleep. Lou once told me that was the best image he had of me: 'a happy peasant, with a boy child at the breast.' The sad thing was, that when we bent together over the cradle, there was always a wall between us, a transparent wall that we could see through, talk through, even smile through, but never reach through to touch each other. Now, perhaps, you will understand why I had a moment of jealousy about you and your wife."

"Perhaps," Cavanagh suggested gently, "perhaps you should finish your pasta and let me tell you something about this Lou Molloy whom you met for the first time on your wedding night."

"How can you possibly know anything about him?"

"He told me himself, when he came aboard the *Salamandra* in Ischia to give me my sailing orders. I'm not quoting you the exact words, but I'll guarantee the message is authentic. He said he needed to talk. He was talking to me because I had been taught the same doctrine as he, about sin, guilt, repentance, new beginnings. He said he had tried to make a confession to Cardinal Spellman in New York, but Spellman had recommended he use another confessor. He shied away from that. He said all he wanted to do was make a clean start with you and found a family that could be proud of Lou Molloy. For God's sake, Giulia! You have to give the man full marks for trying."

"We're talking about a marriage, Cavanagh, not a dog show!"

"Nevertheless, the marriage did last until he died!"

She put down her fork very carefully, wiped her lips with the napkin, then signaled to Luca to clear the platters away and absent himself for a while. Then with more than a touch of impatience, she told Cavanagh:

"There were a number of very good reasons for our staying together. First, my father's position at the Vatican; second, Lou's long and important connections with Cardinal Spellman; third, the terms of the marriage settlement, which would have robbed me and Sandro of millions if I initiated divorce or annulment proceedings against Lou—and in those early years there was no divorce in Italy anyway. The only solution was a civilized live-and-let-live arrangement, which Lou himself proposed.

"He was sitting there, where you are now. We had just finished coffee, Lou told Luca to leave us and asked: 'Giulia, why don't we end this sad comedy and give ourselves and the boy a chance?' Of course, I had to make a little scene and demand to know what sort of an ending he proposed. He shrugged and told me he didn't want to play games, just to keep some dignity and peace in our lives and give Sandro some sense of a united family! I was tempted to make a sharp reply; but the look in his eyes frightened me. I knew that if I said the wrong word, he would strike me. So, we talked quietly and agreed to rearrange our lives on live-and-let-live terms, broad enough to keep the domestic peace, preserve the social hypocrisies and spare young Sandro any experience of conflict in the home.

"After that, the going was easier for all of us. Lou traveled a great deal and spent much time in New York. He had bought an apartment on Park Avenue and installed a housekeeper to run it . . . You'll remember her of course: Lenore Pritchard from the *Salamandra*."

"My God! I wonder what happened to Rodolfo?"

"God knows!" Giulia waved an indifferent hand. "After our breakup, I never stayed in the apartment. I had nothing to do with her, beyond asking her to pass messages to Lou. If I went to New York to see Sandro, I always stayed at the Pierre.

"The fact is, that I was gradually opening up my own social calendar. I had some affairs, not enough to cause a scandal, just enough to keep my confidence up and my skin looking good. Then, a few years before Lou died, I formed a serious attachment with a son of one of the old papal families. He, too, was married, so there was no question of breaking up two homes. We took an apartment in Rome, furnished it to our taste, hired a maid to keep it, and spent our times of liberty there. What Lou's arrangements were, I didn't ask and I didn't care. Sometimes I heard gossip. I shut my ears to it. This was the time of La Dolce Vita. Everybody was playing. Nobody cared."

"What about your father?"

"He died in the early seventies. He and Aunt Lucietta were killed in a car accident on the autostrada. I missed them both terribly, but having a stable love-life helped a great deal."

Cavanagh poured himself some mineral water. The Farnese wine left a sharpish aftertaste on the palate. His comment was noncommittal.

"It sounds like a very civilized arrangement."

"It was. The only hitch came when Lou insisted on the agreement that Sandro should go to school in America and afterwards complete his university education there."

"Not unreasonable, one would have thought."

"Not unreasonable; but I still bitched about it on principle, until I realized that it would make my own Roman affair much easier to manage."

"Is the affair still going?"

"No. I grew out of it and he found someone else. But he did pay me handsomely for the apartment."

Cavanagh reached across the table and imprisoned her restless hands in his own. He asked softly:

"Why are you doing this to yourself?"

"Doing what?"

"Daubing yourself with penitential ashes. Lent is long over. Give yourself a break, for pity's sake. Lou's dead and gone and I'm sure he was never so bad they couldn't find a small corner in heaven for him—which he'd have made twice as big the moment he got there. Your son's a middle-aged man. You're still a lively woman who has had a very good life and is now the chatelaine of the Farnese and Molloy estates, which must be worth a mint of money. Nevertheless, you've got a problem. You think I can help. You've paid my retainer, I am now your attorney and legal counselor. Please, Principessa, let me have your instructions!"

She pulled away from him abruptly and stood up.

"Let's go for a walk. I'll choke if I eat another mouthful. I never believed it would be so hard to say a few simple words."

He offered her his arm and let her lead him down the graveled driveway and across a green lawn to a sunken garden, with a pool, tiled with mosaics. At either end of the pool, there was a stone bench, and around the sides, gardens full of tulips and narcissus in full bloom. She made him sit down while she herself remained standing, a little to his right between the water and the flowers, against a background of blue hills and fleecy clouds. It was a very conscious piece of staging, which reminded him of the old Giulia, posed carefully on the after-rail aboard the *Salamandra*. He smiled his approval, but made no comment. She made a tentative beginning:

". . . Just so you have the time elements right. My husband died in 1980. He was sixty-seven years old. Sandro, my son, was born in 1953, which means he was twenty-seven at the time of my husband's death. Lou died alone in his New York apartment. I was here at the Villa. Sandro was in Rome working at the Secretariat. I heard the news first: Lenore Pritchard called me. The next day Sandro and I flew to New York.

"We found Lou had left everything very tidy for us. His instructions were precise. He wished to be buried beside Giorgios Hadjidakis in the cemetery of the Greek Orthodox community in Boston, where, years ago, he had bought the grave-site. He asked that the final dismissals be given in the Latin and the Orthodox rites. When we arrived in New York, the body was already on its way to Boston to await our arrival. I confess I was shocked and insulted. I said some bad things to Lenore. Sandro had to intervene. Afterwards, he scolded me harshly:

" 'Funerals are for the living, not for the dead. Lenore was his lover long before she became his housekeeper. Giorgios Hadjidakis had been Papa's closest friend. His widow and his children were my friends too—my only family indeed, while I was studying here. For Papa, their house was a refuge when the black moods came on him. He knew he didn't have much life to gamble on. He died of lung cancer. Lenore nursed him almost to the end. So your abuse of her was quite brutal! You owe her an apology. Papa was not an easy patient. Sometimes he was weighed down with guilts about what he saw as his failed marriage to you and his unorthodox parenting of me. I used to tell him neither of you was to blame and that I loved you both. But, Mama, it's time you learned to be kinder to people. I think he deserved better than you offered him!'

"My son's reproach was a harder blow than Lou's death. It made me feel small, mean and very guilty. It made me understand that Lou was a bigger and wiser man than I had taken him for in his lifetime. The funeral was another blow to my pride. The Farnese slept in their marble tombs, while my husband was being buried, by his own choice, in a suburban plot beside the son of a Greek peasant. Lenore was there, with the Hadjidakis family and a few—a surprising few—of Lou's old business friends. I was the outsider, and I knew it. Sandro, my son, was protecting me; but the Hadjidakis family were helping him to bear his own grief and purge it in their embraces, not mine. I had no grief to purge, only a relief that I could not share, and hardly dared admit to myself."

Cavanagh held out his hand to draw her down beside him, but she rejected the gesture abruptly.

"No! Please don't touch me. I have to get through this, before I fall apart."

She gathered herself again, like an athlete making a final leap, then launched herself into the story.

"When we got back to New York, there were the usual conferences with lawyers and accountants, the normal, interminable routines of probate. Before we left for Rome, each of us was handed a sealed envelope. We were told that they contained Lou's last communications. On the outside of each envelope was written: 'Please open this when you are alone and private. Lou.' "

Giulia put her hand in the pocket of her slacks and brought out a folded sheet of note paper which she thrust at Cavanagh:

"This is why I called you here, Cavanagh. Read it!"

Cavanagh took the note, unfolded it and read it. He looked at Giulia. She had turned away and was staring at the bright, mosaic images under the water: octopods and dolphins and Proteus guarding them all. Cavanagh felt a cold hand closing around his heart. The words he uttered were more visible than audible, a frosty whisper of despair:

"Dear Mother of God! You got this letter in 1980, twelve years ago! Why did you leave it so long? Why didn't you do what Lou asked?"

She did not answer. She stood mute and still as a stone image, her hands clasped about her breasts.

Cavanagh was locked in his own solitude. He read and re-read Molloy's letter. Understanding every syllable of every word, but not yet able to grasp it as a coherent whole.

My dear Giulia,

I'm not prepared to die with a lie between us. Sandro should not embark on the life he has chosen, with any part of the truth untold.

All the documents I have signed over the years, affirm that Sandro is my son. There is no evidence that can, or should, prevail against them.

But you know, and I know, that when you married me, you were already pregnant and that the natural father of the child was Bryan Cavanagh. I didn't know it at the time. I was too pre-occupied with my business affairs, too eager to make a happy marriage with you. If you had told me the moon was made of cotton candy, I would have believed you.

Afterwards—what can I say?—I loved the boy so much, I would have killed anyone who told me he was a bastard. In fact, no one ever did, directly. When you and I separated and Lenore came to look after me, it was she, who, one night in bed, told me of your affair with Cavanagh. After that it was a simple matter of mathematics.

My attitude to Sandro never changed. I still loved him and treated him as a son. When I judged—rightly or wrongly—that he should be told the truth, I told him as much as I knew or guessed.

Now, I believe it's your turn to fill in the gaps. If you could bring him and Cavanagh together, without starting a war, it might be the best solution of all. But you must at least talk to Sandro. His life will be out of balance until you do.

I wish I could say I love you. I tried, believe

me. Let's at least have the grace to forgive each other.

Lou.

Cavanagh folded the letter and handed it back to Giulia. She took it without a word and thrust it deep into her pocket. Cavanagh stood up and took her arm.

"Why don't you show me the rest of the place?"

A long time later, while they were walking silently, hand-in-hand under the orchard trees, Cavanagh asked:

"What does Sandro say about all this?"

"Nothing. He has never told me what Lou wrote to him. Until recently, he had never asked me a single question about the matter. It is my guess that Lou told him the simple facts and said that it was my right to explain the rest of it in my own time. There was a great bond between those two—a kind of special chivalry in which I had no share."

"But why have you decided that this is the time? What's special about this day, this week, this month?"

"Because it's an important moment in his life, in his career. I wanted to give him a gift. I asked him what he would like. He said: 'If it could be arranged, without hurt to anyone, I should like to meet my natural father.' "

"And just like that, I'm paid to come here and meet with him—no warning, no preparation! My God, Giulia, you really are an incorrigible bitch! All I know about this man is his name and the fact that he's a thirty-nine-year-old diplomat and you're about to slam us in each other's faces. Not good enough, Principessa! Not good enough by half! If you'll excuse me now, I'll go and pack. You can either call me a taxi or have your chauffeur drive me back to Rome. If my son wants to see me, he'll find me at the Hotel de Ville! . . ."

"Please, Cavanagh! I beg you, don't go like this. It doesn't help. It just drags everything out. Your son—our son—will be here at six tonight to say an evening Mass, talk to you and then have dinner with us."

Cavanagh stared at her, gasping like a grassed trout.

"You told me he was a diplomat?"

"He is, in the Vatican Secretariat of State."

"Oh God! A priest in the family! And himself born on the wrong side of the blanket! Now there's a comedy for you!"

Suddenly, he was laughing, a dry, hiccuping sound that brought tears to his eyes and had no merriment in it at all.

"He's a bishop, Cavanagh. He was consecrated last week to the titular see of Trajanopolis in Phrygia! He expects to be sent abroad very soon as legate, to one of the new East European republics."

"And I'm to be his going-away present!" Cavanagh was not laughing now. A slow, sullen anger was building up inside him. "The Farnese don't change, do they? Last time, it was your father handing me to you, to keep you sweet and compliant until you were safely wedded to Molloy. Now with no warning, with no shred of proof, you endow me with a bastard son—complete with miter and crozier—and you expect me to crush him to my bosom and shout, God be praised! You have to do better than that, Giulia mia! Why, in Christ's name, all those years ago, didn't you tell me you were carrying my child? I wasn't running away from you. I was begging you to marry me!"

"Because I didn't know . . . I just didn't know!"

"Remember when we talked this out in Sardinia? I said I wanted to make a child with you . . ."

"My thought was the same, Cavanagh. I loved you.

I wanted your child, not Lou Molloy's. If I didn't marry you, I'd always have part of you to keep. So, I took the risk; but don't you see, I didn't know I was pregnant until you were gone!

"A week after we left Ischia, I missed my first period. I missed the next one too, which was due the week before we were married. So, this child would make a scandalously early arrival. I talked to Aunt Lucietta. She talked me out of my panic, telling me that lots of women had premature babies. We could certainly make this one look premature, by having a Caesarean. The big, heart-stopping gamble was whether the baby would look like you, with those blue eyes and that ruddy complexion. On this question I had to talk to Papa. He laughed at my fears. All newborn babies looked alike. Once Lou had registered the birth, as father of the child, its paternity would be beyond challenge."

"He was right," said Cavanagh. "In Italian law the document prevails. Your father had really done a thorough job on this marriage. You were all lucky the boy looked like a Farnese. You were also lucky he loved the child—and loved you enough to swallow the shame you put on him."

"That's a brutal thing to say!"

"I'm afraid, Giulia mia, you're the brutal one. Everything in life has to be tailored to your demands!"

"And why not? I paid more than enough for the privilege of being Giulia Farnese!"

"What about Sandro? Why didn't you do as Lou asked and tell him our side of the story?"

"What was there to tell? I fell in love with a man I couldn't have. All I had left of him was a baby with Molloy's name and a medallion the baby used to grasp as he suckled at my breast. Now you're here, you can explain it all to Sandro!"

"No way! No how! I'm leaving!"

He turned on his heel and began striding through the orchard trees back to the house. Giulia followed him, running, and then barred his way, a tiny, imperious figure, formidable in her anger.

"You accepted my retainer, Cavanagh. You asked for my instructions. I have given them to you. Since they are legally and morally reasonable, it seems to me you have a clear duty to carry them out! Mass will be celebrated in the Villa chapel at six this evening. Luca will conduct you there. All the staff will be present. You and Sandro will have time to talk before we dine together at eight. I cannot believe that you will fail your son or me!"

The next moment she was gone, fleeing back to the Villa. Cavanagh made no move to follow her. Instead, he walked slowly back to the pool, squatted by the edge and dangled his fingers in the water, trying to attract one of the fat carp which swam lazily above the images of another age.

At five minutes to six Luca, the majordomo, came to his room to conduct him to the chapel. Luca was garrulous now. This was a special event for the family and the household, a Farnese bishop saying their house-Mass. He was so young for such an honor: not yet forty! It was not impossible that, in twenty years or so, there could be another Farnese pope. At least he would have to get a cardinal's hat . . . This Sandro was a man full of surprises. Before he left for America, he had been a wild boy, hard for his mother to manage. But, once in America with his father, he had settled down beautifully. He had been a fine sportsman: a tennis player, a sailor, a runner. He had graduated in philosophy and humanities: *summa cum laude*. Then, suddenly, poof! He was out of it all and enrolled in the diocesan seminary in New York. Ordained there, he came back to Rome for further studies at the Gregorian University, from whence he was co-opted straight into a position at the Secretariat of State in Vatican City.

Luca's eulogy had to end there, because they were already at the door of the chapel, a small vaulted chamber, designed into the Villa edifice itself and decorated in a subdued Palladian style. Giulia was kneeling at a *prie-dieu* on the left of the nave, with members of the household, maids, gardeners, farm-folk, ranged on both sides behind her. The celebrant stood alone at the altar, vesting himself for the Mass. Luca led Cavanagh to a *prie-dieu* on the right hand side of the nave, level with Giulia, then walked up to the sanctuary to lay out the altar vessels and serve as acolyte.

Cavanagh knelt down and looked at the man whom he had begotten and who was as remote from him as a creature from Mars. However, there was no doubt he was a Farnese. He had the long face, the high forehead, the beaked nose and the full lips of his grandfather and of their ancestor, Pope Paul III, brother of Giulia the Beautiful.

Cavanagh noted with detached approval that he seemed not yet to have acquired the sleek and corpulent look of the desk-bound cleric. He was still slim. His movements at the altar table were measured and precise, his recitation of the vernacular prayers simple and unmannered. The focus of his gaze was somewhere in the center of the room and not on Cavanagh or Giulia. It was an old preacher's trick, to collectivize an audience, but Cavanagh was grateful for it. He was even more grateful when, after the ritual summons to "offer each other the sign of peace," Sandro stepped down and embraced each member of the small congregation, who then exchanged the salute with each other. Giulia crossed to Cavanagh, embraced him, and, as their cheeks touched, she whispered: "Please, Cavanagh! Let us make peace." Cavanagh's anger died. He squeezed her hand in a silent consent and a moment later, stood by her side to receive the consecrated bread and the wine from the chalice. Then he returned to his place, buried his face in his hands and prayed as he had not prayed in years. He was still there when all the worshippers had gone and the Bishop, divested of his hieratic garments, stood beside him and said formally:

"We have to talk, Dr. Cavanagh."

"Indeed we do." Cavanagh got stiffly to his feet.

"I fear," said the Bishop, "I am something of a shock to you."

"And I am an embarrassment to you." Cavanagh managed a weary smile. "Now may we cut the formalities? I need a drink—a strong one!"

"I, too. Let's go to Grandfather's study."

As they walked out of the chapel, Cavanagh groped for another line with which to begin a dialogue. He was not very proud of what he produced.

"Your mother tells me your full name is as much a mouthful as mine is. So, call me Cavanagh. Your mother always did."

"And I'm Sandro, like my grandfather."

In the study, rich with old leather bindings, dark wood and ancestral portraits, a tray was laid with liquor and glasses and ice. Cavanagh settled himself in a deep, leather armchair. Sandro poured a large measure of Scotch for each of them. Cavanagh raised his glass:

"To the truth. Let's have it out between us and be done with it."

"Amen to that," said Sandro, the Bishop.

They drank. Cavanagh said:

"That's a hell of a title you've got yourself: Bishop of Trajanopolis in Phrygia!"

Sandro laughed. It was an open, cheerful sound. "A

big name for no place at all. There's a whole list of these titular sees in the Pontifical Almanach."

"Who picks them for 'the new boys' like you?"

"Theoretically, His Holiness, but in practice, some prelate from the Congregation for Bishops. I'm told you can ask for a vacant title, but you never get what you ask for. It's very Roman. All through your life in the ministry, someone dishes out these little pinpricks just to remind you that you're a man subject to authority. Now tell me, Cavanagh, which of us is going to begin?"

"Well," said Cavanagh, "mine's the shortest and the simplest story. But you'll save me some breath and yourself some boredom, if I know how much Lou Molloy told you about me."

"Quite a lot." He smiled as he said it. "You were a smart-ass Australian—his words, not mine! You had a good war record and a new law degree and you knew how to run a boat."

"So far, it's an accurate report."

"He said you had a good Jesuitical mind, which would either land you in jail or at the top of your profession. He also said you had an easy way with women and were a rough man to fight with. He admired you, Cavanagh. Sometimes I used to think he was reading me the specifications for the son he wanted me to be. That didn't make me like you very much, especially when I learned you'd seduced my mother!"

"When did your father tell you all this?"

"When I informed him I wanted to enter the seminary and become a priest. He wasn't well at the time. He became very agitated and told me I shouldn't do it. We both got very heated. Then he told me I couldn't do it anyway because of some old provision in canon law that illegitimate sons were barred from holy orders."

"That was a hell of a way to break the news!"

"It was, and it nearly broke me. I just didn't know who I was anymore. I'd come to terms with a lot of things: a divided family, my mother's love affairs, my father's aberrant lifestyle. This was one blow too much! I went crazy for a while. I hit the bars. I hit on all the girls I knew and a lot I didn't know. I spent money like water. Lou let me run until I'd exhausted myself and my allowance—which was a very generous one. Then he apologized and tried to explain that, although he loved me dearly, he was tired of living a lie—a whole pack of them in fact. He wanted the record straight between us. I still wasn't sure I understood his motives, but at least we were friends again. He'd gone a step further and asked for a ruling from some canonist or other and had come back with a clear decision: my certificates of birth and baptism, all my life history, confirmed that I was the legitimate son of Lou Molloy.

"However, we were still left with a couple of problems. Lou had to explain how my mother had become pregnant by you. I had to work out how my wild weeks of indulgence matched with my aspirations to a life in the ministry of the Gospel."

"I'd be interested to know how you worked out both problems."

"That's not easy to explain, because you have to understand where Lou's life was heading at this time. These were the early seventies. Lou was in his late fifties, a rich man, an active man, stuck in a time-warp from which he couldn't escape. The America of the fifties had changed beyond recognition, but he had been so busy with his own affairs at home and abroad that he was insulated from the impact of events. He read them only as shock waves on the graphs of financial analysis. His Church had changed too—according to him, for the worse. Pope John XXIII had opened the door to the Left. The Vatican Council had shaken all the old certainties. His marriage was a wreck beyond salvage. Most of his old business associates were dead or retired. Now that I was going into the Church, he felt he had nothing on which to build a new life.

"Lenore, who kept house for him, said to me one day: 'My heart breaks for him, Sandro. He's so desperately lonely. Because of your mother, he's lost his trust in women and his taste for them too. He hasn't even got a steady man-friend anymore. He's talking of building a new boat, so he can go cruising with these young fellows he brings into the house when you're not around. I don't know what will happen to him when you're gone . . .' I didn't know either, Cavanagh."

"Did you ever try to talk to him about it?"

"Yes, I did, several times. He only got angry and told me to keep my nose out of his life. One day, I got angry too and shouted that his life was my life, because I loved him and I hated what he was doing to himself! Finally, it was like breaking through a wall to a prisoner, and finding him huddled in fugue. I coaxed him. I bullied him. I did everything possible to make him talk. Eventually he told me about himself and Hadjidakis. He opened his safe and brought out Hadjidakis's journal. He knew I'd studied Greek and Latin in my humanities course, so he handed me the book and told me:

" '. . . You've had a small taste of hell recently, Sandro. Now read this and see what a real hell looks like. While you're reading it, and making all the judgments that you can't avoid making, write this little note on your shirt cuff. "Even when I was in hell, I thought it was heaven, because I was sharing it with a loving friend." If that makes a grain of sense to you, you'll probably make a good shepherd of souls. If it doesn't, give up the whole idea and go join the bandits like Sindona and Gelli, who are playing games with the Vatican's money; just like the Colonna and the Borgia and the Farnese did in the old days . . .' "

"So," Cavanagh asked, "you read the journal?"

"I read it several times. I was hypnotized."

"But what did you *feel* about it?"

"I laughed. I cried. I wanted to puke. I was shamed. I was angry. Sometimes I wished I had been there to share the sexual adventures with them. Sometimes I had nightmares from which I woke, sweating in the darkness about all the spoiled lives and all the brutal tyrannies of the underworld, which had been my father's playground, and was becoming so again. Looking back, I think the book confirmed me in what I saw as my vocation, to bear some of the human burden, some of Lou Molloy's burden, on my own shoulders."

"Did you tell that to Lou?"

"Not in so many words."

"What did you say to him?"

"I thanked him for letting me read it."

"And . . . ?"

"I put my arms around him and cried. Afterwards, we tore the book apart, put it through Lou's shredder, then dumped it down the furnace chute. Next day we drove to Boston to visit the Hadjidakis family. And that," said Sandro firmly, "is enough about Lou Molloy and me."

"More than enough. I'm grateful for your telling of it."

"So now it's your turn, Cavanagh. What was it between you and my mother?"

"It was love—on my side, at least—on hers, too, I believe. I was young. She was vulnerable, because Lou Molloy wasn't treating her very well and she was just beginning to understand what this marriage might cost her. So, when Molloy left the ship to go to Naples and New York, we became lovers. Giulia's father and her Aunt Lucietta joined in a conspiracy to keep Giulia happy until Molloy returned and led her to the altar."

"I can understand that." Sandro the Bishop frowned, unhappily. "It's all in the grand family tradition! Please, go on."

"I asked Giulia to marry me. I promised her and I promised your grandfather, that if she accepted me I wanted nothing from the family and I would deal with Molloy. If she refused me, I was ready to walk out of her life and create no problems for anyone. Giulia didn't want to make a decision until the last moment. I accepted that, too. In the end, she opted for Molloy; but believe me, if I'd known she was pregnant, I'd have fought the whole of the heavenly host to keep her with me!" He shrugged and spread his hands in a gesture of total defeat. "What more can I say? Your mother's story is her own to tell; but there's one thing I can swear: you, my Lord Bishop of Trajanopolis in Phrygia, are truly a love-child. You were begotten in love, even if you weren't always nurtured in it. I'm just sorry it's too late in the day to give you back a little of what you missed."

"I don't think I missed too much." Sandro poured another shot of whisky for both of them. "What I had was different, that's all. I often wonder whether my mother didn't fare worse than any of us."

Cavanagh permitted himself an ironic smile at the notion. "I'd be interested to hear you explain that pastoral thought, Sandro."

"I know it sounds like a paradox, because now she's free as the birds in the air, with both the Molloy and the Farnese trusts firmly under her control. I've asked her to administer my share along with hers until I can choose the right cause to spend it on. But what I'm really trying to say is that you were the big love of her life, the one hope of happiness she had; she lacked the courage to grasp it. So, all her other affairs, short or long, were pale station lights in a long, dark night of the soul. You, I understand, have found another love and made a happy family together. So, it is as I said: Mama is left alone."

"Are you blaming me for that?"

"Of course not!"

"Giulia still has you."

"I'm afraid she doesn't. I'm in servitude now, to God and to the Church. You know that's not a fiction. I go where I'm sent, do as I'm told. The Farnese line ends with me. The Molloy line, too. Perhaps it's just as well. In today's world, dynasties are out of date. To attempt to revive them or create them is to put new monsters on our planet, which already we are turning into a moonscape." He was silent a moment, hesitating over his next question. He was not smiling when he asked it. "Tell me, Cavanagh, are you still in love with my mother?"

"You'd have made a hell of an inquisitor, Sandro!" said Cavanagh with grim humor. "And you'll probably want to burn me for the answer I'm giving you. No! I'm not in love with your mother. Being in love is a transient state, a malady of youth. You should be over it by your fifties. If you're not, you're in real trouble. Ask me, however, if I love your mother? Yes, I do. The world still lights up a little when I look at her, or think of her. We can still strike fire when we're angry with each other, as we were today. When I thought she was in trouble I came instantly to her call . . . So I guess you could say I love her."

"Would you, if you had the chance, take her back into your life?"

"No, I wouldn't. There's no more room left in my

heart, in my house, or in my life; but I'd rather not have the pain of telling her that."

"She knows it already, Cavanagh." Sandro smiled at him over the rim of his glass. "Just don't let her seduce you into a discussion about it."

"Which brings me to my last question," said Bryan de Courcy Cavanagh. "Where do you and I go from here?"

Alessandro Aloysius Molloy Farnese looked very much the churchman as he put his fingertips together, pursed his full lips and pondered the question. His answer, when it came, was clear as spring water.

"I don't think we go anywhere, Cavanagh. Time, geography, history, are all against us. There is no place for me in your life. There is none for you in mine. I know something about women, a lot about my dear mother. She's a perennial maker of small mischiefs and I doubt if even a seasoned attorney like yourself could cope with her. So, here is what we do. From tonight, the book is closed, shredded and burned; but you will think of me sometimes, as you think of my mother, with love. I will remember you with my mother, every day in my Mass, which is a sacrament of love. That way, I think we'll all have the best of it—and none of us will be a nuisance to the others."

Cavanagh was very near to tears. As always, he tried to conceal his emotion with a joke: "Do you think your mother will agree to that deal?"

"She's the one who constructed it, Cavanagh. In the best Farnese tradition, it's the women who rescue the men, from debt collectors, irate husbands and the public executioner. You will, however, have to perform a small service for my mother."

"Which is?"

"To resign as her attorney. That way she dispenses

with you, not you with her. Also, it may suit you to leave tomorrow instead of Monday . . . With my mother's permission of course!"

"I hope I'm up to all this," said Cavanagh with weary humor. "I'm getting too old for grand opera!" He raised his glass in a final toast:

"To my son; too lately come by, and the mother who bore him! *Slainte!*"

"To my father, well met, at last!" said Sandro. "Hail and farewell!"

As they drained their glasses, the sound of the dinner gong echoed through the halls of the Prince's Villa.

Sandro stood up first. He offered his hand to Cavanagh. With surprising strength, he heaved him out of his armchair into a long, silent embrace. Then they walked together down the tiled corridor to dine with Giulia the Beautiful.